Book of Sands

A NOVEL OF THE ARAB UPRISING

Karim Alrawi

HARPER**AVENUE**

HarperCollins Publishers Ltd
2 Bloor Street East, 20th Floor
Toronto, Ontario, Canada
M4W 1A8

www.harpercollins.ca

Library and Archives Canada Cataloguing in Publication
information is available upon request

ISBN 978-1-44343-445-4

Printed and bound in the United States of America
RRD 9 8 7 6 5 4 3 2 1

PART 1

1

On the morning babies decide not to be born, and mothers cease to give birth, Neda, seven weeks and four days to being ten, late for school, skelters through a flurry of starlings that scatter from the sidewalk, take flight to gather on balconies and rooftops. At the corner of the alley she stops. A wall of concrete slabs, four metres tall, seals off the street. Its pitted surface spray-painted with slogans for an end to the rule of soldiers.

She leans forward. Her satchel slides over her shoulders like the shell on a turtle's back. She gazes through a crack between two slabs at a deserted road strewn with rocks and gutted car wrecks, flotsam on a beach of broken asphalt. Soldiers lounge by sandbags and coils of razor wire. She hears her father call, hurries to him, follows down a side street, takes his hand to cross snarled traffic at a junction with lights that flash all three colours in festive unison. Flights of starlings sweep over minarets and cathedral cupolas, past skyscrapers as sheer as the crystal turrets of a picture-book palace, soar to chase tendrils of cloud, swoop to cut through streets like shards of glass. Lines of traffic knot in gridlock to the river.

From the metro station tides of pedestrians rise through steel-grated stairwells, stop to stare at the chittering swarm along the sidewalk.

Neda feels a shiver of anxiety. "What's going on?"

Her father shakes his head, appears uncertain. He squeezes her hand, stills the moment's apprehension.

In the schoolyard she slips her hands into the pockets of her hoody, bites her lower lip, pretends not to listen as the janitor, a retired army corporal, tells her father of troubles—walls constructed overnight by the military to block streets against protestors gathered from college campuses beyond the bridge of crouching lions. At the city's central square, crowds tore sheets of corrugated steel and scaffolding from construction sites, raised barricades, hung flags from lampposts and banners across buildings that declare: *The People Rise and Tyrants Fall.*

Neda wonders what *tyrants* could mean, looks to her father for an explanation.

The school bell sounds.

Loudspeakers crackle to announce morning assembly cancelled, direct students to their classrooms. Neda joins the flow along the corridor and up the stairs to take her place at her desk. She leans forward in her seat, not casually the way she does most mornings, but to better see what may happen now the yard teems with flocks that gather on boughs and congregate along the sides of buildings.

Tarek waits for the bell to sound for the start of classes before taking leave of his daughter. Outside the school, birds flit then settle along a wall that severs the street. They scrape their claws and peck, as though to chip away at the concrete. He cannot recall when last they gathered in such numbers. He checks his watch, calls his wife on his mobile phone. "Any contractions?"

"It doesn't have to be today."

He detects a note of exasperation in her voice. Yes, he knows the obstetrician only estimated the date, but by that estimate Mona is days late.

She pleads with him, not another morning of calls every half-hour. "I'll phone you when it starts."

He tells her he will go to the ministry, file a request to have the electricity meter read. He has been carrying the bills with him for a week, always finds a reason not to go. Every month he receives an estimate of electricity consumption, which he knows to be inflated. He must pay the invoice regardless, or the power will be cut off, which sometimes happens anyway. He understands the game. He must go, find the man in charge of reading meters, pay him a bribe and only then will his meter be read and the adjustment made to his bill. He hates paying bribes. It makes him feel complicit in the general state of corruption. On the other hand, nothing happens without something extra, and sometimes nothing happens even with the inducement. It is a bell curve of probabilities. Paying simply increases the likelihood of a desired outcome, but then again, not always.

Tarek counts his money, hopes he has enough. It is never just one payment. Always one and another, then another, before he can reach the person who he really needs to pay. Not that any fixed sum constitutes a satisfactory motivator. If he pays more, then maybe he will get an early reading. If he pays too much, they get greedy, think he can afford to be gouged. He does not hold any grudge against the people he has to suborn—bribery is simply the cost of getting anything done these days. Thinking about it sickens him.

He waves down a minibus, catches it downtown. He will have to change buses twice to get to the state power company before they close for the afternoon. The trip to the ministry takes him longer than he anticipates, most of it spent waiting for transport delayed by walls elsewhere in the city. Frustrated by the wait, he walks the last part past more concrete walls, feels like a rat in a labyrinth, hurries past soldiers at the checkpoint by the ministry gates. Seeing him in a rush only makes them want to question him. They demand his identity card. He shows them his receipts, explains he wants his meter read. After more questions, they keep him waiting, because they can, before letting him through.

At the ministry's customer service department, Tarek joins a line bounded on either side by iron rails—a calf corralled at a slaughter-house waiting its turn for the knife. A handwritten sign announces the ministry will close mid-morning because of citywide disruption by protests, birds and walls.

At the small arched glass window, through a circular hole, he makes his request to a man seated in a cubicle that passes for an office. With a clutch of past bills he explains he has been paying estimates but now needs to have his meter read so his payments can be adjusted. He is sure his consumption is significantly less than what he has been charged. Tarek hands him the receipts with enfolded cash. The clerk slips the money into a side drawer of his desk, hands back the receipts with a piece of paper, tells Tarek to go down a couple of corridors to the fourth door on the left. "Give them the paper. They'll see to everything."

Tarek hurries down to the second corridor, past three doors and knocks. Waits, knocks, waits. Presumes here is where he must pay his second bribe. A passing office boy carries a metal tray with a cup of coffee and a glass of water. He says, "They're not in."

Tarek chases after the boy. "Where are they?"

"Out reading meters. They leave early." The boy goes into an office, past a counter with a handwritten sign—*Do Not Enter, Government Employees Only.*

"We're closed to the public." An officious woman glares at Tarek, pulls forward her yellow scarf to make certain every last hair is covered. God forbid a man should see the slightest curl. To think there was once the possibility of his working in such a place with such people, each an autocrat ruling over a desk, phone and filing cabinet, dispensing favours with a rubber stamp and a signature. However difficult his circumstances, at least he works to his own schedule, performing shows for children. Their joys and sorrows so far from the mendacity of a place like this.

He walks back down the corridor past closed doors that all look identical. He has no idea which door he waited at, or in which corridor. With mounting exasperation, he makes his way back to the customer services room with the cattle rails to ask again for directions. The room is crowded, the window to the cubicle closed. The ministry has already stopped serving the public, if they ever did. Well, maybe they did once, but not now, and not for a long time, and only if they're paid extra.

"Come back tomorrow," says a man with a briefcase. "The ministry opens at eight."

"Tomorrow's Friday."

"We close Fridays. Come back mid-week."

Tarek clenches and unclenches his fist as frustration flows to exasperation—God help him and help any person from the ministry that comes his way.

Employees pour out of ministry buildings, shepherded to a line of buses. From the placards being distributed, Tarek assumes they're on their way to a government demonstration. They will be delivered to streets for television cameras to relay images of cheering crowds to counter those on Internet and satellite stations of protests elsewhere in the city. He does not care. He rarely watches television, thinks it lies. One way or another everything is a lie. A lie sent him to the closed office. A lie that if he returns mid-week he will get his meter read. He knows there are still bribes to be paid right down to paying the man who arrives to inspect the meter to make sure he gets an accurate reading. It's like this with everything in this festering corpse of a country. He slaps a lamp-post. It takes a moment for the jolt of pain to register, to bring tears to his eyes. Since his arrest twelve years earlier for participating in a student demonstration, all he ever does is lash out at inanimate objects, then bites his tongue to not make things worse.

He rests his back against a wall of reinforced slabs that spans the street, taps his head against it, considers cracking his skull against the concrete. But what good would that do? Even if by some miracle he could strike the wall hard enough to shift one of the metre-wide blocks a fraction of a centimetre, and if the wall came down after a hundred such strikes, what then? They will just build a new wall, as they have wall after wall after wall actual or virtual, to cut off streets, seal off a man from his neighbour, a husband from his wife, a father from his child. However much of a failure he has been, Mona has stayed with him—a major consolation. Where would he be without her? But now a second child—*I'm so unready*. He turns, leans with his forehead against the concrete slab, blinks as his eyes sting and tears moisten his moustache. God damn everything. How is he going to raise another child when he cannot even pay a bribe to get his meter read? They will not let him do that without humiliation, dragging him back again and again, disrupting his life, day after day, like rubbing a dog's nose in its shit so it knows its master. And what with Mona still not calling to say contractions have started.

He slides down the wall until he crouches, wipes his face with the back of his hand, his moustache matted and damp. So much to do to earn a living, and how to do so with the turmoil and walls blocking his way everywhere he turns? He leans back, confirmed in the knowledge that he is one of the weak preyed upon by the weak. He looks out at the street. The throughway blocked by a wall. Starlings jab at the blocks as though their beaks could crack concrete.

He follows the line of newly built walls, in no hurry to go home, goes from one sealed-off street to another. Some sprayed with slogans—*Down with the Rule of Soldiers*. Others roughly painted with people and children at play, faces, sunrises and rainbows. Images that he barely registers, his mind preoccupied by anxiety and insult. He follows wall after wall with a growing sense of impotence.

He reaches the river, watches the water lap the banks. Black ants track sprigs of vegetation from riverbank to sidewalk. Ahead of him soldiers lay coils of razor wire, block the road with sandbags and an armoured car. They leave a narrow gap wide enough for a single file of traffic. Soldiers stop drivers, check identity papers, drag a man from a blue sedan. A woman steps out of the passenger side, shouts at the soldiers to let her husband go. They point their rifles, yell at her to get into the car, prod with the barrels to force her back. On the rear seat children scream. She gets into the car to comfort them, loudly curses the soldiers, their mothers and fathers, back to the seventh of the seventh generation.

Dragged to open the trunk of his car, the man's shirt rips. He steps back, examines the tear as soldiers search among tools and spare tires. They drag him back, thrust him headfirst into the sedan. He fumbles with his keys, starts the engine. It stutters and stalls. He turns the key again. The engine chugs, then dies. The soldiers back off. Rifles point at the man in the car. The children cry. Their mother shouts at him to get moving. The man leaps out of the car, screams at his wife. She yells at him to get back in. Soldiers train their rifles on the man. He throws the car keys to the ground, shouts at the soldiers—Can't they see what they've done? They've disrespected him in front of his wife and children. He tugs on his torn shirt to show how he has been humiliated, dares them to fire their rifles at him. Drivers turn off their engines. Pedestrians stop to watch. Quiet spreads. Time slows to a stumble. From the lines of dusty flame trees along the broken sidewalk, the chatter of birds rises like the clatter of a child's rattle.

A bilious taste in Tarek's mouth induces torpor, clouds his mind, keeps him rooted to the sidewalk. The man gazes at the stalled traffic with people frozen by the moment that could be his last. Rifles held steady point to the man's chest. He waits out the silence, then smiles triumphant, having stared down death. His look turns to disdain. He takes a deep breath, turns away from the soldiers, picks up the keys from the ground, climbs into his car. The engine engages and the blue sedan moves forward. The stream of vehicles starts up with roars that drown out the birdsong. Soldiers stop another car to search. For a moment it seemed as though the buildings, roads and walls had peeled like a scab to expose a living flesh of trees and birds—a reality of raw potential beneath the actual.

With the image of the man with the torn shirt still clear in his mind, Tarek sinks onto a bench, gazes at the river bearing tangled roots and flotsam from where the water thickens with vegetation close to its source in the south. He feels the clamminess of his skin, the stickiness of the world. He pitches forward to lean over the low iron rail and retches into the slurry at the water's edge, sears his throat and mouth. He remains leaning over the rail until his head clears and the swell of nausea ebbs. He fumbles for a tissue in his jacket pocket, wipes his face, breathes deeply and feels better for the air in his lungs. "*Maalesh*," he murmurs. A knot of a word that can be spoken by way of reassurance, encouragement, apology, irritation, defiance, excuse, pardon, love. A word that fills many a gap in language. A word that, in effect, means nothing. He checks his watch again, rises slowly from the bench, dials home, speaks to Mona. She is well, wishes he would not worry so much about her, tells him Neda's school just called to say they're closing an hour early.

* * *

At a streetside café, Tarek sits at a table with a friend. They order glasses of tea and a backgammon board. His friend wins the first roll of the dice, chooses white. Often when they play, his friend keeps back a pair of counters at the last space to block, for as long as possible, the passage of Tarek's pieces off the board. If the dice goes against him his counters are trapped, but usually the strategy pays off and he wins. Tarek plays more cautiously, prefers to move the rear counters forward first before advancing the front line. Today, his friend appears distracted. From across the narrow metal-topped table Tarek, with a flick of his fingers, hurries him to throw the dice, start the game. His friend wipes his face with the palm of his hand, tosses the dice, reads the numbers, lifts and places the white pieces.

Tarek throws, moves the black counters.

They play in silence, roll the dice in turn, count spaces, try to keep their counters in pairs and threes. His friend, normally circumspect about his work at the state film and television studios, talks, refers to his job as quality control. A euphemism Tarek dislikes but chooses to ignore. His friend reads scripts, withholds or grants approval for scenes to be shot for film or television, watches the rushes before they are edited, stamps the state seal in red wax on cans with reels of film and boxes of videotapes that meet with his approval, confiscates anything deemed too political by State Security or an offence to public morality. For a change, he seems preoccupied, plays a slow defensive game, throws the dice, counts spaces down the right side of the board. "My son's at university."

Yes, Tarek knows the boy. He throws the dice and pairs counters on the left side of the board.

His friend forces a smile, shakes the dice in a cupped fist. Moves his pieces click-clack, miscounts spaces, stops with a counter in his hand, uncertain where he picked it up from, where to place it. He sighs.

Tarek counts spaces for him.

They play and his friend loses.

Tarek sets the counters for a new game. This time, he plays white to his friend's black.

"He's joined the protestors in the square." His friend shakes his head. "I told him, once the army's finished building walls they'll move to clear the streets. What if they use tanks and armoured cars, live ammunition? Can you imagine the bloodshed? More bloodshed." He frowns. "I told him, stay home. Watch movies, play on your computer." He stares with an anguished look.

Yes, Tarek understands. Of course he understands. He feels his friend's distress, plain to read on his face.

"I asked him, what is it you want?" His friend sighs, places his counters. "Freedom isn't real. Life's a toss of the dice. You read the numbers, move to your square, wait for the next throw." His son told him of the tents of blankets and plastic sheets; food kitchens; clinics for the wounded staffed by volunteer doctors. "Who's in charge, I asked him. We are, he said. People get on and do what they have to do to make things work, cook, clean, defend the barricades. I can't imagine how the place functions with nobody in charge. Order without authority. How is that possible?" He gazes at Tarek.

Uncertain what to say, Tarek lays his counters in a line on the board.

"I said, my boy, you're just one person. You can't beat the army. It's a machine. It doesn't care about you, or how you feel." He glances at Tarek again. "I don't want what happened to you back then to happen to him."

Tarek stops playing. He tries not to think of what could have been and what is not. He does not find such thoughts helpful, does not like to enter the world of regrets and wishful thinking, tries as much as possible to stay in the here and now of being a husband and a father. "All things considered I'm as happy as I can be." So, he implicates himself in a lie, but what else can he say? What could he have been capable of had he graduated with a master's degree in mathematics? Maybe earned a doctorate, was awarded a fellowship abroad? There is no limit to what he believes he could have achieved had he been free to live his life.

Tarek picks up the dice from the board, watches his friend struggle to find words to form his thoughts. With a slight gesture of his hand, he signals for his friend to lower his voice. Who knows who could be listening?

His friend leans forward, continues in a hushed tone. "The boy's engaged to be married the summer he graduates. If he's arrested, expelled from university, we'll have to call everything off. How can he afford a dowry, an apartment, everything that's expected? His life will be ruined."

"Did you discuss that with him?"

"He said he was suffocating. Said there's no future with the army a dead weight on everybody's shoulders. I asked how he thought I felt having lived all my life with the same weight around my neck. He said, there's the difference. You put up with it—I won't." Tears well in his eyes.

Tarek rests a hand on his friend's arm.

"Years of humiliation I've put up with so he can live a cleaner, better life than the one I've led. So he can get out of this urinal we've been crawling in like roaches. Where every soldier with a stripe or star on his shoulder can piss on us. The cheating and lying I've done so he won't have to cheat and lie himself. The bribes I've paid and taken. If he's killed it will have been for nothing." He looks at Tarek with bloodshot eyes. "Talk to him. You'll know what to say. You'll know how to explain things. Make him see sense, leave the square before the army goes in."

Tarek gazes at him, unsure how to respond. He feels he owes his friend, but since his own detention he thinks himself a marked man.

"I'm sorry." His friend stumbles on the chair as he rises. "So very sorry. I don't mean to burden you. I'll talk to you later. I'll call. I'll see you maybe next week." He makes his way past the tables for the street, stumbles again, shields his eyes as he steps into the sun.

Tarek stands, stares, wants to call him back, but is silent. He loses sight of his friend in the crowds. Across the sky flights of starlings sweep forward and back like leaves from a bough blown by a storm. Yes, with friendship comes obligation, but what of the risk? A knot of a thought he cannot resolve. He thinks to call Mona to discuss with her what he should do, takes out the phone, sees it is low on credits, hesitates, decides not to dial just yet. He knows she will tell him not to go. It isn't safe. He glances at his watch. Still time before he has to collect Neda.

Tarek waves down a minibus, jumps on as it slows. The stiff plastic seat crackles as he sits. He passes the fare to the driver. Coloured plastic prayer beads dangle from the front mirror. Pasted along the dashboard are cut-out pictures from magazines of singers and actors. The minibus bounces on uneven roads, takes him past boarded-up shops, deserted sidewalks. He gets off, walks by storefronts closing early. Men lower steel shutters, roll down grates, fold forward metal slats, turn keys in padlocks. Armoured troop carriers wait in alleys. A military truck speeds by. Khaki uniforms unload coils of razor wire and sandbags by a barrier that seals off the street. Others stand with automatic rifles slung across their chests.

Old instincts guide Tarek through back streets and alleyways to avoid soldiers and checkpoints. He cuts through the front of buildings, exits through the rear, comes out into a narrow street littered with stones. Along the sidewalk, an old beggar lifts and drags himself with hands and one bent leg, like a crab. His skin tanned with dirt, beard tousled. His scent of urine and of the garbage piles he searches for food every night.

Tarek hurries past, avoids eye contact, with some trepidation makes his way towards a makeshift barricade of corrugated steel sheets stripped from building sites, reinforced with iron rails and upturned black-and-white sentinel boxes that once stood by entrances to government buildings. He stops a short distance from the barrier.

A barricade in the city centre, how is it possible? One of several that seals the square. Beyond it flights of birds rise and settle, flutter between buildings, perch on balconies and windowsills. The street quiet, there seems little danger. But he knows he should not be here. He struggles to decide whether to go forward, to cross the barrier, or leave now, having seen the barricade and the birds. He wants to search for his friend's son, talk the boy into leaving. But would he even know where to look?

He holds the phone, considers calling Mona, to let her know where he is. He glances at the barricade. Once, he would not have hesitated, but these last few years he has learnt to avert his gaze and play safe. He feels an impulse, a faint echo of memories of a desire to perceive things as they are, unconstrained by fear of what may happen—to wind back the years to when he believed he had a future worth living. Then, he thought freedom was all that mattered. Now such recollections come laden with guilt, as though freedom were selfishness.

He looks at the barrier blocking the street, thinks of himself as a reel of film that at the decision point peels a second strip. In one he goes to the barricade and in the other returns home. One world becomes real and the other, not unreal, but a possibility unrealized. He stares at the phone. He should let Mona know where he is. But no, he cannot burden her with a decision that should be his. He pauses. It would be hard to live with the thought he came this far only to turn back. He counts to ten, takes a deep breath. He slips the phone into his pocket, goes forward to the barricade.

The lingering acrid scent and bitter taste of tear gas from the night's confrontation stings, burns his eyes, raises memories of demonstrations from his youth. He raises his arms shoulder high to be searched by young men with scarves pulled over their faces. Their eyes scan the street behind him while they pat him down for concealed weapons. Apologize for doing so. "Welcome to freedom's republic." They pull aside steel sheets and let him through.

The city's central square—to one side the museum and the river—normally congested with crowds and traffic, now is vast in its emptiness, with only scattered clutches of people and flocks of birds. It opens up before him, an expanse that keeps on widening, spreads in all directions to a far horizon of trees and grey buildings. This seeming void induces vertigo, as though he is watching from a great height. Small groups mill about, look as dazed as he feels. Some stand alone, waiting for what? A distance away, a white sheet painted with a red crescent drapes the side of a building. In the still air, he hears bird-chitter from rooftops and trees. Far above him flights of starlings ripple across a blue sky.

He stumbles on tarmac torn from the road to get at the metalling beneath during the night's attacks by riot police. People sleep against shuttered storefronts, huddle with arms crossed about their chests to hold in what warmth still lingers in their tired bodies. On a round patch of grass and trees, with tents and piles of old blankets, animated knots of young people form, separate, then gather again. Crowds bend between speakers, sway towards one then another. Groups form, then disperse to join others clustered in discussions.

At a side street with a barricade of steel sheets and a burnt-out police truck, vendors wheel their barrows, manoeuvre them between piles of rocks and twisted metal to park in the square, he supposes for the evening when crowds will gather after work. Some sell cigarettes and candy, others sandwiches, bottled water and soft drinks. Groups of young people sweep clouds of dust from the street, medical masks on their faces. Others collect trash in black garbage bags. He imagines by nightfall the square will be full of protestors. Security forces will again try to storm the barricades, fire birdshot and cylinders of tear gas. Rocks will fly in both directions.

A young woman asks Tarek to hold open a plastic bag she fills with litter. She takes the bag from him, reads the question in his gaze. "Because this is home until it's over." She leaves to join a group loading black bags of garbage onto a truck.

He struggles to make sense of what he sees, walks slowly, observes the square as though for the first time, approaches the white banner with the red crescent. It marks a field clinic of blankets and plastic sheets strung from lampposts fixed to the side wall of a mosque, its domed roof crested by larks and sparrows. A young medic wears a white hospital coat, latex gloves, sorts into a can gunshot pellets fired by riot police, each the size of a pebble, into another spent cartridges from snipers' rifles collected from rooftops. Empty canisters of tear gas line a bench. Printed on the canisters in clear blue letters warnings on use, instructions for first aid. Piled on the ground by the bench are steel projectiles the size of a man's fist, with one end covered by thick black rubber, lethal enough to split a skull or crack ribs on impact.

Another medic, a blue surgical mask pulled down under his chin, sits on the sidewalk by a body covered by a checkered blanket. "I never trained for this. I thought I'd spend my life writing prescriptions for colds and flu." He looks up at Tarek. "The riot police kept up their attack all night with gas and bullets." He rubs his face as though to wake himself.

Tarek turns back the edge of the blanket, sees a twelve-digit number written on the inside of the dead man's arm.

"The kids at the barricades write their phone numbers on their arms. So their families can be notified." The medic stands. "I should call. Let them know their son's dead." He walks away.

A young woman in jeans approaches, loosens her medic's mask. "Tarek."

He recognizes her—Yara, Mona's young cousin. He thought she was still at medical school.

"I'm interning at the state hospital downtown. The doctors' syndicate asked for volunteers to manage the field clinic. Don't tell Dad. He thinks I'm working the accidents and emergency ward."

Of course, her father, the retired high court judge, would not approve of her being in the square. "If you don't tell Mona you saw me."

"Mutual promise." She breaks a faint smile.

To one side of the tented structure two more bodies lie covered by blankets. He turns down the corners to see if either of them are his friend's son.

"Looking for someone?"

He nods, folds the blankets back to cover the faces.

"Last night State Security used phosphorus gas at suffocating concentrations. Also, snipers." She points to the rooftops.

"It can't be safe for you here."

"Safer at the clinic than at the barricades."

He describes his friend's son, gives her his name. She has seen many who fit the description, agrees to call Tarek if she comes across the young man. They exchange numbers on their mobile phones.

"I'm proud of you." He hugs her. "Be careful."

"Give my love to Mona and Neda." She excuses herself to tend to the wounded.

Tarek wanders through the field clinic, glances at faces, enters the mosque through a side door to see the wounded laying on the carpeted floor. But no, the boy is not here. Once outside, he sits on the curb, stares at birds flitting and pecking in the square, watches people arrive through the barricades, wonders where this will lead, thinks it all so sudden, though knows it not so—not if he considers the years of protests, strikes and demonstrations, none in themselves significant, each barely a puff to ruffle a paper tissue, while the state stood as firm as a stone edifice. Reluctant to leave, though knowing it will soon be time to collect Neda, he recalls his student days of protest—white banners hung on black campus gates, listening to speeches from the university senate steps, and the young women in bright spring colours gathered to watch, some engaging in debate. The square familiar, yet not. Tranquil in the sunlight. Flame trees with clusters of red buds in deep green foliage. Tall buildings with rooftops silvered with flocks of starlings. Expecting, at any moment, Mona to go into labour. He conceives the notion that, to varying degrees, everybody in the square must be thinking the same thought of what next, as though the concept had summoned them here to think it, to give it substance and direction. Is this commitment to an idea that demands to be thought what it means to believe in a truth beyond the lies that are a part of so much of his life?

Loud clangs beaten on the sides of hollow lampposts raise a cacophony of bird cries. Young men run towards the clanging. Tarek follows, sees a dozen soldiers with a tank grind its treads down a side street towards them. A group of young men lock arms before the machine, behind them the makeshift barrier of wood and sheet metal. They know if the tank reaches the square all is over. The tank stops, waits as though for orders from an officer to proceed through the barricade. The beggar Tarek saw earlier huddles in the shadow of a building. Invisible to both sides in his wretchedness, he picks at his hair and beard. A struggle breaks out as soldiers clear the men blocking the tank. The wretched beggar thrusts himself forward. With hands and one foot, he slides crab-like between the soldiers into the caterpillar tracks, crouches between cogwheels. Soldiers panic, shout at him and each other, if the tank moves an inch he'll die. The crowd pushes forward. Does the crab-man know what he is doing, and for what? For them? Even though none of them gave him as much as a glance. Now their lives and the dream of the square depend on him in the serrated wheels of the machine. All fear gone, the crowd presses on to block any motion of the tank, Tarek among them. Some lie in the path of the tracks, others lean against the armoured plates, crawl under the hull. They cannot let the wretch die. If he dies they will die with him. They chant slogans, call on the soldiers to join them.

The soldiers panic, yell to each other, call for orders for what to do. The crowd grows, their chants louder. The soldiers inside the tank climb out, sit on the turret. To move in any direction will cause death beyond any orders they were given.

A man shakes a spray can. It rat-a-tat-tats like a toy gun. He sprays along one side of the tank—*People and Army One Hand*. The soldiers yell at him to go away, he is defacing military property. He continues spraying slogans. The soldiers do not know how to defend themselves against a man with a spray can.

Tarek looks around, in every sense thinks himself lost. He turns from the barricade, glances back towards the square. Not for the first time he feels as though an unseen thread tugs him in a direction he does not want to go, like a character in a story of someone else's making, an element in a set of numbers bracketed by barriers about the square.

2

Omar prays the morning prayers at the airport's masjid, a carpeted room to one side of the duty-free store advertising perfume and whisky. He checks the arrivals board for delays caused by swarms of birds over runways. How he hates those feathered emissaries of the devil—*the malevolent whisperer, whispering in the breasts of men.* They cost him, cause him to lose income waiting for clients. Elderly couples stream through the barriers at passport control. No doubt here to see ancient temples where Moses castigated Pharaoh, and old churches, sites where the child Jesus and his mother stopped during their journey to escape King Herod's massacre of the first-born. They appear perplexed by porters and drivers calling to them, know to find their guide before accepting help from strangers, change currency at the exchange kiosk, aware the rates are better than at hotels.

He speed-dials the dispatcher to say the flight has landed. He holds up a card with the client's name, waits to be found, sees a man in a dark suit wheel a suitcase towards him.

In the back of the cab the client appears jet-lagged, spreads his legs, closes his eyes. Omar slows as they approach the security checkpoint of razor wire and sandbags at the terminal exit. Soldiers check identity papers and passports. It has been a while since he has seen the army out in such force. Bad enough concrete walls have turned the city centre into a maze with traffic congested all the way to the river. His thoughts wave to and fro between tasks he must do today and the condition of his sister, Mona, on the verge of labour. He waits for the call from Tarek that she needs to be taken to the maternity clinic—God willing it will be this evening and not during the day what with more walls and soldiers and having clients to deliver from place to place.

He runs his fingers through his cropped beard, glances at himself in the rear-view mirror. The beard makes him look older than his thirty-seven years—maybe, at times, with the grey hair, as much as ten years older. As his eyes drift from the mirror, he sees legions of starlings chase and spin in sheets above the city centre. It brings to mind verses from scripture—what is the phrasing? Something, something, *birds on the wing a community like those of humans* . . . Something *raised to the heavens by the Almighty*. He kisses his fingertips and touches the holy book on his dashboard—God forgive his poor memory.

The passenger on the back seat opens his eyes. "Why the delay, the soldiers?"

"Security check." To distract the client's attention, and disguise his own unease, Omar gestures at the swarms of birds that swirl above them like tufts of cumulus. He inches the cab forward, stops, waits his turn to be waved through the barrier, counts eleven cars ahead of him, calls Tarek on his mobile phone, asks after Mona. But no, nothing yet.

Omar speed-dials the dispatcher, says he has been delayed. "Should make it in forty-five minutes to the hotel." He turns to the passenger. "Your request was for blondes?"

"Two escorts for this evening."

The boss will not have trouble filling this order. Over the last decade or more, there has been an influx of eastern European women. What does Omar care what foreigners do with each other in hotel rooms? His is a job collecting and delivering clients and women who earn more in an hour with their bodies than he does in a day driving his cab. He feels sullied doing so. But what choice does he have? Lord have mercy. Women are *awra*—the seduction of the eyes, the allurement of sight, the sin of temptation Eve caused Adam. He will not be blinded by woman. He keeps his body unsullied, conscience clear by prayer.

They pass the checkpoint with barely a nod from the officer in a red beret and wraparound sunglasses, speed along the airport road for the city centre. Omar glances at the phone on the passenger seat. He has willed it to ring all morning, but it remains silent. No matter, it will ring when Mona goes into labour.

Once the client is at the hotel, he decides on a late breakfast, stops for a sandwich from a streetside vendor, watches a man sharpen a long knife against a fluted-steel rod. It pleases him to imagine himself one day as skilled with knives, wielding them deftly. Slivers of liver, chopped, cooked with onions and garlic on a hot plate over kerosene burners, drip blood, sizzle in the flames.

At a tap by a garage Omar washes for the noon prayers—face to ears, arms to elbows, feet to ankles. He washes the defilement of sin from his body, the powdered touch and perfumed smell of the women he delivers to clients at night, collects in the morning. If he could, he would rinse their images from his eyes, wash from his memory their giggles and foreign talk—*I seek refuge in the Lord of mankind, Master of mankind, God of mankind*. Between parked cars he lays out the prayer mat from the trunk of his cab—stands, bows and touches the rug with his forehead.

At a gas station he refuels the cab, checks his phone for messages—still no calls from Tarek. If he does not hear from him, he will drop round that evening. He has an hour before he has to collect an escort from the stable, take her to the hotel. The extra cash he earns in tips from ferrying women about the city he saves, thinks if he does not spend it on himself he is not living off sullied gains—maybe, one day, he will donate it to a mosque or charity to gain credit with God for the hereafter. He keeps the money folded in a scarf under the mattress. What he earns is more than enough for himself, though probably not for a family should he, one day, choose to have one, not that the thought appeals much.

Late nights, when he collects the women, thick with the stench of cigarettes and alcohol, from clubs and hotels, they touch him, make salacious jokes, giggle and laugh. He freezes inside, feels humiliated, insulted in his religion. Not that he was always so abstemious. There was a time, when young, he believed in his right to all manner of sin. But he has mended his ways, found God. Still, in truth, he believes all women unclean, menstrual, mendacious, learning deceit from their mothers. He thinks ferrying whores demeaning—but God sets the path for every man. And every path is His, even *the path of those who earned His wrath and are deluded.* God misleads and punishes whomever He wishes, rewards the pious and the prudent. Omar will forgo pleasures on earth to take his reward in heaven where what was once forbidden will be permitted with delights multiplied beyond anything possible in this world.

On days when Omar intends to work late, he has lunch at his apartment, then rests for a couple of hours. The small apartment is barely a room and a kitchen with a flush toilet in a closet, the paper-roll holder screwed to the door, the floor uneven with tiles loose on crumbling concrete. He can afford better, but he has lived here for the past twelve years and cannot be troubled to move. A window in the kitchen and another in the bedroom provide him with all the light and air he needs. A gas heater on the wall warms water. He washes in a basin in the kitchen. A small television tuned to a religious station sits on a shelf by a row of pans, plates and glasses. When not at work he lives in the kitchen, spends his waking hours here before going to sleep in the other room, which has a bed, a side table and wardrobe. He thinks himself comfortable, though he knows others may not find it so. He considers he has done exceptionally well. He is a long way towards paying off his cab, to own the means to his livelihood. He has never been late with monthly instalments. He does not have to pay rental on a car to the company he works for. He is not beholden to anyone. In his mind that earns him respect.

On a shelf by his bed is a copy of the holy book and by its side a framed photograph of his sister and mother. Omar can barely remember his father, who died while he was still a child. He gazes at the picture of his sister. With the years they have drifted apart. He had objected to her marriage to Tarek—initially, for the man's not believing in God, His angels and prophets. But also for having a daughter by another woman out of wedlock. He wonders if Neda even knows her actual mother. Mona threatened never to speak to him if he ever mentioned a word to the girl. But it troubles him that Neda has not been brought up in God's religion, but then she is not his flesh and blood, as Mona's child will be once born. Her pregnancy gives him an opportunity to discharge his duty as brother and uncle. To teach the child about God will assure Omar a place in heaven. The thought gives him comfort.

From under his bed he removes a shoebox. The lid with punched-in holes is held on by rubber bands. He carries the box into the kitchen, places it on the table. He unrolls the bands, lifts off the lid, crumbles stale bread to feed a large cockroach he caught some weeks earlier by the floor drain. The moment he saw it, he knew it was the devil's minion. He was not afraid, for scripture says, *Satan has no authority over those who believe and trust in God*. He named the cockroach Pilgrim, thinks the name neutral, vaguely respectful. Pilgrim remains still as the crumbs scatter in the box. Omar slides the lid on, rolls the rubber bands into place.

Omar lies on his bed with the box beneath, asks Pilgrim what made Satan turn his back on God, and does he ever think to repent? Why has the devil sent his myrmidon to Omar and what does he think he will gain? You wish to make me sin? I know about sin. I did sin before, but no more. My faith is strong. You'll bear witness on the Day of Judgment that even you could not turn me from God's straight path. He laughs at Pilgrim's foolishness. "What can you offer to tempt me in this life that God cannot offer as reward in heaven?"

He pauses to listen for Pilgrim's answer, knows from scripture that Satan speaks in whispers in men's breasts. He reads out loud from sacred texts, stumbles over archaic words whose meaning he can only guess, hopes the sweet-sounding verses will cure Pilgrim's satanic heart, as it once did the *jinn*, creatures born of fire, and brought them to believe in God. He falls asleep waiting for a response. The book rests on his chest, then drops open by his side.

The school bell rings. Neda hesitates to leave the classroom, uncertain what to do, her day, ending early, now unfamiliar. In the playground children feed birds with crumbled cookies and flakes of bread. What if nobody shows to collect her? She considers the question. Not in an overly anxious manner, but seriously, as she would solve a puzzle. She does know the way home, so she really must not worry. Then, as though summoned by her thoughts, but still distant like an echo, she hears her father call. He waves from across the street, weaves his way through slow-moving traffic to the school gate.

"I came as soon as I could." He takes her hand.

"How did you know?"

"A birdie told me."

She grimaces. Daddies are sometimes so silly: school must have called. Besides, she had only asked by way of confirmation.

They cross the street congested with cars. Above them the sky surges in silver waves that flash in the sun, throw forward, fall back, sweep forward again in fitful pulse.

"Has Mummy had Baby?"

"No, not yet."

Neda frowns, glances at him.

He smiles. "Can you help at the theatre?"

She nods. Yes, she knows it is almost time for the regular afternoon performance.

At the Karagoz puppet theatre, once a two-car garage, in an alley shaded by old apartment blocks, Neda reaches for the shutters to close out the afternoon sun from an auditorium of children on cushions and mats. She switches off electric lights, turns on the ceiling fan that whirls currents of air to spin coils of dust. A small black dog spreads itself at the foot of the stage, pants, lays its head on its paws, its eyes heavy from the heat of the room.

Backstage, in the red light of a low-wattage bulb, her father checks the time on his watch. She hears him on the phone to her mother. "Are you all right?"

"I'm reading."

"Contractions?"

"Nothing yet."

"I'll call later."

"No, please. I'll call you."

Neda strikes a match. It breaks, flares in the darkness. Her finger scrapes the striking strip on the box, burns from the friction. She sucks the grazed skin. The next match grates, flares, lights a candle stub in a pool of wax on an old metal saucer. She cups the flame with her hand, sets the candle on a shelf against the back wall. Behind a white muslin screen the size of a single bedspread, she adjusts the rear footlights of lamps on a narrow table, takes the flat puppets, painted and translucent, out of a carved wooden chest, checks their wired joints to make sure the rods are fully secured to their frames, suspends them from hooks on a stand by the back wall to wait their turn. She knows each puppet by name, knows their stories, talks to them. "You'll be fine. Have a great performance."

Children sit cross-legged in rows on rugs, heads resting on palms and knuckles, elbows on knees. Perspiration glistens on faces, reflects like glitter the glow of the screen on which shadows distend, contract, come into focus to take on colour. Behind the cotton sheet, her father, moustache frosted by light, phone by his side set to vibrate in case of a call, speaks for each of the puppets, changes tone and inflection, holds long, thin rods attached to arms, legs and torsos. With a flick of his hand or a turn of a wrist, puppets take flight, ride steeds, wield scimitars. He tells the story of three sisters:

Once there were, though maybe not, three sisters.

One morning, mother-ghoul knocked on their door, sniffed, smiled and said:

Good day, you sweet and lovely little girls,
Your skin like jasmine, your eyes like pearls,
I could gobble you all from your toes to your curls.

The sisters ran and ran as fast as their legs could carry them, from hearth to door to town and city. They rested here, left from there, never more than a single night under the same roof or in the same bed. Then, one day, they came to a crossroad where a bird on a golden bough of a whispering tree chirped:

This way to the road of stoning,

That way to the road of drowning,

And this to the road of no return.

The three sisters decided each should choose a separate path and risk the consequences come what may to search, as they must, for Zahrat al-Maram, the Wishing Rose, with power to repel every evil and break any spell.

"Before we part," said the eldest, "let's bury our pendants at the foot of the whispering tree so should one of us return she'll know who of us is lost and who has made it back."

She buried a turquoise pendant, the middle sister one of red carnelian and the youngest a pendant of golden amber. Then, with tears and hugs, the sisters parted to face whatever ordeals awaited them. Each set one foot before the other down a path not knowing what lay ahead.

Far into the story, her father holds to the screen the crested hoopoe with striped wings, recites its words to the parliament of birds, tells of Mount Qaf, the hinge of sky and earth, where dawn first breaks to spread across a world sustained by the song of the Peacock Angel. When the song stops the world will end. Rustles and chitter from the ceiling interrupt his storytelling. He pauses, then continues with the tale of the three sisters searching for the Wishing Rose in the emerald oasis of the amber desert, where rainbows bloom and the book of all that was or ever will be is hidden.

To signal a change from scene to scene, Neda shakes a tambourine to make a sound like the rustle of leaves, slaps the taut skin with the heel of her hand to clash the jingles on the frame like bells. To adjust the light from day to night she moves lamps away from the screen, drapes others

with a cloth. She brings forward to within her father's easy reach puppets whose turn has come and carries away those whose time has passed.

Bird squalls erupt from above. Her father stops, waits for a lull, then
continues.

She leans against the side wall of the auditorium, gazes at the screen,
chews on the tips of her fingers, thinks of her mother pregnant, wonders
what life will be like once Baby is born—and what if Mummy has twins?
And, oh, if she had two sisters, then the three of them would be wonder-
ing what to do. Who of them to take the road of stoning, and who the
road of drowning, and would she take the road of no return? How she
would urge all three to stay together and not part ways just yet. But once
her two sisters set off each on her own path to who knows where, then
so must she who has shared with them everything in this life from when
she first knew herself with a mind of her own—all will and want, and so
full of curiosity—to find the Wishing Rose.

It is the Wishing Rose that saves her and helps her return to find her
sisters' pendants buried by the whispering tree. Now she must search
for them, solve the riddles, splash water from the golden lake to make
stone into children once again, like the children watching the screen in
the glow of lamplight in her father's Karagoz theatre. His voice clear and
nuanced, his storytelling practised, the puppets as vivid as images on the
pages of a picture book. For the children this is unlike videos and DVDs
they watch at home, pirated and of poor quality, with pictures that
fade and sound that crackles when it can be heard, or television with
interrupted reception, power failures, political speeches and grown-ups
changing channels to catch news reports on satellite stations with their
sad litanies of deaths from countries sister to her own.

A rush of chitter and a chorus of chirps from the rooftop force her
father to stop. He strokes his moustache, checks his watch, waits for the
chattering wave to pass and the children to fall silent. The clatter and
rustling get louder, reverberate against the concrete walls of the old

garage. He glances at Neda, as though to say the noise will not get better, then skips to the end of the story. "Safe and happy to their home the sisters came, so too may you to your homes go the same."

At the window she draws back the shutters to let in light through dusty panes.

Her father comes forward from behind the screen, bows to applause. The children rise from the mats, their eyes and minds still full of story, make their way along the alley to the street. Her father goes out to see what caused the ruckus, watches as flocks alight on the flat roof of the building, then peel in flights towards the sky to return and swarm once more.

An elderly woman laden with shopping bags stops, looks about her. "What're all the birdies for? It's not hygienic all them pigeons. It were better when the building were a garage."

Neda laughs. "The birdies aren't pigeons."

The woman mutters to herself about the world going to pot.

Tarek's phone vibrates. He checks the screen.

"Who's calling?" Neda asks.

He mouths, "Uncle Omar." Above them birds squall. He cups his ear with a hand to speak on the phone.

Backstage, Neda collects the puppets, hangs them on hooks on the wall, lays out the props for the next day's performance. She clears the floor of silver candy wrappers and crinkly cellophane from licorice sticks sold at the grocer's down the street, confident one day, so very soon, when she is fully ten years old, she will be not just the *sandikar* but the *khayali* working her own puppet show. The notion infuses her labours with serious intent.

Tarek's two-bedroom apartment, compact with old furniture, once belonged to his parents. His father died eleven years ago at sixty-four and his mother four years later, he often says of a broken heart. He calls to Neda to hurry, brush her teeth and get to bed. She says she still has to give her mother a nighty-night kiss and get her cuddles.

Tarek spreads a newspaper on the kitchen table, barely glances at the headlines of protests spreading from city to city. He turns the pages, looks for the obituaries—the only section that carries news he trusts. A car mechanic died at the age of fifty-two, mourned by wife and four daughters. Tarek is thirty-four, does not smoke and has cut back on sugar though still takes a spoonful in his tea, hopes for a long life, but knows nothing is certain. Saladin died of a fever at fifty-five. He remembers seeing the movie as a child at the cinema just two blocks from here. He scans the columns and boxes with black borders set in different fonts, finds an obituary of an air force officer who died aged seventy-three, counts several deaths past the age of seventy-five, four past eighty, and feels the odds good that he has years ahead of him.

On maternity leave from the high school where she teaches literature and languages, Mona spends her evenings in a wicker chair on the bedroom balcony. As the breeze chills, she pulls on the knitted shawl about her shoulders. During the weeks of protracted pregnancy, she watched all about her with eyes unfocused and mind distant. At times, when spoken to she responded barely aware of what was said. Her body weighed down, her movements slow and deliberate. She made an effort to be in this life and of it. Some days, on her laptop, she followed her students' postings on their social pages. With the strife and uprisings that start in one place to continue in another, she doubts the world's readiness for her child cupped in the open palms of her pelvis, registering the pressure and pulse of amniotic fluid. Its skin differentiating sound from touch, registering the incessant roar and rumble of her body, her heart's pounding. From sound it acquires an awareness of space as near and far. From the yearning for its mother's voice it learns time is absence and duration, and with that comes the first stirring of mind.

In the last hour or so since sunset the cramps started and, though intermittent, have become more insistent. Mona measures the lag between them, estimates everything in contractions: one to get to the bedroom, another to the washroom and the kitchen. When it is time for Tarek to call Omar—if he can be trusted to arrive on time—it may take three from the apartment to his cab. The clinic another five or six—it is no more than a thirty-minute drive. By a slight turn of her head, she sees Tarek through the open curtains. He packs, unpacks and packs again a cloth bag with clothes she laid out on the bed for her overnight stay. He mutters to himself, his movements abrupt, anxious. Behind him the cot, with new cotton sheets and quilt, borrowed and lent out so many times between relatives and friends she no longer knows who first owned it, not that it matters.

She gasps, catches her breath, pants through the slow wave of pain, exhales in short puffs, anticipates the next pulse, leans back into the cushions of the chair, pants, closes her eyes, keeps puffing. No, she does not feel ready—no, not yet—feels a pulse gather as a coil tightens, wants to disconnect from the rhythm strengthening to childbirth, wishes it like a sound to fall silent. She pants, waits for the spasm, the wave of pain, pants again, opens her eyes, checks her watch. She closes her eyes, puffs and pants for another minute, opens one eye while keeping the other closed, peeks a look at her watch. Still nothing. She puffs for a while longer and then stops, opens both eyes. She calls to Tarek. "It's stopped."

He comes out onto the balcony. "That's all right, isn't it?"

"I guess I'm just not ready." Mona straightens herself in the wicker chair. Framed by shoulder-length black hair, her face is flushed from the brief exertion.

"Shall I call the obstetrician? I could call Yara, if you'd prefer." He bites his lower lip, tugs at one end of his moustache.

"I don't think we need to yet." She takes his hand, places it on her belly, holds it against her, closes her eyes to better sense him and the child connect through her. She thinks together they touch a future immeasurable, so alive and unimaginable in its potential, and a past that draws back through the generations to a time beyond all possible recall. She opens her eyes, asks if he has decided yet to tell Neda about her birth. "We always said we would before having a baby."

He knows she wanted him to broach the subject earlier, but surely Neda is still too young to understand.

"You're the only one to tell her."

Yes, he knows, of course, she is right.

With the night temperature dropping, he helps Mona from the wicker chair to the bedroom. On the bed, she gazes with unfocused eyes at the lights that come on in buildings opposite, yellow phosphorescent and white neon against a backdrop of a sky filling with stars.

He leans forward, kisses her.

She smiles, asks him about going to the ministry to arrange for the meter to be read.

He says he will have to go again, thinks to tell her about the barricades and meeting Yara in the city square, sees the weariness in her eyes and decides it is not time for explanations as to why he took such a risk. Instead, he tells her of the man at the checkpoint with the torn shirt stopped and searched by soldiers, and how the birdsong seemed to tear a gash in the world of concrete and cars.

"What was he thinking, arguing with soldiers?" Mona says. "How terrible for the children trapped in the car."

Tarek, startled by her response, wants her to see through his eyes the moment of restitution just before the man turned back to join his family. As he describes what he witnessed, he senses her far from him, carried away by a wave of misjudged concern. He feels rebuffed. No longer able to confess his going to the square and telling her of how the wretched crab-man had stopped the tank, he falls silent, then says, "I'll go make us some aniseed tea." He touches her arm, relaxes the resistance he felt, feels the connection with her renewed.

He looks in on Neda, curled in bed, folds Grandmother Teta's old quilt over her shoulder, tucks it around her so it does not slip off during the night. The dog sleeps at the foot of the bed. On her desk a matryoshka doll he found for sale in a second-hand market. The babushkas set in a row from largest to smallest to watch over her as she does her homework.

In the kitchen, he boils water to make tea. When at a loss, it is the one thing he knows to do. He brings Mona the amber infusion in a glass on a saucer. She is asleep propped up on pillows. He loosens her clothes, covers her with a blanket, flops into the old reclining armchair he often piles his clothes on before going to bed, gazes at the empty cot. Against the wall a low bookshelf of picture books Mona has collected for the baby, and by it a stack of diapers he buys whenever he sees them on sale. He undoes his belt buckle, stretches his legs. He will sleep here ready for when the cramps start again, to call Omar to drive them to the hospital.

* * *

Tarek's sleep is troubled by shards of memory of his late-night arrest, years earlier. Men in black uniforms took him to a villa by the river, past blast barriers and an iron gate. An elderly man with crystal-thick glasses at a desk wrote down his name, as a receptionist would for a visitor to any government building. Led to a room with pea-green walls and plain chairs, like those at a doctor's surgery, he waited with mounting anxiety.

A quiet-spoken official called his name from the door, led him down a brightly lit corridor. "This your first interrogation?"

"Yes." He rubbed the back of his hand.

"God willing, just a few questions and they'll let you go."

An officer ordered him to sit in a room full of shadows, screamed in his face charges of fermenting civil unrest for participating in a student demonstration, demanded he remove his watch and empty his pockets into a bowl on the desk. Slapped, and slapped again, the slaps seared, knocked him sideways. Perspiration stung his eyes. Held in a chair, cigarettes stubbed into the soft underside of his arm. Smoke rose in fine coils like cotton thread, a singeing, pungent scent. He ground his teeth so as not to make a sound. Struggled to imagine what it was they wanted to know but were not asking. His mind, numbed by blows and burning, dissociated to watch from a distance, recorded every detail in close-up, like a man witnessing an experiment with himself as the rat.

Stripped naked in a cell in a basement lit by a bulb hung from a copper wire, the floor smelling of piss, walls of shit, the stench seared the back of his throat—the pain from the beatings made worse by nausea.

A warden fetched a blanket. "Wrap it around your shoulders. Sleep against the wall. It's not as cold as the floor." He took away an iron pail with an acrid odour and brought back an empty one. In this place such acts passed for kindness.

At dawn, with mounting fear he was taken naked to an interrogation room, felt the chill of stone tiles underfoot. Punched, knocked to the ground, spat and urinated on, beaten with rubber hoses, whipped with wires, he bled in lines of welts.

When some semblance of awareness returned, he was shackled, suspended by his wrists from a hook. To distract his mind from the pain he tried to recall high school anatomy—What is likely to rupture first, the glenohumeral ligaments or the biceps tendon? Damage at the wrists would likely be in the carpus at the lunate and ulna. His body flooded with sweat, lost consciousness. Unchained from the wall, doused with water, placed on an iron bed with cables. For a passing moment a tingling sensation, then a bolt of lightning flashed at the back of his eyes and all was white. In those hours, and the hours to come, his body was a locus of pain beyond anything he had known, beyond any limits he could endure.

He lost all awareness of time, learnt confession is purging. With each confession the pain increased to further extract what still may be hidden. He admitted to everything, anything, no secrets held, no place to keep a secret, made lies into truths just so suffering would stop. When finally exhausted with admissions, wept to be believed, he discovered his interrogators did not care to know what he had to tell, for he had nothing worth telling. Their only purpose was to induce pain. Sentenced by a military tribunal, he spent his first evening of internment at a train station, caged with prisoners in blue uniforms. Armed men led them aboard a cattle car with piles of straw in one corner. The guards locked the sliding doors, lit a storm lamp that cast sharp shadows on the walls of the carriage, smoked, joked, spat on the wagon floor where the prisoners slept. The guards played cards about the storm lamp, made tea on a small kerosene burner that flared under a brass kettle. So easy for a spark to set the wagon alight. If only it would—an act of mercy to put an end to this.

The roar of the lamp and the sound of the burner drowned out the whispers of the prisoners on the mound of straw. They shared names and stories, to be remembered in the likelihood they did not return, and the possibility one of them survived to bear the memory of having met the others.

The train stopped at a small deserted station. Three of the prisoners were let off the cattle car in the dark with their guards. With the doors of the wagon locked, the storm lamp turned down, the guards tried to catch some sleep before the next disembarkation.

He woke to the sound of wagon doors sliding open. Early-morning light poured into a carriage of sweat and stale bodies. He could see only desert from the railway line to the far horizon, pale amber in first light. He dropped from the side of the carriage to dry, stony ground. Train tracks extended forever in both directions. Guards shackled the prisoners. Unused to leg irons they stumbled as they were led to a truck. Small slits high on the sides and at the rear let in air and a streak of light. A bench extended on each side. The truck jolted as the wheels pulled forward.

Prisoners slept on the bench and floor. He leant against the side wall, felt the sun sear through the metal. Soaked in sweat, he dozed, then woke. The heat suffocating. The dry air oppressive. Dust encrusted his skin, stuck to his eyelids and face, coated his cracked lips. He climbed onto a bench, looked out of a slit window, saw a haze of dust and sand, thought he was dead and gone to hell. Seated on the bench, overcome by heat, he fell asleep.

Woken by the sound of the doorbell, Tarek hurries to let Omar in, closes the doors to the bedrooms, whispers that Mona and Neda are asleep, leads him into the living room.

"I was waiting for your call." Omar glares at him.

"It started again then stopped."

"You didn't call."

"It's not the first time she gets close then backs off."

"You know you can call me anytime." Omar's tone betrays hurt at what he believes is Tarek's lack of faith in him.

Tarek thinks Omar takes offence too easily, feels a gap widen between them, apologizes for any hurt caused when none was intended.

Omar places a folded scarf with banknotes on the glass-topped coffee table. "You'll need extra for the clinic."

"We'll be fine."

"Don't shame me. She's my sister."

Tarek refuses the cash—not that they do not need money, but he would rather not be beholden to Omar, or to anybody else for that matter. He appreciates the offer. It is far more than they will need, and Mona's health insurance from the teacher's syndicate should be sufficient.

Adamant on discharging his family obligation, Omar proclaims he will be deeply insulted if Tarek refuses.

Tarek insists Omar keeps his money.

Each in turn feels proprietorial over Mona as wife and sister.

"I swear thrice by God Almighty, I will not take the money back." And Omar having thus sworn, Tarek feels obliged to accept, says he will treat it as a loan to be repaid as soon as he can, thinks it must be the man's savings and feels guilty.

Omar, though triumphant, cannot help feeling antagonistic towards Tarek for making him argue over what by rights is his to give.

As a gesture of reconciliation, Tarek goes into the kitchen to boil water for tea, thinks Omar a decent but, at times, difficult friend.

Omar glances round the room. There are no framed verses from scripture on the walls, no symbols of faith on the shelves, no copies of the sacred text. He does not wish to raise the subject of how his niece is being brought up without religion. He has spoken to his sister, but she ignores him, says, "If God is everywhere, we don't need to go looking for Him." He has yet to think of an adequate response. He checks the time on his phone. Soon, he will have to take women to a hotel for a client. "Call me when Mona starts labour."

Neda, sleepy-eyed, stands by the door to the kitchen, watches the two men. Her father talks to the puppet Haji Ezat. But then Haji Ezat smiles and with that smile is Uncle Omar. "I'm thirsty," she says.

Omar kisses her on the cheek, says he must leave now for work.

Tarek pours Neda a glass of filtered water from a jug in the refrigerator, leads her back to bed.

"Is Mummy having Baby?"

"No, not yet." He kisses her good night, returns to his bedroom.

Undisturbed by contractions, Mona sleeps deeply. In the armchair by her side, Tarek stirs with every sound she makes.

Later that night, with the apartment silent and full of shadows, Neda wakes wrapped in sheets ruffled like surf. Street lights shine through the slats of wooden shutters to her bedroom window, etch ladders across the floor. She hears voices from the street below. The rumble of machines grows louder. Red light pulsates into the room. She pulls aside the sheets, climbs from the bed. She drags the chair from her desk to the window, stands on it to open the shutters. Tall lampposts with duckbill heads cast a fairy-tale saffron glow on the street and sidewalk. A light flashes atop a crane that lifts a large slab of concrete off the back of a flatbed truck, lays it on a row of concrete blocks, with two more completes a wall that truncates the street and casts a dark shadow.

The crane gathers its cables, leaves with the truck.

Neda thinks herself like a picture-book princess trapped in a tower, with walls going up around her, waiting to be rescued by a prince. She closes the shutters, returns to bed, wonders what mysteries the morning will bring, and maybe, just maybe, she really is a princess.

3

With the setting of the sun, a breeze from the desert chills the air. Birds swarm and settle on the boughs of flame trees along the river mercurial in the last of the day's light. For most of the night Omar collects and delivers women to hotels and nightclubs. In between these trips he takes the occasional roadside fare. With the dawn the birds chorus and surge above lofty office towers. They drop in torrents towards congested streets of early-morning traffic, induce in him feelings of unease—Isn't there sufficient strife on earth without the churning of the heavens?

He waits at the airport arrivals hall. Passengers file through glass doors with their luggage on carts to be greeted by relatives and friends. As the crowds thin, he sees an elderly man in a traditional black *bisht* robe braided with gold thread, dark glasses, a black prayer callus on his forehead, prayer beads in one hand. The man rests the other hand on the shoulder of a boy in a brightly coloured shirt and hennaed hair. This must be the Salafi evangelist returning home from his mission to spread the word of God to the infidel abroad. Omar refers respectfully to him as Maulana, helps him with the bags.

Maulana, eyes slits behind sunglasses, sits in the back of Omar's cab with the boy beside him, watches the suitcases being placed in the trunk.

"We've heard concerning the birds." Maulana strokes the boy's thigh, as he would a kitten. "Our flight delayed because of the multitude of flocks."

"Once we're out of the airport, you'll see the chaos they're causing." Omar turns on the ignition.

"Mysterious are the ways of the Lord. My sight is weak, but the boy witnessed them as our plane circled to land. Sheets above the city. Glory be to God."

"Maulana, they've brought downtown to a standstill." The cab pulls out of the parking bay, steers past passengers and porters loading luggage from carts into waiting cars.

"Praise the Lord, then there's the rumours of babes not being born."

Omar has heard the same, but does not believe it. "One calamity isn't enough to occupy people's minds, they have to imagine another to distract themselves from the first."

"But hard to believe the unborn could decide such a thing." Yet, if it is the mothers who are guilty, it would be a heinous case of *nushuz*—the sin of female wilfulness. "Women refusing motherhood in defiance of Almighty God."

"Just gossip. How can any creature defy the will of the Creator?"

"It can only be a test set by the Lord. One sees evidence of his cunning and wisdom in the miracles of scripture. The believer can and but wonder at the knowledge therein—*Presume you man to be without cause? Was he not a flowing droplet then became a clot fashioned and formed and made a pair, male and female.*"

Omar agrees—these lines contain the very essence of every science. He slows for the military checkpoint by the razor wire and sandbags. "Pray for us, Maulana. May God show us mercy from evil caused by the wiles of women." Indeed, woman is *nushuz* and *awra*—wilfulness and temptation.

Maulana nods. Yes, prayer is power. All the good in the world is from prayer. To invoke the Lord is no small matter. He folds about him the *bisht*.

The soldier glances at the identity cards, asks after the boy.

"One of my students and my eyes on the world."

Once past the roadblock, Omar points at the silver streaks in the sky. "Your Eminence. You can see the birds clearly from here."

Maulana asks to stop. "So the boy can witness and but wonder at God's miracle."

They park by the sidewalk to watch the birds swirl and dive.

Maulana strokes the boy's hennaed hair. "Verily this is a sign from the Lord of the Worlds." He peers as tides of starlings rise and fall, collect and scatter and gather again. "It being as the beginning of days when God punished the inequities of men." He recites the verse, "*And He sent upon them a multitude of birds; to cast upon them brimstone; making them as ashen chaff.*"

To Omar the words seem appropriate, though ominous, like a prophecy about to be fulfilled. He feels admiration for Maulana who can with such prescience recognize God's ways. He repeats the verse to himself, nods his approval.

"Remember, God rewards the good with goodness." Maulana leans forward, places a hand on Omar's shoulder. "Tell me you are righteous. You commend the good and disavow evil."

"Yes, of course." How could he not? He prays five times a day and when he can he prays even more by way of thanksgiving to the Lord and remembrance of the prophets. He recites from scripture every night before going to sleep to keep evil at bay and his dreams pure of the devil.

"There's a right way and a wrong way to recite scripture." Maulana smiles knowingly.

Yes, of course, Omar takes lessons at a local masjid. "I go as often as I can after evening prayers."

To drive the clients to their downtown apartment he tries to avoid the walls around the city centre. Despite Maulana's insistence he refuses to accept a tip. "It's an honour, Your Eminence." He drives off feeling refreshed by his proximity to goodness, calls the dispatcher, who says a client wants to see the Hanging Church in the old city. Pick up in thirty minutes.

Yes, he can make it.

That afternoon Omar drives to a shopping mall a young man and the boy with hennaed hair. The older of the two is verbose and commanding, while the younger, languid, speaks more with his eyes, seems often with his glances to solicit and reprove his companion. Before leaving the cab the older one takes Omar's phone number so he can call him when they are done. He asks if Omar can arrange for some *bango*. "How much?"

"Twenty-five grams of black."

Omar knows where to go. Sometimes the women he drives ask for hashish. He always sells it to them at a markup, makes a little more when they tip him for his troubles. He does not think himself dishonest. It is the nature of doing business to charge a little extra with every transaction.

The young men spend an hour at the mall, call Omar to collect them. In the cab he gives them the *bango*. He shortchanges them on the weight and the price, but they do not seem to notice or care. From how they have shopped, he can tell money is not an issue. They have bought several brightly coloured shirts, makeup, kohl and lipstick. On the back seat, as Omar drives, the young man paints the boy's face, adds red to the lips, powder to the cheeks.

"He's pretty, don't you think? Like spices and honey. A mouth like a rosebud." He kisses his fingertips, runs them along the boy's lips.

Omar glances in the rear-view mirror. The boy, androgynous with the makeup, does appear strangely attractive. He smiles demurely at Omar, who thinks he is being teased, even tempted. But, as sometimes with the women he delivers to hotels when they bait him, he feels not so much enticement as humiliation that they should presume to play with him, to lure him and then, he is certain, reject him. He feels the muscles tighten across his chest. He takes a deep, unsteady breath. The young man strokes the boy's face. "Not even the *ghulam* of paradise could be as pretty. Don't you say I'm right?" The cab stops in traffic diverted by soldiers in the red berets and arm bands of military police. In the rearview mirror the boy does not appear to Omar to be pretty—well, not as a girl can be pretty—but innocent, somehow, knowing too with carnal knowledge beyond that of a child, for he is not a child, but yes, attractive, and strangely so. In the mirror the boy smiles at Omar, seems to blush, shyly averts his eyes, then looks up again.

Omar glances at concrete slabs that close off side streets. The walls were not there just a day ago. The young man laughs, recites:

Your glances pierce my heart,
I die, bleeding fast-flowing tears.

Omar recognizes the poem, an Andalusian classic taught at high school, though does not remember any of it to recite.

"Yes, look, look, don't his glances just pierce your heart?" The young man giggles, adds more powder to the boy's face, brush strokes of blush to his cheeks, brazens his appearance.

Omar feels a moment's vulnerability he takes for weakness. It summons vague, disjointed images of childhood. A memory too dense to picture clearly of a day when, thirteen or so, he sat at a streetside café, in imitation of men much older, smoked a shisha pipe, watched kids play soccer in the alley. Then, he does not recall how, he was in the bathroom of his parents' apartment, the local barber wiped with a rag blood from a straight razor. Mona, maybe seven years old, screamed and sobbed as she lay on the stone tiles. Their mother held a wad of cotton between his sister's legs. The cotton spotted the floor red as they carried the child to bed.

"It was time for her cleansing." His mother rinsed the bathroom tiles. "Better done while she's still young." At the wall the grouting stained red. In the cab, he grimaces, tries to contain conflicting emotions, stares at the traffic ahead, attends to the sounds of car horns. Still the young man's voice lures him to the boy. He yields, glances again as the two kiss with mouths open. Omar watches in the rear-view mirror, uncertain whether he thinks what they do is sinful. At their apartment building they blow Omar a parting kiss, laugh and giggle on the way to the elevator, wipe off the makeup with a newly purchased shirt.

To avoid the congested traffic, and muttering to himself in a temper, Omar drives down a narrow side street, only to find himself facing a concrete wall. He tries to reverse, but cars have followed him and now try to turn in the confined space between buildings. Drivers honk horns, yell at each other to be careful. He waits for the cars blocking him to leave. Perspiration builds on his forehead as he tries to clear his mind of the voices flirting and teasing. He recites, *I implore the Lord of the firmament to shield me from the evil He has created.* He repeats the line, hears it echo louder in his head, beats the steering wheel with his fists. He throws himself back in the seat, stares at the narrow strip of sky as swaths of birds flash between apartment blocks with balcony stacked above balcony and windows shuttered. He rocks in his seat until he calms. He kisses the tips of his fingers, strokes the sacred book on the dashboard, keeps murmuring to it lines from scripture as though it is alive and needs placating.

His ring tone sounds the call to prayer, broadcasting his piety before every telephone conversation. The dispatcher says the military have just announced a dusk-to-dawn curfew until further notice. He advises Omar to finish work early and get himself home. First the birds, then the walls and now this—how is a driver to earn a living?

When Omar calls Tarek to ask after Mona, there is no reply. He speed-dials the home phone. Mona answers, tells him she is fine. He demands to know if she is resting and doing everything her doctor told her. She must remember she is responsible for the child she bears, entrusted to her by God.

She tells him she was asleep and he woke her, and, besides, "It's not your baby." She ends the call. He stares at the phone as the screen dims to show the time in luminous numerals. He considers calling back, having an argument, but he feels too drained for a fight, must conserve his energy to keep the teasing voices from returning. He slips the phone into his pocket. He has time before curfew to go to the mosque and pray. God give him guidance. Maybe then his mind will clear and his passions settle—prayer brings repose. He has heard it said and believes it so.

Once in his apartment Omar thinks of the evening's income he has lost, estimates the fares and tips he would have earned driving women to hotels and nightclubs. He flakes the tobacco from a cigarette, with a penknife scrapes black *bango* from a pressed block he keeps in a matchbox in a kitchen drawer, rolls himself a joint, lights it and smokes.

He wonders what the boy he drove from the mall is doing now. He thinks of the boy's soft complexion, his black eyes circled in kohl and his hair hennaed. He inhales *bango* to numb thought and desire.

In his bedroom Omar removes the shoebox from under the bed, takes it into the kitchen, places it on the table, slides back the lid, feeds the cockroach stale bread crumbs. As he does so, he recalls the sacred verse recited by Maulana of birds, brimstone and ashen chaff. He knows the story, having learnt it at school, of how birds, doing God's bidding, cast burning stones on Abraha the Abyssinian with his mighty elephant. Thinking of Abraha makes him think of Satan too proud to obey God's command. But then an unfamiliar voice cuts across his thinking with unexpected force—*Or was Satan's rebellion not jealousy, but an excessive love of God?* Omar stops crumbling the bread, surprised by the notion, wonders how such a question could occur to him. He inhales on the joint, stares at Pilgrim. "Is it possible to love God too much?"

Once you know Him, is it possible to love Him enough?

Is this thought, this voice, coming to him from Pilgrim? Omar takes another draw on the *bango*. "Satan disobeyed God's command to bow to Adam."

To bow to other than God is idolatry.

"Satan was punished by banishment and the promise of an eternity of hell."

A test of fidelity and how true his love of God.

Omar argues that Satan's rebellion was apostasy at its worse, defiance of God's will.

But Satan was the first of God's creation and so the one most like his creator, who most knows his Lord. In every way the very son and Holy Spirit of God. He knew he was being tested and knew what was expected, and so for the sake of his love of his Lord complied despite the cost. He, of all God's creation, took on the burden of His love and suffers for it and, on the Day of Judgment, will be rewarded to sit at God's right side.

"He is the enemy of men, tempts us to the crooked path."

To test your faith as God requires him. Tests men as he was tested.

"To what purpose?"

To separate the seeds of heaven from the chaff to be burned to ashes in hell.

Omar sits back in his chair. Yes, burned like Abraha and his army in the desert. Now Pilgrim is making sense.

Satan gives men a chance for redemption by proving their love of God. Without the temptation of sin there would be no proof of faith. Satan is the good soul's redeemer.

Omar sucks deeply on the *bango*, gazes at Pilgrim. He slips the lid back on the box. He needs time to consider these thoughts and their implication.

With school over early, Neda waits for her father in the yard. The old janitor sits on a chair by the gate. A hen by its hutch, he watches over a brood of children now so used to flocks of birds in the playground they barely pay them any attention. He nods at Tarek when he arrives, calls to Neda. She runs to join her father, who waves down a minibus.

Neda stands on the side of a hill, all stone and sand. Spread before her is the ancient necropolis of domed mausoleums and masjids of the City of the Dead. Beyond it Saladin's Citadel, built to withstand a crusader's siege, and beyond that tower blocks, spires and minarets of the city above which silver flights swing to and fro in waving pennants. About her a salvage yard strewn with carcasses of machines, iron entrails in heaps with skeletal frames, rusted car shells like skulls, mounds of twisted steel. It is as though a great monster flattened a mall, stomped on the stores one by one to reduce each to a pile of mangled debris. Whatever survives in any semblance of its original form is surrounded by shattered and distorted shapes. She walks around stacks of tubes for plumbing, car exhausts, bent metal, some charred and melted. Mounds of washing machines and old television sets block her way, obscure a path pockmarked by stagnant pools of water and oil. Handwritten signs point to one heap or another with some vague description. She thinks of herself as a little red dot in a computer game of mazes that has to find its way to escape a gobbling Pac-Man.

Two men in string vests feed a machine that crushes and compacts scrap before spewing it into a smelting oven. Thick, oily smoke rises from a furnace. Discarded to one side is a large metal box coloured red and green. Her father examines the binocular eyepiece on the box—lenses held in place with rubber rings—then lifts the lid to look inside at cogs attached to a crankshaft and axle. He checks the clip-holders connected to notches on a central rod with fitments for wheels by the lens cylinder. A crank turns the axle, spins the wheels. A drum at the end of the shaft with a loose cog rattles against the sides. At the back, a sound box with a music machine of turning grooved cylinders with sets of metal pins.

"What is it?"

Her father tells her when he was about her age he attended a saint's day *moulid*. On open ground, away from the prayer recitals and circles of chanters, were swings and a Ferris wheel with red and green cradles shaped like bathtubs, stands of popcorn, cotton candy, and sugarcane crushed to juice in wringers. Everywhere a blaze of coloured lights. From a stall he bought a red sugar doll wrapped in crimped crêpe paper. Fire-eaters spat flames. A strongman in chains tore steel sheets with his bare hands as a magician conjured coins and a pigeon from a scarf. A group of *gnawa* played the five-stringed *sentir* and large *qaraqib* casta-nets, sang stories of days long past. Beyond the fortune teller's stand and the palm reader's tent, a man rotated a handle on the side of a painted box. For a coin Tarek peered into the eyepiece, watched figures float before him in scenes from distant lands. His whole world turned, and he knew nothing would ever contain his sense of wonder.

"I'll sell it for scrap." The salvage-yard dealer approaches from a hut by the crushing machine, with the back of his hand saws the last of his lunch from his face. He smells of raw onions.

Neda thinks the man looks like funny Mr. Turyaki the puppet.

Her father feigns disinterest, asks Mr. Turyaki if he has another box in better condition.

"What's wrong with this one?"

"It's broken."

"They don't make machines like this anymore. Cogs solid brass. There's quality for you."

Her father shakes his head. No, he does not have money to waste on toys. Mr. Turyaki shows him a velvet-padded storage case with wheels of coloured glass, another with tubes. "Original picture wheels and music cylinders. Priceless. Yours if you buy the box." He grins at Neda. "She your daughter? God bless. Such a beautiful child."

Neda smiles, moves closer to her father. He tucks her to his side with an arm over her shoulder, as a goose wings a gosling.

Her father tells Mr. Turyaki to put the box and cases aside for later.

Mr. Turyaki follows them past mounds of pipes and plumbing. Neda thinks he smells a sale and does not want to lose the scent.

"Business has been good lately." He glances around as though not wishing to jinx his luck or, God forbid, appear desperate for lack of customers because of the troubles.

By heaps of old refrigerators, car bodies and parts, her father stops by a van.

"Just brought it in. 2CV AK400, 600 cc. Great condition."

Neda's father nods, and Mr. Turyaki goes to fetch the keys to the ignition. Her father asks her what she thinks. Will this do to tour the puppet shows?

Red with corrugated sides, headlights like tipped cups, number plates above the back doors, tail lights red. A bump on one side—poor little AK got hurt. "AK needs a good wash."

Her father reads the mileage on the dial, kicks the tires, slides his fingers into the wheel hubs to check brake pads, looks under the van for leaks, opens the hood, measures oil on the dipstick, radiator full of coolant, inspects the cast-iron cylinder head for cracks or signs of a blown gasket, unscrews spark plugs to check their condition—plates black with carbon. He disputes with Mr. Turyaki the condition of the plugs.

Neda climbs into the back of the van. Its grooved floor is uncomfortable to sit on. Through the side window she watches the two men haggle.

Mr. Turyaki takes a handful of spark plugs stripped from wrecks. "How many do you want?" He drops them on the hood of the van. "Should last you a lifetime."

Her father shakes his head. He sighs, as though he thinks it a really bad idea to buy a van in this condition.

"Trust me, you won't find one as good for the price." Mr. Turyaki sounds as though he is doing them a favour.

"High mileage."

"Low considering its age."

Her father opens the driver's door, frowns as if to say, *This is all too risky*. The cabin is musty. On the dashboard is a cedar-tree-shaped air freshener, stale with the years. He turns on the wipers. They scrape across the windshield.

"It hardly rains," says Mr. Turyaki.

"I'll need it when it does."

"You won't want to drive when it rains. The roads aren't safe."

"If the roads aren't safe I'll want to keep driving."

The engine starts with a single turn of the key. Her father presses his foot to the pedal. The van roars and shakes. The exhaust rattles. The engine sounds like gunfire.

Her father gets the Box of Wonders with all the wheels and cylinders thrown in to seal the deal. He shakes hands with Mr. Turyaki, who sighs and complains that the sale has been daylight robbery and how his loss is their gain.

Neda climbs from the back into the passenger seat.

"Ready?" Her father adjusts the rear-view mirror.

She cannot believe they have their own van—and red too. How cool.

It has been a while since her father has driven. He furrows his brow, scrunches up his face in mock concentration. Neda grins, then glances out the window. What will Mr. Turyaki think?

They drive out of the yard, stop at the end of a street of two- and three-storey buildings. They can cut through the old cemetery to get to the Autostrad and the Ring Road, or take side streets to avoid the necropolis.

Her father holds out a coin. Neda calls heads for the City of the Dead. He flips the coin, slaps it on the back of his hand. Heads it is.

"So heads, in this universe, we go to the City of the Dead." Neda says. "If tails we go the other way, and that would be an alternate universe."

"Yes, in a nutshell that is quantum mechanics." Well, near enough a version of it.

"But how do we know which one is really us?"

"Both are us. We're ourselves, but different with every choice we make in every universe."

"So how many us's are there?"

"We're all of the selves of all of our choices."

She frowns. She thought she understood when he explained the other day about Dr. Schrödinger's cat, but now she is not at all sure.

They drive through the streets of the old cemetery, a suburb in all but name with electricity and piped water. The land between walled mausoleums built up with low-rise apartment blocks of brick and yellow sandstone. Neda reads out the names on charnel houses.

AK waits by a patch of open ground as boys playing soccer in bare feet run after a ball, their shoes neatly placed against the curb to avoid scuffing.

Neda watches the sky gather shadows above skyscrapers, ripple with silver swaths and effervesce like surf. "Can we stop at Teta's?"

"We should do a quick shop before we go home."

"We're so close." She gives him a pleading look, and he succumbs.

They turn down a narrow path between rose-coloured stone walls, park AK. Her father bangs with the flat of his hand on a tall sheet-metal gate. The sound sends sparrows fluttering from trees around them. An elderly man opens the gate, greets her father, waves to Neda, removes from his belt a large key ring, leads them to a domed mausoleum. They stop by a trapdoor that leads down a flight of stairs to the ancestral crypt where the bones of her grandmother lay on a stone shelf.

"I want to speak to Teta alone." Neda glances at her father as though he intrudes on a private conversation.

He waits in the courtyard, checks the time on his watch.

Neda whispers to Teta, who she knows must be listening. The other night in her room, she stood on tippytoes, pirouetted. She likes the word *pirouette*. How it rolls off the tongue. She pirouetted until she was so dizzy the room spun and spun. She fell back on the bed with Teta's homemade quilt, heard the tick-tock of the living room clock and the chimes of the hour, closed her eyes, between strikes made a wish Mummy's baby would not arrive just yet—*I didn't mean never, just not yet*. Now Baby is days late and Neda feels so very bad. So now she would like Teta, who must have special powers from being in heaven, to make things right and just as they should be.

AK drives past old city ruins, follows the ancient aqueduct raised on high stone arches lined with chorusing flocks, takes the ramp to cross the river to avoid the walls downtown. By the bus station billboards advertise household goods and mobile phones, with posters of the old president defaced and torn during recent protests. Between buildings Neda glimpses the main square with protestors' tents and at the museum army tanks and soldiers. Tomorrow, she will have something to talk about at school.

Her father looks over his shoulder, waits for a lull in oncoming traffic, turns down a side street. All about them starlings and sparrows scatter to make way for a hot and tired AK. Her father parks by a store selling coffee from dark wood chests. The beans in the roasting drum rattle like loose change. The scent fills the sidewalk. Neda watches a starling fly into the store, land on a high shelf, flutter to another perch before finding its way out again.

At the next store, her father asks the woman behind the counter if she has phone cards for sale. He tried this morning downtown without success. Neda presses her face against a glass display cabinet to peer at mobile phones shaped like cartoon characters, others as hands and feet.

"We haven't had a delivery in days." The woman tells him he should try one of the kiosks selling cigarettes at the street corner. "They have their own suppliers."

At a kiosk a bearded man as old as Abraham sells her father what he says is his last card for a twenty percent markup.

Neda scratches off the silver foil to the code, dials the number. When the recorded voice tells her she keys in the digits, gets the confirmation message. She hands the phone to her father charged with enough credits for a month.

Bearded Abraham says, "They've stopped distributing cards so the kids in the square can't call and text each other."

"Who have?"

The man shakes his head, glowers at her father. "So are you one of the Sleepers in the Cave who wakes after a hundred years with no idea what's going on? The army, of course."

"Yes, thank you." Her father says he knows the story from scripture, learnt it as a child at school.

From stores along the street he buys two packets of diapers, as they are still on special offer, and a tub of baby ointment. Neda has not seen this brand before. He pays for bread, eggs, cheese and honey, then buys sardines and canned meat. He argues with the shop assistant over the cost of everything.

"Supply and demand." The assistant shrugs. "People hoarding."

From another store he buys cans of beans, chickpeas, cooking oil and more bread. He says they can keep the extra bread in the freezer. But no rice for sale. If she sees any she is to tell him. He pays for the late edition from a boy selling newspapers spread on sheets of cardboard on the sidewalk. Boxed in red in one corner of the front page, next to an article on the arrest of protestors and another on a decree forbidding abetting the spread of birds in the city's open spaces, is a notice of curfew. He checks his watch. "We should head back." He speed-dials, waits, then flips the phone closed. "Your mother's not answering."

He manoeuvres the van past broken stones, bricks and potholes.

"Careful, you'll hurt AK," says Neda.

He gives her a reproving glance, tells her to dial home. She does, but still no answer. From her father's troubled look she pictures ambulances, emergency rooms, and rushing to maternity wards at hospitals in search of her mother the way she has seen people do on the early-evening soaps.

Traffic moves slowly along the main road. Soldiers take up positions on side streets, wait to enforce curfew. AK arrives at the alley teeming with birds, drives slowly through a flurry of feathers that parts and then comes together in its wake.

As Neda's father unloads the shopping, the old woman comes down the stairs, complains that something should be done about the pigeons. "They crap all over my washing worse than bat shit. I can't hang anything out the window. I have to hump it all to the rooftop lines. My legs aren't what they used to be heaving up and down those stairs."

"They're not pigeons," Neda says.

The woman stares at the flocks in the alley and along balconies and power lines between buildings. "They shit same as pigeons."

"They're nothing to do with us." Tarek hands Neda a bag of shopping.

"Do something or I'll report you to the authorities. It's outrageous what you theatre types get up to." Neda helps her father carry the shopping up the stairs. They stop on the landing for him to catch his breath. He complains he is not as fit as he used to be. There was a time, years ago, he went running morning and evening. Outside their front door he fumbles with his keys as the maid from the apartment opposite leaves.

Neda stops her. "You promised me the story of the girl who spoke in starlings and sparrows." Yes, she did the other day, but now there's no time. She is so sorry, but she has to catch the last bus to make it home before curfew.

Mona in her dressing gown opens the door. Bleary-eyed, she appears to have woken from a deep sleep.

Tarek, all worry a moment ago, now, in her presence, just wants to hug her knowing she is safe.

"We called," Neda says with a frown.

"Sorry, darling. I was very tired."

He takes a deep breath, then says, "There's curfew tonight."

"I heard on television."

"Guess what?" Neda's eyes widen. "We bought a van. Now we can take the puppets out everywhere."

"Time to do your homework." He wants to talk to her mother.

Neda huffs, says it is not fair. "I just got home."

While Neda tells her mother about the van, he goes into the kitchen, unpacks the shopping, stacks cans in cupboards; perishables he places in the refrigerator. He asks for news of anything happening in the world, prefers to hear it from Mona rather than directly from television. She can filter out the obvious falsehoods.

In the bedroom he serves her a glass of aniseed tea. She stares at the pile of diapers by the crib. He sees she thinks his shopping excessive. He asks about her day. She shows him a hardback novel in English she is reading with the title *April March*. On the dustcover the author's name, Herbert Quain, printed in bold serif. A front page, with serrated edges rough-cut by a knife, bears a copyright date, 1936. She found it among her old classroom papers, thinks she bought it from a stall at the second-hand book market by the Opera Gardens when she was last there, months ago. Usually, she buys only mystery novels in English, reads to the first or second murder, then skims to the end. But she does not think this is one of those kind of stories.

In the kitchen Tarek fries ground meat with onions and garlic, mixes it with rigatoni in a deep oven dish. He does not follow recipes, prefers to recall how his mother cooked for him as a boy when he paid little attention to cooking. Consequently, he can never remember all the ingredients or proportions of anything. He improvises, and so the food he cooks never tastes quite the way he expects it to. Some nights he orders in pizza.

The dog, though fed only an hour earlier, gets between his feet, as though it has not eaten for days, hopes he will drop some of whatever he is cooking. Food never tastes as good as when stolen off the floor. He pours the cheese sauce, pink with paprika, over the pasta—Neda likes the colour. He grinds more cheese over the top, places the casserole in the oven. He slices cucumber. Pats dry the lettuce in a kitchen towel, places it in the refrigerator to chill, to add last thing to the salad.

He takes Mona her dinner on a tray to the bedroom, calls to Neda, "Dinner's ready."

She flops into a chair at the table, looks down at her plate. Sullen, this evening more so than usual. He thinks she feels justified, given he made her do her homework as soon as she was home, and, as she would say, with not a moment to herself.

He serves her the macaroni cheese, places the salad bowl on the table.

Neda pokes at the pasta and the melted cheese, pushes the lumps to one side, slides her fork around the plate, swirls patterns in the pink sauce.

He may not know why such moods come over her, but he can see her satisfied trying to rile him.

She fixes him with a stern gaze. "What exactly is in the pasta?"

"Ground beef."

"I think I'm vegetarian."

"So was the cow."

She rolls her eyes. "You've said that before. You could at least be original." She stabs the rigatoni with her fork. The congealed cheese sauce stretches from the plate like elastic. The dog at her feet, under the table, waits for her to slip it some part of her dinner to lick from her fingers.

Tarek finishes cleaning the kitchen, goes into the living room, finds Neda asleep snuggled up to Mona reading *April March*. He carries Neda to bed, tucks her in.

She wakes, smiles, murmurs, "Tell me a story."

"All right. God created the world as plain as a pearl. Then the Peacock Angel gave it colour. That is why we have rainbows and flowers."

"No, a real story. Tell me the story of the three sisters."

The dog jumps up on the covers, lies down as though ready to listen. Most nights it sleeps at the foot of Neda's bed, some nights on the living room couch.

"I'll tell you how the three sisters were born."

Yes, she likes that story, even though she has heard it before and thinks it sad.

Once there was, though maybe not, a widow who wanted a child. She burned frankincense and scattered barley to attract the Simurgh, the phoenix that nests among the ash cones of the amber desert. When the bird appeared, she plucked a tail feather. To get its feather back, the Simurgh carried the widow to the great upside-down tree that roots in air, with branches that grow into the earth. She said to the tree, "You must give me of your fruit so I may have a child." The tree rustled its leaves and whispered, "If I do, you must share with the wind everything you eat." The widow agreed. The tree dropped a fruit from a branch. The widow carried it home, soaked it in honey. In the morning, she had a most beautiful baby girl whose smile filled the house with golden lilies. Sometime later, the widow returned to the tree and said her first child needed a sister. The upside-down tree gave another of its fruit. She soaked it in morning dew and had a daughter whose laugh brought showers of rose petals. When the widow went to the tree a third time, she was given a fruit she soaked in milk for a child that cried tears of jasmine.

Every night the widow took a portion of what she had eaten and placed it on the roof of her house to share with the wind. One day, she found a barley seed, and bit on it. Too late she remembered her promise to the great upside-down tree. That evening, the breeze blew through her like mist and her three daughters were left with only each other to care for.

Neda is sorry for the sisters for having lost their mother to the wind.

Tarek kisses her good night with an extra kiss as reparation for making her sad.

He joins Mona on the bedroom balcony. The breeze from the desert clears the day's air thick with the exhaust of traffic. These are good nights to sit out, before the season when the air greys with smoke from burning rice husks in fields to the north. He turns to look at her leaning into the wicker chair and for a moment each feels resplendent and confirmed in the other's gaze.

He tells her of spending the morning looking for phone cards to charge his phone, of bearded Abraham and the rush to get back before curfew. He thinks to mention the barricades at the city square, but is not sure he can give her an adequate explanation for why he went. Instead he tells her of buying the van and his plans to tour the puppet shows.

"Do you ever wish life was different?" she asks.

"Well, yes, maybe." He tells her at university he had developed a passion for set theory and wanted to pursue the subject so rigorously founded on axioms.

She says she thought all mathematics, one way or another, was based on axioms. What does she know, teaching literature at high school? But why set theory in particular?

He tries to explain that set theory is reason applied to everything, from the most mundane act of counting to the most fundamental questions of existence. His explanations lose her.

"I love you very much." She takes his hand.

"Love is the void element in every set."

"You're saying love is nothing?"

No, not what he meant. He says the void—virtual and unlimited potential, the foundation of all that is known though itself unknown—cannot be measured or counted. Everything derives from the void insofar as everything is potential before becoming actual.

"So everything is based on love." She likes that, smiles. Her face lights up, eyes brighten.

With an impulsive urgency, he wants to fold his arms about her, thinks he loves her with unrequited desperation.

"But how can you be certain set theory's axioms are true?"

"Well, no system can be fully grounded. So I suppose it's partly an act of faith."

Oh, surely not. He cannot possibly mean that mathematics is founded on faith.

"There's the incompleteness theorem to prove it. No formal system can be both consistent and complete. There is always something that escapes being structured, can only be assumed but can't be proven."

"Is there really an axiom of faith?"

"It's an axiom of choice derived from the Russell paradox."

"And what is that?"

"The paradox of choosing between situations of equal circumstance."

"But if equal, they could all be equally wrong and every choice would be a mistake."

"The paradox is phrased as choosing between identical socks."

"You're really not serious?" She laughs. "You can't be."

Puzzled by her laugh, he falls silent, then feels his heart lighten and reaches over to hug her.

Tarek wakes in the old armchair in the bedroom with the apartment dark. He switches on a small table light so as not to disturb Mona in bed. He looks through boxes of old papers, finds the letters he once wrote her and those he received during his stay in prison. Letters written knowing they would be read by his jailers, short and lacking in emotion, with an occasional line of a mathematical equation. He takes the letters to the living room, lays them in a row on the table.

The first includes an equation adapted by Mona from a textbook. It reads, $M \cap T \Rightarrow n$. He took it to mean Mona, M, would share, $\cap$, responsibility with him, T, for Neda, n.

On a clean sheet of paper from a notepad he keeps by the telephone, he copies the equation onto the first line. Below it he writes the equation from the second letter, in which he replied, $n \in T \Leftrightarrow n \in M$, then added $T \Leftrightarrow M$. As Neda is a part of, $\in$, Tarek, so she is of Mona, if they are both to be true to each other.

In the next letter she wrote, $M \cup T = \cup \{ M, T \}$, restating her love and that together they will face life's challenges.

He answered with, $\forall \{ n + m \} \cong M(n) \therefore M(n) \lor T \because \neg T$. He feels disconnected, $\lor$, from Mona and Neda, whom he thinks of as family. He misses them and cannot help feeling negated, $\neg$, as a result.

He copies out the equations each on a separate line.

Mona wrote back, $\forall m : M \subseteq T \Rightarrow \forall t : T \subseteq M(n) \because \forall \{ n + m + t \} : \Leftrightarrow M(n)$. All of her is part of him, as every part of him is part of her and Neda. They may be separated, but are one despite everything.

He responded, $\{ T \land M \} \in I$. He loves her infinitely.

At the bottom of the last letter from Mona is $t \notin M(n) \land T \not\subseteq M(n) = \varnothing$, written as they awaited the end of the appeal process and the verdict. She was afraid to lose him, feared her bond with him severed. Full of foreboding, she added, $(\neg T \Leftrightarrow n \cap m) = \varnothing$. The hearts of Neda and Mona are empty without him.

Tarek completes copying out the equations. He cannot think what to call it. A love poem, maybe? Yes, he thinks so, as evidenced since by their years together. Poetry more passionate than any he has ever read, or imagines could be written.

$$M \cap T \Rightarrow n$$
$$n \in T \Leftrightarrow n \in M, T \Leftrightarrow M$$
$$M \cup T = \cup \{ M, T \}$$
$$\forall \{ n + m \} \cong M(n) \therefore M(n) \vee T \because \neg T$$
$$\forall m : M \subseteq T \Rightarrow \forall t : T \subseteq M(n) \because \forall \{ n + m + t \} : \Leftrightarrow M(n)$$
$$\{ T \wedge M \} \in I$$
$$t \notin M(n) \wedge T \not\subset M(n) = \varnothing$$
$$(\neg T \Leftrightarrow n \cap m) = \varnothing$$

He folds the paper, puts it on the dresser for the morning, when he will place it in his wallet. A memento, not of a time of pain and loss, but of how love can endure and overcome.

4

Most nights when Mona wakes she takes Tarek's hand in hers and only then sleep returns. But tonight she gets up and goes into the living room, sinks into the couch, leans into the cushions. With her laptop she searches Herbert Quain on the Internet. A brief entry in *Wikipedia* describes him as Irish from Roscommon, a chronicler of entropic disintegration. A review by an Argentinian writer discusses how in *April March* memory conflicts with perception, leads to character dissolution into unattributable thoughts and dialogue that merges with the voice of the narrator.

The notion of selves fractured and dissolved troubles Mona, reminds her of when, much younger, she recognized parts of herself as needy and longed to lose herself in love, and yet was so fearful of where this could lead. How often she had thought she would like to sever her weaknesses and start life over with only strength. Drawn by the blue light of the computer screen, the dog enters from Neda's room. It jumps onto the couch, rests its head on her lap. In the still darkness of the apartment, Mona recalls as a child playing soccer with boys in the alley. She tackled and ran with the ball. Omar called her to him, took her hand, smelt of tobacco from a shisha he had smoked at a café, led her to their apartment. In the washroom the local barber waved a razor over the flame of a cigarette lighter. The pain of the cut, like needles to her brain. In bed, she awoke with sheets soaked in blood. Nothing can persuade her of the power of an idea more than knowing a mother can harm her child thinking she does good by God.

Her first time with Tarek, with any man—would she feel anything? But the cut had not been so deep as to prevent all sensation. And soon she learnt there is more to love than a single act however much it may be repeated for intimacy and pleasure. Through her relationship with Tarek she discovered that the facets of herself that were yielding and giving were those that made it possible for her to live through love for others, as they lived through love of her, and that the love she expended came back so much richer.

With breakfast over, Tarek calls his daughter in the bathroom. She has five minutes to leave for school.

She sighs, adds red butterfly clips to her hair.

He pours himself black tea.

"Ahm," he hears her say to draw his attention.

She stands at the kitchen door with her hands on her hips, like pretty girls do in soap operas when mad at somebody or other for being kept waiting. Her satchel over her shoulders. "You'll make me late." She rolls her eyes.

"Yes, very funny," he responds drily.

It has been days since Tarek went to the Karagoz theatre. Every morning he expects the birds to have migrated, to leave him with the task

of cleaning up their mess and fixing any damage done to the building. Every day they roost and racket in the alley is an afternoon of lost
income. At least the school still pays Mona's maternity benefit. It is all
that keeps them afloat in these times of protests, curfews and walls.

At a café he watches men play backgammon at tables too narrow
for the box boards. With every fourth or fifth throw, the dice bounce
off the sides onto the sidewalk. His mind drifts back to the square. He
should return, show solidarity with the protestors. He could phone Yara
to ask after his friend's son, but is sure she would have called him had
she found the young man. He lets himself be distracted by conversation about the birds' arrival and their eventual departure, and talk of
the walls that have made a labyrinth of the city. He listens to opinions
that cast everything in the heavy shadow of doubt and raise the spectre
of great conspiracies. Men toss dice, slap counters on boards, order tea
to tables, tell stories back and forth, all little more than rumours, over
and under the roll and peal of unregulated traffic. In the to-and-fro of
chitchat, he quickly loses track of who said what to whom. Snippets,
elaborated on by passersby, collect credence as they transmit from table
to table, café to café, thicken to ink to run as news in the next day's press.

On his way back, he stops at the theatre, stares at the birds that
form a shivering skin on the building. Won't they ever leave? He hesitates to open the front door, afraid they might invade the auditorium,
cause damage to stage and puppets. How would he ever get them out?
He takes a narrow path around the back of the building, dark from the
shadows of surrounding apartment blocks. He counts keys on a ring to
find the right one, removes the padlock and iron ribs that cage the doorway, lays an open palm on the door, as though to feel for a pulse. Wood
should have the feel of bark, with grain in tidal patterns, a living scent
that lingers. Difficult to believe that sap once ran through this. He eases
open the door stiff at the hinges. In this room he repairs puppets and

constructs new scenery for the tales he performs. Stacked in one corner by the Box of Wonders, moving picture projectors and magic lanterns wait to be fixed. On the walls, faded posters of animation movies from the 1930s—*Mish Mish Effendi* and *Farfoor the Fool.* Through the shuttered window, in thin threads of sunlight dust spins, rises and falls. Sets of hand tools hang from a rack along a wall by a worktable—shears and blades to cut and trim, sanders and files to smooth and prepare leather.

Tarek sits at the table by the window, sorts through a carved wooden box with coloured buttons and rough, uneven-shaped pebbles of copal and amber he uses to decorate puppets. He selects a nugget of yellow copal, holds it up to catch the light from the window, sees cavities inside it. This he can heat in rapeseed oil to collapse the bubbles to starbursts. He can split the stone into two, shape them into teardrop earrings for Neda's tenth birthday. He puts it aside, looks for another piece for a pendant.

He places the nuggets in a row on the table, turns on an ultraviolet desk lamp. They fluoresce gold and orange. With magnifying glasses, lenses like half-saucers, he inspects the stones in black light, turns the nuggets around, one at a time, selects a dull stone the size of a large pebble to polish, clears the surface roughness with a small riffler file, smooths it with sandpaper to a light rusty hue. This will complement nicely the copal earrings. His fingers burn, smell of pinewood from the amber. He detects a shadow at the pebble's centre, drips paraffin oil on the polished stone. It clears for a moment to transparent. He holds it to the light, sees an inclusion in the nugget, cannot make out the shape. He polishes the pebble with a cotton cloth, inspects it. There, to one side, is a speck of something. With a ten-times loupe, he sees a tiny moth with wings raised like an angel. The ribbed lines along the wings, thorax and abdomen whole, legs intact—beautiful in its completeness caught seemingly in mid-flight. With a jeweller's hammer and flat-headed chisel he taps the nugget, splits off a flake with the inclusion, shapes a droplet against his thumb with a wire thread coiled between index fingers. The wire cuts into the skin. From a small pot on the table, he rubs tobacco ash on the amber to enhance colour, polishes it with a soft cotton buff, wipes it with olive oil for lustre. In a side drawer to the table he finds a reel of silver wire to shape with small pinch-pliers a pendent cradle. With a silver chain it will be perfect for Neda. He slips the pendant into a small velvet pouch to take home.

Birdsong and chirps from the rooftop interrupt him. The tips of his fingers burn from the sandpaper. Blood lines the cuticles from where he held the coiled wire, now black under the nail plate. He presses his thumb to the tip of his forefinger. Blood swells like ink from the nib of a pen.

With the Box of Wonders on the worktable, he removes a slat from the top to inspect the mechanism for damage, runs his hand along the shaft from the crank. Missing is the belt coupling the musical drum to the picture wheel. The outside of the box could do with fresh paint. The binocular eyepiece, smeared with dirt, needs cleaning. He inspects the padded case of glass wheels. As a child, when first he saw such discs, they were called picture crystals. Each crystal cost a coin to watch.

He hears sounds from the auditorium, opens the inside door, turns on the backstage lights. Birds panicked flutter from corner to corner, collide with stage set and screen, settle on prop stands and frames. He looks about, but cannot see how they got in. Excrement, white phosphorescence, crusts the puppets left out after the last performance. Corrosive stains streak and discolour the leather figures. He picks through the damage of upturned props and puppets scattered on the floor, knows he will have to buy fresh leather to make them anew, such waste and expense.

* * *

Neda in a blue bathing suit sits by the side of a swimming pool. Her feet ripple the water. Boys leap into the pool. She hunches her shoulders, turns away to avoid the splashes. Children swim the width of the shallow end. She slides down the side until her toes touch the bottom, bobs to keep her head above the water. With eyes open, she sinks under, slips into a silent world, spreads her arms, turns, watches bubbles run from her nose to the surface. Light spots from the ceiling dissolve in shafts to the floor, reflect off the blue and white tiles. She rises for air with blood-shot eyes.

Delivered by her friend's mother in a black sedan to the corner of the alley thick with birds, Neda collects from the rear passenger seat her backpack with damp towel and swimsuit, waves goodbye. The wall of concrete slabs in the street has flowered rhizomes of colours in flowing patterns that obliterate yesterday's slogans calling for the fall of tyrants. At one end of the wall a young woman she recognizes for a neighbour climbs a ladder, leans over to photograph with a mobile phone what is beyond. By the wall a group of high school kids wait with pots of paints and brushes. She knows them, knows some better than others for having siblings her age.

A young woman sees her watching. "We're painting what's on the other side."

"Like there's no wall," says another. "Like we don't see it."

How cool to paint a wall invisible.

The first woman says, "You're with us, right?" She winks and Neda smiles, feels ever so special for being chosen. "I'll draw the outlines and you fill in the colours." She shows Neda the photograph on her phone. "See, this is what we're painting."

"Like we don't care them building walls," says the second woman.

They hand Neda a pair of latex gloves to keep her hands from being stained, tie a plastic apron about her waist that hangs down to her feet, stir colours in cans with sticks—black and white for curb stones, orange and yellow for sidewalk paving. They paint lines low down on the concrete blocks, as though the sidewalk runs through the wall.

Tarek leaves the theatre, locks and shutters the back door, crosses away from where the birds are nesting. He sees a line of young men and women paint the street in perspective on slabs of concrete wall, among them Neda. He recognizes them as his neighbours' children, feels reassured that they will keep an eye on his daughter, thinks he should have made it back home in time for her arrival, assumes she must have come looking for him but was distracted.

A young woman steps back to better view what she painted, moves closer to the wall, adds a line or two, stops, gazes at the sketch of a face. The group works purposefully in silence to dissolve the concrete with images of parked cars, to make the slabs transparent. Tarek sits on the curb, struggles to formulate a notion, to grasp what they must think is the purpose of their labours. He can comprehend why they would protest and occupy the square—it is what he would have done at their age. But he would never have thought to paint walls. The sense of their efforts eludes him. Yet his own daughter seems to understand, and so naturally as to be one of them. He watches the paint turn the plain wall into trees and a sidewalk that extends to a horizon yet to be outlined. He wonders if what he sees is something he has never seen before—a revolt by youth against ugliness.

* * *

In the bathroom, after her shower, Neda brushes her teeth, stares in the mirror as she bites the tips of her fingers. Really, they could not be any redder. In her mother's bedroom she keeps her hands behind her back, asks, "How's Baby?"

"Baby is fine."

"Is Baby mad at us?"

"Oh, sweetheart, are you afraid we won't love you?"

"Well, maybe not as much."

"We can only love you more."

But really, really, she says, could that be true?

"Yes, of course."

But Neda cannot sleep from thinking about Baby not being born.

Her mother tells her that eggs and larvae of many kinds of butterflies can remain dormant for months and sometimes for years because it's not yet safe for them to be born. "It's called diapause." Special hormones inhibit the development of butterfly larvae until the time is right. "If so for butterflies, why not for babies?"

Neda hugs her mother, rests a cheek against her to listen to Baby, to feel it move.

Tucked up all cuddly in bed, she asks her father about the meaning of the slogans on city walls. "What is tyrant?"

He kisses her forehead, says now is time for sleep.

But no, not yet, he has to tell her a bedtime story.

The dog jumps up, spreads itself on Teta's quilt.

"I'm out of stories."

She pleads with him, says she cannot sleep without a story.

He pauses for a wisp of a tale to form, then says, "Well, once there was though maybe not." He sits on the edge of the bed, tells her of the great lord of the *afrit*, evil spirits born of smoke from the tar pits of the desert, who rose to be Grand Marshal of all the armies in the land. The *afrit* lord

collected about him the greatest marabouts, with cowry shells and knucklebones, iron bracelets on their wrists, prayer beads in their hands, who
recited scripture like they recited spells. Whatever the *afrit* lord saw he
coveted. Whatever he coveted he took until everything was his and the
people, in ignorance and poverty, lived in servitude to him, the mind and
spirit of the fatherland that stretched like a corpse at his feet from the
foothills that fed the great river to the delta that fans to the sea. His court-
iers lived in dread, for he held them all in mind, sustained and nourished
them with his thoughts. Should he stop thinking of them, at any moment,
they could disappear.

Tales were told of the *afrit* lord. Of how he separated the ocean into
dry land. Turned on and off the light of the sun. The wind carried to
him every whisper. For anyone who doubted he could commit such
feats, hundreds, thousands, swore they had seen it with their own eyes,
or knew of someone who had.

Yet, despite all the great powers at his command, every age must
come to an end, for death does not forgo its right to set the limits to
every life. And so the *afrit* lord lived, died and lay in state.

Her father describes the great alabaster hall and the corpse, with pale
parchment skin glazed like wax, in his coffin. He tells her of the nights of
prayers and praise with marabouts composing eulogies plagiarized from
the epics of ancient poets. All that was said about the Grand Marshal
was lies made true by repetition. With the last of the heroics recited, the
hall of state fell silent. Crystal chandeliers cast their light under a dome
of lapis lazuli and marble walls with gold inscription.

People gathered in the city's central square to wait for news of a new
beginning. They surged through streets, a torrent that beat against buildings, eddied one way then another, flowed to the tug of a great tide. As
days passed, they felt a sense of release, as though waking from a dream
to recover their senses. The cadaver of the Grand Marshal festered in its

opulent coffin, pestilential under the heat of chandeliers. Its odour grew putrid. Panic spread in the great hall. Just when all appeared lost, miracle upon miracles, the corpse stirred. The dead resurrected, as he did with each of his previous incarnations. The *afrit* lord, his spirit renewed by death, had graciously returned for another life term. The brotherhood of marabouts murmured prayers, burned incense, clacked prayer beads in praise of the resurrection. The government announced a month of jubilation with celebrations of praise of the Grand Marshal accompanied by fireworks in every town and city. As the stupor of the resurrection spread, the great river flowed with milk and honey. The sun smiled in golden showers of lotus petals. The moon sprinkled jasmine bells. On televisions people watched the adoration of the newly risen leader. In villages the barely human rejoiced in poverty and hunger to thank the *afrit* lord for the brevity of their lives. How intolerable it would be if they were to live any longer. So gladly they bequeath their health and years to him.

"I don't like this story." Neda's expression is vaguely pugilistic, eyes reduced to slits, lips tightly pursed.

"Sorry, I'll think of a better one for tomorrow night." By way of recompense, he offers to show her some magic. He tears a strip down one side of a newspaper, holds it up, turns it about so she can see the sheet has a back and a front. He wets the ends of the strip with spittle, turns and loops it so that the ends of opposite faces touch, pinches them together to form a Möbius band, a twisty-eight symbol of infinity.

Neda knows about infinity. A place where numbers end, parallel lines meet, and all the roadside curbs and railway tracks that go in all directions come together. It really must be quite a messy place.

He runs a finger along the outer surface from the seam all the way round. The finger traverses both sides of the band without leaving the paper, returns to where it started. "You see, both faces of the page are now one. No inside, no outside. Front is back and back is front. Magic."

Neda screws up her face in pensive gaze. He went from inside to out-side and back again. How can he lose one side of a sheet of paper? She runs the tip of her finger along the surface of the Möbius band, laughs to see it traverse both sides.

Mona naked and wet from the shower folds a towel about her hair, gives it a couple of turns, lets it drape down her back, slips a dressing gown on. In front of the bathroom mirror, she wipes off the lines of kohl around her eyes so they don't smear in her sleep. She does not think her-self pretty, not since being a child would she say she was pretty, but she thinks herself, with some help of makeup and a few accessories, present-ably attractive. Yes, she will permit herself that much of a compliment. She watches Tarek in the living room wipe with a soft damp cloth glass discs, the picture crystals of the Box of Wonders. He lays them in rows of story order on the dining table. She feels overwhelmed by a wish that life could be kinder to him. He looks up at her, as though drawn by her thoughts, and she feels caught in his gaze. At that moment all she wants is to make love to him.

On satellite TV stations they watch reports of the spread of pro-tests. Then, more out of habit than conviction that anything said would be true or worth watching, they change channels to the local news to gaze blankly at the usual round of government ministers doing this and that and nothing in particular, after which the anchor introduces an investigative report, as part of the program's ongoing search into causes of the birds' arrival. Images appear of silver flights across the sky and flocks in the streets. Cars move cautiously through blizzards of feathers and fluttering birds. The camera cuts to a reporter in an alley with a black bobble-head microphone. She talks about a puppet show recently performed in a small theatre where the first swarms of birds appeared. "We came to interview a young eyewitness." She holds the microphone to a boy who nods to her questions of what the performance was about and how the birds descended like a storm on the theatre when the hoopoe lit up the screen to give its speech to the parliament of birds about the Peacock Angel who lives on Mount Qaf. Tarek recognizes the elderly woman from the previous day as she interrupts the child. "They shit, if you'll pardon my saying so, all over my lovely washed cottons. Every day I have to shifty up four flights of stairs with a basket of wet washing. The alley stinks like a crap-house with all the pigeon poop. An angel wouldn't put up with it, if you'll pardon me. I mean no disrespect to the Lord and His heavenly legion. And all from the goings-on at that theatre. It's them thespians what with their hoopoes and sparrows and all sorts of other kinds of pigeons and you know the shitting just doesn't stop. Pigeon poo over everything. I'd be stinkin' rich if shit were money."

"And there you have it." The reporter nods at the camera. "Stay tuned over the coming evenings as we continue our investigation of the Karagoz theatre."

The anchor says they have been in contact with the Ministry of Interior. He reads from a prepared statement. "The ministry is investigating all possible causes for the blight afflicting our city, and will apprehend and punish all those responsible."

Tarek switches off the television with the remote control, stares at the screen as it greys then pops to black. He tugs at the ends of his moustache.

"You're not worried, are you?" Mona asks.

"A little worried, actually anxious, like rising panic." He sits back in the armchair, rubs the back of his hand, stares at his reflection on the blank screen.

"About the news report?"

"Not so much, but if they discover I went to the square."

She stares at him.

"I meant to tell you."

"Somebody'll have seen you."

"That's why I'm worried."

"Tarek, I can't, not again, with you in prison, with a baby, and Neda to care for. I don't know I have it in me to go through that again."

"Do you think they'll find out?"

She is not sure. She needs time to think.

"I'll phone Omar."

"No, don't."

What can possibly be wrong with calling her brother?

"You can't trust him, not with something like this."

He watches her, reads her meaning, feels the ground give way under him, struggles with the thought as it turns, inverts almost ten years of friendship.

"I wish I could trust him. But in my heart I don't." Her tears well, catch the light. "You should leave for somewhere safe before they're sure who they're looking for."

"I can't leave you pregnant."

"The birds will migrate soon enough. Then nobody'll care about an old story on television."

"How will you cope?"

"I'll be fine. The neighbours will help and my uncle, though retired, still has connections."

Oh yes, the old judge, Yara's father, who did not want Mona to marry him and wanted him to remain in prison forever—that uncle?

"Maybe they won't arrest you. But they'll take Neda, hold her until I give myself up."

He is right. Who knows what they would do to the child. Her being so young would mean nothing to them. "Take Neda with you. If they catch you they won't want her. My uncle will let me know when you can return. He was hard on us back then, but blood matters."

"You're blood. Neda and I, we're not."

"I'll do my best with him." She shivers, takes a deep breath, then puffs to control the waves of distress.

In the kitchen by the burners, Tarek stares at the blue and yellow flames under a saucepan of water. So now, after ten years, the wheel turns to bring him back to where it all started, and all for what?

He watches Mona in the bedroom empty her purse on the bed, take out from a box the money they put aside for the baby, add to it what remains of the cash Omar lent them. He knows she will insist he take it all, feels he has failed Neda and the unborn child as a father and Mona as a husband.

He gazes at the brick wall of the house opposite as the windowpane steams up from the boiling water. If he stays, both Mona and Neda are at risk. If he leaves, Mona may have their child without him. His mind drifts through the events of the past few days—the square, the birds, the walls of concrete, the barricades and the crab-man in the treads of the tank. Yara and his friend's son in the square. Once more he feels as though a path has bifurcated before him, and he is uncertain which direction to take. He struggles to clear his mind, tells himself to think logically. Yes, the incompleteness theorem—no formal system can be both consistent and complete. The mathematical impossibility of absolute control gives him hope that freedom is possible. And of course Mona is right: the sooner he leaves, the better for everybody. And once the birds depart everything will return to normal—the stagnation of daily routine, the mindlessness of habit. Then he can be with his family. He turns off the burners, pours tea into two glasses, goes to join Mona in the living room.

PART 2

5

In the steel light of dawn, AK cuts through the yellow haze cast by tall lampposts in deserted streets. In the passenger seat, Neda rests her chin on raised knees, wraps her arms about her legs, struggles to stay awake. The dog by her side leans forward with paws on the dashboard, glances at passing side streets that disappear into shadows. With the spread of sunlight, birdsong breaks from trees along the sidewalk, echoes off the sides of buildings. From rooftops sheets of birds cleave from the concrete to the sky.

With bleary eyes, Neda peers at her father. "You shaved your moustache."

"Time for a change, I suppose."

She squints. "How do I know it's you?"

"I'm more than my moustache."

"I'll miss school." She sighs, turns to the side window. Her tone as of one who has fought day and night for an education and now has been robbed of a hard-won promise.

"*Maalesh*, you can catch up when we get back."

"Where are we going?"

"It's an adventure."

"What kind of an adventure?" She purses her lips, looks at him as though he is withholding vital information. Besides she knows winter is not really the season for adventures.

He shrugs, smiles, glances at his watch.

She rests her chin on her knees, gazes blankly out the window.

He places the phone on the dashboard, as though expecting a call, checks the time again on his wristwatch.

From the flyover her father takes the fork for the desert road. Neda complains they should have tossed a coin first. How else can they be certain they are on the correct road, let alone in the right universe, and not some alternate one? She sucks her teeth.

AK slows as they approach an army checkpoint.

Razor wire coiled about a steel frame of *Xs* closes off the middle of the road. To either side of them are low walls of sandbags with concrete blast barriers. Ahead, five cars wait. In the opposite direction trucks stop to be searched. The dog on Neda's lap yaps at the sight of soldiers. She holds on to it as a soldier checks her father's identity card and driver's licence. Another opens the back of the van, moves aside the jerry can with gasoline, an emergency supply for the journey, lifts folded blankets to check underneath a carton of bottled water, by it Neda's backpack full of her clothes, and a box with cans of sardines and vegetables—anything her father could find in the kitchen he thought her mother could spare—and sandwiches in plastic wrap they made that morning.

The dog barks until the soldier closes the back door. Another, an automatic rifle slung over one shoulder, looks under the chassis with a mirror at the end of a steel pole, runs it first one way, then the other. His olive uniform is not of conscripts in the city. At the sandbags, an officer in a black beret and sunglasses waves them on, stops the next car.

* * *

Past the city's outskirts, the last of the concrete and red brick buildings, dust blows in wisps across the tarmac. Nests of tumbleweed spin and chase after the van like giant spiders in its slipstream. The steady motion induces sleep. Neda closes her eyes. Tarek drives along a black river of a road through a landscape of low, undulating amber hills; beyond them the great stone plateau. Dust clouds billow above the tabletop. On each side of the tarmac, low dark shrubs and clumps of blond grass intersperse floes of rocks and pools of sand whose colours change from grey to red with the spread of morning. Dust plumes from distant vehicles obscure the horizon. He slows and stops on the hard shoulder of the highway, parks in the shade of a grove of guava trees. He watches his daughter sleep, calls Mona to let her know they are safely out of the city.

She tells him of reports on the Internet of births being delayed.

"What's that supposed to mean?"

"I'm not sure, but the thought of being indefinitely pregnant is too exhausting to contemplate."

"Surely not indefinitely?" He cannot believe she just said that.

"I don't recall how it's being phrased."

He feels a wave of panic, needs time to process the thought, promises to call back later. Neda, sleepy-eyed, says it sounds like the you-know theory.

"What does?"

"Like Schrödinger's cat being dead in one universe and alive in another."

"Decoherence theory?"

"In one universe babies are born, in another they're not. We're in the not."

"Where'd you get that idea from?"

"You told me about alternate universes."

"So now we're debating quantum mechanics? I can't believe we're having this conversation." What has got into the child? He is still trying to make sense of what her mother just said on the phone. She shrugs. "I'm just saying."

"Enough Schrödinger's cat." It serves him right for putting ideas into the girl's head. It's one thing to think decoherence of universes, but quite another to live it.

They travel a highway alongside a river by fields of tall clover and alfalfa, turn off to climb a road to raised ground, park by the side of a track. They leave the dog in the van, walk down a path to a house of yellow stone and mud brick obscured by a fence of palm fronds and trees. A traditional split-barrel roof, open at both ends, lets in breeze during the day; closed at night, it retains heat. Tarek knocks at the door, waits for an answer, hears none. Neda follows him round the side of the house to the backyard. An elderly woman holds a long, thin brush to a large canvas on an easel by a flame tree with bright red buds in clusters of green foliage. Before her the ground dips to fields. Beyond them a lake extends to cliffs, hills and desert.

"How wonderful. You're here already." The woman motions them to approach, kisses Tarek on the cheeks. "It's been years, you bad boy. This your angel?"

Tarek introduces Neda to Maryam, who gazes at her, as though dredging memory.

"Yes, that is her. So lovely." She turns to the easel, waves her brush like a wand. The tree, outlined in light dabs of brown and olive on a canvas grid-lined in pencil, stands solitary against the blue of the sky. She shakes her head. "It's unbalanced, don't you think?"

Tarek steps back to get a fuller view of the canvas.

"I should have centred it lower."

Neda moves closer to him, leans her head to one side to better see as he sees.

Maryam grips Tarek's arm, tugs him in closer. "Look from here. I'll have to crop it to fit the canvas."

Tarek shrugs, rests a hand on Neda's shoulder.

"No, no, I'll have to start again. Foreground to background. Paint over." Maryam turns to Neda. "And you, young lady, what do you think?"

"I'm not sure."

"Of course, you agree with your father. You need a mind of your own." She drops the brush on a small table of paints and brushes, wipes her hands on a cloth stained with colours. "I might as well stop. This time of year the light's only good for two or three hours in the morning."

"You don't use photographs?" Tarek asks.

No, she most certainly does not use a camera. That, she says, would be like painting preplanned, with no chance for discovery, and besides, nothing lives in space frozen without the effects of time.

Neda leans shyly against her father. "But doesn't the tree grow as you paint it?"

"The girl's smart, asks a good question. I can tell she's your daughter." Maryam nods at Tarek.

"Is there any doubt?"

She laughs. And yes, the tree changes as it grows with new leaves and buds. "I paint from life what I see, on the day I see it, for however long it takes me to paint it."

She points to a metre ruler by the side of the tree for Neda to fetch. Tarek holds it horizontally against the canvas. She draws a new centre-line several centimetres below the original. "Tomorrow, I'll re-centre the image."

"But why?" Neda looks up at her.

"Well, you see, from this point everything spreads out to fill the canvas. So the centre's the heart." She taps Neda's chest with the end of the long brush. "Always know your heart, young lady. Best advice you'll ever get."

Neda nods, thinks she understands.

Tarek helps spread a plastic cover smudged with paint over the canvas to shade it from the sun.

Maryam leads them through glass doors to her studio with large windows overlooking fields and river. A thick morning mist tempers the shades of green of an orchard of palm trees cut across by telephone wires.

Canvases lean against the white walls, flame with colours. She shows Neda paintings of landscapes and portraits of village women working fields.

"You'll stay a while?" she asks Tarek.

"I need a favour."

Maryam nods, turns to Neda. "Are you hungry? Of course you are. You're always hungry at your age. There's cookies in the kitchen. Help yourself while I talk to your father. I haven't seen him in ages."

Tarek waits for Neda to leave the room, then says in a quiet voice he needs somewhere safe for his daughter.

"You can both stay here for as long as you want. Who's to know?"

"It would be better for you and Neda if I'm not around."

"You want to leave the child with me?"

"There's no one else I trust enough to ask."

"For how long?"

"I'm not sure."

"She's so young. It's . . . well, it's a responsibility you're asking." She rearranges some brushes on the worktable. "Stay the night. Let me think it over."

In the studio Neda sits on the floor, paints on a sheet of paper in bright colours birds, trees and AK on a winding road like a figure eight.

Maryam clears the worktable of brushes, papers and tubes of paint. She lays out snacks.

"Will you be a darling and help me," she says to Tarek. She nods at a canvas loosely spread over a large wooden frame on the floor. "Have you talked to Kasem?"

"I haven't seen him in years." Tarek stretches the canvas across the frame, folds the fabric over the edge, nails it along one side with light taps of a hammer.

"You should talk to him."

"I would like to. It's Kasem who holds the grudge."

"It is time you two made up." She pours herself a cup of coffee. "I hardly see him these days. But then I'm only his mother."

"This isn't about Kasem and me."

She gazes at Neda, sips her coffee, purses her lips.

"So, where is he?"

She shrugs, looks away.

"You don't think he or Leila would want to help?"

Maryam sighs. "He called two nights ago. They're on their way to Sidi Adi, in the mountains."

Tarek nods, turns the frame on another side, tugs the edge of the canvas, folds it, nails it against the wood.

"Have you told her yet?"

"About staying?"

She glances at him as though he is being deliberately obtuse. She lowers her voice. "About her birth, silly boy."

"It's not time with Mona pregnant."

"It's you she'll be upset with when she does find out."

He knows she is right. But Neda will have questions and he does not have answers and then what? "I can't just yet."

"She's your daughter."

"Yes, she is. I wish you wouldn't say it like you don't believe it."

"Is that what you're afraid of? If she knows Mona's not her mother, she might doubt you're her father?"

"Maybe. It's a risk."

"Only if you think she mightn't be." She watches him beat another nail into the canvas frame. "How is life in the city?"

"As well as can be expected." He describes what has happened since the birds arrived in unprecedented numbers—concrete walls, curfews, protests in the central square.

"I don't suppose quantum mechanics has an explanation." She smiles, and he recognizes her teasing. Well, since she brought up the subject, he tells her of how light can radicalize cryptochrome molecules at the back of a bird's retina. The quantum entanglement of electrons induces chemical reactions that influence the signals to a bird's brain and thus its sense of time and place.

"My fault, I shouldn't have asked." She pours herself more coffee.

After lunch they go for a walk alongside fields of clover and sugarcane to the lake. Neda runs ahead with the dog.

"How's Mona's pregnancy?"

"She's doing well. Due any day now."

"I've been reading on the Internet about babies past their due date. Speculation it's a neurological dysfunction of the pelvic muscles, something like Bell's palsy."

Blood drains from his face. "Wouldn't they know if it is?"

"Well, the good news is recovery from Bell's palsy's often full and spontaneous." She sounds almost casual.

A sickening feeling returns to Tarek.

"But really, what's the probability so many pregnant women would catch the same virus at the same time?"

He cannot be sure, but then he has always thought statistics a black art—calculation in the service of bureaucracy. Manipulation that reduces knowledge to numbers, quality to quantity, equates truth with opinion. That kind of mathematics was never his strength, nor his interest. "Anything's statistically possible. The question is, how likely?" In this case, he would think not very likely if at all.

That evening Neda sleeps on the couch in the living room, a quilt pulled around her. The dog lies on the rug. Tarek and Maryam sit in the studio with glass doors open to the flame tree in the yard. Tarek drinks ginger tea from a short fluted glass as she shows him her paintings of village girls.

"They grow up quickly. By twelve, many are married."

The girls gaze out of the canvases. Their eyes defiant, in a way accusatory.

"If Neda stays it'll be for the shortest time possible. I just can't tell you how long that will be."

"I can manage. After all, she's near enough family."

Neda stands in her nightgown in the moonlight. She shivers, and tears run down her face. "I dreamt I was all alone. Don't leave me."

"I won't." He goes to hug her.

"I heard you." She sobs with cheeks burning. "Don't go without me."

"I promise I won't if you don't want me to." He leads her back to the couch in the living room.

"You promise. Promise me, you promise."

"I promise. I won't leave you."

He tucks her under the sheets on the couch, sits by her, holds her hand until she falls asleep.

* * *

With the morning sun warm through the windscreen, Neda sleeps in the passenger seat, the dog on her lap. Tarek pulls off the black tarmac onto a concrete shoulder, clears a space in the back of the van, carries his daughter from her seat, lays her on a spread blanket, folds another into a pillow for her head. She murmurs she is not sleepy, rolls onto her side asleep. Tarek drives onto the road. The dog stands on its hind legs, its front paws on the dashboard. Majestic, lord of all it sees. It stares out the window at the world rushing forward to meet them.

Mid-morning they approach a knoll of palm trees at the edge of a village. People congregate by a parked truck with a white canvas top painted with a red crescent. At the foot of the knoll men with shovels dig at the sides of a pit. Tarek knows what this is, feels conflicted by the need to continue and the desire to witness the excavation.

He stops past the dirt track that leads to the village. He waits, stares blankly ahead. Then, seemingly from no conscious thought, the decision happens. He reverses the van, turns off the road, drives along the dusty track to park in the broken shade of tall shrubs by a palm grove. He feels as though he steps sideways, crosses from one world into another—trespasses on territory close and familiar but not fully his own.

A boy sits in the shadow of a tree, his boots the black inner tubes of old tires tied with rope about his ankles. He watches with vacant eyes goats graze their way between cacti and acacia.

At the pit, plastic sheets lie weighed down at the corners by rocks. Men in white hard hats, dusty blue one-piece suits with zippers up the front, gloves and ankle-length boots work with picks. Beneath the hard, dry surface, the ground is moist and soft. The men unearth corpses, bones and broken skulls like clay-encrusted fossils.

Women in black, old men by their side, stand or crouch by the cra-ter's edge, watch the bodies brought up from the excavation. How long have they waited to see the exhumation of uncles, brothers, fathers, moth-ers, daughters? Men and women lost, alive only as thoughts. They travel from excavation to excavation, site to site, search for family and friends gone without trace. Maybe this is the wrong grave, not the one their loved ones are buried in. And by whom? The army, State Security, foreign con-tractors, who knows anymore? First the killings, then, with time, bodies exhumed, files opened, promises made of justice and retribution, then files close, promises forgotten as another round begins of the disappeared.

The watchers wait as the disinterred bodies are drawn from the earth like tubular shoots shorn from a great taproot of suffering that just keeps growing. Corpses, discoloured flesh clinging to bone, searched for identification papers in wallets and pockets, rings, visible markings noted, teeth fillings counted. Bodies numbered with metal plates, details entered into ledgers, photographed, wrapped in plastic sheets, then stacked into the Red Crescent truck. Most of the victims unknown, no reason given for their murder, not that it matters anymore. The purpose for death clear, as simple as a dog urinates or defecates, killing to mark territory with corpses.

Some of the observers squat, lean forward, stare with blank expres-sions. They poke at a shoe, pull at a piece of torn clothing, pick up a dis-carded object lying half-buried in the mud, turn it about to see whether they recognize it, who it might have belonged to, before casting it back where they found it. Others stand and watch then wander to where an orderly in glasses sits at a foldaway table. He takes notes in an open binder like a clerk counts warehouse deliveries in, then counts them out again. They listen to the descriptions of bodies, repeat a name when they hear it read from an identity card or document. Every so often people melt away in the haze and others arrive.

In places the ground is rich with tiny treasures. At Tarek's feet something glints. He kneels, picks it up. A pair of wireframe glasses bent out of shape with lenses missing. The kind of cheap glasses fashionable when he was a student. He wipes mud from the nosepiece, rubs the wire arms between his thumb and fingers, crumbles the dry soil, folds the frame, puts it to one side by a stone for safekeeping, as though its owner may one day return. A pink plastic comb lies part buried, several of its teeth missing. The kind of comb Neda has back home. He scrapes off the crusted dirt, feels a terrible emptiness.

He knows such pits pockmark the region, from ocean to river to desert to mountains—all the corpses alike, in various stages of decomposition, with little evidence in any of the graves to distinguish the murdered one from another. In places, when the ground is broken, bodies give off the scent of chlorine and phosphorus. In these pits could be buried any one of several of the disappeared the searchers once knew as family or friends, many loved by them since childhood. Hopeless to think they will find their remains. Still, they stop at every excavation. The sense of loss and sorrow draws them, not just their own but that of others. Every mound, a likely grave, waits to bring forth its dead. Each pit, an open mouth of corpses. He gazes at the faces about him, knows he cannot comfort them—each loss unique and incommensurable. Their grief starts where words fail and fade to silence.

"Maybe they'll find my father's body here," a woman says. "Then his spirit will be at peace."

Those about her nod. Each hopes the same for their own lost, feels the need, ever stronger, to seek out these sites, share the pain, wait for the names to be read of the disinterred.

As noon approaches, with the heat, groups of observers disperse for the shade of makeshift shelters of canvas spread between old acacia trees and tent poles. Tarek watches the Red Crescent workers cover the pit with tarpaulin to protect from the sun the remains of buried corpses.

* * *

Still drowsy, Neda watches from the back of the van flights of starlings burst from the open mouth of the pit, as though released from the earth where they were nesting. They muster above the crater with its mounds of upturned earth. A man finishes marking bones with yellow numbered signs on steel stakes, climbs out as another photographs what appear to be pale mannequins wrapped in plastic sheets. She struggles to comprehend what it is she sees as the pit is gradually covered by black canvas.

In a village, at an adobe shack with palm tree rafters, under a canopy of palm fronds, Tarek orders tea for himself, a lemon soda for his daughter, her skin tinselled by pinpricks of sunlight. The heat stills the air, bakes the earth. Pinned to the wall over the serving counter are pictures torn from magazines of mountains and oceans fading to grey from smoke off blazing gas burners and steam from brass kettles.

Tea arrives in a squat tumbler with a heap of sugar left unstirred. The bottle of soda, kept in a bucket of water, is not as chilled as Neda would like. She pulls a face. Tarek holds the tumbler by the rim, pours the tea into a saucer to cool, the way he sees others do, sips it sweet on the tongue, hot on the palate. It burns his dry, cracked lips.

Neda gives him a sidelong glance. "I miss Mummy."

"I miss her too."

"I don't want her to forget us."

"You remember quantum mechanics. It doesn't matter how far apart particles are. Once entangled, they continue to relate."

Neda nods, sips from her straw, appears mildly reassured that science is on her side. She asks if they will be home in time for her birthday.

"Well, maybe." Tarek pays the man by the kettles.

She lets the dog out of the van. It runs in circles, then stops to urinate by a thorn bush.

Tarek calls her, holds up the mobile phone for her to dial home.

So as not to take any chances with phones being tapped, Tarek and Mona agreed to speak only through their daughter. He tells Neda of the rules of the game when talking to Mummy. At no time is she to mention his name. If she must, then refer to him only as Cousin.

"The maid from next door is visiting," Neda tells him. "No contractions, no baby." She wants to talk about the journey so far, but he puts a finger to his lips. Her mother says there was a phone call that morning. Tarek understands. State Security want him to present himself for interrogation. He has forty-eight hours, maybe a day longer, before they will likely follow up with another call or a visit by an officer to his apartment. He tells himself he was right to leave, but now he worries for Mona, hopes her uncle's connections are enough to afford her protection. Yet he does not know what else they could have done. He climbs into the van, waits for his daughter to finish talking. Only one day apart and already he finds the separation from Mona hard to bear.

"We're being followed." Neda fastens her seatbelt in the van.

His heart misses a beat.

She points to the sky. Above them a silver gash cuts across the blue.

"Birds migrating." He sighs, sinks back into his seat, his heart still racing.

The van moves forward on the dust track past patches of green fields irrigated by wells and occasional rainfall. Along the side of the deserted track flowers lift yellow bell-heads, others star-like and blue with thin long stems. Every so often in the distance, men appear tending droves of flat-tailed sheep branded with henna. The van continues past a shrubby knoll flecked by the sun. A lone stone house blazes green cacti and silver-leaf acacia, the last before they cross from arid ground to desert, from the dirt road back onto the highway. The great stone plateau towers in the distance, a shelf raised from a sea of sand. It extends far to the horizon, grows closer with every passing hour. In its shadow swatches of purple shade to indigo before melting to black. Tarek points ahead. "Those are mountains."

Neda's eyes grow wider.

He realizes this must be the first time she has seen mountains. "One of them is called Sidi Adi."

The road, as straight as a book's spine, on either side dunes folding like pages, turns misty with gusts that blow across in waves. Neda winds up the side window as they drive through squalls of sand that sting her eyes and cake her tongue. "I don't find driving amusing."

"You're not driving."

"It's like infinity going nowhere."

"We are going somewhere."

"Like where?"

"Like to the mountains, that's where."

"Well at least now I know." She huffs and crosses her arms.

They drive for another hour through a landscape that barely changes except for the light getting brighter and the earth paler, bleached by the sun. The dog, overcome by the heat, sleeps in the back of the van on a blanket.

While his daughter stares blankly out the side window, her hair turbulent in the breeze, Tarek speed-dials Yara's number, thinks her phone unlikely to be monitored. When she answers he tells her he and Neda had to leave, asks her to contact Mona. "See how she's doing. Baby's due any day."

Yes, of course, Yara will keep in touch. And yes, she is still in the square, but will be leaving in about an hour. She needs a shower and a change of clothing. A hot meal will do her good.

He flips the phone closed. Neda points ahead to a woman by the side of the road. The woman squats under a shelter of a sheet and sticks by a pile of white slabs like marble.

"What's she doing?" asks Neda.

"Selling salt."

The woman stands as the van draws to a stop. By slabs of rock salt is a pale stone rosette, its whorl of crystal platelets looking like petals.

"It's so pretty." Neda gazes at the desert rose.

Tarek asks the price of a nugget of salt, pays without haggling, asks the woman where the salt came from.

She waves across the great stone plateau. "From Wadi Melleh."

How did she bring so much with her from Salt Valley?

"My husband drives a truck."

Neda asks him if the desert rose is the Zahrat al-Maram, the Wishing Rose the three sisters went in search of.

"I suppose so." He sees the pleading look on her face, says the rosette may crumble in the back of the van. "How about we buy one on our way back home?"

The word *home* reassures and she nods. "For my birthday?"

"If you want."

He asks the woman the way to the mountain of Sidi Adi.

She waves her hand in the direction they are headed—but still a ways to go.

In the van Neda holds the nugget in the sunlight from the side window to better see rainbows in its crystals. She places it on the dashboard so the dog does not lick itself sick. "Why'd you buy salt?"

"For when we're in the mountains."

She kisses her teeth. Well, how was she to know they needed salt to go to the mountains?

He drives onto the empty highway.

"Do you think the lady has babies?"

Yes, very possibly, but then again not everybody has babies.

"Well, it's not my fault." She sits back in her seat, stares at the horizon that seemingly resists getting closer.

"What isn't?" He feels a space open between them.

"What you said about her not having babies."

"I wasn't blaming you." He wonders why she would think that. He only meant people can have complicated lives. How can he explain? He checks his watch, says it's time for a snack, parks in a clearing by the side of the road. Neda huffs, sits stubbornly cross-armed in her seat.

"Oh, come on, let's eat something."

"You're always picking on me."

"I'm really not."

"You think everything's always my fault."

To be arguing is not a good start to the day with a long journey still ahead of them. As his daughter lets the dog out of the back of the van and fetches the sandwiches they made that morning, Tarek searches for a piece of paper. He thinks he can explain to her better what he meant using symbols in place of words. There would be less room for ambiguity and confusion. He takes out the page from his wallet with the mathematical poem. On the reverse side he writes:

$$\Phi = \Omega + \sigma$$

He studies the equation, then adds an integration sign and divides by a variable:

$$\Phi = \int \{ \Omega + (\sigma / \eta) \}$$

He shows her the equation. Let phi, Φ, be an individual personality comprising omega, Ω, an inborn character predisposition, sigma, σ, an unsaturated variable representing accommodation to one's environment, and eta, η, resistance to change, say, to growing up—a Peter Pan complex. An increase in value signifies growth, a decrease, immaturity. The integration sign stands for the cumulative effect of discrete moments from birth to the present.

Neda stares blankly at the equation. What was that about Peter Pan? She has seen the movie, recalls the characters of Tinker Bell and Wendy. "So you think omega is me when I was a baby?"

Well, no, he says, that's not exactly what he meant. Not an addition of one part of a personality to another, but only written so by way of illustration. He thinks it would have been better to write the equation with a double-headed arrow in place of the positive sign to imply interaction. But then, maybe it should be a summation sign and not integration. Now it seems too complicated to correct and explain.

His daughter gazes at the symbols as though the brevity of the statement lends it the authority of a spell. She asks if the woman selling salt is some part of sigma. If so, does it mean that having been seen by Neda she is now a part of her?

Sort of, he says, but it's not really what he meant.

"Isn't it weird to think people can be inside me?"

Not so strange. "We were all once inside our mummies' tummies."

She furrows her brow, pulls a face, says it would be exhausting to be burdened with people inside her like her matryoshka doll bloated with babushkas.

The more Tarek considers the equation, the more he thinks it inadequate, if not misleading, perhaps even false. Surely there is no omega as such and no sigma or eta, only a constant flux. In what part of the equation does the emotional and volitional self reside? What part of himself is revealed when he looks into a mirror, or at a photograph of himself, or is held by another's gaze? How is that self experienced as an exterior that acts in the world and informs his thoughts? He feels confused, unable to explain himself to his daughter. He folds the sheet of paper back into his wallet. "We'll talk about it later."

With the passing hours shadows lengthen, light fades. Neda leans to one side, rests her head against the door frame, closes her eyes. She is so unbelievably bored with the drive—the flat landscape and the ever-distant mountains and the sky with the occasional moving patches of grey, flocks of some whatnots, like flotsam, or the black shadow of a soaring predator. It's all so, and more so, of the same old sameness.

As the van approaches the great stone plateau, trucks increase on the road, puff oily fumes from rusted exhausts. Neda complains she wants a shower, wishes she were home. With the monotony of the journey she falls silent then asleep in her seat. Tarek checks her fastened seatbelt. For long periods, as he drives, his mind goes blank. Every so often he checks the time on his wristwatch.

Once close to the great stone plateau they slow to drive past where the tarmac road ends, past a cluster of trees as squat as shrubs. Farther along a gravel road, clouds of dust rise from where men break rocks in trenches. Machines with scoops scrape and level earth to extend the road. Trucks come and go with rubble. Tarek follows a sign for a detour along an uneven side track, turns the van away from the roadworks, keeps driving. The jolting track wakes Neda. Dazed from sleep, she sees ahead of her bundles of indigo and red float in haze from earth pounded by the last of the day's sun. Figures coalesce; like Karagoz puppets they emerge from shadows to take on shape and colour on a screen. From the musical instruments on their backs they must be travelling *gnawa*. An old man guided by a young woman, a third by their side, they glide in and out of billows of yellow dust.

Tarek slows the van. "Shall we give them a ride?"

Sleepily she nods.

Tarek stops a short distance ahead, watches the *gnawa* in the rear-view mirror. It takes a moment for him to recognize each of them— Yaqzan the *muallem* who leads the songs. Leila the *shawafa* with the *qaraqib* castanets, and the other her husband, Kasem, the *qawwal* who plays the stringed *sentir*.

He steps out of the van, waits as they approach. The dog on Neda's lap, puzzled by the swatches of colour in the dust cloud, cocks its head to one side then the other, watches as it would the approach of a flock of birds of exotic plumage.

The young woman in the blue dress laughs, turns to the old man, says, "I don't believe it. It's Tarek."

The old man nods and smiles, leans on the woman's arm as they glide forward.

In the long shadow of a flat-pad cactus, Neda and her father share a meal from the back of AK with the *gnawa*. The ground smells like smoke from the day's heat. A short distance away the worksite blows dust. Neda calls the dog as it chases grasshoppers from the silver lances of dry desert grass and moths from prickly shrubs. It returns to rest by her side.

"Such a sweet girl." Leila smiles. Neda, who enjoys the compliment, decides she likes the *gnawa* lady even more than she thought possible for somebody she has only just met. All shyness, she leans against her father, rests her head on him. He puts an arm around her and she feels comforted, confirmed in her goodness.

Yaqzan eats slowly, holds the food close to his mouth.

Leila whispers to Neda how the old man, so advanced in years, his sight restricted to the corners of his eyes, can see clearly only in dreams. Several days ago, he dreamt they must go to the mountains. Since then they have been travelling, catching rides on trucks.

"Why the mountains?" Neda peers at Leila.

"At Sidi Adi is the sanctuary of the seven angels."

Neda says she has never been to the mountains but knows of them from geography lessons at school and from her father's stories of Mount Qaf, home of the Peacock Angel. She is sure going to the mountains would be lots more like an adventure than driving on desert roads to who knows where.

"We'll take you to Sidi Adi." Her father places bread in Yaqzan's hand.

"We don't want you to go out of your way," Leila says.

"You won't find another ride from here this evening, maybe not for days." Her father glances from the empty road to the clouds of dust from the worksite behind them.

Kasem removes a packet of cigarettes from his pocket. "We rely on serendipity," he says.

Her father smiles. "And the use of cellphones."

Kasem stares blankly at him, then nods. Yes, he says, he did call his mother some days ago. He turns away, looks back at the road. "So far it's been serendipity."

"I'm so very sure we were meant to meet." Neda smiles at Leila, who winks at her. She thinks it way cool to be winked at by a grown-up.

"We'll be fine," Kasem says. "There'll be trucks by eventually."

"I don't see any." Neda looks both ways along the road from horizon to horizon, all desert.

"Please." Leila rests a hand on Kasem's arm. "I don't want to spend the night here."

Kasem shrugs.

The dog pants, its tongue covered with sand. Her father cracks the screw-top on a bottle from inside AK, pours water into a bowl. The dog laps and slurps as it drinks. Her father hands a bottle of water to Neda to give Yaqzan. He offers another to Leila.

Yaqzan thanks Neda, calls her a spirit pure as an angel.

Kasem taps a cigarette out of the crumpled packet, holds it in his hand as though undecided whether to light up or not.

Her father reorganizes the back of the van to make room for the *gnawa* with their instruments.

"Is the sanctuary of the angels like the City of the Dead?" It troubles Neda to think she might have to sleep next to corpses.

"Nobody should fear death," says Yaqzan. "All that lives is the breath of the Almighty in its ebb and flow. God breathed on clay to give life to Adam. God's spirit is in the world, as our thoughts are in the words we speak. Spirit, like thought, cannot be destroyed."

"But what about babies not wanting to be born?"

"Oh," Leila says, "but babies will be born when the time is right." She cannot imagine otherwise.

"Death leads to rebirth." Yaqzan is certain, for where else can spirits go but shed one body to enrobe in another? "A single life span is not enough for a spirit to achieve self-knowledge." He leans against the side of AK to stand. "Every spirit experiences every kind of life until it discovers its true nature." He steadies himself. "Only then can a spirit depart the world to meet the face of God."

"Like rain returns to the ocean." Leila folds a blanket on the floor of the van to sit on.

"Enrobing must be so, by natural justice and reason. It is attested to in scripture." Yaqzan nods as he speaks.

Her father says such beliefs are based on faith, and there is always some doubt with faith. But what about Kasem? Surely he has not changed so much in ten years to believe in spirits reborn life after life?

Kasem shrugs, fidgets with the cigarette, dangles it unlit between his fingers, says ten years is long enough for any man's ideas to change. Tarek, he says, knew him a lifetime ago, when he was a kid fresh out of high school. "Think of the waste of those years. The best of a generation jailed, murdered or fled. The rest too afraid to think or imagine anything other than what we were told." He walks away, strikes a match. The flame flares, burns the tip of his finger. He drops the match in the sand, lights the cigarette with a second match.

Neda watches, curious what he meant. She thinks the *gnawa* so seriously mysterious she would never have believed her father would know them.

Tarek apologizes to Leila for upsetting her husband.

"He never talks about those years." She goes to Kasem, rests a hand on his shoulder. They watch the sun burn at the horizon.

Neda asks Yaqzan about the tattoo, like a flight of birds, in the soft flesh of his hand between thumb and forefinger. Ah, she must mean the *kutrai* of sun and seven stars of the Pleiades tattooed when he was a child with pinpricks of lampblack mixed with goat's milk. It stung and bled, then crusted, healed with the years to a dull blue. "A symbol of the Peacock Angel and the seven angels that rule the world."

So the Peacock Angel is real after all. She tells him she thought it only true in stories.

"It is true *because* it's in stories." Yaqzan smiles.

"We should leave before it gets too dark to drive." Her father collects the blanket and the remains of the meal to stack in AK. "We'll find a place to spend the night." He helps Yaqzan to the passenger seat. Neda rides in the back with the dog, Leila and Kasem beside the jerry can, bags and instruments.

"Why're you going to Sidi Adi?" Neda asks Leila.

The *gnawa* will perform at the *moulid*, the saint's day festival.

Neda asks Leila if she has sisters or brothers.

"I had two sisters."

"Where are they?"

"Gone."

Neda feels sad for having asked. If only she had the Wishing Rose like in the stories, then Leila might find the talking bird by the whispering tree and from there they could go in search of her sisters.

Her father turns on the engine, shifts gear out of neutral. AK moves forward to cut through the gathering dusk. The detour they took off the highway curves back past where the roadworks end, past machines that level stony ground, raise saffron clouds under bright floodlights on steel towers bathing the worksite in an icy glow. The setting sun smears an orange stain across the sky.

The van's headlights dimly light the road ahead. Yaqzan sleeps slumped in the passenger seat. Tarek glances in the rear-view mirror to see Neda and Leila whispering as Kasem dozes, his back against the side of the van, his legs outstretched. The dog rests its head and one paw on his knee. A little later his daughter sleeps, her head on Leila's lap. Tarek looks to the side to see if anything is coming along branching tracks from villages hidden below hills as black as the dunes on both sides. The van drives past trucks and cars that appear out of darkness, blind him for a moment with their headlights, release palls of dust in their wake.

In the thickness of night Tarek has no sense of where they are anymore. In the distance lights flicker from electric bulbs powered by generators and from oil-filled lanterns. They pass rows of huts in places where he cannot imagine people have a cause to be. Maybe, here somebody once sank a well, watered a patch of land, so others followed, built huts, grazed goats, exchanged milk for water, meat for grain.

In the dark, by the side of the road, Yaqzan relieves himself. Kasem smokes away from the van. The tip of the cigarette glows with each inhalation, dims then glows like a lizard's eye blinks. Neda sleeps on Leila's lap.

"We still have a way to go." Tarek refills the tank with gasoline from the jerry can.

"You and Mona have done a wonderful job." Leila strokes Neda's hair. "The child's such a delight."

"Seeing you together, it's clear she has your features. Reham's too." Tarek tightens the lid on the can, returns it to the back of the van.

Leila agrees the child has something of her mother's looks. "The eyes, don't you think?"

"The eyes of the daughters of the House of Majid."

"I never blamed you for leaving when you did."

"I had no choice." He is grateful for her understanding. Or is it forgiveness?

As Yaqzan settles in the passenger seat, Tarek borrows Leila's phone to call Mona, thinks it safer than to use his own. The line is clear. Mona asks after Neda. He tells her she sleeps. Mona reminds him he agreed to speak to her only through their daughter. "It's just not worth taking chances."

He stiffens as he listens, but then softens as he tells himself she is right. He promises her he will be more careful, says he expects once they skirt the great stone plateau on their way to the mountains telephone reception will be poor, if not intermittent.

"Omar phoned. I said you were away for a few days. Please don't take his calls."

Omar *had* called. Tarek had recognized the number when it lit up on his phone while he was driving. No, he hadn't answered. She says the neighbours sent their maid around for an hour to clean the apartment. They said they would do so every day until he returns. "Everything will work out. I know it will."

He wishes he shared her faith in the world. He wants to say, given the way everything is, a second child might not be a good idea, and immediately feels guilty for having such doubts.

"I spoke to my uncle," Mona tells him. "He'll call back in a couple of days to arrange a time we can meet. I didn't want to press him. He'll get suspicious and might say no."

Yes, he knows the old judge can be difficult and frankly doubts he will help.

It is past midnight when Tarek stops the van at a fuelling station at the edge of a small one-road dusty town with two- and three-storey buildings—red brick, windows ill-fitted with frames and glass, the flat roofs thick with sheaves of straw to insulate against the sun during the day, keep the warmth in at night. Street lights give out a pale haze that fades to black as it spreads to the road. From a red sentinel pump with a white head, Tarek fills the tank and the jerry can.

Kasem asks the attendant for somewhere to spend the night, gets directions to a nearby *khana* with rooms to rent.

They take two rooms—one for Neda, Tarek and Yaqzan, the other for Leila and Kasem. The rooms are small and poorly lit. Bare bulbs give out a yellow glow. In bed Neda asks Yaqzan about the mountains of his childhood. He tells her of fields with mulberry trees where, as a child her age, maybe younger, he gathered red poppies and golden crocuses for his mother to boil for dyes in copper cauldrons on open fires.

She asks why he is going to the sanctuary of the angels.

"In a dream, I was instructed to ask at the shrine of Sidi Adi about my new mother." He would like to meet her in this life, before death and rebirth.

Neda's eyes could not open wider. It would be just so amazing to know one's mother before being born.

In the lobby of the *khana* Tarek, too exhausted from driving to sleep, sips a glass of chamomile tea he thinks of, since childhood, as vaguely medicinal. Through the lobby's glass window the streets are dark. The burning tip of a cigarette glows where Kasem sits on a bench. When he comes inside, Tarek says, "I need to talk about Neda."

"*Now* you need to talk about Neda? Where were you when her mother needed you?"

Tarek freezes as Kasem steps past him for the stairs. Does he deserve such rebuke? Why doesn't Kasem take a moment to see what happened through Tarek's eyes? He didn't choose to leave Reham, promised to return—and for a long time blamed himself for failing to do so.

6

Omar wakes to his phone sounding the call to prayer. He does not recognize the number on the screen, turns off the ringer, goes into the kitchen to wash his face. He boils water in a small funnel pan, adds ground coffee and a heaped spoonful of sugar. Birds on the windowsill squawk as they fight for a perch. He throws the shutters open to scatter them, closes it to keep them out. At the kitchen table he sips his coffee. The phone vibrates. It is the same number as before. He answers. A young man asks if he is available for a job for Maulana. If so he is to be at the apartment in an hour.

Omar parks in the street, pays a man to keep the birds from settling on the roof and hood of the cab—the new profession of bird chaser, another way of gouging money from drivers. The elevator doors are locked. Not a tenant, he does not have a key. He climbs the stairs to the seventh floor. Out of breath, he is let into the apartment. A young man tells him to wait as Maulana completes a lesson to his students seated on a couch and cushions on the floor. Omar stands against the back wall, wonders if he will be compensated for time wasted.

"*Men are a degree above women,*" Maulana quotes scripture. "What, you may wonder, is a degree? It can be little and it can be much. Not less nor equal to, but above. Above means more. More means better." He pauses to make his point. "Howbeit, and in what manner is a woman less? Less in body? Yes, she is less in strength. Less in spirit? Yes, that too. That much is meant, by way of metaphor said, Eve created from Adam's rib. A woman's strength and wisdom come from the man by her side. Her father and brothers in the first place, and but after them her husband. Her spirit from the spirit of the men in her family—anything else is *nushuz*, wilfulness. Thus, her ignominy is their ignominy. Her dishonour, their dishonour." He speaks of the terrible burden of shame—an affliction that cannot be borne without a heavy price. When a man is dishonoured, the dishonour is his. When a woman is dishonoured, the dishonour is that of her family and all who know her. Anyone aggrieved can rightfully claim recompense for the sullying of their honour. Hence, her dishonour must be more severely punished than that of a man. He talks of circumcision—the Abrahamic covenant shared by all believers marked on the body by a cut. For a man the cut exposes his organ. When a woman is cut, it is to remove the thorn of desire from her flesh. God gave Abraham wives and concubines. Thus, so did He confirm in principle a man's right to, and his responsibility for, many women.

"What then is to be learnt from the stories God tells in holy scripture?" The cornerstone of social order is the relationship between man and woman. Man is reason. Woman is other than man, as Satan is God's other. "The God of Abraham is one, and all otherness is falsehood. Woman's subservience to man has been ordained by God. When woman disobeys, she is *nushuz* and aligns herself with the devil. And what does Satan do but seduce. By her very being, woman is seductress. To fight the devil in the guise of woman, God permits a husband to beat a wilful wife." Maulana recites the verse from scripture.

He speaks of the promiscuous increase in birds whose numbers overwhelm the city. "Howbeit, we know from holy text and must wonder, the Lord sent swarms of birds to cast brimstone on Abraha the Abyssinian with his elephant in the desert. The Lord did so but as warning and sign that the Prophet, God's prayers and peace be upon him, was but soon to begin his mission. And so we do ask what lessons from then for now? For lo, the birds return to signal this new age of ignorance and disorder, of sacrifice and struggle, in which once more there be strife between believer and the infidel."

Omar thinks it true—the birds are an evil omen and the line between sin and piety is but a hair's breadth.

The lesson over, Maulana asks Omar to drive four of the students home. In the street Omar finds birds settled on the roof of his cab. He argues with the bird chaser, curses him, demands back the money he paid, eventually gives up. The young men in the cab insist he stop by a kiosk selling newspapers and magazines. The young man in the passenger seat talks to the vendor, pays him, takes a rolled-up magazine. As they drive off, he flashes the cover of a bare-breasted woman and giggles, passes it to the three in the back. They hoot and applaud.

They giggle and quote from scripture. *Men are a power over women by the degree God has favoured some over others.* Yes, yes and then there is this too, *As for those from whom you fear* nushuz, *admonish them, do not sleep with them, beat them.* They pass around the magazine as they discuss the times they live in and whether the signs are those of the end of days, as Maulana claims. Ah, what would they willingly sacrifice to wrestle Satan in the guise of any one of these women, to purge them of wilfulness, to turn them to God's true religion with the tool God gave each of them, and what moves they would do to convert a woman to plead for redemption. They laugh and tease each other with admonishments, mimic Maulana's inflections and intonation.

In a temper Omar tells the young men to respect Maulana and his teachings. Where can they find such wisdom in this day and age? He drops them off downtown, calls the dispatcher for the next assignment.

Told to report back to the main office, he arrives apprehensive. The secretary says the company has obtained a curfew exemption permit for him.

"How come?"

"You provide an essential service."

He laughs. And since when was driving whores to clubs and hotels an essential service?

The dispatch manager hands him the permit, points at the signature. "A general in State Security. Son of a bitch." He grins. "We applied for exemptions for all our drivers, but you're the only one so far. You must have a relative in the army, or maybe do them favours." He looks suspiciously at Omar.

"Well, actually, my uncle is a retired high court judge." Omar sits on an old couch with collapsed springs. Should he be concerned or grateful for the permit? He shrugs and smiles. His phone vibrates. Maulana's number lights up.

Omar waits for the doctor to finish examining Maulana. He glances at the boy he drove to the mall, seated in an armchair, kohl around his eyes, his hair dyed and nails stained with henna. He plays with a gamepad in front of a television, presses buttons to gun down soldiers hiding in ruins. Omar watches. Who does the kid imagine himself—a virtual Bin Laden fighting infidel Crusaders? Omar excuses himself to go to the washroom. As he urinates, a small cockroach, as still as an ink blot, watches from the shower drain. Omar sits on the toilet, dials Mona's number, asks when will Tarek be back.

"I'm not sure."

"I'll come around. It's not right you being on your own without a man."

"Don't start with me."

He argues that as her brother—her guardian—he should know what she does and who she sees.

She interrupts, brusquely says she is not a child in need of a guardian. "Next you'll say I'm *awra*."

"I didn't say anything about *awra*."

She will phone when she needs him to fulfill his brotherly duties. Until then, she will not be taking his calls. She hangs up before he can respond.

He glares at the phone, snaps it closed. There was a time when women respected men. But in this insane topsy-turvy world any woman thinks she can tell any man what to do—Please God, I didn't say my sister is *awra*.

The doctor asks if the young man with hennaed hair can use a syringe to inject insulin. Yes, the boy knows how. The doctor will leave a prescription. He examines the dark prayer bump on Maulana's forehead—swollen like a third eye, blinded and black—asks if it has recently changed shape or colour.

"A wonder and a blessing from the Lord. It has been the same for the last twenty years or more."

The doctor's father and grandfather both prayed daily yet never developed such black protrusions on their foreheads. Most likely a callus, induced by repeated trauma from deliberate impact compounded by abrasion. But he cannot discount the possibility of acanthosis nigricans, a sign of insulin resistance prevalent among type 2 diabetes patients. The hyperpigmentation a possible sign of paraneoplastic syndrome indicative of lung or gastric carcinoma. He asks Maulana if he smokes.

"The occasional cigarette to relax the nerves in the evenings."

"Any digestive problems?"

"No, thanks be to God, and praise be to Him. Though pickled fish can cause indigestion."

The doctor nods, packs away his instruments into his bag.

Maulana has noticed the doctor does not temper his diagnosis by expressions of "God willing" or references to scripture, suspects the doctor may be agnostic or, God forbid, worse, an atheist. For that reason he does not tell him that on the Day of Judgment, when graves give forth their burden and the sun and moon are extinguished by angels, the prayer callus on his forehead will shine a divine light to guide the faithful, risen from their graves, on the path to the gates of paradise. He imagines it will be like the light of lanterns carried by children during the month of Ramadan when they go round to their neighbours' apartments asking for cake and candy in return for telling a riddle-me-rhyme. Then with the light shining forth from his forehead all the world will wonder and know him for one of the righteous for whom a place has been reserved for eternity by the side of the Lord.

For days Maulana has been troubled by a condition he would like to broach with the doctor, but dares not. When he defecates, his feces come alive in the bowl. It took several days of careful observation before he could be certain that what he defecates are cockroaches. As much as he tries, by varying diet and multiplying purgatives, he cannot stop excreting roaches. To avoid embarrassment he defecates at night. Quick shits followed by a flush, but not fast enough to stop the whiskered parasites from escaping up the sides of the bowl. The infestation spreads to the landing and the stairwell. The neighbours complained, called the health inspector, who identified Maulana's apartment as the source of the pestilence and obtrusion to the housing unit.

After the doctor's departure, Maulana waits on the landing outside his apartment, folds about him his black *bisht*, watches two fumigators in grey jumpsuits and rubber boots rise in the elevator to his floor. They roll a cylinder on wheels into the apartment, don gas masks, seal the windows with green tape, prepare to spray, room by room, clouds of white powder pumped from the cylinder. Omar and the boy carry suitcases down to the sidewalk.

Omar drives them to a hotel for the night, rants at the birds for messing his cab and causing delays all across the city. Every night he covers the cab in newspapers, but still the poop seeps through to stain the paintwork. He stops by automated glass doors to the hotel lobby, helps load the bags onto security scanners.

Most mornings, when alone, Mona has the television on with the sound down low. This morning she turns up the volume to listen to an obstetrician talk of Pitocin, Cervidil and Cytotec prescribed and administered intravenously or inserted into the vaginas of mothers past their due date, but even so babies refuse to be born. This he takes as evidence that the cause is not the mothers. God forbid he should impute such blame to them—*beneath whose feet lay the gates of paradise.* No, not *nushuz*, as some rumours claim. He assures his viewers, with a self-deprecating sideways glance at the camera, but a concerted resistance of the unborn to birthing. Whenever amniotomy was attempted it had to be discontinued, as babies born by this method, and by caesarean section, died soon after. The mothers and fetuses when left alone showed no signs of distress and no cause for alarm—heart rates regular, fetal movement normal. His tone takes on a certain gravitas as he warns mothers of an increased risk of placental abruption, but so far there have been no reported cases.

On a talk show, a gynecologist maintains his professional right to a woman's body. With due erudition he appeals to historical precedent, to when concubinage was the norm and a woman's body the ward of men. Of course, this was no poor reflection on the women of the day but simply due to the fact that an educated man knows what is best for a woman. A gynecologist such as himself—he pauses to make his point with a smile—is more knowledgeable of a woman's body than she can possibly be. And, of course, with knowledge comes responsibility. The profession obligated to society at large—he nods for emphasis—to manage women's bodies so that they may procreate future generations, the flesh and blood of the nation. He reassures viewers that modern science will find the cause of and solution to why babies are not being born.

On another program, a university professor describes how his research categorically proves that bird-chitter disturbs the nervous system of the young, drives them to rebellious behaviour. "The plasticity of the brain is impaired by high-pitched twittering." It is unnatural for humans to be in such close proximity to birds. The human race has evolved to live in cities, where low rumbling sounds are the norm.

Mona changes channels to a panel of theologians and philosophers who debate the significance of the unborn's willpower and its implication for understanding the greater evolutionary process from single-cell amoeba to *Homo sapiens*. The moderator asserts that if it can be shown the unborn have willpower greater than the force of nature, then evolution cannot be an unconscious Darwinian roll of the dice, but rather is an act of creation by a greater sentient being, meaning, with all due reverence, Almighty God. The theologians agree, declare the babies' deferred birth evidence of divine intelligence, giving meaning and purpose to existence—proof of the inherent moral character of the universe. The philosophers prevaricate over the significance of the words chosen, protest gendered pronouns in reference to God, speak of the relativity of all things and the falsity of the real in a world engineered by humans, insist on an evolutionary will-to-life that does not require the intervention of a divine being—God must remain in parentheses.

Early morning at the *khana*, Tarek goes to settle his bill, discovers that Kasem has already paid. He asks a young man at the reception desk for directions. The man shrugs, glances around before he continues— according to television reports, communications towers and power lines are down between here and Sidi Adi with roads blocked and casualties in the mountain areas.

"How serious the troubles?"

The young man does not know, but then in a hushed voice speaks of protests in villages, fighting in some places between army and rebels.

In the courtyard Kasem smokes, turns his back on Tarek. When Yaqzan and Leila arrive he pinches the end of the cigarette, drops the burning tip to the ground, puts the stub into his pocket to smoke later. Tarek helps Yaqzan and Leila load their instruments into the van. Neda carries the *qaraqib* castanets for Leila, the cups larger than the palms of her hands.

* * *

In the distance mountains rise and float over a dawn mist. The van speeds past fields of loam. Chugging engines raise groundwater to irrigate low-lying crops, pump to galvanized cisterns that run with pipes like rhizomes from rootstock alongside ploughed furrows. Neda asks Leila if she knows the story of the girl who spoke in starlings and sparrows—the tale the maid from next door had promised to tell her. But Leila does not know the story.

Kasem takes the crushed cigarette with the ragged end out of his pocket, pats it into shape, places it between his lips, searches his pockets for matches, finds them tucked into the cigarette packet where he put them earlier that morning.

"You're not smoking here." Leila snatches the packet from him, leans over Yaqzan, slips it into the glove compartment.

Kasem sighs, removes the raggedy cigarette from his lips, leans back against the side of the van, strokes the dog by his side.

Past the fallows and partway across an expanse of scrubland, a sudden cloud soars from shrubs alongside the road. Whirling swarms of locust, each the length of a man's hand, abdomens red as brimstone, slap against the windshield with a sound like breaking eggs, blur Tarek's vision with yellow mucus. He turns on the windscreen wiper, squirts fluid, smears slime across the glass.

Neda, startled, leans forward to look over Yaqzan's shoulder. She asks Leila if this is the part of the journey where spells are cast and riddles have to be solved.

Leila winks at her. "I have something for you." She searches through the sack with her belongings, removes a spiral shell with a shiny pink lip wrapped in a scarf for safekeeping.

Neda listens to the whispers deep in the shell. "What's it saying?"

"Someday you'll know."

* * *

Mid-afternoon, along a road once cut by caravans, past fields with stones flaked like shale, they approach the foothills.

An army roadblock appears through dust and desert haze.

A soldier peers through the side window, sees Yaqzan with the dog on his lap and the others in the back with musical instruments. He asks for identity cards, inspects them, tells Kasem to get out of the van.

"What's the problem?" Tarek says, nods to Kasem to stay put. He knows once Kasem is taken the questions begin, and they may be forced to leave without him.

"His identity card should state served or exempt from military service." Tarek cannot say that Kasem did not do his military service because ten years ago they were both in prison for taking part in a student demonstration. No, that would not help. He argues for the soldier to raise the barrier, to let them through.

"You'll have to wait for the captain." The soldier turns away.

Tarek slips money from the glove compartment into Kasem's packet of cigarettes, steps out of the car, takes the soldier aside, offers him the packet, lights a cigarette for him.

The soldier takes the packet, slips the money into his pocket, gazes at Neda with Kasem, then, as though he cannot imagine the *sentir* and *qaraqib* being a danger to anybody but the *gnawa*, waves the van through the roadblock. "Go, before the captain comes out."

Leila sighs with relief, her flushed face on the verge of tears.

Neda gazes out the rear window as the checkpoint recedes into a haze of dust behind them.

"Those were my cigarettes you gave away," Kasem mutters.

"If you say another word I'll slap you." Leila glares at him, then turns to Tarek. "You keep driving." Neda grins, full of admiration for Leila.

Yaqzan laughs.

* * *

At a truck stop, Tarek dials Yara's number, asks for news of the city, the birds and the walls.

Yara says everything is much as it was before he left. "We're not leaving the square until the military agrees to free elections." She has spoken to Mona and everything is well with her. She will visit soon.

He feels reassured to know the two of them are in touch.

Boys sell soft drinks from buckets and tea from brass kettles. Kasem calls one of them over, buys off him a cigarette.

Tarek asks directions from a group of truckers.

One says that for the last couple of days the roads were blocked with fallen rocks and rubble. "The army's sweeping the hills for rebels."

Tarek asks about the sanctuary at Sidi Adi.

The truckers shake their heads. They have not heard anything.

The van rolls forward onto the road.

"Will we ever get there?" Neda's tone exasperated.

"We'll be fine once we're at Sidi Adi," Leila says.

To entertain Neda, Yaqzan tells her of his childhood in the mountains, of summer days waved golden. Fields of tulips. Mulberry trees with leaves like frosted glass and boughs threaded with spiders' webs that caught the morning light and hung with dew like an abacus. Autumn skies crimped by winds in folds of white and grey. Winter snow, bright and crisp, etched with cuneiforms of bird prints. Spring storms broke the banks of streams. Fish beat against the mud in shallow nooks. At school he sat on a floor of rush mats, listened to stories of the ancestors—the first created of Adam's spittle before Eve was born of his rib—the first spirits to enrobe in flesh, the most beloved by the Peacock Angel.

He tells her of the sanctuary of Sidi Adi. Its ribbed conical spires of pale stone screened by a filigree of golden leaves in the day's first light. On the outside wall, by heavy wooden doors, a carved snake stained with soot and lampblack in remembrance of the serpent that during the great flood sealed with its body the crack in Noah's ark. Crescent and stars etched in the disc of the sun above the great door. Bouquets of tulips and crocuses, gathered in season, dried and crumbling to brown sheaves hung above the stone portal. On the first day of spring families gathered with cakes and candies they shared with children carrying leaf-shaped lanterns of olive oil which when lit cast a gossamer light that flickered like fireflies until the dawn filled with birdsong.

They drive in the dark. The night air is humid with the scent of vegetation after a day of scorched dust. They reach a village lit by electric bulbs strung on wires across narrow streets, a labyrinth on the side of the mountain. They turn off the road for a track that leads them past a row of single-storey houses, stop on clear ground in a bend against a mud-brick wall. Kasem helps Leila down from the van. She stretches and bends her back. She calls to a group of women in a lantern-lit courtyard threshing stalks of grain with knotted-rope flails, asks if there is anywhere to get something to eat and spend the night. A woman stops work, comes forward, describes the way to a nearby *khana.*

At an open-air café, under bright bulbs strung along courtyard walls, men smoke shisha pipes and drink tea. A woman squats by kettles on flaring burners. A young man in a leather apron refreshes charcoal in the burning bowls of shishas. Tarek collects chairs around two tables pushed together. Kasem talks to the woman, orders meals and a shisha for himself to smoke.

Tarek asks about the troubles, the damage and the number of casualties. The men know nothing more than they have heard on the radio. They are sure there must be casualties. There always are when there are troubles. Besides, wherever there are soldiers, there have to be casualties.

Tarek and Neda take the leftovers of their meal to the dog in the van. It wakes and barks when it sees them. Tarek pours it some water. "He's getting too old for all this travelling."

"Poor thing." She strokes the dog. Its eyes brighten with her touch.

Only two bars of signal strength out of five show on Tarek's phone. Neda calls her mother to say good night. She glances at him. "Mummy says, no news for Cousin." He nods, satisfied.

When they get back to the café's courtyard with blankets from the van, young men are questioning Kasem. They carry knives and sticks. Leila, tears in her eyes, calls Neda to her at Yaqzan's table away from the armed men.

Neda takes Leila's hand, squeezes it.

Tarek goes to the men surrounding Kasem. "What's the problem?"

They are the newly formed village militia. They want to know where the *gnawa* are from, where they are going and when they will be leaving. The men raise their voices, demand answers to different questions asked all at once.

"We'd like to spend the night here, then leave in the morning."

Two of the men take Tarek aside, quiz him away from Kasem, demand to see his identity card.

"Is the child yours?"

"Yes, she's my daughter."

"And the woman?"

"She's his wife."

"Not the girl's mother?"

"No."

They hold up his identity card to the light, want to know why he shaved his moustache. The questions continue a while longer with one group clustered about Tarek, the other around Kasem. The groups confer. The man who led the interrogation comes forward, shakes hands with Tarek and Kasem, apologizes for the degree of suspicion. "We have to take precautions. It's our homes we're protecting."

Kasem asks if he can have a cigarette.

The man stares at him, then takes out a half-empty packet from his pocket, offers it to Kasem, who takes two cigarettes. "One for now, the other for later." The men leave, wishing the *gnawa* a good evening and safe travel.

"You just had to ask for a smoke?" Tarek cannot understand what Kasem was thinking. "What if he knifed you instead?"

"They were as afraid of us as we were of them." Kasem slips a cigarette between his lips. "If anything happens to me, take Leila and Yaqzan to Sidi Adi."

"If we leave you anywhere, you'll likely end up arrested or dead."

"I can take care of myself." Kasem walks off, lights the cigarette.

Tarek helps Leila lay the bedding in the yard by the kitchen of the café. "If anything happens to me, promise you'll take care of Neda."

"You don't have to ask. She's like my daughter."

Tarek nods, reassured, but thinks this journey a mistake that may yet cost them dearly.

Tarek wakes to a night still with stars. The moon a thin sliver of a crescent tarnished by smoke from distant fires that light up the sky. Flames, like shoals of golden koi, weave in and out of faraway ruins, flap tails of flame in the dark, feed on brash and rubble. He hears the scraping of cicadas.

Leila, swaddled in a blanket, turns on her side. "You awake?"

"I'm a light sleeper."

They watch the fires burn along the horizon.

"Is Yaqzan the reason you and Kasem are going to Sidi Adi?"

"One reason." She is quiet for a moment. "We want to have a baby. We haven't had much luck. They say a wish made at Sidi Adi can help."

The van climbs the side of the mountain, picks up speed past a sheer face of grey rock, passes the occasional truck, bus and car. The road narrows, turns sharply back on itself. Tarek pulls to one side close to the cliff face to let by a truck. Many of the houses clustered into villages seem to grow from the sides of stone escarpments. In places, rows of buildings turned to rubble spill clothes and furnishings along the hillside in a blaze of colours against the grey of stone and dry shrubs.

"What caused this?" Neda asks.

"The army, most likely." Kasem strokes the dog resting by his side.

She gazes from the rear window at men and women clearing stones and rocks. Children play in an orchard of lime trees. "It's so very sad."

Leila hugs her.

Tarek slows the van to a stop beside two boys carrying a large flat-screen television. He asks the way. The boys are not sure. Here is all they know.

Kasem asks where they are going.

"We've lost power, but our uncle's house has electricity."

"We're taking him the television."

They need to fix a satellite dish to their uncle's roof in time for tonight's soccer match.

Tarek offers them a ride.

They decline, say they can cut across country and, besides, their uncle's house is closer this way and not the way he is going.

Tarek drives past fields with women working. He stops, calls out to them, asks if the road is blocked up ahead. One of the women shields her eyes from the sun as it breaks through thin cloud. "It's blocked for a ways. Take the track at the next fork and you can cut back to the road further up." She points to a path barely wide enough for the van.

"Was your house damaged?" Yaqzan asks.

The army searched homes for weapons, she says. They blew up the houses of those they accused of supporting rebels.

Kasem leans forward over Yaqzan's seat so he can speak through the side window. "Are people leaving?"

"Some families."

"Where to?"

"Anywhere they think is safe. Some to the city, others to the coast."

"What about you?"

"I have to irrigate the fields or else there'll be no crops to feed us this year."

"Where's your husband?" Yaqzan asks.

"Helping the neighbours."

Yaqzan wishes her good fortune and God's protection.

"Next left." She points up ahead.

Neda waves to the women in the fields from the back window as the van moves forward, picks up speed.

At the fork they turn sharp left to climb the side of the hill, stop as a flock of sheep swarms over a broken stone wall to block their path. Tarek waits as boys run to shoo the sheep to a field to make room for them to pass.

* * *

Before the turn in the track to rejoin the tarmac road, they stop for lunch at a village café. Old men sit on mats in the shade of a tree. Tarek slips his shoes off to join them, greets the men. He orders meals for himself, his daughter and the *gnawa*. They are served rice and vegetables in bowls with tea in short stout tumblers. Tarek counts out his money. Leila pleads with him to let them pay, swears that unless he agrees, she will make her own way to Sidi Adi, even if she has to walk there alone through this maze of villages and hills. They argue. He knows they cannot have much money, but they know neither does he. Finally, he agrees to split the bill for meals and let the *gnawa* share the cost of gasoline.

A woman wires an old television to a box on the wall. Men sit around and watch, sip their tea and stare at the blank screen that greys from black then lights up with white specks like snow and lines that rotate downwards and then roll back up. She turns dials on the side of the television, slaps it, gives up. "I'll tune it later."

The men complain later may be too late. They want to watch the soccer match and fear there will be no reception.

"It's not on for a couple of hours." She throws her hands up in the air. "I've work to do and you want to be fed."

Tarek asks the men the safest way to Sidi Adi.

"These days, nowhere's safe."

An old man speaks of the blast that tore apart his house. "The army says they're defending the nation, the rebels fight for God. And what are we, chaff?" He speaks of deaths, friends and family he has had to bury.

Kasem says he will go feed the dog. He will wait in the van until everybody is ready to leave.

"Can I come?" Neda feels sadness like a weight on everything, not like any sadness she has known before. She feels it heavy on Kasem, takes his hand. He hesitates, appears surprised by her touch, pulls away, relents, holds her hand. They leave together.

Tarek listens to stories of grief, aware that listening is all he can do to help.

At the van, Kasem smokes in short inhalations. "It's a miserable bitch of a world." He throws the cigarette aside, climbs into the back by Neda and Leila.

Tarek searches his bag for the small pouch in which he placed the amber pendant he made for his daughter's birthday. He had all but forgotten about it on the journey. He hangs the pendant about her neck with a silver chain Mona gave him. She gazes at the winged inclusion. "It's an angel."

"To keep you safe."

She hugs him, holds on to him. Tears moisten his neck.

"What's the matter?"

"I miss Mummy. I don't like it here."

"We'll go home soon, as soon as we can."

She squeezes him tightly.

They stop by a cluster of huts nestled in a cleft of the mountain above fields of barley. Neda phones her mother. Sound fades in and out. Mona says she is well. The neighbour's maid is a godsend. She does all the shopping on her way in the morning and even helps with the cooking.

Neda asks about the baby.

"Baby's resting inside Mummy's tummy and everything's fine." Mona tells them of a visit by a uniformed State Security officer who wanted to know when Cousin will return. She hopes to meet with her uncle soon and hopefully will have better news to report.

AK makes its way past rows of broken houses, fronts and sides mounds of brick and stone. People clamber over rubble, extend sheets of plastic, rugs and blankets from poles for shelter. Every so often a house stands as though untouched by conflict. Everywhere birds peck and hop in the debris, settle on loose hanging power lines, perch along the tops of half-demolished walls sheared to ruins. The dog, its hind legs on Yaqzan's lap, leans forward to watch the chaos through the passenger window. Silent, it seems to recognize that nothing is as it should be. At the edge of a village, black flags mark a fresh grave. A body wrapped in a white sheet lies on the dark soil, awaiting burial.

Neda struggles to comprehend the grief she sees about her. "It's so really random."

Leila sorts through the baggage to find a bottle of water, drinks, offers the bottle to Kasem. Neda lays her head on Leila's breast, falls asleep. She awakes restless, returns to the back window, watches children playing in and around the debris of destroyed homes. A girl alone among the brick and stone lifts her head. Her cheeks swell. Her mouth opens, widens as though for a scream. Then, slowly, with wings pointed forward a tiny starling flutters out, flies upwards, followed by another. More children raise their heads as though in chorus. From open mouths, in ones and twos and then more rapidly, tiny birds emerge with wings flapping— starlings, swallows, martins, so many of all kinds. Neda cannot count them, nor imagine how they can be in bodies no larger than her own, and several so much smaller. Birds pour into the sky. She turns to call Leila to the window, but both she and Kasem are asleep against the sides of the van. When Neda looks back through the window they are past the village, picking up speed through open fields. Above the ruins grey clusters soar and spin, billow and gather in endless flow.

At the outskirts of a village they wait for the road ahead to be cleared, sit in silence in a café under the stern gaze of locals—faces morose and suspicious. The television turned down low plays images of soccer fans inside a stadium. Neda asks for the phone to call her mother to tell her what she saw of children and birds. Her father turns on his phone. No bars show on the screen. The line does not connect. He slips the phone back into his pocket, concerned that from here on there will be no connection. When he asks the way to Sidi Adi, everybody, even the children, offers directions. They should follow the road around the mountain. Just keep going. Cross the high valley.

The teams run onto the pitch. The volume is turned up. The auditorium fills with chants and roars. The referee tosses a coin. Everybody in the café ignores the strangers, their attention engaged by the start of the match.

In the back of the van, Neda leans her head on Leila's shoulder, asks about the name of the shrine.

"Sidi Adi was one of God's chosen on earth," says Yaqzan. "For the sake of his saints God works miracles."

That evening, with light fading, they discuss whether to sleep out or spend the night at a village.

"We shouldn't keep driving once it's dark." Tarek is concerned they might run into an army patrol.

"I don't think stopping at a village will be any safer," Kasem says.

"We're best off the road and alone." Leila's tone is final.

They drive for another hour, then continue over rough ground to stop by tall rocks along the mountainside, sheltered from view. With a thin scattering of clouds, the night should be warm enough to sleep out. Tarek sorts the bedding, pulls out the blankets. Yaqzan, tired from the drive, decides to sleep early in the back of the van. Leila spreads a blanket for him to lie on, wraps another around him. Tarek opens a bottle of water, drinks, takes from his wallet the sheet of paper with the mathematical poem, gazes at it, then slips it back into his pocket. Unable to call Mona, he feels this is his most direct connection with her.

"How do you stay so calm?" Kasem's words break harshly into Tarek's thoughts. "I can't get all the images of hurt out of my head."

Tarek thinks himself anything if not troubled. "My world is what fits in this van. Anything else happens in an alternate universe beyond my control. I'm not responsible for it. It's how I've survived these ten years."

Kasem glares at him, clenches his teeth. "Well, I didn't choose the world I was born into."

"Your priority should be to keep Leila safe so she can have your child."

"That's really none of your business."

Tarek thinks he has had all he can take of Kasem, tosses him a blanket from the back of the van.

Kasem walks away along the side of a stony incline. He stoops to break off a twig from a dry shrub, chews on it, spits out the bitter sap. He sits alone, stares at the setting sun with the blanket pulled about his shoulders.

Tarek grabs a bottle of water from the van, walks over to Kasem, throws him the bottle. He stares at Kasem, dares him to respond, then returns to the van to collect a blanket for himself.

Neda and Leila lie together by flowering shrubs and a tree with large red corollas on branches that reach to the sky. At any moment, it could rain jasmine and honeysuckle. Starlings swarm about the crown of the tree, swirl in legions high above, chase the leader in a spiral wave that sweeps up then drops to settle on boughs, raise a chorus to fall silent with the gathering dusk.

As the sky darkens, Neda and Leila take turns making up names for constellations, watch for falling stars.

"Tell me a story," Neda says as Tarek bends over to kiss her good night.

"Before you were born your mother ate rose petals so she would have a beautiful baby. You were born of roses."

Neda smiles. Yes, this really is her most favourite of all her father's stories.

Leila turns to him. "We'll be safe once we arrive at Sidi Adi."

He had thought so, but is no longer certain.

Once everybody is settled, Tarek wraps himself in a blanket and thinks of Mona. He pictures her in their apartment, reading or watching television, or just as likely asleep. He wakes in the night to a calm of grass, trees and stars in a vast expanse of blackness. He feels a measure to the stillness—a drift and flow as with a wave. Distant and imminent like sound, yet silent, it extends from mountains and valleys to horizon, sky and stars. The fabric and rhythm of all that is.

7

With every rise of ground they travel, Tarek checks his phone for a connection. On the side of a hill a single bar flickers. He stops the van and dials Mona's number, calls Neda to join him by the side of the road. The line cuts out before the call connects. He tries again a couple of times, then gives up. Neda's eyes tear—it is so unfair, the phone not working.

As Tarek drives, to distract Neda from thoughts of her mother, Yaqzan tells the story of when as a boy he left the mountains with his sister, Fadia, for a valley cleft in the side of the great stone plateau. At dawn the sun rose over sheets of copper sand and rocks banked in great waves against the amber arc of the sky, shot quicksilver across the waters of a lake that welled from the side of the escarpment. Clusters of white-washed adobe huts formed a village from whose fields the breeze bore the scent of jasmine to the dry odourless air of the desert.

In a mosque by a sand barrier of tamarind trees and cacti the boy sat on a floor of rush mats. About him men as tall as palm trees rolled strings of honey-coloured beads between fingers and thumbs, their whispers like a breeze rustling the leaves of an open book. On a raised dais the Wali, God's shadow on earth with authority over all believers, his name recited in prayers alongside those of the prophets—praise and prayers be upon them—preached war by the valley's farmers on Tibu grazers from oases far in the desert. That night the heads of the Tibu dead were hung in trees as feed for crows and nests for wasps.

In weekly sermons the Wali instructed his congregation on justice in this life that, assuredly, led to paradise in the next. He spoke of the hourglass as the image of man's destiny—the sands above, the predetermined future, those below, the past. The present a fleeting moment as one tense passes to another—God's day of final judgment the gravity point that draws all to it. With his eloquence as undeniable as his message irrefutable, the teachings of God's shadow imprinted on the boy's mind as a pen inscribed a tablet.

After evening prayers, the boy brought oil for the mosque's lanterns, poured ink from iron filings and lampblack into a small pot by a set of reed quills for the Wali to record his visions in *The Book of Knowledge*. "Can I read what you've written?"

"It's not for the eyes of the living. It's an account of what's to come."

"How can you know?"

"If my community holds to my teachings then the future will be as I foresee it."

One night, as the boy prepared the lanterns, the Wali saw the blue tattooed *kutrai* of sun and stars between his thumb and forefinger. "You bear the sign of the Peacock Angel."

"The spirit of mercy whose tears extinguish the fires of hell, my lord Wali."

"Do you believe in the enrobing of spirits after death?"

"The Prophet said, *People sleep, should they die they awaken.*"

"An errant reading. Should they die to the falsehoods of the world they will awaken to God's truth."

"It says in scripture, *And you were dead and He brought you back to life; and He shall cause you to die and shall bring you back to life, and in the end shall gather you to Himself."*

"Dead to the Lord and now alive in His teachings."

"If God and the angels will it, a person who dies may return enrobed in new flesh. The old stories tell us so."

"If stories are in holy scripture, then it's best people read them in the sacred texts. If they are not, then, like graven images, they are falsehoods and lies and must not be spoken."

On the first day of the Feast of Abraham, Yaqzan's sister, Fadia, was taken with the girls of the valley to the lake for cleansing. The cut made, she cried, was carried to the water, a rag held to her wound. With the coming of night, he watched as moths caught in lantern flames flared to rise as ash.

At dawn Fadia's body, as stiff as a chrysalis, was wrapped in white sheets and taken for burial.

"Don't," Leila says. "You'll give us nightmares."

"But please." Neda pulls a sulky face. "I want to hear the story."

One day the boy met a gypsy trader selling magnets and microscopes, and a silver disc etched with leaves and vines, a flap sprung open to reveal two hands that moved around a dial.

"It's a clock," the gypsy trader said. "A machine to carry in your pocket to track time." The boy bartered for the watch his throwing knife, with its long, curved blades protruding at angles from the central shaft.

In the months that followed, he listened to the ticking of the watch, realized time now knew the valley, and knowing it had asserted its order. Rains came only when Aldebaran rose in the constellation of Taurus. Plants that once flourished all year round grew only in season. Stars once fixed in the firmaments now traversed the heavens. The static order of duration, once measured by sand running through an hourglass, changed to one that moved in cycles.

Over the next few months, the Wali appeared to age and weaken. One night he fell into a fever, covered himself in blankets. His followers whispered that *afrit* called *marid* fed on the Wali's spirit, driving him to death. In the olive light of a lantern, the Wali beckoned the boy, whispered to him, "Men are sheep. Every flock must have its shepherd. There will come another after me. Remember me to him." In return for a promise, he granted the boy the power to bring rain to the valley.

"Then what happened to the Wali?" asked Neda.

"He is buried in the valley now lost to the desert."

Next-door's maid arrives at the apartment, unpacks the shopping, complains prices remain scorchingly high. "They say because of the protests the old president's going. The barricades will come down and the birds will leave." Of course, once everything gets back to normal it will all need a good clean. It means more work for her and a little extra money, which helps. Especially as she has children of her own and it's such a long bus ride home in the evenings. Then there's all the cleaning she has to do in her shanty and the next day's cooking so her daughters can have their dinners ready once they're back from school. She has to keep one day ahead of herself and sometimes several days and that really isn't so easy. The eldest of course helps, but at an age when boys are a distraction—so worrisome, as if she doesn't have enough to think about without having to wonder what the girl is up to. Oh, she shouldn't be talking so freely. She is so sorry for going on like this. But God willing, things will be as they should. Though who knows what may happen next?

Mona nods, listens to the maid as to an echo in days hollow without those she loves. In the kitchen the maid puts the shopping away—cans in cupboards, fruit and vegetables on racks in the refrigerator. She has found a jar of the pickled herrings Mona craved the other day, shows it off with pride, explains how she had to ask at several stores. "You'd never have found it yourself. You have to know where to look."

Mona thanks her, though the taste is no longer with her. For the last two days she has yearned for mango ice cream—a flavour from her childhood. Then a question she has meant to ask comes to her, "What is your name?"

"Heba."

"Heba, I'd like it if you call me Mona."

"I can't. It wouldn't be right."

"I'm Mona."

"Mona." Heba pauses to weigh the sound as she speaks it, to sense how it fits the new mistress. "The flame on the kitchen cooker burns low. You'll need a new cylinder of butane."

Mona nods. Maybe the supplier will call round in time to bring a full one. But then, with all the troubles, who knows when that might be?

Mona wakes from a nap with a start, certain of something missing. She reaches to her side, realizes she is alone. She lies still, listens to muffled street sounds, tries to bridge the distance between her and Tarek.

She sometimes wondered what would have happened to either of them if, when she was a student, she had not volunteered to write to a political prisoner, and had not drawn his name by chance, one among several, from a list provided by a lawyer.

From the chest of drawers she removes the small bundle of letters she exchanged with Tarek when he was in the city penitentiary awaiting his appeal for clemency after two years in a prison camp.

She sorts through the envelopes, stops to read the letters with the mathematical symbols, struggles to recall what the equations mean. The first of them she wrote after Neda was brought into her life, barely weeks old. She could no more refuse the child than she could abandon Tarek once she knew him and began to love him.

Alone most of the day, for several days in the apartment, she no longer thinks she knows herself. In Tarek's gaze she felt herself confirmed. As much as she misses him, misses his touch, she misses the quiet immediacy of their silences together. A shared innocence, as everything is innocent before the overlay of words. Strange to think she could ever really trust another person enough to love them. Her first night with him she awoke, rested her head on his chest, felt his warmth on her cheek. His closed eyes flickered and she thought him dreaming, wondered what he saw that she could not. Yes, this was what she wanted—comfort and ease with another, and a world yet to be discovered.

A cat's persistent mew draws her to the apartment door. A stray looks up from the mat, pleads to be fed. Its belly swollen hangs low, sways pregnant. What does she have for it? Maybe milk, and the jar of pickled herrings brought by Heba.

From the field clinic by the side of the mosque, Yara watches armoured personnel carriers approach, then stop beyond the barricades. They change positions, creep forward, then roll back, never more than by three or four metres. At night they offer cover to groups of State Security men out of uniform and street gangs recruited by the military. The men attack with stones and petrol bombs thrown over the barriers of sheet metal and scaffolding. Along the side of the museum at the far perimeter of the square, tanks stopped when people climbed into the caterpillar tracks or lay in their way. Now, old and young sit with blankets pulled about their shoulders against cogwheels. Others bring food and bottles of water, wait to take turns with them. Like the young men at the barricades Yara writes her phone number on the inside of her arm. Every evening she goes over the figures with a ballpoint pen to make sure they are clear to read. Every morning she calls home to reassure her father she is alive and well, pretends she is at the emergency ward of the city hospital, knows he pretends to believe her.

She calls Mona, asks how she is doing and can she come round for an hour or so.

Mona sits on the edge of the bed, watches Yara shower and then dress in a pair of her jeans and a blouse.

"The numbers keep growing," Yara tells her. "Something happens to people once they're there. They stop being afraid. Start thinking for themselves in ways they hadn't before."

"I worry. I can't afford to lose both you and Tarek."

"We've had enough of soldiers."

"That's like saying you want to change the world."

"What's wrong with that?"

Tears well in Mona's eyes.

Yara hugs her, holds her until the sobs become the steady in-out, in-out of Mona's breath.

* * *

Through a pass between tall outcrops of rock, AK travels along a road that zigzags past the side of a mountain to a high valley. The stony landscape, with strips of green and patches of yellow in the sun, turns a deep russet in the shadows. At this altitude the air chills with every passing cloud.

"Sidi Adi is the heart of the world," Yaqzan says.

Yes, Neda can see why he would say that. Here the soil, thin as skin, covers rock white as bone. Veins of water break in streams, then submerge again.

They continue along the track, every so often pass solitary stone houses sheltered among tall mulberry trees. Outcrops of rocks appear flint grey, by the roadside dark red. As they alter direction for the mountainside the landscape changes once more, from a plain punctuated by dry shrubs to fields of tall grass. Late morning, they pull up to a drystone wall, stop by four parked cars and a taxicab. Neda and her father feed the dog, leave it in the van with a fresh bowl of water, follow the *gnawa* on a path past stone houses. They walk slowly, fall behind. As they crest a hill, through trees they see below in a valley the fluted stone spires of the sanctuary of Sidi Adi. Beyond it mountains of dark stone with large shrubs that grip the earth like fists. Ahead of them, the *gnawa* enter the yellow stone courtyard of the sanctuary. Their robes flutter in a light breeze like butterflies in a field of corn.

At the entrance to the sanctuary Tarek reads the inscription to Neda: "In the name of God, the Merciful, the Compassionate." He removes his shoes and socks, Neda her sandals. Tarek carries his shoes heel to toe in one hand, runs the other along the black snake carved on the outside wall. They proceed through a narrow corridor to a chamber with the tombs of the seven angels each covered in a cloth of different colour, knots tied at each corner. Leila stands by the blue angel's banner, calls Neda to her, tells her to untie a corner knot, then tells her to retie it so that her wishes come true.

Neda closes her eyes, touches her pendant, unties the knot, in a whisper asks the angels to help her find the Wishing Rose to break the spell that stops babies being born so Mummy can have her baby, Yaqzan find his new mother and Kasem give up smoking because Leila wants him to.

From the tombs of angels a corridor leads past a low, narrow door to the sanctum of Sidi Adi and farther to a sacred spring that murmurs a constant prayer. Leila shows Neda the nugget of salt her father bought from the woman at the side of the road, says they should place it as an offering in the stream.

Tarek stoops through the door to the sanctum. At the centre of the room, dimly lit by oil lamps, a wrought iron grate surrounds a raised block covered by a woven rug. Tied to the grate are coloured threads and ribbons. A man murmurs an invocation; another incants a prayer. Tarek thinks it all superstition, an expression of pent-up emotion and magical thinking. He sits in thick shadow, leans against the wall to one side of the entrance, closes his eyes overcome by exhaustion.

He wakes to see Leila at the grate. In tears she wipes her face with the back of her hand. She unties coloured threads from the iron grille, gathers them, by a lantern braids the threads into a single cord.

Neda, by his side, leans her head on him. He puts his arm around her. She looks up and smiles. "You were sleeping."

He nods, still drowsy.

Yaqzan sits against the wall close by Tarek.

"Have you found what you're looking for?" Tarek asks him.

"Too soon," says Yaqzan. "Maybe tonight Sidi Adi will be gracious."

* * *

In the courtyard to the sanctuary Kasem tells Tarek, "I've reserved two rooms at the *khana* by where we parked. One's for you and Neda. I thought it best before the evening and people arrive for the *moulid*."

Among the houses clustered by the sanctuary, Tarek and Neda find a small restaurant still open for lunch serving skewers of lamb and chicken with flatbread and salad. Leila joins them as they wait to be served. A man in a black apron removes from a refrigerator marinated meat in a large metal bowl, cuts and skewers it with onion slices, lays it on charcoal burners. The meat drips marinade, smokes the small, dark shack.

Neda eats grilled chicken strips wrapped in flatbread. Since leaving home, she is less picky with her food. Today, she eats everything served with the sandwich, including the garlic sauce in a small paper cup. "Do you think birds really evolved from dinosaurs?"

Tarek shrugs. "I suppose."

"Chickens too?"

"Maybe."

"They must have been big chickens."

"You mean like Tyrannosaurus Chickens?"

She bites into her sandwich, drips garlic sauce, wipes her face with a paper napkin. "Maybe Brontosaurus Chickens."

"Maybe they evolved from small dinosaurs."

"Like what?"

"Tiny-saurus Rex."

She rolls her eyes.

"Some dinosaurs were small." He tries to sound convincing.

"Those were lizards. Don't you know anything about reptiles?"

Leila supposes lizard is what one would call a small dinosaur.

Tarek asks a waiter for bones for the dog. They give him a handful wrapped in newspaper. As the waiter brings tea to their table, Neda takes the bones to the van.

"Do you wish you'd kept her?" Tarek watches the dog fight a bone.

"Reham would have wanted her to be with her father." Leila would never go against her sister's wishes.

Yes, he understands, but still, Leila may have felt the child was as much hers as his. After all, he had left, as Kasem keeps reminding him.

"Had you refused to take her it would have been different."

He calls the waiter to pay.

Leila shows him the coloured threads she braided in the sanctuary. "It's a *dezi* for Mona's baby to wear about its neck to protect it from evil." She turns and knots the *dezi* about his wrist—its threads red, blue and golden.

"What about yours?"

"I'll make one when I know I'm pregnant."

Buses arrive. People descend in brightly coloured shirts and dresses to make their way to the shrine.

Leila calls to Neda, tells her they should collect flowers to place in the sanctuary.

"Like Yaqzan did when he was a boy?"

"Just like Yaqzan."

Tarek buys a packet of cigarettes from a man setting up a stand by the car park. He returns to the sanctuary courtyard in search of Kasem, sits in the sun on the pale flagstones, his back against a low stone wall. An elderly woman scatters bread crumbs. Swallows and martins hop and peck the ground. Kasem arrives from the *khana*, carries the stringed *sentir* across his back and two sets of *qaraqib*. Tarek holds up the cigarettes to draw Kasem's attention. "A packet to make up for the one I gave away."

"I've given up smoking."

"Given up, or giving up?"

"All right, giving up." Kasem rips the top off the packet, shakes out a cigarette.

"I don't recall. Did you smoke in the camp?"

"When I could get cigarettes. Otherwise it was *bango*."

Yes, occasionally Tarek did too.

Kasem sits, lights the cigarette, closes his eyes. The lines on his face soften as he inhales.

"How long have you and Leila been trying?"

Kasem sits, exhales smoke. "Leila thinks being here will help."

Tarek watches the shadows spread from the hilltops with the sun slipping towards the horizon. "Do you still blame me for Reham's death?"

"Blame's a strong word."

"What word would you use?"

Kasem nips the burning tip from the cigarette. It glows as it drops on a flagstone. He slips the unfinished cigarette into his jacket pocket. "I want to thank you for what you did at the checkpoint and then again in the village. It was a risk you took. Fact is I'd die sooner than go back to prison."

"I can't go back either."

"The day we met you and Neda, I wasn't expecting, never expected, to see you again."

"Serendipity, I suppose."

"I suppose." Kasem gazes at the mountains, then turns to Tarek. "At the prison camp, I felt you'd betrayed us. Taken your freedom and left us."

"It wasn't like that."

"It's what I felt." Kasem stands, leaves to fetch Yaqzan from the sanctuary.

Tarek remains in the courtyard, feels the last of the day's warmth on his face and arms. His mind drifts to memories of Reham. Their time together so surreptitious and fleeting, every thought or feeling gained an unbearable intensity—*I have tried to forget you. Thought the memory of you unfaithfulness to Mona. When I did think of you, I couldn't stop all of me wanting all of you.* He wonders what Mona is doing—probably reading her novel unless Yara is with her. He closes his eyes, recalls water foaming from a bed of pebbles along an outcrop of tall grey rocks. Chilled underground, a stream flowed ice cold, started as a narrow rivulet, spread to the width of a river. Mona lay against the prow of a rowboat. Her hand over the side ran ripples in the stream. He bent to the oars. Once away from the banks shipped the sculls, slipped from the board to lie beside her. She dripped water from the tips of her fingers onto his arms and face hot from the sun, flushed with exertion. She laughed as he ducked the droplets.

They floated past willow branches that glanced the water's edge, drifted to shallows shaded by trees. The hull grated on pebbles to the river's gentle flow and ebb. He watched her sleep under leaves gilded by the sun. Then, he was as close to her as he has ever been. His happiness a measure of all happiness past and to come.

The truck carried the prisoners across the great stone plateau from the train line to a border post where guards stood ready with bolt-action rifles. Once the back door of the wagon opened they dragged them out by their chains—barely alive from hours in the heat and thirst of the journey.

Sheets and blankets dispensed, the prisoners were led to their cells, served the first day's meal of lentils and rice on metal plates, water from an unglazed urn. All the next day they shifted rubble, cleared mounds of sand, placed stone upon stone, fetched water from a well to mix with cement for the concrete to construct walls around walls around the prison block.

Within a week more prisoners arrived to share the burden. The guards sat in the shade of the barracks, barely paid the prisoners any attention, smoked *bango* grown in the valley and dried in the sun. They giggled as their heads lightened, watched prisoners stumble and trip over stones and leg irons as day after day they built walls.

Working in the heat of the sun, the prisoners took off their shirts, their chests and backs awash with sweat. Their bodies marked with scars, purple tumescent welts and black bruises.

"What caused these?"

"Wires and hoses."

"And those?"

"Acid burns."

The prisoners told of punishments endured during interrogation. They talked of pain—wounds that pulsated and ached long after beatings had stopped, of lightning that flashed in the brain, of liquid that burned in the bloodstream. They talked of pain beyond the guards' comprehension. Knowing what the prisoners had endured induced a strange respect. Then, one day, the guards removed the ankle chains. A few days later they no longer pressed the men to finish building walls. After all, to where would they escape? There was nothing but desert to the very horizon and beyond.

Tarek was among the first prisoners to arrive, Kasem one of the last. They shared a cell. Kasem's mother, a painter with friends in the Ministry of Culture, arranged to send him packets of ground coffee with the quarterly dispatch to the camp. When Tarek went running, morning and evening, Kasem boiled water in a can over a fire of twigs, served coffee on Tarek's return. Often, he thought he owed Kasem his sanity, along with the endless supply of coffee.

* * *

Late afternoon and into the early evening, taxis and cars bring people from villages in the mountains to Sidi Adi. Tarek watches buses drop off families at the edge of the courtyard, then return to the car park to wait out the night. What was once an empty space fills with children. He would enjoy having Mona here with him—maybe next year, or the year after with Neda and the newborn. He watches his daughter. Her face is not as he once knew it, at times now unfamiliar. Away from Mona, she no longer sees herself through her mother's eyes, chooses instead to be seen in Leila's image.

At one end of the courtyard, Kasem has set up for the night's performance. He sits on the ground, the *sentir* on his lap. As he tunes it, Leila demonstrates to Neda how to hold the *qaraqib*, how to clack it in rhythm with the singing. Yaqzan sits cross-legged, listens to Leila and Neda, smiles and nods to their conversation.

As darkness spreads from horizon to horizon, flickering oil lamps light the courtyard. Neda claps the *qaraqib* by Leila's side. Kasem plays the *sentir*. Yaqzan sways as he murmurs, rehearses his words. Tarek leans against the sanctuary wall, watches Neda, thinks she could so easily be mistaken for Leila and Kasem's daughter. How Leila must have loved her sister to part with the child. And how Mona must have loved him to be willing to keep his daughter.

The open space of the courtyard, strung with lamps, fills with families. A short distance from a large mulberry tree, its leaves golden in the light of lanterns hung from its branches, children play on swings and slides. Tarek stands to catch a glimpse of Neda through the gathering. She sits cross-legged on the ground, moves to the music, appears and disappears like a candle's flicker between the crowd collecting about the *gnawa*. She strikes the spoon-shaped *qaraqib* with as firm resolve as she worked the puppets at the Karagoz theatre. He had not seen it before—nor wanted to, he supposes—but how determined she is in all she does. He smiles to think he will be no match for her once she is older.

Tarek listens to talk of soldiers and rebels, and of refugees making their way farther into the mountains or seeking refuge along the coastal plain. How much longer before Sidi Adi is overtaken by the troubles? To stay with the *gnawa* is the best option for Neda should anything happen to him.

As the evening wears on Neda tires. When Tarek goes to her, she protests that she wants to stay with Leila, starts to cry. She holds on to him as he lifts her and carries her back to the *khana*. She is asleep by the time they reach their room. As he undresses her to slip on her nightgown, he finds the spiral shell Leila gave her, thinks it familiar, but then thinks not. Places it by the pendant on the side table, tucks Neda into bed, watches over her as she sleeps, thinks her returned to him as he has always known her—a serious child, inwardly calm, sweet and gentle.

8

Morning sunlight streams through the windows of the airport arrivals lounge. Omar holds up a sign with the name *Nathan*.

The elderly client looks tired. He hands his suitcase to Omar, clips shades onto his glasses. He speaks of his flight from Toronto delayed eight hours because of bad weather in London. Some information would have been helpful, but the British have yet to learn the rudiments of good customer service, left him in a crowded lounge with no indication of when his plane would take off, if ever. Then the delayed landing because of swarms of starlings over the runway.

Omar rolls the suitcase along the polished stone-tiled floor to glass doors leading to the car park, complains of the blight he has had to endure for weeks of birds knowing no decency, soiling everything, disrupting the life of decent folk. The authorities tried everything from phosphorus gas to poisoned bait, but still the flocks keep gathering. And what's worse, their twitter has done something to people's brains, driven them into the streets to camp in the city's main square. Ministries shut down for days, public services ground to a halt, power outages and fuel scarce at gas stations. His company has laid off drivers. He is kept on because of his curfew permit.

On the flight over Nathan read in the newspaper the old dictator has resigned.

Omar waves a hand in the air. So the old autocrat's gone, but the square's still occupied with protestors making new demands. "Now they want freedom and democracy." He laughs drily. "It's not democracy we need, but God's law as laid down in scripture." It's time the army stepped in to impose some discipline, get the economy moving again. He says all this in broken English, locks the suitcase in the trunk of the cab, falls silent when he realizes the client has settled into the back seat and can no longer hear him. In the cab, Omar asks the name of the hotel to drive to. The client checks his watch, digs deep into the breast pocket of his jacket, fumbles with a piece of paper, reads the address of a cemetery. "I'm late for a funeral."

As Omar waits in a line of cars to leave the car park through the army checkpoint, he calls the dispatcher, asks for directions.

"Take the Autostrad. Then exit at Bassatine before the Ring Road." It's nowhere Omar has been to recently. "Once you're there ask for the cemetery of the Jews."

Omar never even knew there was a cemetery for Jews, cannot imagine what a Jew would look like, cannot think of having ever met one, thinks he would know if he had.

They approach Saladin's Citadel, take the ramp for the Autostrad, head south. From the shantytowns along the side of hills at the city's edge, flights of silver flow to the sky, roll in waves, turn, crest and break into streaks of spindrift that scatter and gather.

Once off the Autostrad the cab enters narrow streets of unfinished red brick buildings made narrower by parked cars. Children play and vendors sell wares from carts pulled by mules. Goats graze amid the garbage in alleyways. Omar feels himself slipping back in time to an earlier age, thinks it simply wrong the foreign client should see such sights before he can admire modern malls and skyscrapers. "Here life hard." He apologizes for the poverty about them. He parks in a line of cars by a broken wall, leads the client to a metal gate and into the cemetery. Before them, hundreds of stone cubes a metre or so wide, slabs two metres long, lay scattered across an expanse of dry earth. A dog paces between stone blocks, watches, seemingly mistrustful.

By one wall the grounds drown in black acrid water from a burst sewage pipe. Some distance away, henna, juniper and palm trees shield the cemetery from concrete buildings beyond the wall. Between the stone blocks clumps of scrub grass, dry shrubs and red bougainvillea mask Omar's view of men and women in black congregating beyond tall, narrow stone structures, some domed, others arched like doorways. The men wear black skullcaps and dark glasses. The client tells Omar to wait for him, unfolds a yarmulke from his inside pocket, adjusts it with both hands on his head. He continues along a dry mud path between gravestones and mausoleums to where the mourners, some carrying flowers, take turns to scatter earth with a shovel over a coffin laid in a pit. A man in a black suit and tie recites from a book. Omar tries to make sense of the sounds he thinks should be familiar yet are not—*El malei rachamim, shochayn bam'romim*. He watches the client move into the small crowd to take his turn to shovel dirt into the grave.

At the hotel, a bellhop helps with the suitcases. Omar waits until the client is through the glass doors and the security check to the lobby. As he drives back to the hotel gates, he recognizes the driver by a cab in the car park, wonders which of the girls is working—unusual for them this early in the day. He drives out of the hotel, stops by the sidewalk, adjusts his side mirror to watch the lobby, waits.

The cellphone vibrates. It is the boy from Maulana's apartment. He wants to be taken to a mall. "Which mall?"

"Any mall."

"To buy what?"

"Transformers."

"Electrical supplies?"

"No, Autobots, Decepticons, like in the movie. For my collection."

In no mood to be teased, Omar says he is busy with a client.

The boy pleads he is bored of spending all day in the apartment, and trapped in the evenings by curfew. "Anything to get out if only for an hour." Besides, he needs more *bango*. "What you got last time was so good."

"Not now, I can't."

In the side mirror Omar sees one of the blondes he sometimes delivers appear from the hotel lobby. She stops under the awning, looking so pretty in the sunlight. She lights a cigarette, glances around for her ride. She inhales several times in quick succession on the cigarette, drops it to the ground, walks over to the driver by the parked cab. She lights another cigarette before climbing into the back seat. Omar slides down below the dashboard so as not to be seen as they drive past.

That evening from Maulana's apartment Omar collects three bearded men with prayer calluses on their foreheads, their expressions stern. He drives through deserted streets to the central square. At an army checkpoint he shows his permit and is waved through. Tanks and armoured cars wait in side streets. In the city centre he stops again to show his permit. Before they reach the square he parks in an alley. From the back of the cab the men take orange hard hats and metre-long metal tubes, swing them like scimitars, make swishing sounds. Omar watches by the cab, worried they may scratch the paintwork. From where he stands, he can see the tents of the protestors, white under neon street lights, past barricades of metal sheeting.

The group leader tilts his head, pulls his scarf up to cover his face. The others do the same. "You can come with us or leave."

For the moment Omar has nothing better to do. "I'll have to leave if the dispatcher calls with a fare." But he thinks it unlikely given the curfew.

They pass lines of soldiers in khaki with plastic shields wielding long black clubs. The officers in black uniforms. Now he understands the game. First, the hard hat warriors with metal tubes attack in God's name. Then the riot police will follow to clear the protestors from the square. For now the hard hats are with the army, but Omar is certain, soon enough, God will turn against the generals.

They proceed down a side street and join a group of men carrying crates of bottles with newspaper stoppers smelling of gasoline. Ahead, Omar sees an armoured personnel carrier parked a short distance from a barricade. Men hide behind the vehicle, light paper fuses, hurl bottles over a barrier of sheet metal behind which protestors shelter. Flames pool and flare on the tarmac, give out black smoke.

Soldiers have secured an area by the museum. From here Omar can see the street aglow in orange flames. The air is thick with tear gas fired from the turrets of armoured cars patrolling between sidewalks with rival groups of stone throwers. The gas constricts Omar's throat and chest. His eyes burn. He holds an arm across his face and inhales through the fabric of his jacket. The men pull their scarves tighter, walk faster. At an iron barrier guarded by black-uniformed State Security men they stop, then pass one at a time.

"He's with us." The group leader waves Omar through. "Wait here. We'll let you know when we need you."

Omar watches bearded men gather with wooden staves and rocks by the museum walls. There are rippling black pools on the sidewalk. He thinks it is oil, realizes it is blood, fed on by tiny roaches from the gutters. He feels a moment's revulsion, moves towards a crowd congregating by the gatehouse. He hears shouts and screams from within. State Security officers with shotguns stand by. The beards beat a young man to the ground, punch and kick him as he writhes on the concrete. A State Security officer turns his back to the assault, talks into his transceiver. Riot police fire canisters of gas and rounds of birdshot at protestors trapped between buildings. Every so often a wave of hard hats wielding metal tubes and wooden staves surges from the museum wall, through the State Security barriers. They drag a protestor back, beat him until he collapses. Officers arrive to arrest the prisoner. Omar's phone sounds the call to prayer. He reads the dispatcher's number. Too exhilarated, he ignores the call, turns off the ringer. Another protestor is dragged through the barriers to the museum wall, beaten, clothes torn, bleeds from his face and mouth. He sobs as he tries to reason, screams as he pleads between beatings. Omar feels a surge of excitement, watches the terror on the man's face as speech splinters into whimpers and cries. A metal tube cracks his skull with a sound like wood snapping. He drops to the ground. A crowd of hard hats and beards kick the body, stamp and spit. They scream at Omar to join them.

A young woman in a medic's white coat and blue gauze mask hanging loosely about her neck, reluctantly accompanied by a State Security officer, argues with the men to let her treat the unconscious man. They swear at her—whose side is she on? They insist on seeing her identity card, mock her name as they read and repeat it out loud, demand to know her religion. Are you Buddhist, Baha'i, Christian, Muslim? And where is your husband and guardian? She contends her right to examine the body. The officer threatens to call for soldiers to subdue the hard hats and beards unless the medic can examine the man, says he does not want a death on his watch. They shout at the medic and the officer.

Boisterous, but afraid to defy a man in black uniform, they turn their attention to another protestor wrenched through the barriers, beaten against the wall. What with the noise and the dark and not having seen her in at least, what, a couple of years, Omar is uncertain whether the medic is, or could be, his cousin Yara. He pulls his scarf across his face, backs up into the shadows. She sees him staring at her, wants to know what he is looking at. "Who are you? Are you with them?" No, he is not with anybody, he says, just a hired driver.

"So why are you still here?"

Flustered, he does not know what to answer, asks her the same question.

"Why do you suppose? Can't you see I'm a doctor?"

Over the din of the crowd and the sound of shotgun fire, a voice calls for the driver.

She says to him, "If you are with them, shame on you."

A young man forces his way through the crowd, grabs Omar by the arm. "You've got to take one of ours to hospital." Omar can barely make out the words over the thud-thud of gas canisters, the crack and whoosh of lead shot. They weave their way past a group of beards throwing stones and State Security men loading shotguns with cartridges. At the barrier, a young man squats, holds a rag to the side of his head. Blood runs down his face, mats his beard. Three men lift him by his legs and arms, follow Omar to his cab. They lay the wounded man on the back seat. Blood leaks through the rag he presses to his head. One of the men gets into the front passenger seat, leans over to check the wound.

At the hospital gates the soldiers in red berets and arm bands let the cab through. The wounded man is taken on a wheelchair to the emergency ward.

The phone vibrates in Omar's pocket. He flips it open, hears the voice of the dispatcher.

"Where are you?"

"At the military hospital." He has a pickup in twenty minutes, one of the blondes from a hotel downtown.

Omar parks away from the street lights within sight of the hotel, recognizes the young woman as she steps out under yellow awning light. It is the same woman he saw this morning. Dyed blond and peachy skin well powdered. Doubtlessly, she smells of gardenias or some such scent to mask the stench of the men she has been with. She does not see him, waits, lights a cigarette, inhales, lets her arm drop to her side. He thinks she looks tired. He can imagine from what. He feels disgust, having left good men sacrificing blood to clear the square, to fetch a whore all sin and pollution. How is it he has to do such shit to earn a living while she looks so pretty, when, by God's law, the *awra* should be stoned?

The cab crawls forward into the light. She sees him, throws the cigarette aside, gets into the back seat. He glances into the rear-view mirror at her soft white neck with a silver necklace. "Tonight good bunga bunga party?" He laughs drily. She glares at him, then looks down to her bag, finds a cigarette and lighter. The tip of the cigarette glows red in the mirror. He drives away from the hotel. "Money good tonight?"

"I get baksheesh. Your boss, he get money." She inhales on her cigarette.

He cannot read her any more than he can read the thoughts of a dog. Her skin cool white like a lizard's. Her eyes ice. He cannot imagine what she must think and how she feels—as alien to him as Satan is to his godliness. "I take you home."

"Home to Ukraine?" She stares at him in the mirror, defiant, not in any way wanton, he thinks, but as though she sees herself a degree above him. "Ukraine too far to drive. To where you stay."

"Get passport from your boss and I go."

"Then you give me what? You give me money? You give me sex?" He shakes his head. "I no need woman money, no woman fuck."

"You fucker. Fuck yourself." She turns away to the side window.

All the nights he has driven women to and from hotels, listened to their teasing, their complaints, drunk and sober. He slams his foot on the brake, shifts into neutral, all he sees is white, he turns to tell her what he thinks of her and how she will go to hell to burn forever. Her slap knocks him back against the side window. He blanks out for a moment. When he turns again she is gone. He looks around at the empty street and sidewalk, cannot see for darkness. He cannot let her get away, has to find her. But how in these black and empty streets? She could be calling the dispatcher for another car. If she reports him he will be fired. Drivers are not to mess with the women. What if she runs away? The hotel doorman will say he arrived on time and she got into his cab. They will think he is responsible. Maybe think he is pimping her. God knows who takes a cut of the money she makes—some army general or high-ranking official. They will make his life not worth living. He throws himself against the seat, rocks back and forth, thrusts himself hard against the headrest, drops his head onto the steering wheel. Tears soak his beard. He feels so tired, so fed up with everything.

Then, there she stands by the car finishing her cigarette.

He wipes the moisture from his face with his hand, rubs his wet beard. "Miss, mademoiselle. I'm sorry. I no mean what you think I say."

She drops the cigarette stub. "I go in car, you drive."

He nods and starts the engine.

She gets into the back seat. "You take me now to where I stay."

"Yes, I take you."

Though his face still burns where she slapped him, he feels a calmness he has not felt all this night, and not since he cannot be sure when. He glances at her in the rear-view mirror. Whatever he may have thought of her, he thinks there is also beauty in the woman, a kind of strength. Maybe that is what draws his eyes to her.

He wonders if, possibly, she sees him as attractive, even exotic, but then thinks probably not. Though if she got to know him she might respect him a little. Maybe, one day, even admire him for being manly and godly, on the path of the prophets, wise with their teachings.

She glances up, sees him looking at her. "You keep face in front when you drive. If you put face back, I slap more hard and make you really sad."

Omar smiles, feels himself lighten. "I take you back where you stay. You safe with Omar." He engages the engine and moves forward into the dark, empty street.

"Fucker, you no safe, just you drive."

He laughs and shifts gear into third.

Mid-morning, Tarek drives out of Sidi Adi, follows Yaqzan's directions to where he says they will find his new mother. The signal returns to his phone. He and Neda devise a variation on their game whereby she phones her mother, talks a while, then he takes the phone and listens without speaking.

Mona tells Neda that she misses her. Now more than halfway through the novel *April March* she finds it hard going, but can't find another to read because bookshops are closed with the continued street disturbances and the whatnot with the unborn babies and all the birds all over the place. Heba, such a blessing, helped hang net curtains to keep the birds from the apartment. She has heard in some parts of the city people have resorted to wire mesh on their windows. When Neda hands her father the phone, Mona speaks of the previous night's battle in the square—several deaths and scores injured. "Things may be changing. I'll have a better idea once I see my uncle."

With his phone almost out of power, Tarek texts Yara, "U OK?"

She responds, "ok thx holding firm."

Their first night out of Sidi Adi, they sleep in a field by an acacia tree, its leaves crystalline in the moonlight. Tarek's eyes tear and sting as he sleeps. In dreams, his hands fill with hours like coins that drain like sand. He wakes in a state of confusion. Where is he? In the distance, village huts bud in tallow light.

He draws the blanket about his shoulders, looks to where his daughter sleeps in AK—a pale shipwreck under stars as bright as dice. He stands to clear his head, sees Leila alone by the van.

"Can't sleep," she says. She points to a cluster of stars. "The Pleiades. The seven sisters."

"A good omen for Yaqzan finding his new mother?"

"A sign of good weather for a while longer." She says Yaqzan spent much of the night at Sidi Adi asking strangers where he might find a woman he described in some detail. "He claims to have seen her in a vision. He sounds so certain, I can almost believe him."

"The notion's hard to accept."

"I think he's looking for something else."

"Meaning what?"

"We were three sisters. Salma has been missing since before Neda was born."

He remembers Salma at the apiary by the valley lake, and the mats she soaked at the well to place on the hives to cool them on summer days. He asks if it is possible to find a woman who went missing so many years ago.

Leila shrugs. "In truth, I've never stopped searching."

"It seems he hasn't either." What kind of quest is this? It could go on forever. He feels such sadness in Leila. He cannot get himself to say he thinks the whole venture pointless. Instead, he asks, "Would you want to be reborn?"

She says she cannot imagine herself wanting rebirth after rebirth. This life is enough for her. When she dies she wants to cross the Sirat, the golden thread that binds this world to the next. Life can end, time return to its shell, her spirit rest in the black milk of the sky, far from the light of stars. Better that than enrobing to endure loss after loss of those she loves for time after time. To lose Salma then Reham was pain enough for eternity.

They drive the day, under turbid skies, through villages, one much like another. Every so often they stop to perform and collect money for a meal. Early evening, in a dusty square lit by a street lamp, on a circular patch of dirt trodden bald of grass, Leila sits with *qaraqib* on her lap, helps Neda fit them to her hands. Kasem tightens and tunes the strings on the *sentir*. They wait for Yaqzan to start the recital in his dry, raspy voice. Tarek waves to Leila. She sees him, nods and claps the *qaraqib*. He leaves for the *khana* at the corner of the square.

In the dark lobby, he raps his knuckles on the unattended desk. An old man appears from the shadows.

"We'll take two rooms for the night," he says.

"Payment in advance." The man points to a charge sheet on the wall.

The rooms are up two flights of stairs at the back of the building. The unlit corridor smells of sweat. Tarek drops down on the hard bed in a room lit by a small dull bulb in a plastic skirted lampshade. It hangs from a wire lined with black flies. Cold perspiration breaks across his body, soaks his clothes. He strips, lies on the coarse blanket. His skin burns. He crawls between the sheets. All day he has been assailed by thoughts of Mona, murmured to her when alone, thought of her on the drive on dusty roads to villages where they stopped for Yaqzan to ask about a woman he says sells honey and for directions to places he describes as though familiar to him.

Tarek wakes to darkness, feels more tired than before he slept, listens, hears sounds from the street outside, holds his breath, thinks for a moment he is back in the prison cell he shared with Kasem. He lies still, tries to control his breathing, certain that people are listening, watching, staring through the walls, even in the darkness can see him. He knows it is not true, tries to dismiss the notion of being observed, a result of exhaustion, maybe a memory of his internment now returning. His mind overrun with vague, empty thoughts, he closes his eyes. Half in sleep, he sees himself inside a deep cavern, wandering through the blackness of granite passages to a cave with flues hewn by means beyond his knowing. Shadows play on the floor and walls. Figures form, distend, dissolve. The cavern opens to a starlit sky. Mona's black hair flows before him like the night. Blown by the breeze, it floats to the stars. He reaches for her into a thick and viscous sky.

When he wakes it is to the hushed voice of Leila telling him that Neda is asleep in the other bed. He sits up, his head congested with images, to see Leila fold the sheets over Neda's shoulders.

"I worry she'll get too attached to me and be hurt when we part."

"I worry about everything. One more worry won't make a difference."

Leila smiles. Yes, she knows there is always something to worry about with children. She thanks Tarek for the sacrifice of his time and energy in helping them with their search.

"I feel I owe it to you and Kasem."

"You don't owe us. You shouldn't think that way." She closes the door behind her.

He lies down, stares at the ceiling, waits for the darkness to overwhelm him and sleep to return.

In the morning they stop by the roadside so Kasem can pick fruit from the flat pads of a cactus. With a knife he tops and peels a prickly pear, offers it to Neda. She does not much like the taste, but smiles and eats it. He removes the spikes from pears to store in the van for later.

Tarek calls Yara. She is leaving the square to return equipment to the hospital. He asks after his friend's son. Did she ever find the boy?

"No, but everybody's leaving. They trust the military will keep its word. That there'll be elections and a civilian government."

"And you don't?"

"Our strength is in numbers. We should remain in the square until elections are held, but not enough people are listening."

That afternoon black plumes from distant fires thicken to blot out the sky. Tarek stops to ask directions at a shack by the side of the road with a large sign advertising diet soda. Neda asks for a drink of anything cold and fizzy. The woman behind the counter has no bottled drinks. She lights two of three kerosene burners set on flagstones to boil water for tea.

"So why the sign?" Neda pouts, goes back to the van to let the dog out for a run.

The woman spoons tea into two small kettles, wipes glasses on a rag, sets them on a tray. On a raised shelf a radio broadcasts news of fighting in the mountains. The broadcaster lists the numbers of army casualties, names villages destroyed.

For hours they keep west of the smoke, black in the night sky. Not thinking it safe to stop, nor wishing to attract attention, they drive with headlights off. Yaqzan sleeps. When he is awake his confidence seems irrepressible.

By dawn they arrive at a town in a dip that drops to a flat stretch of grey rock, a volcanic crater scooped out of a side of the great stone plateau. Neda wakes as the van rolls down the track past rows of houses, parks by the side of a walled building. In the back of the van she dresses in an indigo gown that Leila hemmed for her. With kohl around her eyes and henna in her hair she looks like Leila must have at her age. Tarek locks the dog in the back of the van with a bowl of water. It stands on its hind legs, stares through the window.

They stop for something to eat at a small restaurant.

Yaqzan, his vision a vague halo of sight at the rim of a circle of blindness, moves between tables, describes a young woman, asks after her, listens and nods, then asks more questions.

"Doesn't he ever stop?" Tarek thinks Yaqzan is strangely obsessed on a hopeless quest.

"He has the scent of something." Kasem sips his tea "He's racing against an hourglass almost empty." He taps on a saucer his half-smoked cigarette, its tip black with ash.

After breakfast Kasem stands alone, smokes as Neda helps Leila set up the instruments for a performance by the entrance to the market square crowded with people coming and going. Tarek watches them, thinks a recurring thought—should anything happen to him on this journey, who will tell his daughter of her birth and his story with Reham? He would not want to leave the telling to Kasem. It really is time to have that talk. He calls her to him, leads her to the van. She sits in the passenger seat, the dog on her lap, waits to hear what is so important he cannot talk about it in front of others.

"You know the story of Zulhima, the woman warrior, how she was brought up by shepherds when really she was a princess."

Of course. She remembers the puppet all gold and silver with eyes of amber wielding a scimitar. It's one of her most absolute favourites.

"Well, you're a bit like Zulhima."

She settles in her seat, waits for him to continue. He stares ahead, rubs his face with his hand. Where to begin a story he has always avoided telling?

"What about Zulhima?" Her eyes widen with anticipation.

He swallows air. "We don't have time. You don't want to miss your performance with the *gnawa*."

"You were going to tell me about being a princess."

He says this town has the best prices for leather. He has to buy enough to make new puppets, replacements for those destroyed by the birds. "Don't you want new puppets?"

But what about her story? He leads her complaining back to the town square filling with people and animals brought to market, leaves her seated between Leila and Kasem. He walks narrow streets past men herding goats and lines of cattle. Lost among buildings of corrugated iron and mud brick, shaded from the sun, he emerges into a place where women tend fires. A man lays one end of a tire into a fire until it burns a deep orange flame with thick, oily smoke, picks it up with an iron hook, carries it between huts to a clearing, throws it into a pit that ignites and billows black fumes. All around, smoke sumps with mounds of garbage fuel more fires. Flames leap and lick the rims of pits. Goats with slit throats gurgle blood.

Men twist and turn bodies that swell and stiffen in fire craters to burn them clean of hair. Everywhere the stench of scorched hides. Children go from pit to pit with cans of water for sale to parched workers. Men dark with soot pull burnt carcasses from flames, scrape them with flat blades to remove layers of blackened skin. At baths of turbid water, women scrub cadavers with wire brushes, clean hides to a light tan. Everywhere the smell of death—blood, urine and burnt hair.

Tarek looks about him to find a way back. With growing nausea, he loses all sense of direction. Past heaped corpses of goats, he enters the circle of cattle slaughter with rows upon rows of severed heads propped up on chopped-off horns. Farther into the square, men tug on ropes to trip bulls tethered by hind legs, tumble them to the ground. A bull discharges a golden stream, lows as it struggles to hold its head up. Its hooves slip in slurries of blood and urine. Barefooted boys leap on fallen behemoths to keep them down as men grip horns, slit throats. Contorted bodies struggle for last gasps. Everything the colour of excrement. A dull ocean with breakers of cattle, women, men, boys. Death reflects frozen in the eyes of the slaughtered. In their tear ducts flies suck brine and spawn. The slippage from life to death to life continuous, all-becoming, a constant churning.

Meat carvers roll bodies onto their backs with legs upright like masts, trim carcasses with thin long blades, cut along hind legs to the belly, peel back skin, strip flesh and fat. Dripping ribcages, carried on men's shoulders like rugs, washed in overflowing basins. Rows of shanks and hocks strung from poles like sacks. Full legs hang from hooks by Achilles tendons. All around, traders bargain for animal parts. Boys, in torn clothes encrusted in sweat, pull bloodied carts. Tarek steps on softness that gives underfoot. A lung sodden with blood wheezes as it deflates. A toothless man, as lean as death, squats to boil water for tea on a kerosene burner, offers a glass to Tarek, who sickens at the sight. Whores lean against walls, bare their breasts, lift their skirts, uncover swollen bellies, beckon to dark alleys.

Tarek stumbles into a clearing, stops to catch his breath. He enters through high stone walls the quiet of a tanner's yard. In the sunlight, fresh skins drape like sheets of cloth, pile on the ground like mats. Farther away, lime pits milky white, grey in the shadows. The air above the pits caustic, the sky clear blue. Sunk in the ground, dye pits of bright pigments—reds, blues, purples—like giant paint pots awaiting the dip of a brush, missing only the canvas to take colour and give form.

He sits on a stone ledge that juts from the side of the wall, waits for the sickness to pass.

"What can I do you for?" A master tanner wipes his stained hands, coarse like tree bark, on his apron.

Tarek leans against the wall, takes a deep breath to clear his head. Remembers the puppets he has to replace. "I'm looking for good top grain, sanded and finished."

"I've all you need. Full, top and split." The man points to a row of open sheds with mounds of treated hides. "Over there brained, next shed vegetable tanned. Pick what you want. You'll get a good price."

Tarek needs leather to take dyes in bright colours.

"Vegetable tans will do you best." The man leads Tarek to piles of different grades, calls to a boy to help Tarek sort and pick.

The leather must be firm enough to hold the puppets' shapes, yet clear and translucent to let through the light once painted.

"You'll need to bleach the skins."

Yes, Tarek knows.

The man tells the boy to fetch tea for the client, excuses himself to get back to work.

Tarek searches the leather stacks, sips the sweet black tea when it arrives. He takes his time as he tries to estimate his needs.

When he is done, the tanner looks through the sheaf of skins, folds them like the leaves of a book, states a price. Tarek offers him half of what he asked.

The man stares at him with a look of hurt pride. "I'm giving you a good price."

"All right, but give me a discount."

The man counts again the strips, pauses, then offers a better price.

Tarek counts out his money while the boy loads the leather onto a handcart to deliver to the parked van.

9

Omar collects Nathan from his hotel. The client asks to be taken to
the Ben Ezra Synagogue. Omar calls the dispatcher for an address.

"By the Hanging Church," the dispatcher says.

Omar knows where that is. He has taken clients to the church.

In the cab, trapped between walls across streets and soldiers direct-
ing traffic in a one-way system, Omar listens to the client tell of his first
visit to the country as a postdoctoral student from the University of
Toronto. Then, he discovered in the desert rock inscriptions that read *Al*
for god, *Ab* for father, and the phrase *rise and toil*. Along an escarpment
he came to the ruins of buildings with rough hieroglyphs on short stelae
defaced by graffiti. A short distance from the site was the entrance to
a mineshaft. He had tried to picture the ancient town as it would have
been two or three thousand years ago, maybe older for all he could tell.
He wondered where roads would have run and where people got their
water. In a notebook he sketched a plan of what he imagined was the
layout of streets and houses. So far from any centre of civilization, the
town would have had to trade with tribes migrating across the barren
expanse. The idea of interface, transition and memory became a guiding notion that led to his study of Judah Halevi's *Book of the Khazars*,
preserved in the collection from the Ben Ezra Synagogue. His annotated

edition of the original in Judeo-Arabic, with commentary on the derived Hebrew by Judah ibn Tibbon, has since become the standard text.

Omar detects a self-congratulatory tone in the client's telling, though he does not understand the pride in rummaging through ancient ruins and editing texts. They drive alongside the river to avoid the walls downtown, turn into tight little streets. Omar, as affable as he can be with clients, asks if the client is, maybe, an antiques dealer?

The client says he is a university teacher and scholar of old manuscripts. He talks of *The Treatise of the Pool*, by Obadyah, the grandson of the great Maimonides. A work of Judeo-Muslim pietism only seven pages of which were known to exist. "I think I've identified another three from microfiche of the loose-leaf collection from the synagogue's *genizah*." He explains that for hundreds of years pages bearing God's name were never thrown away, but stored in the *genizah*, a cemetery of sorts for discarded texts.

Omar is impressed that such respect for God should exist even among non-believers.

The client adds that Ben Ezra is the purported site where Pharaoh's wife found baby Moses in a bed of reeds. Omar knows the story, is surprised to hear the location is a synagogue where Rabbi Maimonides taught many Jews their religion. He smiles and nods, thinks it impolite to correct the client. After all, everybody knows the Jews left at the time of Pharaoh, as recorded in scripture.

They park at the rear of the synagogue. Sagging wires hang low from a side wall to a pole. A man arrives. Omar recognizes him from the funeral. The man shakes the client's hand, leads him into the building. Omar remains outside, uncertain whether it would be right for him to follow. He watches an elderly gardener tending plants against the railing of the yard. A flame tree casts a shadow against the pale stone of the building. A short broadleaf banana tree grows over the outside wall. He wonders how long the old man has been tending the garden, asks him if people come to pray. The man shrugs. "Not often, anymore." Though, as a child, he witnessed the synagogue overflow into the street on the Sabbath.

Omar detects no trace of deceit in the man's eyes or voice. But how could there have been such numbers of Jews to worship here? He asks about the funeral the other day.

"Rabbi Samuel managed the affairs of the synagogue. May he rest in peace."

Where would these Jews have come from? He thinks his view of the world upturned, in some way he himself threatened. The thought draws him to the doorway of the synagogue. He stands at the threshold in shadows to a hall with a marble floor. Grey-and-white columns support balconies along side walls. Before him a marble mastaba with a headstone and gold lettering and beyond it a raised platform with steps. Ceiling and walls decorated in Moorish style, windows in stained glass, lights hanging from wheels about the columns. What is this place, neither mosque nor church? Too disturbed to venture farther, he gazes with unease at the cherry-red latticework at the far end of the room where the client and the man nod and talk quietly together.

Heba joins a crowd by the sheet-metal gates to the butane depository. On a billboard above the building is a poster of an army marshal in sunshades. Now that is a face she has not seen before. She wonders if he will be the new president. God willing, he will be better than the one just gone.

She has carried from Mona's apartment the empty metre-tall steel cylinder balanced horizontally on her head. It has been a twenty-minute walk, and though empty the cylinder is heavy. She lets it down, stands it on the ground. "Is the warehouse out of gas?"

A man next to her shrugs. He has been waiting since early morning and is now late for work. Frankly, he says, when has there not been a shortage of cooking gas? For the last thirty years there has been one kind of shortage or another. "Shortages get better, shortages get worse," but always a shortage. "They do it on purpose to keep people at each other's throats while they rob the country blind."

A boy lights a cigarette by a No Smoking sign. The man glares at him. The boy shrugs. "What? I'll stop once the truck arrives."

She watches the cars move slowly outside the grounds of the depository. The side streets congested with people and traffic. Wouldn't a car be such a convenience with a cylinder to carry. But then some people live like the sun in the sky, while others are ground dry like dust. Not that she resents anybody's good fortune. She knows God has apportioned *to each according to His will and no more than a soul can endure.* She is grateful for what she has. Glad to have learnt not to think of the future. Though she would like to imagine her children have a future. She worries about her youngest. Soon it will be time for her to get cleansed. If she could find a doctor or a nurse to do the cut, that would be so much better than one of the local women, or the barber on her street. If there is another way to protect a girl from *nushuz* she would do it. Yes, what is the saying? With great happiness—and her daughters are that to her—there is always some anguish. Then there is the story told her, as a child, by her mother how God created Happiness so we would each know the promise of paradise. How does it go? On the last day of creation, Happiness was born out of every perfection. The angels loved her for bringing joy to all things. But only God is perfect and nothing created can share in His perfection. And so one day Happiness felt a pain in her side. The angels saw a tiny rib deformed in her body. They cast out the rib they called Anguish, and Happiness was well again. But, resentful at being abandoned, Anguish follows in Happiness's shadow to spread anxiety and sadness.

A man in blue overalls appears at the depository gates chained together from the inside. He waves people to be quiet. "The delivery truck hasn't arrived. You can leave your cylinders and take a receipt, come back tomorrow." He hushes the shouts of protest. The boy whispers to Heba to wait. When almost everybody has left, he goes and talks to the man at the gates. The boy returns. "He'll sell us cylinders for a markup."

"How did you know?"

"They always keep some aside for the black market."

Heba drags the steel cylinder to the gates, exchanges it for a full one. She does not know how she is going to explain the price rise to the mistress, hopes she will be understanding. The boy helps her lift the cylinder onto her head, and she balances it on its side on a folded rag she uses as a cushioning pad.

The apartment bell pierces the quiet of the morning. Mona opens the front door to two men in black leather jackets. They introduce themselves as State Security officers. They ask for Tarek. Mona tells them her husband is away on business. They say he is to call them on his return—a routine inquiry. Nothing to be concerned about. She mentions, as if in passing, that her uncle is a retired high court judge. Yes, they know of her uncle. They will try not to disturb her again, as she is pregnant, but if they do not hear from her husband in the next few days they will send somebody round to make further enquiries. They hand her a card with a phone number for Tarek to call.

Once they leave, she phones Omar.

He says he has to deliver a client to the mall, agrees to collect her in about an hour.

In the kitchen Heba turns a spanner to tighten the tube from the stove to the new gas cylinder. She strikes a match and holds it over the connection, then runs the flame up and down the tube to check for leaks.

At Maulana's apartment Omar waits for the boy to get ready, thinks to ask Maulana if it is permissible for a believer to serve a Jew, wants to say he suspects he has been driving one in his cab, and is it permitted for a believer to do so without sin? Instead, he asks if it is true that scripture describes Jews as People of the Book, the mother book in heaven of which all sacred texts are versions?

"You know the story of the prophet Moses, may peace be upon him." Maulana's gaze makes Omar uncomfortable. "He meets the stranger by the two seas. The stranger but sinks a boat, kills a child, repairs a wall. Moses protests for lack of understanding and is reprimanded. Don't be as Moses, who let his heart misguide him."

Omar, unsettled by being compared to Moses, struggles to grasp the relevance of the story. He decides he will recite an extra prayer that evening at the mosque. God will understand his need to earn a living, especially in these uncertain times.

In the cab the boy pays Omar for a block of *bango* wrapped in foil. "Let's go somewhere we can smoke."

Omar drives to where the Ring Road crosses the river, parks on the concrete foundation of a deserted building site. He rolls a joint, lights it, inhales and hands it to the boy. They smoke in silence. Omar leans back in his seat, his mind blank, his body numb. The boy reaches a hand between Omar's legs. Omar watches, as though it is another's body that hardens to the boy's touch. The boy unzips his trousers, rubs him until he comes.

From the street below her apartment, Omar phones Mona, tells her he has nowhere to park. She should come down when she is ready. He watches her descend the stairs, step by step, and climb into the front passenger seat. As she struggles to loop the seatbelt across her body to fit the buckle into the latch, he complains that Tarek has not returned his calls. She says his phone is out of credits. Because of the troubles, he has not been able to buy a card to recharge it. She is surprised how easy it is to lie to Omar.

On a billboard, above the butcher's store opposite, the new marshal in sunshades gazes into the distance—the image of a farsighted visionary. Omar argues with a bird chaser over the stains on the car roof from when he was last here.

A woman sorts through the iron bins beside the building. She picks food from the garbage for a child holding open a plastic bag. Mona wonders by what margin of fortune is she separated from this woman. She taps Omar's arm. Too distracted to pay her any attention, he works himself into a temper reprimanding the bird chaser for being a parasite on drivers, may God damn his kind. Mona leans forward, opens the glove compartment, gathers a handful of change, hands it to the woman.

"I can't believe you did that," Omar shouts. "All day I pick up people who don't have change for fares."

She sinks back into the seat, looks out the side window.

As he drives, Omar says he won't visit their uncle. He has fares to collect and cannot afford to waste time with the old man who will only reprimand him for spending his life driving cabs.

At the fifth floor of her uncle's building, the security guard assigned to the retired judge opens the elevator's concertina metal door, rings the bell to the apartment, waits for the manservant to let Mona in. Her uncle sits opposite the television, mutes it with a remote, rises from his armchair, smiles and waves her to a seat next to his.

When was the last time she saw him? It must be almost a year since his wife died. The apartment was crowded with relatives and friends, lawyers and their wives. Then, she thought him laden with grief, drawn into himself like some beast constrained by hurt turning about itself in its lair.

They exchange pleasantries. He thanks her for the visit.

She asks how he is.

He is as well as can be expected considering his poor health, and the chaos in the country. His investments have taken a hit with the troubles—not good for him on a pension.

She wonders if he thinks she is here to borrow money.

He opens a box decorated in an arabesque of mother-of-pearl, offers her bonbons wrapped in shiny coloured paper that crinkles as she takes one out of politeness. "How do you pass the time with your pregnancy?"

"I read."

"Still foreign novels?"

Yes, but translations are not always available, and foreign books so expensive she buys them used.

"When I was younger I used to read novels."

She glances at him, not sure where he may be steering the conversation. Since when was he interested in literature?

"Back then the stories spoke of duty and community. Now everybody wants to talk about freedom. Don't people have duties anymore?"

"Do you mean duty or responsibility?"

"You're right to ask. Words change their meanings. Why is that?"

"I don't know." She is afraid to be drawn into a conversation that will make her request for help harder.

"People think they're speaking the same language because they're using the same words, but they're not. Duty, a kind of caring, comes to mean obedience. Freedom means licence."

"Will there be democratic elections? An elected president?"

"You've seen the billboards."

"Replacing one marshal with another won't solve anything."

"You're right. We don't need to suck a lemon twice to know it is bitter."

She stares at him, having never heard him speak so frankly. She knows the expression—a different soldier, but the same rule of soldiers. She asks after Yara.

"She's a resident at a hospital downtown. They keep her busy."

Yes, she knows the kind of hours young doctors have to work in state hospitals and for so little pay.

"We grow up twice, once with our parents and another time with our children." He closes his eyes. "We've turned our children against us. And now we're killing them." He turns back to her. "When is the baby due?"

"When Tarek returns."

"I always thought you could do better."

She has no wish to argue. Only she knows how unhappy she was in her parents' home, how spiritless she felt. "You know the saying, a mother will dig a well with a needle if she has to."

Yes, he knows the aphorism, waits to hear what she has to ask of him, knows it will be a request for the child's sake, which makes it more difficult for him to refuse, joined to her by family bonds of duty, obligation and blood. She gazes at the raised veins along the backs of his hands. The skin once clear discoloured in patches she takes as signs of a slippage towards death, feels a surge of tenderness for him. She tells him of the interview on television about the birds at the Karagoz theatre, of Tarek's going to the square and the two visits by State Security. He says the first visit would have been a routine inquiry, possibly, as a result of the television report, the second because they think they have some evidence against her husband.

He tells her he cannot make promises, but she is not to worry. He pauses, shakes his head. "Of course, you do understand there is no recourse in law. No rule of law in matters of State Security." But, even so, he knows officers he can talk to. Maybe they can help.

Once home, Mona discovers the cat with a litter. It lies on its side against the foot of the couch. Five kittens suckle at its nipples.

It is evening before Tarek parks at the ship breakers' camp by the shores of the tranquil sea, green upon green and turquoise in the deep. Gentle ripples run to the horizon past sepulchral vessels that wait to beach for scrap.

From the van, Neda watches an old cargo ship sail towards the sands. It cuts a wreath of white carnations through still green waters. Its hull stained with rust rides high, shows along its side painted depth markers. Its propellers protrude from the water, churn white spume against a rudder that looks impossibly small for such a great ship. The cutwater rams the beach, slides onto the sands. The propellers churn slurry. Giant anchors and chains drop from portholes at the fore of the prow. Lines of men reach the hull, lift the anchors, drag them to winches. Great machines belch a black liquid smoke, turn large drums to draw the steel hulk, link by fisted link, along the sandbank blackened by oil and the burn of cutting torches. Men climb the chains to get into the hold and onto the deck, haul up cutters' cylinders with pulleys mounted on the bow. They work like ants on a washed-up carcass.

"Are you sure this is the place?" Leila sounds doubtful as she gazes at the worksite.

Yaqzan nods. "She's here. We'll find my new mother in the morning."

At the site manager's office Tarek negotiates for somewhere to spend the night.

By the van, Neda watches men toss lit rags into the hold of an empty ship. "What're they doing?"

Kasem lights a cigarette. "Making sure it's safe before they start work."

Fires of gas and chemicals blaze as men wait, boil small kettles for tea held over the flames of welding torches. Above them on the ship's deck a foreman yells instructions to teams of cutters—where to burn through seams and where to torch the plates. Crews of breakers on the beach hook up cables and chains to winches for when the steel plates are pierced.

Directed by the site manager, Tarek drives the van to a whitewashed hut of corrugated metal and cinder blocks. Leila and Neda help Yaqzan to a string bed to rest, while Kasem and Tarek unload their belongings.

That night, outside the hut, Neda sits with her father, Yaqzan and Leila. Kasem boils water for tea on a kerosene burner. Wires leak electricity to light the huts on the site. In the distance torches flare about a ship's hull. Too excited to go to sleep, Neda makes a Möbius band from a strip of newspaper. She shows it to Leila, runs her finger along the single face of the twisted loop. "Whatever way you go you always end up home. It's magic."

"It must be." Leila laughs.

Neda holds her pendant up to the electric light, peers through at the winged inclusion. "Are angels *really* real?"

Yaqzan turns to her. "Insofar as angels may be personifications of archetypes, they may be real."

She does not understand, looks to her father, who says, "In mathematics archetypes are axiomatic examples. But maybe Yaqzan means something else."

"Archetypes give form to spirit," Yaqzan says. "Each of us is a composite of different qualities, never wholly of any one archetype."

Leila nods at Neda. "Listen carefully to Yaqzan. Everything he says is from the old wisdom."

Neda glances at her father, who shrugs and smiles.

Kasem places tumblers with glass as thick as oyster shells by the burner.

"Are they real in the sense of physically in this world?" asks Yaqzan. "Can we see them, touch them, taste them? In that sense archetypes are nothingness and nowhere. We can only intuit the specific archetypes that form us as limitations and possibilities, inclinations to think and act in certain ways."

Her father asks Yaqzan if he means archetypes are God's thoughts.

"Only God is eternal. Before the beginning, there was only God. Then God became substance and spirit and from that came myriad multiples we call the universe."

Tarek nods. He thinks he understands, but not enough to know if he agrees.

"I believe in a universe we can measure and put into words."

"God is beyond what language can describe or minds comprehend. Beyond all categories of being. Absolute and perfect, God is one and all-knowing."

Her father frowns. Neda knows he disagrees and is silent so as not to offend Yaqzan.

Kasem flakes dried sage leaves into the kettle on the kerosene burner, waits for a break in the conversation to serve the tea.

To change the subject, Neda asks how Yaqzan can be so very sure of rebirth.

"As we are spirit, we share in God's eternity. So, we may enrobe and repeat in large measure as we were when first we entered the world. With each repetition we shed what was specific to our previous existence. What remains and matures is both unique to each of us and eternal. What the old masters called the red sulphur of the soul."

"So when does it stop?" Neda thinks the number of rebirths must be important.

"Possibly when a spirit has been enlightened with knowledge enough, or cannot bear to know more." Yaqzan sips his tea.

She likes the idea that each spirit sets its own limit, but worries Yaqzan will not be reborn if the spell she cast is not broken soon. She would confess, but who can she tell of the terrible thing she has done, and what good would it do if she did?

Yaqzan stands, gropes his way into the hut towards the string bed against the wall. Leila heats flatbread on the serrated top of a large can placed on the burner, flips the bread over and turns off the flame.

"Will Yaqzan know you when he's reborn?" Neda asks her.

"He may, if he is born *natiq* with memory of his former self." Leila slices a tomato and a red onion, adds a small block of cheese to a plate.

"If he doesn't, will you be sad?"

"It's not about me. It's what he needs to be at peace."

Neda takes the plate to Yaqzan, watches him as he eats in bed. "Do you know if your rebirth will be boy or girl?"

"It will be as it will be. To be whole a spirit must experience all manner of otherness."

That night, Neda sleeps on cushions by Leila's side in the hut. The sound from the cutting torches disturbs her. The breeze is heavy with the vegetative scent of the sea mixed with that of burning oil. She wakes at first light, her skin dry, hair stiff with salt spray. Her father takes her to join a line of men at a large iron cistern that holds fresh water for the camp. At the taps he soaps his hair and the stubble on his face. "Maybe I'll regrow my moustache."

She pulls a face.

"All right," he laughs. "I'll shave."

As much as she enjoys being with the *gnawa*, she wishes she could have a nice long shower with lots of hot water and shampoo that smells of strawberries. "When can we go home?"

"We promised to help Yaqzan find his new mother."

She sighs, rolls her eyes. She knows that, but how long will it take? She gazes out at the sea pale and silver in the early-morning light.

A tanker plies still waters, heads for a terminal of squat cylinders and tall cranes on concrete jetties far from the ship breakers. Along a tall wire fence that surrounds the harbour, plastic sheets and old blankets, held up at corners by rough wooden poles, shade gaunt figures. Vacant eyes of seated and recumbent bodies of women, children and the elderly stare at Neda riding on her father's shoulders. Leila leads Yaqzan by the hand. They pick their way between bundles of belongings wrapped in sheets and woven palm-frond baskets. Neda watches men gather at distant wire gates. "What are they doing?"

"Looking for work," her father says.

Yaqzan nods. "She is here."

"Can you be sure?" asks Leila.

"How do you know?" Neda asks.

"I feel it."

She agrees. What else is there to trust except one's feelings?

"Not long, not long," he says.

They reach the end of the camp and Yaqzan has not found the woman who will be the mother of his next enrobing.

"Are you tired?" Tarek asks Neda. "Do you want to turn back?" She reads his tone as hesitant, uncertain whether the search will ever be over.

She shakes her head, sure they must be close. She so wants to find Yaqzan's new mother. She rubs her pendant, implores the angel inside the amber to please, oh please, grant Yaqzan his wish.

"She is somewhere ahead of us." Yaqzan stumbles in the sand. "We'll know her when we see her."

Before them, shipwrecked on the beach, is a great split hull of a rusted cargo vessel. The stern, brown in the sun and saline spray, rides the dunes like waves. Beyond, the beach extends to desert.

"Is she there?" Neda steadies herself on her father's shoulders.

"It's there or nowhere," says her father.

Leila shrugs. Even she seems weary of the quest.

Neda can see children swim far into the sun-speckled water to gather the jetsam of passing ships into crates lashed to old car tires.

Leila leads Yaqzan towards the rusted hull, huge in its solitude against a blue sky. Their progress slows in the white sand. They reach the remains of the old vessel. It towers above them, like a giant sundial. In its shadow a knot of women and children shelter to catch the breeze off the sea.

Leila guides Yaqzan by the arm as they mount a dune.

Yaqzan glances sidewards at the first person they come to seated in the shade of the hull. "Where are people from?"

The woman looks up. "Everywhere." She shrugs. "Escaping the troubles."

They move among the seated and sleeping figures. Leila describes to Yaqzan what she sees. He listens and nods, keeps moving on.

Sunlight cuts a sharp line across the sand.

A young woman in a dark blue gown stands alone at the edge of the shadow. The *tarha* she normally wears over her head hangs loosely from her shoulders. She stares out to sea, then sits in the sand. As they approach, she raises the *tarha* to cover her hair.

"I think it's her," whispers Leila. "My God, it's so like her. I'm afraid to go any closer."

"Leave me here," Yaqzan says. "Let the child come with me."

Leila releases him, steps back.

Tarek lets Neda down from his shoulders. She takes Yaqzan's hand. They go forward to where the woman sits.

"Is it her?" Tarek asks.

"She's looking away. I can't see her face. I'm not sure." Leila stares at the woman. "I think it could be her."

Tarek tries to recall the times he had seen Salma by the apiary in the valley. His memory of her so unclear. Yaqzan, his hand on Neda's shoulder, sinks down by the woman's side. "What's your name?"

"Salma." She barely glances at him.

"Salma, do you have sisters?"

She turns to him, appears puzzled by the question, stares at Neda as though struggling to reclaim a memory long lost.

Leila starts to cry, leans on Tarek's chest. "It is her."

Tarek tries to lead Leila to where the woman sits.

"I'm too afraid. What if she doesn't recognize me?"

Tarek guides her forward.

She drops to her knees in front of Salma. "I'm Leila. Do you remember me?"

The woman gazes at her.

"Maybe you don't know me, but you, I recognize you."

Salma's face flushes. She chokes back a sob. "I thought you were all gone. The valley no more."

Leila hugs her. She holds Salma until the crying stops. "We've been looking. For years I've looked for you."

"No survivors. That's all we heard. And Reham, where is she?"

"I'll tell you everything."

"The child . . . Do I know her?"

"Later, later, but first, have you eaten?"

Salma shakes her head. She has not had a meal since morning.

"Where's your home? How did you get here? How do you live?"

"I keep a few hives to sell wax and honey. My husband drives a truck, takes what work he can find."

"We don't have much, but we'll bring you what we have." Leila pulls away to see Salma's face, then hugs her again. She says to Neda, "Have Kasem fetch what he can."

Yaqzan stands. "I feel like I'm floating." He laughs. He sounds so like a child, it brings more tears to Leila's eyes. "I am not sad," she says. "I'm happy. Believe me, I'm happy. I've found my sister."

They leave Leila with Salma, make their way through the makeshift camp back to the worksite of ship breakers.

Neda holds Yaqzan's hand. "Is she really the one?" Yaqzan nods and smiles. "Salma will be the mother of my rebirth."

* * *

At the hut, Kasem collects bread and cheese to take to Salma. Neda insists on going back with him.

"First, I'll make us tea," Tarek says, to give Neda time to rest.

She waits outside the hut, listens to the deep whispers in the shell Leila gave her.

"I am at peace," says Yaqzan. "There'll be no sediment from this life to contaminate the next."

"No regrets?"

"Every mistake is a regret, a burden one carries unless made right by recompense." Yaqzan lies down on the bed, pulls the blanket over him. "We are our choices, the risks we take and sacrifices we make." He is asleep before the water boils.

Kasem wraps the bread and cheese in newspaper. "You can't let Neda come with me," he says to Tarek. "She might find out from something Salma says. It's not right she hears it from anybody but you."

Yes, Kasem is right. Once he leaves, Tarek will try again to speak to his daughter.

He finds her crying by the side of the hut. "Uncle Kasem wouldn't take me with him. It's not fair. I'm fed up. I want to go home."

"AK is home."

"No, it's not. I want my real home. I so miss Mummy."

"There's something we must talk about."

"I know, I know," she sobs.

He feels himself go cold. "What do you know?"

She tells him she is a terrible person. She has done something so bad, so very bad. She cast a spell, not that she meant it to be a never-to-be-broken spell, just, she thought, an ordinary spell, and now Yaqzan will never be reborn and Mummy and Leila will never have their babies.

"You know Mummy loves you very much."

She knows that, but maybe not anymore once her mother knows of the spell.

"Love is not like that. Mummy will never stop loving you for any reason." He tells her of how one day he was sent to a faraway place on the great stone plateau. There he spent his days alone.

"It's where you met Uncle Kasem."

"Yes," and there he was in love with Auntie Leila's sister—a young woman by the name of Reham.

"Where is she now?"

Well, Reham became pregnant and he had to leave to go far away from her. Then something terrible happened. She died after having the baby. Auntie Leila and Uncle Kasem took the child and went in search of him. He was in prison in the city appealing his sentence. That was when Mummy started writing him letters to make him feel better. Then, when she saw the baby, she fell in love with her. He married Mummy so they could be the baby's parents. "That baby is you."

Neda stares at him.

"What matters is you are very loved by both of us."

"So Mummy is not my mother." She speaks deliberately, as though working through a riddle.

"She is your mother."

"But not really."

"Yes, really and in every way that matters."

She stares out to sea. The play of light on the water holds her gaze. She turns back to him. "Are you really my father?"

Yes, he most certainly is, and very happy to be so.

"How can I be sure?"

"You can be sure of that."

"And if my first mother hadn't died?"

"She did, and you needed another mother, and I fell in love with a woman who loves you very much."

"It's like a puzzle," she says.

"I should have told you earlier."

She squints at him. "So why didn't you?"

"I suppose I was afraid you wouldn't understand."

"What makes me really mad"—Neda fixes him with a hard look—"is that everybody knew I had two mothers and I didn't."

"Well, not everybody. In fact, almost nobody knows." Tarek feels his body lighten, as though a cord that bound him tightly has snapped and he is free. He takes a deep breath, exhales.

"So, now," she says, "you really must help me find a way to break the spell on babies."

"How do you suppose we do that?"

"We need the Wishing Rose."

"Yes, of course, but where do we find it?"

"We already did." She reminds him of the woman by the roadside selling salt and a desert rose.

Yes, he remembers her. She came from a place called Salt Valley in the stone plateau. "It can't be far from here."

"Can we go?"

He cannot imagine it being an easy drive.

"It's really, *really* important."

"There's nothing magic can do that science can't do better."

"Like what?"

He reads anxiety in her eyes. He does not understand what the importance can be for her of a stone with a clustered array of platelets, but then thinks his understanding is not important. "I'll ask the way to Salt Valley." He says Neda should stay with Auntie Leila and get to know her auntie Salma while he goes to find the Wishing Rose.

"Then can we go home?"

"Maybe, then we can."

She nods, satisfied. She needs time, anyway, to think about how special it makes her having two mummies when all her friends have only one.

For now she is comforted, but tonight she will cry in her sleep. For years she will find herself in tears and not know why. The tears will come and go for no apparent reason. Then one day the tears will stop.

Early morning, at the water's edge the dog wets its paws, sniffs the white spume and sneezes, shakes its head and barks, chases a wave as it ebbs, runs from its surge. Neda follows a crab along the salt-encrusted rise of sand to a rock pool. It will not play with her, takes cover in a crag under still, clear water. Its legs show like bare knuckles on a clenched fist. Neda takes out the shell Leila gave her, dips it in the pool to return its silvery sheen, thinks it pretty as it catches the sun in rings of colour.

In the shade of the beached ship's rusted hull, like a great conch shell, Leila braids Neda's hair. Salma scrubs pots with sand, rinses them at the water's edge. Neda likes how the two women treat her more like a sister than a child. She wonders if Mummy's baby will be a girl or a boy, and how she cannot wait to have a brother or sister of her own. She complains when Leila braids her hair so tight it hurts.

Salma places the pots in the sun to dry, sits by Neda and Leila in the shadow of the broken hull. She nudges her sister aside. "Let me take a look." She loosens the braid. "You're out of practice." She lightly slaps Leila's hand.

Leila laughs.

Neda feels Salma's touch gentle as she braids her hair. "Is it true you keep bees?"

"I have a couple of hives. I used to have many more."

"Don't they sting?"

Salma tells her that God created men out of clay and then gave them the world to care for. But they didn't care for flowers and trees nor for the land and what grew on it. They cared only for what they could tear from rocks with axes and the soil with ploughs. When God saw that the world was dying, He turned to the *jinn*, but they were too busy exploring the plains of time to think of jasmine and oleander. The angels, too busy decorating the skies with constellations of stars, had no interest in fig and olive trees. So God created the bees to care for what was neglected. That is why to care for bees is to care for the world.

Alone on a dune, between the breakers' worksite and the beached ship, Tarek watches a dark shape in the tranquil green waters bob like flotsam. It comes closer to the shore. The figure reaches the shallows and stands. A boy, his skin dark from the sun, drags by a rope a crate that floats on an inner tube. He draws it onto the sand, empties his haul at the water's edge. Tarek watches him sort empty bottles, cans and pieces of plastic jettisoned by passing ships.

What the boy does not want he throws back to sea. The rest he loads into the crate, drags it past Tarek, heads for a rise of land beyond the beach. Coarse wild grass crowns the incline. The boy struggles, bare feet sink into the sand. With a hand clutching tall reeds he pulls himself up the slope. Tarek follows along the steep of stone and sand. Beyond the crest, sheets of crystallized salt crack underfoot like ice. Ahead he sees the remains of a fishermen's hut long abandoned. Roof-less walls, like white stalagmites of salt, rise towards a blue-enamelled sky. On the rise, the breeze from the sea cools the heat of the sun. Here the sands are desert coral, bleached splinters of bone and pale shell fragments. Against a ruin of a corner wall he sees a shelter of driftwood and plastic sheets.

"What do you want?" The boy kneels by the crate.

"To see where you live."

The boy shrugs, empties the contents of the crate in a heap.

"What do you do with the things you collect?"

"Sell them."

"Who to?"

"People need bottles."

Tarek watches the boy sort his collection.

"You work breaking old ships?"

"No, I tell stories."

"What kind of stories?"

"All sorts of stories."

The boy clinks the bottles as he stacks the larger ones at the bottom of a sack. "What good is telling stories?"

"Well, for a start, people often tell stories about people they care about to people they love."

The boy counts bottles.

"And when we're gone, it's often all that's left."

The boy shrugs. He has no time for stories or thoughts of death.

Tarek sits in the sand, watches the boy estimate his wealth from the day's harvest. Behind him the great stone plateau still and vast as the sea.

PART 3

10

In slow-breaking early-morning light, at the apiary by the lake in a valley cut in the side of the great stone plateau, Reham watched the stranger run along the escarpment. He ran as though he saw little and cared to see even less. A rhythmic steady pace carried him forward through the mist, past figures that coalesced like ink blots bled from shadows—villagers on their way to fields or mosque.

By the hives, her younger sisters, Salma and Leila, collected full combs in old metal buckets. Their long *tarhas* pulled high across their faces for protection from bees sluggish in the cool air and drowsy from the smoke Salma fanned with goose feathers from a censer into the stacks. A speckled mare grazed in the shade of a flame tree. In the bee-keeper's hut Reham steamed the combs for honey and wax. The room filled with the scent of flowers. From the window she saw the stranger standing by the well. She stepped out to make sure her sisters were not troubled by his presence. Her *tarha* hung loose off her shoulders. She glanced at him, then slowly raised her *tarha* to cover her hair and face, as was only proper. She read his gaze to mean he found her pleasing, felt flattered for being seventeen and desired by a man not of the village, attractive and in his early twenties.

He apologized for troubling her, said he was thirsty.

She called Leila to draw water from the well to fill the ladle for him to drink.

He said his name was Tarek.

She responded hers Reham of the House of Majid. "My sisters, Leila and Salma."

"We see you running this time most mornings," Leila said, and asked if he was from the prison on the stone plateau.

Yes, arrested for being a bad mathematician.

Unsure what he meant, Reham adjusted her *tarha*, said they had work to do. Like most people in the valley she was not sure if it was a good idea to talk to prisoners, even if they appeared more lost souls than dangerous.

Once by the hives, in the broken shade of a white-petalled oleander, she stopped to watch the young man climb the path along the escarpment back to the stone walls of the prison camp. She continued with Leila up a steep path between rocky outcrops to a narrow opening hidden in the rock face of the stone plateau.

She stooped to enter the hollow. It took a moment for her eyes to adjust to the dark cavern, to see the walls decorated with images in red, white and black of gazelles, ibex, longhorn buffalo and animals whose names she did not know for having never seen. Farther along, crimson figures of men with bows and spears. Lower down on the rocks, ochre figures swam, while others dived into what appeared to be an amber ocean. She gazed at pictures painted long before the Bedouin of the House of Majid discovered the valley. In the cool air of the cave she waited for Leila to join her in this their safe and secret place. On the floor of the cave she found a spiral shell with a shiny pink lip and a top that peaked like a minaret. She wiped the sand from it, placed it on a ledge to one side out of harm's way.

With Leila well hidden in a recess of the cave, Reham stood watch outside, below her the lake hemmed by fields crimped in furrows. She knelt, slipped her hand through the sand, let it run between her fingers, lifted a bee that struggled to shake the dust from its back. It jittered in her palm, raised itself to hover, then flew towards a row of hives nestled in the folds of the escarpment, sheltered in the shade of flame trees.

At the apiary, Salma spread wet palm-frond mats on the hives to keep them cool, added rocks to secure them against the wind. She glanced up, saw Reham wave to her somebody was approaching.

Along the path from the village, Umaya in a red dress decorated with white cowry shells led five women followed by a gaggle of girls with long white shawls. She stopped short of the hives, flicked a horse-tail swat to and fro, called to Salma, "We're here for the young sister." As everybody well knew, a child's sex must be etched on her body before it is fixed at puberty by nature. Uncut, a girl's appetites may become feral, God forbid, like those of a man. The sisters were late with Leila, so terribly late. "You're taking a great risk waiting this long for her cleansing."

"As we said before, we sisters have decided not to have Leila cut." Salma remained by the hives with the bees about her.

"You daughters of the House of Majid lack foresight. You think the rules don't apply to you. Why wait another year?" The women and girls lined up behind Umaya. She whipped her swat about her. "Don't force us to search the apiary. You are one and we are many."

Salma lifted the top off a hive.

Umaya hesitated, waved her fly swat, then with renewed resolve led the way forward along the track.

Salma tumbled the hive down the slope, spilling a swarm of bees.

The girls shrieked.

She toppled a second hive. "It is you who are few. We are many."

Umaya shouted at the women to catch the girls as they screamed and ran, shook the dust from the soles of her sandals to show her contempt for Salma, swiped her swat at her. "This will cost you more than you know."

By the edge of the lake before a gathering crowd, Umaya dug a row of shallow pits with a ground-axe. Girls waited their turn. Women beat tambourines and sang. For Umaya the singing was an uplifting celebration of empowerment that strengthened her resolve, confirmed her in the knowledge that what she did was right.

The children approached the water's edge, sobbed with fear and anticipation of pain, having witnessed the cleansing of sisters and cousins. Umaya felt for them. How could she not when she loved them so dearly? This was the hardest part, not least for her. She steeled herself to make the first cut. A girl brought forward, held about the waist with arms pinioned to her sides by two of the women, pressed to the ground, her legs forced apart. Umaya unsheathed the blade. With a steady hand she sliced from the top of the vaginal cleft through the clitoris and folds of labia.

The girl wailed, struggled to free her arms and legs, kicked and flailed, fought as Umaya cut. The other girls fluttered to and fro, wailed, tried to break free from the line. With the girl's wound washed with water brought from the lake in a shallow gourd, Umaya sealed the bleeding at the opening of the vagina with needle and thread, packed mud over the cut to speed clotting. A woman bore away the barely conscious child to her mother. Umaya buried the trim of flesh and bloodied rags in a pit. The next girl writhed as she was held. Umaya cursed under her breath. It was a strain when they did not acquiesce. A girl broke free of the line, ran for the lake. Women waded in to stop her before she reached the deep waters, black in the shadow of the stone face of the escarpment, where the *ghawas*, spirits of the lake, hid by day away from the light.

Umaya worked with speed, concerned the girls should not harm themselves by struggling. She pitied them the necessary suffering to become women. What could she do, but be light and swift with the blade? She looked into each girl's eyes to know her stripped of everything by terror and pain. She could tell which of them, later in life, would be trouble, and the kind of trouble they would likely be. She would know how to read them when, as women, they came to her for talismans and spells.

The morning's task over, Umaya returned the gelding knife to Agha Hashem at his compound. His knives were sharper than any she could purchase in the valley. His blades did not rust to risk poisoning the children's blood. In the yard Nufal, Hashem's foreman, honed a set of knives, his skin crusted in dust and perspiration. He worked a foot-pedal that turned a wheel with spokes on a tripod. A leather belt spun a circular grinding stone. He laid a knife to the stone. Steel screeched. Silver sparks fanned in a shower to the ground. Umaya complained about the girls she had cleansed, as she always did every year—This one too feisty, that one would not stop screaming, another kept kicking, while others wriggled, spat and fought.

Agha Hashem nodded as he took his payment for the rental of the blade from the money Umaya received for the excisions. He asked about Leila. "Was the child cleansed?"

No, but Umaya will try again next year.

The Agha thought he had been clear. This year there should be no exceptions.

"That Salma's crazy. She set swarms of bees on us."

As a village elder he cannot approve such behaviour from a woman.

"Yes, but for a horse to be ridden it must first be broken."

He knows the expression. An unruly girl needs a strict husband.

Umaya flicked her fly swat. "There's no easy way to break a girl like that."

"A woman can always be broken."

Umaya had not meant to disagree. She meant no disrespect to Agha Hashem.

In the shade of prison walls on the stone plateau, Kasem heated water in a can on a nest of twigs and scraps of paper. He spooned in ground coffee, stirred and waited for it to froth and rise before pouring it into cups for Tarek and himself. On a flat board marked in sections for backgammon, they tossed knucklebones for dice, moved stone chips for counters. A prison guard called to Kasem, told him he had been hired out to assist in the compound of a village elder, the valley's rainmaker, a man by the name of Yaqzan.

For the next several days, as Kasem made his way to the rainmaker's compound to replant the yard in time for the change in seasons, he watched surveyors in teams of two, each with a mule loaded with equipment and supplies, survey the valley. They measured angles, lengths, moved from point to point with tall numbered sticks and plumb lines, developed a grid of degrees and distances, laid chains and read dips and rises through rotating telescopic sights of three-legged theodolites. They recorded everything in ledgers bound in black leather. To shield their eyes from the sun, the mules wore straw hats through which their long ears protruded. Mules with hats became a subject of merriment for the people of the village, to be recalled long after the surveyors completed their task and departed. "When mules wear hats" caught on as an expression for a time when the implausible became possible, and the world seemed to lose its mooring with nothing as it should be.

Days when Reham was at the apiary, Tarek would stop to ask for water. On mornings she was alone to churn honey, or melt wax to mould into candles, she draped her *tarha* across her shoulders and left her face uncovered. She thought him sombre, at times sullen, not the type to commit a crime deserving of prison. She asked about life away from the valley. He would respond in short answers as though shy and respectful in her presence. One morning, to provoke him, she asked if city girls were cut and sutured like girls in the village. He paused, said he thought the practice still prevalent, though probably less so than in the past.

She told him she had something to share, but he must keep it secret. She led him along a steep incline of sand and stone to a crevice between rocks to a narrow opening. She stooped to step into the hollow rock face. It took a moment for their eyes to adjust to the dark cavern, to see the walls decorated with ibex and men with spears.

"Do you have anything like this in the city?"

No, he had not seen anything like it before.

She said as a child she imagined the images were *jinn* who came alive at night to gather and hunt across these walls. She had thought they had been dreamt by the great spirit of the earth and the dreams trapped in the cavern.

He smiled. No, he did not think so. "These were painted by people an age ago when the desert was grassland." He supposed each of the figures had a story to tell—"If only we knew how to reach them."

"At least I made you smile." She handed him the spiral shell she had found and left on the ledge. "Maybe they'll whisper to you what you want to know."

He held it to his ear. "I hear them." He paused, gazed at her. "They say I should kiss you."

She blushed, then closed her eyes and waited for him to touch her.

Late morning, in the *majlis* room of his compound, Yaqzan—the valley's venerable rainmaker, first among the elders, respected by all who knew him, tolerably wealthy, unblemished in character, master of his household and his women—studied a scroll spread on the floor by a stranger in khaki uniform with a dark visor, as unblinking as a scorpion's eye. He did not know what to make of the signs, symbols, gridlines, the markings and numbers in black and red on the unfurled sheet. His eyes glided over the surface unable to penetrate to the meaning of the figures and the letters that formed words he stutteringly read as place names. He thought it like listening to speech in a strange dialect. Just as one sound became intelligible, promising an epiphany of sorts, other sounds confounded and confused to make him realize he understood nothing. He tried to catch a glimpse of the stranger's eyes under the glass mask—it was disconcerting the stranger should choose to hide his sight—but how else could Yaqzan tell if the man seated in his house could be trusted?

When the other elders arrived, they removed their sandals and *mar-quob* shoes at the door, a customary courtesy, a show of respect. The stranger kept his black boots on. He wore a knife in a scabbard on his belt, as he would among infidels.

Kasem brought in from the kitchen brass bowls of rosewater with floating petals for the guests to wash the dust from their hands and faces. He served mint tea in pear-shaped glasses, placed a burning censer on the rug to rid the room of malevolent spirits. Thin coils of sandalwood smoke rose from the burner, folded about the ceiling.

Yaqzan watched with a deep foreboding the turning black threads, certain they foretold the fate of the valley. A man more skilled than himself could read words in whorls of smoke, just as the prophet Daniel, may peace be upon him, had read them on Belshazzar the Chaldean's wall. So much knowledge had been lost with the passing of the generations and more will be lost when he too joins the ancestors before the all-seeing face of God.

As the stranger, in a tone of knowing self-satisfaction, pointed out what the symbols, letters and lines meant on the large sheet of paper spread on the floor, the disparate, seemingly irrelevant markings on the drawing coalesced into meaningful patterns—the oasis, a cranny between ridges of escarpment, lake, fields, village, sand barrier of trees, the sea of dunes that flowed to the great river, the purple hills and scattered oases, some barely known by name, linked by caravan routes and roads marked in dots and dashes across plains and fields of sand and stone to the very ends of the earth. The rainmaker stared with wonder at the world unfolded, laid bare, its secret paths and hidden places unveiled. What he had experienced in discontinuous fragments, in discrete substantive actuality—the oasis, the sandy slopes of the escarpment and parts of the great stone plateau—now formed a continuous whole, a single view he could grasp at a glance and retain in his mind.

He recognized the vastness of the great desert, life as a flicker, a momentary flash, felt the anxiety of insignificance and a deep sadness. His eyes drifted from the map to read the thoughts on the faces of the other elders. Agha Hashem, who owned fields from the edge of the lake to the escarpment, stared at the markings on the sheet and thought his holdings diminished by the sweep of the desert, felt the need to find a woman with land to marry to increase his worth. Sabri, the owner of the mill turned by blinkered mules that ground sorghum and wheat to bake in his ovens to be sold as bread, wondered at the price of grain in the green ribbon along the great river. Mahmoud, who rented a truck to carry goods to his store in the village, ran his eyes along the lines of dots and dashes, and under his breath calculated the cost of transportation from point to point and wondered how much richer he would be if he could trade across such an expanse.

The stranger explained that soon the prison on the stone plateau would be replaced by a border post, the prisoners repatriated to city penitentiaries where they can serve out or appeal their sentences. "The job of the border guard is to secure the borders." The stranger raised his head, adjusted the dark visor.

"How will we know where the borders are?" Sabri asked.

"They're drawn on the map."

The baker wanted to know whether the people of the valley would find themselves with walls where once there was only open space.

The stranger assured him no walls would be built. But men must learn to respect the invisible boundaries. That is all.

"We know nothing of borders and how they are managed," Yaqzan said.

"You'll learn."

The venerable rainmaker was unused at his age to being spoken to in such a manner by a man many years younger, and in front of the other elders.

Agha Hashem said he spoke for everybody present when he welcomed the stranger and wished him well in the valley. "How should we address you?"

"I am an officer of the border guard. You can call me Corporal Aboud."

The baker asked the corporal about the glass mask he wore over his eyes, whether there was anything wrong with his sight.

"With this visor I can see in the brightest light."

Mahmoud, surprised such a device sufficient against a power as great as the sun, stroked his beard.

The corporal rolled up the map to bring the meeting to a close.

Once the stranger had left, Yaqzan marvelled at the vanity of the man whose affectations seemed unbounded and whose presence, he was sure, would lead to nothing but trouble.

"If there are border guards, then next they'll build a road." Mahmoud's voice dark and wise fell to a hush. "There may be profit in it."

Sabri disagreed, talked anxiously of borders and how invisible lines would hem in the world, stifle life in the valley. With the principle of invisibility accepted, there would be rules they would be expected to respect and yet knew nothing about, and maybe, even, never would. If a man inadvertently transgressed the invisibles, he would be guilty and not even know it. By virtue of a line, what was once the same in its continuity would be different in its contiguity. The valley had done fine for itself without invisible lines and men in uniforms to enforce them. And now they had a corporal—he wagged his finger, no less—stationed among them.

At night in his first wife's bed, Yaqzan dreamt of making love to a girl in a field. In his dream his mouth rattled. He spat teeth, woke in a flood of perspiration. He waited for his heart to settle its pounding, went to a carved chest of tamarind wood in the corner of the room, removed the leather pouch in which he kept the old pocket watch etched with leaves—still since the Wali's death. He turned it about in his hand, carefully placed it back in the chest. One day, he will awaken time again, but not now, not yet.

At dawn, he crossed his fields to reach the mosque. He saw a dark bundle in the lake as though shorn free from shadows under the stone ledge of the escarpment. He waded in, struggled to pull the drifting mass ashore, laid it on the soft black soil. The body of a child—a long red *tarha* hung loosely about her shoulders, the flesh pale fish skin, swollen from a night in icy water. He avoided her gaze. Death sees with the eyes of the dead. He rested under the great doum palm the children of the village call the upside-down tree. He closed his eyes, thought the corpse a sign of impending calamity. When he looked again the girl's body was gone. He could see no trace of her, felt confusion before leaving to pray for rain to fill the wells.

Later that morning, Yaqzan sat under a red arabesque canopy musty with the odour of dust scorched by the sun, sipped tea through kelp-like leaves of mint. He watched the young man, Kasem, he had hired from the prison corral a flock of Awassi sheep to pens of thorn branches pleached and latched by stakes to the ground. Yaqzan trusted him more than he did the local men who worked his flock, their honesty always in contention. The shearers paid by the number of sheep shorn, the bundlers by the bale, could not be relied upon to count accurately or to charge him fairly for their labour.

In the pens, buyers made blue marks on notepads with blunt lead pencils moistened by licks that stained their tongues green. They ran their hands through fleece to feel for softness and length. The wool, once sheared and baled, was rolled to the cantilevered arm of a cast-iron scale and weighed, the poundage recorded in ledgers. Buyers negotiated the price with Yaqzan.

"Sixteen bales at discount. Discount from ten."

"Discount from twenty." Confident of a sale, he would not condescend to bargain.

The earth, bleached and crushed by the sun to a fine powder, felt dry as dust between his fingers. Yaqzan scanned the horizon for signs of an impending storm. He knew the many names of the winds—the soaring sheets of sands called *aalam*, and the flying *sagagid*, the blustering *haboob* and the fifty-day *khamasin*, the rolling winds of the *hibli*, the *semoum*, the *nafkhat* and the *harmattan*. He could tell which swirls of dust were caused by mischievous sand-demons and those that would become great maelstroms whipped up by battles between *afrit* and *jinn* with scimitars that flashed lightning. Other times thin columns of spinning dust formed at the horizon, spread their skirts, gathered up clouds of sand that rose to the sky to tumble into the valley, shrouded everything in a jaundiced haze through which the sun smouldered and leaked like a bloodstain. With the air noxious, the people of the oasis shuttered their windows and sealed their doors until days later the dust settled and the air cleared. Then the men congregated in the village mosque for thanksgiving prayers. For they had all heard recited from scripture how once fierce winds had obliterated the tribes of Aad and the fabled city of Iram with its many lofty pillars. So too the people of Thamud, who cultivated gardens in the desert and hewed cities out of rock that were thought to endure until the end of time.

* * *

With the day's trading over, Yaqzan made his way to the marabout, who with deep knowledge of the world of *jinn* wore a cowry-shell necklace, iron rings on his arm. His magic great enough to have his own *kuni* servant spirit. The marabout sat cross-legged with an incense burner by his side in the shade of a fig tree with mats of palm fronds across the branches to screen him from the sun. When Yaqzan arrived, he rose to show respect to one so venerable as the valley's rainmaker. Yaqzan asked about the marabout's recent journey to the scattered oases of the great desert, listened to him speak of scant rainfall to the south and dry waterholes. When he deemed the moment right, he asked if any family had that day lost a daughter by drowning in the lake. The marabout had heard nothing.

To avoid having to explain his question, Yaqzan told him of the girl he made love to in his dream.

"Such a dream suggests a fear of dying."

No, Yaqzan did not fear death, but every year it did get harder to bring rain to the valley. As rainmaker, he felt his powers wane, feared the loss of respect that comes with failure. He tired of the great burden he shouldered alone and for so long. "I have waited for a new Wali to arise, to relieve me of my covenant, to appoint another in my place, but this has not happened."

The marabout closed his eyes, traced with his fingers figures in the sand, read the markings as signs from the ancestors, announced that the rainmaker's mission was not over. "Only when the new Wali arrives will the curve of time find its horizon, and as the pages turn the book of sky and earth will close and a new age begin." He struck iron with flint to ignite the incense in the burner, commanded the *kuni* spirit to guide him to the lords of the *jinn*, called upon each of them by name, chattered, shook and shivered, cast a handful of cowry shells, stared intently at them, declared the old man had need for a son to share the burden of his covenant.

Yaqzan sighed. With both his wives past childbearing age, how was he expected to have a son?

Sons extend their father's shadow, give life to his name. "The ancestors require that you take another wife."

How could the ancestors require such a thing of him? Such foolishness to even think it possible.

"The fate of this valley hangs by a thread and you are that thread. The thread must not be broken."

As burdened as he felt with the gravity of his obligations and the weight of the world, Yaqzan could not countenance the idea of another marriage.

"The ancestors will not be denied. Your dream was clear. The cowry shells confirm it." The marabout spoke of a man's obligation to those who have passed away and responsibility for those yet to come.

Yaqzan pleaded. At his age a new wife would be a millstone for him to bear. Let the ancestors choose somebody else to inherit the burden and let him spend his final days in peace and prayer.

By cowry shells and traces in sand the ancestors repeated their demand. The rainmaker must comply.

Wearied by argument, and unable to defy their authority or refute their reason, Yaqzan acquiesced on condition he leave the search for a suitable bride to the marabout. "I ask only that she be capable of bearing me a child."

The marabout will consult with Umaya for a suitable bride for the venerable rainmaker. He would do so with caution, knowing her to be capricious and dangerous for the black book she kept with the names of those she cursed. Anyone who believed themselves afflicted by her visited the marabout. For a fee he gave them a candle etched with a line of scripture. When the candle burned to a pool of wax their names faded from Umaya's book.

* * *

That evening Yaqzan told his two wives that he planned to marry. He expected protests, but instead, the women exchanged glances, sucked their teeth, turned away to the kitchen. They kneaded dough to rise overnight and bake in the yard the next morning. Well, they presumed him a fool, so what? He did not expect sense from them. He knew at their age any jealousy they once felt for one another had given way to solidarity against him, and often despite all reason. He believed he had been a good husband and, if truth be told, a fine father. Now, he must think of the future of the valley until the coming of the next Wali.

When his daughters heard from their mothers that their father planned to take a third wife, they arrived at his compound with their children in phalanxes. They berated him, said he had lost his senses—too ripe in years to be mocked by neighbours for adding another bride to his household. Who had ever heard of such a thing at his age?

His face reddened at their audacity to speak to him in such a manner. As patiently as he could, he recounted his oath to the Wali, to whom they owed everything. They should meet with the marabout, who could explain to them the importance of the pledge he made as a boy.

"Who is the marabout to be consulted on family matters?" How outrageous to discuss such a subject with a stranger. "Let it be one of our children."

But the child had to be conceived for the sake of the covenant.

"What is it to us a promise made before we were born?"

Why could they not see how the Wali's return was the future that structured the present and gave meaning to the past?

The daughters slapped one hand upon the other in gestures of incredulity, said, as when the world confounds the senses and is beyond all reason, "There is no means nor power except by God."

"Now is the time when mules wear hats."

11

All night the speckled mare stomped her hooves against the stable's mud-packed floor. The scent from her body and the pungent odour of urine on the bedding straw signalled her time. The mare beat and pounded against the door of the stall, whined and chomped.

Under a sky still crimson with the dawn, Reham fed and watered the mare, led her out to the sheepfold from when in better times the sisters owned a drove. The mare tossed her head, pulled on the harness, panted and snorted. She resisted being led to the enclosure, stamped, threw up sand. In the pen, she butted the walls with her shoulders, first one side, then the other, whipped her mane across the crest of her neck, snapped her tail. A fine mist formed along her back.

With the air still cool, the three sisters watched Agha Hashem arrive on his pale stallion with his man Nufal. Hashem, beaked nose and gaunt, his beard hennaed black and red to disguise the grey, dismounted, straightened his turban, let one end drop onto his shoulder in the rakish manner of younger men. Reham had heard it said, as much as Agha Hashem loved himself, he loved that stallion.

The mare, in the sheepfold, clenched and released her vulva. Nufal led the stallion to her. The stallion bared its teeth, reared and lunged onto the mare, gripped her back with fetlocks pressed to her sides. Its shaft extended an arm's length. The mare staggered, steadied herself under its weight. After several thrusts, the stallion withdrew, dripped silver globules in the sand.

Nufal drew the stallion from the pen to rub down and saddle for the return journey to Agha Hashem's stable.

"Your land along the escarpment is barren." Agha Hashem gazed at Reham. "If you sunk wells, it would all be good for grazing."

"We don't have goats or sheep to justify the cost."

"But I do." He smiled. "So much grazing land would earn a good income for a husband."

Several evenings later, Reham waited for Tarek by the well. Together in the cave of images she told him of her meeting with the marabout and the marriage proposal from the venerable rainmaker. She had accepted, believed this the only way to shield herself and her sisters from a man like Agha Hashem, who with three wives was now looking for a fourth. She had heard of how most evenings before he went to Mama Sara's coffeehouse for his arak and shisha, he stopped at the one-room hut by the truck stop where Hayat, the village wet nurse, lived. It was said the girl spent her days standing over burning censers calling on the *jinn* lords to make her fertile. She bought tree medicine from Umaya to make her full with Hashem's child. But everybody knew Agha Hashem would marry only for land and Hayat had none to her name.

"You know as well as I do, there's no future to our relationship. You could be sent away at any time. I need protection for myself and my sisters and you can't offer me that. I wish it were different but that's the truth of it." She said once she was married, Tarek would not see her again. "I will miss you. Please don't make this harder for me than it has to be." She thought she saw the terrible gate of marriage open and all she could do was enter and let it close behind her to shut off the world she had known and the one she had hoped for.

For days after, when alone in his cell, Tarek lay on his bed, closed his eyes, imagined himself floating from his bed, suspended in still air, no ceiling above, no walls around him, disembodied mind, intellect without sensation.

With the sun barely risen, and again at dusk with the earth in shadow, he ran on the great stone plateau, pounded the ground to pulverize his thoughts and exhaust his body. Curious for news of the world beyond, he collected scraps of newspaper, casual litter carried by winds from waste heaps of towns by the great river, shreds caught in tumbleweed, yellowed by the sun, buried by sand, uncovered and blown farther by fresh gusts across an expanse of dunes and sand sheets. Some remnants discarded by truck drivers going to and from the valley. Evenings in his cell he sorted and stored the scraps in a cardboard box, listed them by topic and date in a notebook he bartered from the owner of the village general store in return for a morning's labour.

He imagined the shreds of paper clues to the world's unfolding. Analyzed with sufficient rigour, the fragments might yield a pattern. With enough data he might derive an equation to describe the news events in the form of a wave—the height of the crest the significance, symmetry the degree of stability, the width of the base duration. As best as his memory served him, he wrote the formula for the universal unfolding of a singularity. For a measure of order, he applied functional terms derived from a morphogenic system. With an impossible task to attempt, he gained a sense of purpose. Hell seemed bearable.

* * *

At the bride's house, Yaqzan sat upright by a mound of cushions with a neatly wrapped turban on his head. His brown polished *marquob* shoes smelt of fresh leather, placed heel to toe on the floor by the door. His moustache and beard groomed with beeswax, hennaed to moderate the grey. Rattled and shaken by the trip on the buggy from the village to the escarpment, yet mindful of his status and the gravity of the day's mission, he tried to appear composed and of manly vigour sufficient to make the young woman the mother of his child.

His two wives, intent on intimidating the sisters with their finery, wore silver wrist and ankle bracelets. They noted with satisfaction the child to be engaged had sturdy limbs. "Raw-boned, peasant stock," murmured the second wife to the first. A girl accustomed to labour. They spoke of their lives and the many tasks needed doing about the compound. Their words sweet, their tone caustic.

Reham agreed to the marriage on conditions she had negotiated with the marabout. Yaqzan would be her sisters' guardian, as though they were his own daughters. But no decision would be taken concerning them without her consent. Her terms to be written into the marriage contract.

"Your sisters will be as my daughters," Yaqzan repeated by way of confirmation.

The date of the wedding was discussed, as Leila served the wives sage tea and squares of flat cake baked with diced figs soaked in honey. After the customary insistence and polite refusal, thrice both ways, the wives with restrained smiles succumbed to the enticement.

When the visit was over the two women sat in the back seat of the rental buggy under a retractable canopy to return to their compound in the village. Yaqzan sat next to the driver. The wives talked of how they would devise chores and divvy up labour for the new wife. Over the clip-clop of the mule's iron-shod hooves, they reminded their husband of how they never denied him when he came to their beds. Had they ever refused him? He should not forget their fecundity when they were young.

He ignored them, excused their resentment.

At the village market, the wives stopped to haggle for a mound of limes packed into baskets of woven palm fronds. In their kitchen, they pickled the limes in large jars with rock salt, garlic and cloves. After a month the swollen fruit tasted as bitter as tears. For as long as the limes lasted, the wives ate of them, to deepen their well of sorrow.

In the days before her wedding, Reham looked at fabrics and makeup. Her sisters advised her saffron and red were most definitely her colours. Visiting neighbours congratulated her on entering the world of woman-hood. They spoke of the mysteries of marriage and of men, of how best to manage a husband and warned of the jealousy of other wives.

"Use the early years of marriage when you are your husband's favourite to win as many concessions as you can."

"First break the talons of the most jealous wife."

"Flirt with him in front of the other wives."

"Make them know he likes you best."

"Treat them with obvious sufferance."

"Don't let their tears stop you getting what you want."

The women giggled and blushed as they spoke of men.

"A woman can have a mind to many things, but a man's mind is only on one."

"A man thinks with the head between his legs."

"A head with no brain."

"A stork with two eggs."

"A rooster with one eye."

"A snail with a soft shell."

Reham smiled to mask the icy feeling that gripped her. The world beyond her home so vast, and she little more than a leaf shed from a once great tree so ill prepared for all that could happen. Her evenings with her sisters spent recounting, more through grief than joy, stories of their childhood.

The women swarmed about her, bees about their queen, instructed her on womanly wiles, relived their own wedding nights, assailed her with stories of how to pleasure her husband to win him to her side. But she must never forget to guard his honour. With marriage the risk of shame increased manyfold. They whispered of girls who disappeared from the valley after rumours of secret trysts. A woman must guard against love, the enemy of honour that leads astray, that brings ruin in its wake.

Umaya arrived with ground cochineal mixed in beeswax to blush the young woman's cheeks, colour red her lips and nails. She prepared henna to stain Reham's hands and feet in filigree patterns. The women whispered that Umaya understood the secrets of desire, for she had seduced a lord of the *afrit* and learnt from him the power of spells.

"Your skin takes henna well." Umaya drew rosettes and arabesques on Reham's hands. With a wooden quill she etched sweeping whirls and speckled patterns along the girl's arms and feet that Leila said looked like vines. Salma thought them more like bee stings. Wrapped in a camel-hair blanket, Reham squatted over a shallow pit of burning sandalwood. The smoke imprinted its scent on her body, fixed the henna to her skin. She spent her last hours at home reinforcing in memory images of house and garden—the cracked tiles and flaked blue paint, the patchwork plots of vegetables, sage and thyme, trees of pomegranate and tamarind, and the apiary at the edge of the escarpment.

On the evening of the wedding, the bridal party collected at the sisters' compound to set out along the road to the village. Reham sat swaddled in black in a buggy decorated in tinsel with silver charms of stars and crescents. Small brass bells jingled as the carriage swayed. The breeze, green with the scent of the fields, lifted her skirt, tugged at the black wrap around her breasts. She knew this day was an end of sorts; with dawn would come a new beginning.

The sunset burnished the horizon with a momentary flash before darkness. Oil lanterns flared in orange flames on tall staffs under stars that spread like hoarfrost and a moon as pale as parchment. A small band with drums, tambourines and bamboo flutes led the procession, collected guests from the shadows by doors that flashed light like flames from oven grates. They walked alongside the buggy by the lake hemmed by reeds flecked with fireflies, made their way past arbours of bougain-villea. In lantern light the red blossoms scattered on the bride's lap and at her feet glowed like embers.

At Yaqzan's compound men collected in the open courtyard. The women congregated inside the house. The oldest wife remained in her room. What did it matter to her whether her husband took another bride? After all, she had lived through this before with all the pain she could bear. This time let the second wife feel humiliated, as she spends the evening at the gate to the compound dabbing her bloodshot eyes with handkerchiefs as large as bedsheets, greeting wedding guests like a grieving widow at a wake.

* * *

Reham took her seat on the dais in an armchair of carved tamarind, thought herself a child lost at a *moulid*. By her side the groom, as old as Abraham, eyes leaden with exhaustion from the day's preparations and the anxiety of the event. After recitations from scripture and the repetition of vows, a ram was slaughtered. Its blood ran across the doorstep, coagulated in the dirt.

In the bedroom, her husband told her to undress, extinguish the candle when she was ready for him. He absented himself in the *majlis* room to drink the potion of yohimbe given him by the marabout to strengthen his seed and ensure he produced a boy worthy of his father. In bed, he struggled to remove the last of her garments, rolled onto her trembling naked body, pushed and pressed, could not penetrate her. She sobbed. He stopped, lay on his back, stared at the ceiling, explained that with his previous two brides he had the vigour to burst their sutured vaginas with his fingers and follow through with the thrust of his shaft. But, alas, at his age, he lacked the strength to breach the seam. Though he did not have the heart to cause her pain on their first night, if by morning they did not show blood on the sheets there would be gossip, most certainly by his wives doubting his manhood, worse still the bride's innocence. He recalled the advice he had been given to split a pomegranate on his wedding night. He forgot to do so—a stupid superstition. He shuffled to the kitchen, returned with a trimming knife.

Reham stared at the blade in the light from the window. She trembled, felt cold.

He forced her legs apart, eased the blade into the seam. She writhed in the darkness, screamed, sobbed as he climbed on top of her to insert himself into her fresh wound. Her warm blood flowed along his scrotum and thighs, lubricated his penetration. She pleaded for him to stop, tossed from side to side, her face wet with tears. He thrust to come, to discharge himself in her and be done. He tried, gave up, pulled out, rolled onto his side away from her. His shaft shrivelled, all desire gone. Shadows played on the walls, condensed, separated and coalesced into grotesque shapes to the sound of the band loud from the yard. He closed his eyes, fell into a deep sleep brought on by fatigue and the yohimbe potion.

Blood ran from the cut between Reham's legs. The coloured lights in the courtyard leapt across the walls through the partially shuttered window. She eased herself off the bed, struggled to the washroom, sat on the cold floor with a cloth pressed against her thighs to soak and slow the bleeding, leant back against the wall, felt her head lighten. Her mind slipped in and out of consciousness. The shadows cast by the window rose and fell accompanied by the squalls of the band. How long will this horror last until it seemed normal, until she no longer felt dread at her husband's approach? For now she had discharged her obligation, bloodied the sheets to be hung on a line in the courtyard, proof she had bled on the marriage altar.

All the next day the hemorrhaging continued. Reham could barely support herself to and from the washroom. That night her husband came to her bed, but her bleeding drove him back to the second wife's room. The next morning, fearing for his young bride, Yaqzan sent for Umaya. In her understanding of roots, bark and sap he saw the limits of his own knowledge of stars, storms and scripture. Umaya gave Reham a balm made of the juices of the prickly pear cactus and beeswax to calm the inflammation and seal the wound. She urged Yaqzan to give his wife time to heal before he tried with her again. He protested. He was not to blame for his wife's condition, caused by the cleansing and not by anything he had done. After all, he did not care, one way or another, if girls were cut and sutured. It was all a matter of custom. Why should he take the blame? Such matters were best left to women to decide upon and arrange. He did not interfere in women's matters.

After the first month of marriage, Reham made the customary visit of the new wife to her old home. That morning she took a rental buggy, arrived with gifts from Yaqzan for her sisters. She spent the day reliving a life forever lost. She spoke to Salma of her disgust at having the old man touch her. For how much longer will she endure him until pregnancy provided her an excuse and relief? And what if he were impotent, would she be blamed, and then who would protect her and her sisters from the likes of Agha Hashem?

Tarek stopped for water from the well at the apiary, saw a spiral shell by the side of the ladle. Uncertain if there was significance to the discovery, he climbed the steep incline of sand and stone to the painted cavern.

As his eyes adjusted to the darkness in the cave he saw the images of animals and men with bows circling a fire. A shadow split from the rock face, came towards him. He recognized Reham's touch as she drew him to her.

They kissed.

She let his hands move down her body, leant against him. For the first time let him undress her. They made love in silence. Their bodies alive to each other.

Once they had come, he lay on his back on the cave floor, closed his eyes to retain for as long as he could the sensation of release and pleasure. When he opened them she was gone.

In the dark, the figures on the walls swayed as they gazed at him.

* * *

Every day in the courtyard of the compound the two wives watched the young woman thread her loom with fresh yarn, beat down the weft with a comb that made a tinkling sound like bells. They talked to her about the weaving, complained of the outrageous effrontery—weaving rugs as though it did not matter if anybody saw her. What could she be thinking? What must the neighbours be saying, to see her weave rugs when rugs can be bought from itinerant traders?

To their irritation, she paid them no heed, as if they were foolish, would you believe, and she the one with all the airs and graces from an ancient and noble line. They shook their heads as they glanced at each other. They spoke to their husband to tell the girl she must be rid of the loom, but he would not, glad she had something that kept her in the compound within his sight.

They murmured to Kasem that the girl was, after all, Sahrawi—Bedouin, you know. It was all so very shaming. Whereas, they were Baqara, cattle-herder stock—to be sure, fine well-bred folk. Of course, they believed themselves vindicated, for the rug weaving could only confirm that the young woman was never a suitable choice for their husband. So foolish with age he had taken for a bride a child younger than his own daughters. Not that they blamed him, really, being a man so under the influence of the marabout, who should have known better than to encourage such a marriage.

When Umaya arrived with Hayat, Yaqzan rose from his chair in the shade of the fig tree to greet her, called the two wives to prepare tea for the guests.

"Hayat will be a wet nurse for the child," Umaya said.

"Too early for that." What with the young wife's bleeding, and her frailty, he had left her alone these past few weeks.

"The young wife is with seed." Umaya straightened the *tarha* on her head by way of emphasis.

How was that possible?

"Penetration need not be frequent nor complete to result in pregnancy."

He dared not believe, but neither did he want to show disrespect by openly doubting.

"Her urine brings forth eggs from frogs."

The old man, almost giddy, marvelled at his vigour and potency. His feelings of tenderness and concern for the new wife increased.

Umaya stated a price for Hayat's milk. "It's the wet nurse that gives life to the valley."

Yaqzan protested that he was not a rich man. But after some haggling he relented, agreed to Umaya's price. He will provide a place for the wet nurse and meals during the breastfeeding period. He will apportion for Hayat meat and fat from every slaughter of ewe and ram from now until the birth.

"You will not find one with milk as sweet."

"I count on you to choose the best."

"I'll bring her to you as soon as the child is born."

He pressed the commission fee discreetly into Umaya's hand as she left with Hayat, then called Kasem, told him to be mindful of the young wife. She must not be allowed to clean or cook and certainly not carry water from the well, nor bake bread in the sun. Her meals were to be served at the loom. He sat in the shade of the old fig tree, bit on a bitter green olive, sucked the brine from the flesh and felt justified before God.

12

By Yaqzan's fields Kasem tossed grain in a tambourine sifter, made sounds like scraping cicadas. It took the early part of the morning to clear seed from the granary floor, collect husks for animal feed. In the shade of a shelter of palm fronds and hemp cloth, he strapped a padded collar to the neck of a blinkered mule to turn a grinding stone. The flour, gathered in sacks, he stacked against the back wall of the granary. Pinpricks of sun through the palm-frond ceiling burned his skin. He rubbed his face and arms to stop the itching.

He unloaded the sacks from the mule at the rainmaker's compound, carried them to a storage room by the kitchen, watched the young wife as she worked the loom with the shuttle, beat down the weft with a comb, ran threads of new colours through the warp, her skill at making patterns magical. A girl stopped at the gates to the compound, hugged and kissed the new wife. The *tarha* slipped from the girl's face to her shoulders. Kasem's cheeks flamed as he watched her.

That evening at the cellblock he boiled water on a bundle of twigs to make coffee, poured two stout glasses for himself and Tarek. He watched another group of prisoners loaded onto a truck to be relocated. "Do you think soon it will be our turn?" Tarek sipped his coffee.

"They're shuffling us like a deck of cards. Whether we stay or go, we'll still be in prison."

"At this rate, it's only a matter of weeks and there'll be none of us left here."

Tarek shrugged.

Kasem stirred his black coffee, watched the truck move with a trail of dust through the prison gates. He said that morning, at Yaqzan's compound, he saw a girl with the sweetest smile, overheard her name was Leila.

Tarek recognized the trace of feelings left unspoken, thought Kasem smitten.

"I'm not in love."

"What would you call it?"

Kasem did not know. "Maybe, in like."

That night after lights out, they lay on their beds in their cell, waited for the sounds to die of guards rattling doors in the corridor. Kasem asked what love was like.

"I don't know I can describe it."

"What I feel is like an ache."

"Yes, it can be like that."

Yaqzan sat in the yard, regarded his wives at work. The one weaved, the other two kneaded and pounded dough. He sucked on a green olive, watched as a large black dog settled outside the gate, rested its head on its paws, stared at him. At first he thought nothing of it, but then began to worry the animal may be an evil omen. He threw a stone at it.

The dog ignored his bad aim.

He yelled at it to leave, waved his walking staff.

The dog barely raised its head to acknowledge his efforts.

He called to a group of children, offered to reward them to chase the creature away.

They screamed and waved their arms, but the dog paid no heed.

The old man called Kasem, told him to spend more time in the compound to keep an eye on the dog.

The older wives took pleasure in Kasem's company. They told him stories of the valley, whispered of the ghoul stones on the great stone plateau, feared by *jinn* and *afrit* as much as by men, their force primitive, from a time when the world was all void and darkness. A man whose shadow fell upon the stones would have his spirit sucked from him. They told him stories in hushed tones of how a hyena's spittle caused leprosy, turned humans into hyenas. "Once, and not so long ago, a child was found in a hyena's litter." That was how they knew the stories true—hyenas copulate with men.

In the yard of the rainmaker's compound, the marabout recited spells and charted the unborn child's fate based on the date of conception and the throw of cowry shells. He predicted the child would be a boy, sound of mind and body. Yaqzan, pleased with the prognostication, ordered his wives to slaughter a sheep. The two women wielded long knives, carved and divided the flesh from the bone. They squatted on low stools, collected coils of fat in a basin, set aside a generous portion of meat for Hayat, another for the marabout for his intercession with the ancestors. The remainder to be distributed to the poor by way of thanksgiving.

Yaqzan asked the marabout about the black dog.

The marabout tossed the dog a bone red from the carcass. It stared at him with eyes held low. He shook his rattle, muttered words in the language of the *jinn*, led the dog to the yard. It took a position by the side of the loom. The marabout assured Yaqzan there was nothing to fear. "*Jinn* protectors of the unborn, called *nadir*, are known to take the shape of dogs."

With the morning light clear and the breeze gentle, Reham asked Kasem to take the rugs she had woven to the lakeside. Spread on the water, they soaked, then sank to the pebbled bed. Barefooted, Kasem trod them clean. With the *nadir* dog by her side she watched from the bank, recalled the stories her mother had told her—stories every woman in the valley knew—of how in the Garden of Eden childbirth was a pleasure and all children were born to Eve as twins. On the day Eve ate the fruit of the forbidden tree, she felt shame at her easy fertility. She hid the second of every twin. When the angel came to the Garden to admonish her, only half the children were counted, expelled with Eve to become enrobed in flesh. The hidden children remained to become spirit companions to those on earth. These are the *qareen*. A fetus, more spirit than flesh, is closer to its *qareen* than to its own mother. Many mothers had lost children stillborn, their spirits sloughed off their bodies, enticed to the spirit realm by jealous *qareen*.

As Kasem trod each rug in turn, removed it from the water to dry in the sun, Reham went to the great doum tree festooned, by young people from the village for loves lost or yet unfound, with ribbons that fluttered in a breeze off the lake. She thought to tie a ribbon for Tarek. But stopped, surprised by the notion. She had not imagined she felt that way about him. How strange to realize by making love she had fallen just a little in love. She smiled, felt lightened by the thought.

From the clay by the side of the tree she moulded a doll, laid it in the waters of the lake as an offering to the *qareen* to spare her child. On the face of the lake a fine mist formed. For a moment she felt foreboding, reached for the clay figurine. It crumbled in her hands to a copper stream.

On the days Reham visited her sisters, she left the spiral shell by the side of the well at the apiary for Tarek to know she waited at the cave of images by the rocky outcrop. There they made love. The *nadir* dog lay guard outside the cave in the shade of the escarpment.

Tarek told her he may soon be transferred from the prison camp to the city to appeal his sentence—how he wished to leave to gain his freedom and yet desired to stay to be with her.

She moved away, gave her back to him as she dressed. "I knew one day you'd leave." She smoothed her hair with both hands, drew the *tarha* across her shoulders. She turned to him. "I *will* miss you."

He was surprised by the sadness in her voice.

She lifted the *tarha* over her head. "I think I might be in love with you."

Yes, he knows. The risks she took to be with him too great to be explained otherwise. Fearful for her safety, should their liaison ever be discovered, he could not confide their relationship even to Kasem, thinking to burden him unfair. The responsibility too great—a casual word misspoken and overheard sufficient to justify her death for betraying her marriage vows.

* * *

When at night Yaqzan went to his young wife's room to plead his right to share her bed, she would refuse, said she feared losing the child. When he became insistent, the *nadir* dog growled and bared its teeth, as though he were a stranger.

The two older wives listened with satisfaction to his protests, tinkled tea glasses with spoons to let him know they overheard, made comments within earshot. They recalled the days when their husband had eyes only for them. Both thought him not the man he used to be. "A real man doesn't need a girl to make his tail stand." On that they both agreed. It was true they had only given him daughters. But it broke their hearts to recall the boys who died in childbirth. Of course, that may not have been their fault, for a child received its flesh from its mother's uterine blood, its bones from its father's seed. If bones were weak the child would not survive.

At Mama Sara's coffeehouse, Yaqzan bit on the soft wood of his shisha's mouthpiece, inhaled smoke from tobacco in the burning bowl, cooled as it bubbled through water. He comforted himself with the knowledge that it was the season of Canopus in the Scorpius constellation—a treacherous star. Another month or so before its malevolence could be moderated by Sirius. Then might be the time to try again with the young wife.

Nufal, Agha Hashem's foreman, approached Yaqzan, bowed his head respectfully, asked to speak to him on a matter of importance to his master. Yaqzan nodded, listened to how Agha Hashem desired to wed one of the daughters of the House of Majid of whom Yaqzan by virtue of marriage was guardian. "Will you grant consent for him to take Salma?"

Yaqzan sighed. The Agha could ask for anything of him, but not this. He had promised as part of his contract with Reham to shelter her sisters from all such proposals until they were ready to marry. "Tell Agha Hashem it is too soon."

Nufal explained the Agha did not like to be denied.

Yaqzan understood, but the time was not right. He dismissed Nufal, turned aside to Mama Sara, a woman grown large with the wisdom of the world, to complain of his wives. She advised him that once the child was born the young wife would be more willing, and the older wives more forgiving.

"That's how it is. Believe me, I know." She laughed, slapped her thigh as she often did when the hilarity of the moment overcame her sense of decorum.

He thought her right, sighed, inhaled on his shisha, talked of the *nadir* dog that still troubled his days. "I'll never have peace with that dog around."

"Don't worry about the dog. There are men who'll take care of it for you." She raised her voice and glanced around the room at nodding heads befuddled by arak.

He shrugged, asked for more tobacco for his shisha.

Mama Sara called Zainab, the serving girl. "Where is that child?"

Mama Sara learnt to make arak by fermenting dates with baking soda sealed in jars buried in sand under a hot sun. With her profits she built the coffeehouse and a room to store arak and merisa beer brewed from sorghum grown in the valley. With thought only for what was best for business, she encouraged Zainab to go for turns with clients. For those prepared to pay a little extra she had curtained off a ledge by the kitchen with a thin cotton mattress. She taught the girl to protect herself by inserting a ball of bezoar stones and cotton soaked in vinegar. Should the girl become pregnant, Umaya had the most efficacious potions of tree medicine. Mama Sara watched Zainab carefully, for nothing would ruin her business more than if the child fell in love, and nothing made that more likely than for her to have time on her hands.

Unseen in the tamarind trees by the coffeehouse, small, mischievous spirits called *dulla*, a genus of *afrit*, were drawn by the acrid scent of stale beer and arak. Every night, Zainab wiped down the tables to keep away the wasps that supped on droplets of spilt beer, and left a bowl of merisa by the back door for the *dulla*. As she slept on the mattress on the ledge with the curtain closed, the *dulla*, drunk from the beer, climbed into her bed, curled up under the sheets and stroked the secret parts of her body. Then, Zainab's dreams brought on hot flushes.

In the house by the edge of the escarpment, once so full with Reham's presence, Leila rattled like a coin in a brass cup. At first light, she climbed the ladder of a cob tower to reach pigeon nests, to collect eggs for breakfast. The small windows afforded her a clear view of the valley. Some mornings she would see Hayat cross the fields, make her way back from the border post to her shack by the truck stop. This morning, she saw Nufal, Agha Hashem's foreman, watch the wet nurse from the shadows of a bower of palm trees. Hayat increased her pace, just short of running. The soft clay of the fields slowed her. Nufal ran through a cane patch to block her way. She screamed at him to leave her alone. He shouted, shook his head, gripped her wrist, accused her of spending the night with the corporal. She demanded to know why she shouldn't do as she pleased.

"You do what Agha Hashem tells you."

"If he wants me he'll have to marry me." She pulled away, ran past Nufal towards the village.

Leila collected eggs, hurried down the ladder to tell Salma what she had seen.

That morning, Yaqzan woke to loud screams. His head heavy with sleep, he did not pause to wrap a turban about his head, ran barefooted into the yard. The *nadir* dog lay on the ground by the gate. Flies collected about its fractured skull, fed on dark coagulated blood. The young wife sobbed. She glared at him, rage in her eyes. He wanted to say that he had done nothing—he did not kill the *nadir*. Surely she knew, at his age, he did not have the strength. He tried to reason with her. Had the dog not been sent by the *jinn* lords to protect his child? Why would he harm it?

Her screams raised the neighbours, drew them to the compound.

Yaqzan looked around at the crowd. A gaggle of children climbed the walls to his yard. Women gathered, crows to peck at carrion, their black *tarhas* pulled over their heads covered their looks of scorn and muffled their whispers. Their eyes pierced him. He stared at the young wife. He had brought her into his home, given her everything, a handsome dowry, his patience and consideration. In return, she incited his wives to disrespect him, made a fool of him, an elder, the valley's rainmaker, reduced him in the sight of the village. How dare she behave this way with him. All he had done was show her kindness and in return she had shamed him.

Her scream jolted his brain.

He slapped her face.

She reeled to the ground. The *tarha* flew from her.

The neighbourhood women berated him. The shamefulness of a man exposing his wife's face to strangers, and in such a savage manner.

"Beats his wife in public."

"And she pregnant with his child."

They shouted at him to leave the young woman alone. Their husbands tried to corral them, each his several wives and children, back to their compounds.

Reham raised herself from the ground, her sight hardened on Yaqzan. "A curse upon your eyes for striking me."

Yaqzan's older wives scurried into the yard, terrified to see their husband in such a rage. He yelled at them to clean up the corpse and blood of the accursed *nadir*, shouted at the young wife to get herself in the house, to cover her hair and face like a decent woman, turned on the neighbours, ordered them to leave his yard before he fetched his walking staff and cudgelled them one by one for trespass. The courtyard emptied faster than it filled.

In black wraps, the two wives visited Umaya in her shack lit by rush candles. The air heavy with the scent of burning myrrh from a charcoal censer. Both women struggled to sit on the ground without tipping like urns. The older wife told Umaya they had come to consult her about their husband. Umaya had heard of how the venerable rainmaker had chastised the young woman. But God granted men permission to beat an errant wife. So no blame could be apportioned to the elder for doing so. A man is free to act within his rights.

Of course, they would not think to dispute the word of God, but what next? Would their husband beat them? "The young wife is driving him out of his mind."

"So you want him to be blind to her?"

The two wives thought Umaya had expressed their wish more precisely than they could have. "What can we do?"

"Cast a spell so he'll not see her and so not desire her."

Yes, they would like a spell to return their husband to them.

Umaya took a piece of paper from a small wooden box, drew stars, numbers and letters, placed it on the floor in front of the two women, muttered an incantation, folded the paper, handed it to the oldest wife.

Back at their compound, the wives doused themselves with rosewater to lose the scent of myrrh that had insinuated itself into their clothes and hair. They chose the mirror in the second wife's bedroom, the largest in the house, for Umaya's spell. They squeezed the folded piece of paper with its secret symbols between the silvered back of the mirror and the wooden frame.

Evening prayers over, Yaqzan returned from the village mosque with a basket woven of palm fronds. He called Kasem to give the basket to the young wife at the loom in the yard. He watched from the shadows as Reham undid the frond ties, paused, then lifted from the basket a white kitten with eyes barely open. She stroked it, held it to her breast. He nodded to himself. Yes, he will make his peace with her, convince the young wife of his innocence in the dog's death. But she too must realize she treated him poorly. He would give her time to learn, for she was a child, bearing his child, and had yet to understand what it meant to be the wife of an elder.

* * *

Over the next several days the two older wives watched their husband as his mind flickered between lucidity and forgetfulness. In the yard, they kneaded dough, joked about the old man's confusion and the little tricks they could play on the young woman to force her to leave.

"This was never her home and never will be."

"Let her learn to be a phantom, as she made us phantoms to our own husband."

The two wives beat and wrung the washing carried in tubs from the well to hang on a rope drawn between the branches of trees in the yard. Their disconcerting chatter, with words as hard as pebbles, disturbed Yaqzan, shattered his fragile train of thought. He left the yard for the house, wandered into the first wife's room, searched in the tamarind chest among his old belongings, found the old pocket watch given him as a boy. In the *majlis* room he sat on a bank of cushions, cupped the watch in his hand, pressed the sides of the bezel. The front piece flipped open to reveal the glass face, the hands stopped decades earlier. He pulled on the grooved lever at the top of the silver disc, turned the hands backwards and forwards. He wound the ball-head, felt the spring tighten until it would not turn. A deep sadness overwhelmed him. Tears ran down his face.

Through a cloud of moisture, he glimpsed a movement, lifted his head to see a girl seated on a cushion near him. Her eyes held down. Her head covered by a red *tarha*. He had not heard her enter. She raised her head and he felt chilled by the look in her eyes.

"Do I know you?"

She glanced at the watch.

"It's started again." He stared at the watch's moving hands. When he looked up, the girl was gone. He went out into the yard where his two wives laid dough in flat pats on a baking stone in the sun. He asked where the young girl went. They exchanged puzzled glances. They had not seen anybody. Who could he mean? They kissed their teeth, glanced at each other. For a moment he thought he must be going mad, shook his head, told himself he was dreaming and all was well—the sky azure, the sun golden, no dust swirls to herald a storm on the horizon. The season no longer ruled by Canopus, these nights good with Sirius rising high in the heavens. He sat on his chair in the shade of the fig tree. Time slipped away as his mind filled to its horizon with recollections. There were the days of youth spent swimming in the lake by the rocky outcrops of the stone plateau, playing by the great doum palm adorned with ribbons. The year of the Wali who led the war on the Tibu grazers, his marriages and births of his children, their marriages too, and deaths. Joy and grief all displayed to him. The world he had experienced and recollected all presence, with him at its centre. As he turned one way and another he observed a life well spent.

He slipped an olive into his mouth, sucked on it, rolled it on his tongue. The brine burned along the gum line. The kitten, a chrysanthemum wreath, curled on his lap. He glanced at the watch. The hands crept around the dial, from second to second, minute to minute. He saw his wives working in the yard. They were distant, farther from him than his memories. His mind, fine and whole, gave over to reverie, as the sun warmed him through a filigree of shadows cast by the leaves of the fig tree.

Occasionally, as he sat in the yard, puzzlement came to the old man's eyes. He struggled to recall or make sense of a notion that lingered at the edge of consciousness, never revealing itself to him—a thought that something was missing, maybe misplaced, but he could not think what. Moments of confusion became more common. Then, like a man who walked in his sleep, or was awake in a dream, forgetfulness stayed with him. He saw objects that he knew had names, but the names escaped him.

Early one morning, under a sky laden with the last vestiges of night, Kasem found Yaqzan in his nightshirt, his bare feet sunk into the black soil of the fields.

"Where am I?"

Kasem took the old man by the hand, led him through village streets, to his compound. "Now you're home."

"I don't know." Tears welled in his eyes. "I can't remember."

Kasem guided him into the house, helped him dress, wrapped a turban on the old man's head.

"I have a crack in my mind. Thoughts fall through and are lost."

Kasem took Yaqzan into the yard to the fig tree where often he sat to suck on bitter green olives and watch the world through the gate to his compound. Yaqzan stared at the leggy whatever before him with upright sticks that curved to a flat palm-frond platform. The old man struggled to name the thing. If he could find the name he would know it and knowing it would know its use. But his mind, too brittle or too broken, could not discover the name to repeat for a meaning lost among the debris of words cluttered and heaped in memory.

"You can sit on the chair."

"Chair," echoed Yaqzan. Yes, now he knew it. He shuffled forward, steadied himself with a hand on the trunk of the tree, and sat.

That evening, Yaqzan watched Kasem cover the loom to keep the yarn dry from morning dew. A bright light flared at the southern horizon. Not the warm glow of sunrise, but a cold white frost. Too early for dawn—Sirius had not set, Venus yet to rise. He waited for a new star to reveal itself, a second sun above the stone plateau. There was no movement at the cut of earth and sky, the horizon frozen with a crust of ice. He felt the ground shiver beneath him. In the village dogs barked, disturbed by the unnatural glow and the earth's faint tremor. People came out of their houses, wondered if a star had fallen or the earth caught fire.

At the prison camp, an officer read out Tarek's name among those selected for case review. He was ordered to pack and report to the military van parked by the gates. In his cell, he asked Kasem to tell Reham he had been transferred.

"How do you know her?" All the hours Kasem spent speaking of Leila and not once had Tarek mentioned her sister. "Why didn't you tell me? Don't you trust me?"

"Just do me the favour."

"With no explanation?"

"I don't have time."

"You're not going to give me a reason?"

"Reason? What reason do you have in mind?" Tarek gathered his clothes, flung them on the bed to pack.

"A reason like is there something going on I don't know about?"

"There's no reason. Absolutely no reason for anything. Everything's degrees of contingency. My meeting you, my meeting her, serendipity." He stopped, stared at Kasem. "This is my chance for appeal and early release. What do you want me to do? Turn it down? Spend the rest of my life in a prison camp? That won't do her or me any good. And when the order comes through for you, you'll go. You won't have a choice."

Kasem glared at him. "At least I don't lie to my friends." He walked out of the cell.

Tarek slammed his fist against the wall, felt the jolt of pain through his arm. Blood welled along the torn skin of knuckles and fingers, darkened under the nail plates. He threw the last of his clothes into a canvas sack, drew the strings to close it tight, carried it out to the waiting truck.

13

The evening the wives conferred, decided their husband had lost what strength of mind remained to him, they told Reham to pack and leave. The next morning Leila brought the mare to the yard. Pregnant with the stallion's foal, it swayed as it climbed the path to the compound. Kasem laid the rugs she had woven across the mare's back, strapped her belongings to its sides.

Neighbours came out to watch. Their eyes questioning—What could cause a pregnant wife to leave her husband? What reason to cast her out? Sides taken in glances and whispers. But Reham knew, regardless of blame, they would assume the shame must be Yaqzan's for failing to manage his women. How could he ever be respected? His judgment poor, his authority questionable—a weak husband only brings ruin on his home and all who trust him.

Once outside the village they stopped to rest in the shade of a silver-leaf acacia. Reham said she was thirsty. Leila went to fetch a goat-skin sack hung from the side of the mare. She smiled at Kasem, grateful for his help. His cheeks flushed and his look softened. Reham thought the young man's eyes bestowed beauty on her sister. Leila, held by his gaze, seemed to lighten before she drew herself away to deliver the water.

* * *

In the darkness of an unfamiliar room, Salma woke on a thinly padded mattress and a sheet that reeked of sweat and stale beer. Her body ached, her mind confused. She heard the distant call of a desert lark, judged herself far from the escarpment. She leant against the door. It would not open, probably bolted from the outside. Through a crack she saw Nufal load empty urns onto a flatbed cart, heard Mama Sara, "I don't want to be blamed for damage to what's his."

"I'll be back to collect when he's ready." Nufal lifted an urn to the cart.

"Can't he find somewhere else for her?"

"He needs time to make arrangements."

Mama Sara insisted on an extra urn of beer by way of compensation for her troubles. Nufal promised to deliver on his return.

"Make it two, or better three to celebrate the happy occasion."

He laughed, led the wagon away. Its wheels creaked along the path.

Salma pounded on the door.

In the coffeehouse, Zainab served the clients shisha and arak. When she heard the girl bang on the door and scream, she recalled she had made a lot less fuss when she had started with Mama Sara. Still, she resented the thought the girl may be here to compete with her for clients.

Corporal Aboud arrived in khaki uniform and visor, wanted a turn with Zainab.

"There's no mattress on the ledge." She felt a fresh surge of resentment. "I'm not doing it without a mattress."

"Well, get the mattress."

"I can't. It's with the new girl." And besides, she said, she had promised Nufal he would be first that evening.

Aboud had taken a great dislike to this bull of a man—though not a person he would pick a fight with sober—for berating Hayat for spending her nights at the border post with him. What business was it of Hashem's foreman who Hayat chose to sleep with? He drank his arak, and drank a couple more. He went to the back of the coffeehouse to urinate against the wall, unbuckled his belt, heard the girl shout to be let out. There was nobody in the yard. He unbolted the door to the storeroom, stepped into the dark, removed the visor, waited for his eyes to adjust, smelt the stench from the old mattress mixed with stale beer from stored urns. Through cracks in the ceiling, fractured light reflected off the girl's moist skin. She tried to push past him. He thrust her back. She fell against the wall. He grabbed her hair, licked the perspiration off her neck and face. She punched, lashed at him with arms and legs, fought with her whole body, clawed with broken nails, beat with clenched fists. With his weight he forced her to the ground. She kicked, spun and twisted, threw her head back, thought she saw a movement, a ripple in the darkness, felt herself subtracted from the figure of a girl on a mattress, watched from a distance in the shadows a child pound with raw fists the humped body of an animal gorging on her.

Aboud rose off the girl, welts along his neck and shoulders, bruises on his back, swayed for a moment from the arak he had drunk. He squatted by the door, defecated, closed his eyes to savour the pleasure of release. He opened them as the girl swung a bottle at his head. He ducked. It shattered on the wall. Tiny shards of glass gashed the side of his face, drew blood he tasted in his mouth. The arak from the bottle stung the cuts, burned his eyes. He stumbled out of the room, threw himself against the door, bolted it. She thrust against it. His body flooded perspiration. He buckled his belt, wiped the blood from his face, made his way back to the coffeehouse.

In the darkness, Salma smashed bottles and clay urns against the wall, scattered splinters of broken glass on the ground, selected the largest, sharpest shards to place by the mattress, tore the thin sheet to strips to tie about her hands to grip the blades. She lay down to muster her strength, waited for the door to open, the next person to enter. Against the far wall a silver shape slipped along the bricks, then stopped, a scorpion likely flushed from the wall by the winds of a rising storm.

Nufal drank Mama Sara's famous arak to celebrate Agha Hashem's impending marriage to Salma of the House of Majid.

Zainab asked Aboud about the blood on his face. He laughed, said it was from the new girl.

Nufal suddenly sobered. "What girl?"

"The one in the storeroom."

Nufal stared at the corporal, unable to read him with the visor covering his eyes. He could not believe the man would be so crazy as to joke like that. Did he have no idea what Agha Hashem was capable of? Unsteady, he hurried to the yard, pulled back the bolt on the storeroom door, left it open for light, grabbed the girl by the arm to examine her for damage. The glass on the floor pierced his sandals, cut his feet. As he glanced down, she lunged for him. He felt a shooting pain in his belly and chest, fell back against the wall. His eyes widened to see himself pierced by clay shards running with blood. The girl grabbed more blades from the mattress, flung herself on him. Pain tore through him. He tried to shout, but blood frothed in his throat. His legs gave way and he slid down the wall.

Her hands and dress stained with his blood, Selma stared at him, thought he must have been a pretty child. She stepped back, then threw herself at the door, ran into the thickening fog of dust and sand whipped up by winds from the desert.

In the shadows of the trees of the sand barrier the *dulla* spirits watched, chattered in excitement at the mischief they could cause. Disguised as cats, they could crouch on drunken men's laps, sip their beer and whisper many a rumour about Nufal's death.

As the sun set, Yaqzan sat under the fig tree in his yard, the kitten asleep on his lap. He waited for it to wake of its own accord, dipped the tip of his finger into a bowl of milk thick with cream for it to lick. The southern light burned along the horizon. Its cause and meaning not apparent. From time to time he felt the earth gently quake. From the dull copper of the moon, this was a night for a storm.

Sabri the baker arrived to call Yaqzan to a meeting at Agha Hashem's compound. It was a matter of great urgency. He bobbed his head as he spoke. Yaqzan demurred, said it was not a night to be out. The baker did not have time to argue, hurried to notify the other elders.

Agha Hashem, his face as grave as stone, spoke before the elders of his foreman murdered by one of Mama Sara's girls, asked for their opinions on what should be done. Sabri's head bobbed left and right—With all due respect, nobody had witnessed the murder to be sure the girl, whoever she was, did anything. After all, a man like Nufal must have had enemies. The girl could have witnessed the murder then fled out of fear of herself being killed or falsely accused. "We need witnesses, most certainly we do."

Mahmoud, who owned the village general store, asked, "If she should escape, who of us would feel safe in his bed from his own women?"

From his yard Hashem watched, through thickening dust clouds, the dull glow of search party lanterns. "The law is not about right or wrong. It is about deterrent for the greater good. The girl must be stoned so men can sleep peacefully at night."

The baker wobbled his head. "It has never been done before in the valley."

"First the girl must be found," Mahmoud said with a troubled look.

The baker shook his head. This was ever so serious. He was not used to taking decisions on matters of life and death.

"A pit must be dug." Mahmoud gazed at the elders.

"A yawning pit invites a death," cautioned the baker. "If dug there must be a stoning. There's no escaping that." Oh, he did so hate dealing with such issues.

Mahmoud stroked his beard. "What if we don't find the girl?" Hashem had already taken the precaution of ordering his men to fetch Hayat. He was tired of her complaints and attempts to malign him. Tonight, regardless of guilt, there must be retribution.

Salma stumbled across fields of black soil that clung to her feet like grasping fists, continued over stones and rocks towards the lake. Behind her she saw the flaxen light of search parties, heard dogs bay, knew they had caught her scent—only time before they reached her. The burning torches gathered in the dark, turned away from the village towards the fields. The moon floated like an open mouth in the lake, beyond it the blackness cast by the shadow of the escarpment. She waded into the water.

Flickering lights approached the dark banks. She sank in deeper, trod the current to keep afloat, heard the voices of men at the lake's edge complain of the dark, speak of fear of the *ghawas*, spirits that lurk in the deep, as they strained their eyes. Dogs barked on the banks. A man picked up a stone, threw it far into the gloom. The rock splashed away from her. She kicked to get to deeper water. Rocks struck the water wide of her. She struggled for the centre of the lake where the air was clear and the moon beckoned. Translucent forms moved about her, gently stroked her, carried her to the deep. She floated, closed her eyes, soothed by the songs of the *ghawas*.

Hearing the beckoning sound of kettledrums, Yaqzan struggled to dress himself, called for Kasem. They walked through deserted village streets. At the horizon, the white light burned steadily through a thick dust shroud. They approached the crowds by the truck stop. Men carried burning torches. The smoke added darkness to darkness. Agha Hashem, raised on a mound of earth with the other elders on either side of him, spoke of God's law. The wind tossed his words with dust. The Agha said the God of Abraham abhorred sin, and no sin was greater than that of a woman killing a man—*We have given you command of her*. He quoted the verse in full. From that first ordinance all others followed. He picked a stone from the pile at his feet, hurled it into the pit.

Hashem's men drove the crowd forward to the pit's edge, urged them to cast stones.

Yaqzan recognized Hayat's voice plead she had done nothing, she had been a wet nurse to many a child in the village, fed them from her own breast milk. As the stones fell, she screamed curses on Hashem and all his progeny back to the ugly ape of an ancestor that copulated with

Eve to give birth to his poisonous line. She shouted she was pregnant with his child—bore him a son. But it was too late for the lie to save her. A rock struck her. She dropped to her knees. More bore down to bury her.

With rocks spent, and silence from the pit, the crowd dispersed. Yaqzan watched men shovel dirt to cover the corpse. They worked slowly, all urgency gone. If only Yaqzan's mind were whole again to make more sense of everything. What happened that God should require Hashem to punish the sinner for Him? What presumption on the Agha's part to appropriate God's will and right to judge. But where was God when His authority was usurped? Where was God, if God there is? He felt a cold emptiness inside him.

He gazed into the pit, discerned a movement in its depths, a tremor in the darkness. He struggled to see more clearly, strained his eyes. A figure coalesced in the shadows, moved in the blackness of the crater. How could anything have survived? He willed it to look up, to show its face. It turned to gaze at him. He knew her, the girl in the *majlis* of his house as he held the watch. Now he was certain she was the same child he saw drowned in the lake those months earlier. There she was before him. Then, just as she had appeared, she dissolved into darkness and was gone. He swayed at the edge of the pit. Kasem gripped him before he fell. The Agha's men heaped the last of the earth into the pit, beat it flat with shovels.

By the reeds at the edge of a strand of marshland, Umaya lit a fire with rushes to warm Salma's blood, watched her skin catch the amber glow of flames to regain colour, wondered how much Agha Hashem would pay her if she brought him the girl. Whatever he paid he would still be in her debt. But whatever the Agha offered would not be enough for her to forget Hayat, nor to forgive him for her death. "Child, you cannot stay in the village."

Salma said she had nowhere else to go.

"Don't cry. This isn't the time for it." Umaya said she felt weary of life in the valley. She had stayed long past her time, knowing once she left, all spells would be broken. In her heart she grieved for Hayat. "You're a better person, but I did love her."

In a dusty clearing at the edge of the village, Salma, covered in a wrap given her by Umaya, waited by a truck painted green and red in floral patterns that coiled round the sides to reach full bloom in bouquets on the hood and about the windscreen.

Umaya called to a child playing by the side of the *khana*. "Do you know who I am?"

"Yes, Umaya."

"You're to take a message to the daughters of the House of Majid. Tell them their sister is safe, but has left, never to return."

The boy nodded.

"Your eyes are mine. Don't make me curse you blind for failing."

The boy promised on both his eyes he would do exactly as she said. Even a child so young had heard of the terrible spells Umaya had learnt from the *afrit* lord who was once her lover.

The driver, hungover from a night of drinking, arrived from the *khana*, agreed to take the two women as far as the river road. They climbed onto the bed of the truck. He locked the sides and back quarter panels, drew a tarpaulin over the skeletal frame to shade them from the sun once it had risen.

The truck moved off in the half-light, picked up speed. Salma watched the valley recede, disappear below the rise of the stone plateau. She leant against the cabin wall and slept.

* * *

In season, it was not unusual for Salma to stay late at the apiary to churn and store honey. That evening, with the air thick with dust, Reham and Leila waited in the stable for the mare to give birth. Her belly swollen, she lay on her side on dry straw. Her hind legs twitched. She staggered onto her hooves. She had been up and down several times, swayed and paced, lay down on her side before standing, then lay down again.

Reham glanced at Leila seated on the mud-packed floor, by her side a lantern. "We should get back to the house, shutter the windows until the dust storm passes."

The mare shuddered. A moist, translucent balloon billowed from her rump. The foal's front hooves and fetlocks showed. Leila gripped them, tugged, felt a moment's resistance, leant back with all her weight. Suddenly, seemingly from nowhere, a foal lay bedraggled on the straw, about it the torn transparent sac. The mare stood, turned, licked the foal along its neck, nudged it with its muzzle, licked and nudged.

14

For days, since the stoning, Yaqzan had not slept. His mind churned and troubled him with thoughts he could not put into words. Early morning in the yard of his compound, the oldest wife served him black tea in a tall tumbler. He watched the leaves on the fig tree shiver, felt a slight tremor beneath his feet as though the earth were sighing.

In the *majlis* room the two wives drank their tea and talked of their daughters, reminisced about their grandchildren. They were interrupted by the tinkling of spoons. The house filled with the high-pitched hum of rims and edges of all things glass. The two women glanced at each other. The humming and tinkling increased in pitch until, in quick succession, windows, tumblers and mirrors exploded, ripped through clothes and skin with shards like shrapnel that shattered against furnishings and walls. The screams of the two women brought the neighbours to their door. Blood ran from cuts to the wives' faces, arms and legs. Barefooted, they froze, afraid to take a step with the floors and rugs covered with a fine scatter of glass that sparkled like spittle in the sunlight. Room after room bore signs of devastation—windows broken, mirrors shattered. The neighbours lit censers of myrrh, purged with smoke the washroom and kitchen, damp places where *afrit* may hide, to drive away any that may have caused the calamity.

* * *

The glazier arrived with two mules bearing wooden frames with panes of glass tied with rope. He worked window by window, removed the remaining shards, scraped the wood with a flat blade, fitted panes with fresh putty kneaded and rolled into long soft cords.

In the yard, the two wives sat in hazy sunlight, picked at the fine spray of sharp granules in their skin. The kitten climbed onto the old man's lap in the shade of the old fig tree. Yaqzan stroked its fur warm from the morning sun. "Where is she?" he asked. "Was she hurt?"

The two wives exchanged glances. "Who do you mean?"

The young wife, of course.

"What do we know? She returned to her sisters."

He stared blankly at them. How can a wife, pregnant with her husband's child, leave home without his consent? Why would she do so, when her home is here with him?

"Instead of thanking us for protecting your honour all these years, you question us like sinners."

"You're a fool refusing to admit what everybody knows."

"At your age wanting another wife and child." They clucked and shook their heads.

"You've daughters with children of their own and granddaughters to be wed."

"Your duty's to your name."

"Prized, passed on, generation upon generation."

"A man your age should be thinking of his grave, not his bed."

"What have you done?" His voice barely above a whisper. What must the neighbours be saying? What must the village be thinking? Such shame on a husband that his wife should leave him, and she pregnant. They must think the child not his and he a cuckold. They will question the paternity of his other children. Never has he been so weak and powerless, never felt his age such a burden. His wives' words, hammer blows. His frail mind a ruin—a house fallen in upon itself. Its contents spilt in the dirt.

Then, he saw her by his side, the child from the lake, the girl in the pit. "Help me. I'm losing my mind."

"I know," she said.

"Who are you?"

"Fadia."

He struggled to recall who he knew by that name, to reclaim a memory long buried. "My sister Fadia?"

"They took me to the lake for cleansing. The bleeding wouldn't stop."

"Yes, I remember." How could he have forgotten?

He no longer heard his wives as they berated him. Their voices washed past him. He followed Fadia out of the compound, paid no heed to the people who greeted him in the street, who stopped to exchange pleasantries. He followed the shadow of the girl as it flashed and flitted on walls and paths in front of him, led him on out of the village to the treeline of the sand barrier. Then on past the tamarind and cacti to where the world was desert to the far perimeters of the earth. She beckoned him farther. He crossed the edge of desolation, kept walking until he was far from the valley. Between towering dunes, in the great void of the sand sheets, he stopped, faced the sun, stared at its burning centre—coiling fire churned air and sky, flames licked about the rim, spiralled one way then another, turned in, then spun out of the bright liquid mercurial core. This was all that was real, the desert, the sun, burning light—the rest lies, false hopes and deception. He stared at the glowing eye as it burned the earth about him, turned all to dust. Its fires shot through him, scorched retina, optical tissue, withered nerves, reached deep inside him. Then, as a pyre whose heart has turned to ash, he crumpled, fell into himself, to smoulder like spent cinders.

* * *

Kasem woke at the cellblock, washed at the well by the border post, left for Yaqzan's compound. The two wives told him they had not seen the old man all morning. "Try the coffeehouse." They combed tiny shards from each other's hair as the glazier fit silvered glass to mirror frames.

In the yard of the coffeehouse, Mama Sara pressed a red cockerel to a flat stone, cut off its head with a long knife, held the cockerel by its neck to drain blood on the ground by the storeroom where Nufal died, repeated incantations she learnt as a child to ward off ill fortune that comes with a violent death. She hoped Nufal's spirit, appeased by the effort and expense, would not haunt the place to frighten away her customers. No, she had not seen the venerable rainmaker for at least a day or more. Kasem went through the village to the fields, to where sheep and goats were kept in pens, and still no sign of the old man. Late afternoon by the sand barrier, he gazed out to the desert. Surely the rainmaker would not venture past the cacti and tamarind trees. Beyond this line was death. He walked to the rise of a dune. In a scooped-out hollow he saw a bundle, a hunched shape like a wounded animal. He slid down the slope. His feet sank into hot sand. The wretched figure appeared barely alive. The face and body burnt, hands and feet swollen, misshapen, raw flesh blistered.

Kasem helped the wretch stand, recognized him, took the old man's weight against his body. They struggled to the top of the dune, every part of them aflame from the sun. They went through the sand barrier of trees close to the Wali's old mosque. The old man murmured he could go no farther. In the shade of the building brought to ruin by winds and neglect, Kasem cleared the ground of rocks, helped Yaqzan sit. He wet a rag from the well, patted the burns on the old man's face, dripped water onto his cracked lips. It was only then he realized the old man was blind.

At the compound, Kasem took food from the kitchen, a goatskin of water and a sheet from several in the first wife's room. The wives so used to him about the yard, and too busy with their own afflictions, barely noticed him come and go. They inveighed against Umaya for abandoning the valley when she was most needed.

At the ruins of the Wali's mosque Yaqzan ate, as Kasem tore strips from the sheet to bandage his swollen hands and feet. With the evening, in a rasping voice the old man asked, what of the southern lights? Yes, as the sun set the lights came on as bright as from an open brazier. The old man asked for a walking staff. Kasem searched among the tamarind trees of the sand barrier, found a broken branch to strip.

As Yaqzan felt the cool night breeze, he stood, leant on the staff, stumbled a few steps forward, raised his head to the darkness. There was a time when he knew the stars, could read them as clear as words— red Canopus rose at dawn in months of sudden storms, Sirius ascended when palm trees bud and again at harvest time, Antares heralded hot winds, Aldebaran the sowing of winter grain. Now they were no clearer than ink blots. "You'll take me to the lights."

"It's too far to go."

"No, not far." The lights were from the Firaq gorge, a barren chasm in the stone plateau. Its wells run dry, not good for much, not even grazing, home to the silver ants. In the heat of the day their bodies shimmered like droplets of water, attracted thirsty prey. They swarmed and stripped flesh from bone.

"Why go?"

"It may be the light of the Wali shining forth."

But surely any new Wali would arrive at the valley and not the Firaq gorge. The old man should wait until, in better health and greater strength, he can commit to such a journey.

"Scripture says of the People of the Cave, *You would think them awake, when they were asleep. When we awakened them, they asked each other, How long have we been here?* I've lived my life like the sleepers in the cave, watched for shadows, not knowing if I'm awake or asleep. I need to know the truth. Only at the Firaq gorge will I find it."

Kasem argued he did not know the way.

Yaqzan swore by what life remained him he would go alone if he must, resolved nothing would stop him. "With you as my eyes we can make it safely."

With great reluctance Kasem led the old man through the barrier of trees and cacti across the sands. Long shadows darkened the hollows between lines of dunes. They kept a steady pace, stopped briefly to drink from the goatskin sack. Kasem described the stars, their positions, watched for where the southern lights shone brightest. The old man listened, occasionally changed direction, orientated himself by Kasem's descriptions. Now they had started there was no stopping to rest and nowhere to shelter. Late at night, they turned a ridge, saw the lights as clear as flames. They continued past several small *wadis*, followed the line of the plateau, then climbed the escarpment to get above the gorge. As they reached the stone plains they felt the ground tremor, heard pounding muffled by the sides of the defile loud above the plateau.

From the edge of the rock face, Kasem described what he saw in the gorge—great wheels turned, hammers nodded on tall frames, high pillars blazed with lights. Great machines ate the sides of the cliff, scooped rubble with steel jaws to drop into giant wagons with wheels the size of houses.

The old man prodded the ground with his staff, moved to the edge of the cliff, swayed as though to cast himself from the rocks. Kasem held him back. Yaqzan struggled, swung his staff like a cudgel, uttered grunts and cries before collapsing on the ground, all strength drained. He remained still as thoughts corroded what faith he had left. There were men who died before their time, and there were those who lived long after they should have gone. He said the machines that lit the gorge and fed off the cliff face were disfiguring the earth beyond recovery and renewal. Such destruction can only mean the breaking of the wheel of time, the cycle that with each turn marked a new age for which God sent a shepherd for his people. Bereft of divine guidance, how will men know their way? How will they find meaning in life? Living sequentially from moment to moment, as time extended onward in a line to an undetermined future, how would they live without the guiding light of a wali? Without hope of return there could only be despair. Yaqzan rose, leant on his staff. "We must get back before the sun rises."

Corporal Aboud sat outside the border post, drank arak, watched a dying fire of brushwood. The arak thickened his head. In the flames, he saw shapes form and break in leaps and flashes. The wood crackled, spat sparks like fireflies. He lit a *bango* reefer. A cool breeze came off the stone plateau. Flames seethed beneath a surface of cinders. He threw a branch onto the fire, waited for the wood to ignite before adding another. It kindled in the flames, then rippled alive with ants. Their bodies exploded in tiny flares. He stared at them, distracted by their deaths from thoughts that gnawed at him. For days, he felt with increased certainty Agha Hashem had killed Hayat as an affront to him. He thought of his pride as a corporal of the border guard and how he could not leave the offence unpunished. Why should he fear Hashem now that Nufal was done away, and by a girl?

In the cold light of the southern horizon, his mind raddled by arak and *bango*, Aboud took a shovel, clambered down the escarpment slope to sandy ground, to the mound of stones that marked where the Tibu killed by the Wali an age ago were buried. Their heads severed as feed for wasps and ravens. He shovelled to reach the remains of corpses wrapped in rotting winding cloth, carried the bundles of bones back to the fire, cast bone after bone into the flames, called upon the *afrit* lords to hear him, to release the spirits of the Tibu dead, inveighed against Agha Hashem. As the stench of the burning bones filled the air, the smoke thickened, rose, dropped in clouds that rolled on the sand, coalesced into the shapes of hyenas with short, stocky bodies and large jaws. The flames died. The smoke thinned. The hyenas rose from the sand, approached Aboud, their heads held to one side. At the border post, Aboud loaded his service-issue bolt-action rifle, took a box of cartridges, led the hyenas to the village.

At Hashem's compound the lead hyena crushed the skull of the watchman at the gate. The hyenas entered the house, searched out Hashem's wives, each in her room. They crushed skulls, broke bones with their great jaws, savaged all who tried to escape. The scent of blood burned in their nostrils. Children and wives woke to the sight of death, screamed in terror. Daughters and sons, servants and maids cried and ran from the house for the compound gates. In the yard, Aboud watched, lit a *bango* reefer. Those the hyenas did not fell, he shot—men, women, children. Hashem came out in his nightshirt, pleaded with Aboud. "Take what you want, my house, my land, spare my life."

Aboud shot a child as he ran crying across the yard.

"Not the children," Hashem sobbed. "They are my shadow. They bear my name."

Aboud raised the rifle, shot Hashem in the face. What does he care for Hashem's shadow and the longevity of his name? He watched the hyenas feed on the flesh of the dying, inhaled deeply on the *bango*, saw with bloodshot eyes the Angel of Death, large and fleet, swoop through the rooms of the house and across the yard, a lightning scythe harvesting souls, scattering shadows. Hashem's family, his wives, children, the husbands and wives of his children, the grandchildren down to the youngest, barely two years old, breastfed by Hayat, slaughtered. No man or woman related, by blood or service, to the Hashem household survived the slaughter—not a single person spared to one day honour or avenge the Hashem name.

As the hyenas gnawed on the bones of the dead, Aboud searched the stable, took the stallion into the yard, a trophy and reminder to all in the valley that he was the scourge of the House of Hashem. The main building in the compound, ignited by a fallen lantern, spat flames. The straw on the roof of the stable flared. The hyenas ran from the blaze. Flames reflected red in their eyes. The stallion smelt the stench of hyenas and fire, tugged, pulled free of Aboud's grip, bolted. If he cannot have the stallion then better it be dead. He raised his rifle, but too late. The stallion leapt the yard wall and was gone.

A while after Aboud departed with the hyenas, the people of the village emerged from their houses with lanterns to gather the remains of the dead. Fires had scorched the earth in tattoo patterns, reduced the compound to plumes of smoke.

15

Kasem and Yaqzan reached the valley as dawn broke. They stopped for water at the apiary well on the escarpment. Kasem helped Yaqzan to the beekeeper's hut, settled him on cushions. Yaqzan whispered to Kasem to go to his compound, fetch him *The Book of Knowledge*, wrapped in cloth, tied with rope, kept in the tamarind chest in the first wife's room.

The wives protested. "Why doesn't he collect it himself?"

"What do you want with a book anyway?"

"It's not worth anything, is it?"

When Kasem returned to the hut, Yaqzan was asleep. He placed the book on the table where honey once churned was stored in jars for sale.

At the well Kasem did as he had seen Salma do most mornings. He soaked mats to place on the hives to cool them in the day's heat. In the distance wisps of sand spun along the horizon. Was this a sign of a storm or just a passing dust devil? If a storm it could be here by the evening. Then again, the storm may bypass the valley. Yaqzan would know, but Kasem did not have the heart to wake him.

In the hut, he ate, lay down on the floor to rest, slept for several hours, woke mid-afternoon. Yaqzan had woken, eaten some of the food Kasem had left for him, then gone back to sleep. Kasem went out to the sun shelter of palm-frond mats tied to a criss-crossed frame of bamboo stalks. He brewed tea in a kettle on twigs of scrubs and thorns, saw Sabri the baker on his mule at the foot of the escarpment, waved to him to draw his attention away from the hut.

"If you're on your way to buy honey, the sisters aren't here to sell."

"I wish that was my reason. We're holding a wake for the House of Hashem." He whispered of the terrible calamity that befell them, a fire burned down their home as they slept. "Some say a pack of hyenas, no less, attacked the compound." He bent his head towards Kasem. "Gunshots were heard. A terrible carnage." Furtively, he glanced around as though expecting to see the beasts lurking in rocks about the stone plateau. He tugged at the bridle, kicked the sides of the mule to take him back to the village.

In the hut Yaqzan was awake. Kasem told him what he had heard. He will attend the arrangements at the village mosque to find out more, return once the funeral is over.

At the mosque, the marabout led recitations from scripture. Prayers held for the souls of the deceased were followed by more recitations. At sunset the funeral party took the slow climb along the side of the stone plateau to the burial ground where the remains of the dead wrapped in shrouds were laid to rest.

It was dark when Kasem returned along the path from the village. The night breeze smelt of burnt dust—a sign of an impending sandstorm. He climbed the escarpment back to the apiary. Along the path, he saw Leila. Her face flushed and sombre, her eyes tearful. She ran to him. "I've been searching forever for you. I was at the hives but you weren't there. I went to Yaqzan's compound but couldn't find you. And then I went back to the apiary. There was somebody asleep in the hut, but it wasn't you. I didn't know where to look."

"I was at the mosque."

"Hurry, please hurry." She ran ahead of him to her compound by the lake at the foot of the escarpment. The house stood silent and dark but for a light in a window. They could hear the mare in the stable. It stomped its hooves on the mud-packed floor, snorted. Leila ran to Reham's room. In bed, Reham appeared pallid in the oily glow of a lantern. By her side, a baby slept in a cot on a lamb's fleece, covered by a thin blanket. Leila stopped by the child, gently lifted it in her arms. Kasem went closer to the bed, uncertain whether to wake Reham, to tell her they were here, then decided he should not. Her face waxen, exhausted from giving birth. She slept so peacefully, like a fairy-tale princess waiting for a kiss to be woken.

"It's a girl." Leila rocked the baby. "I was sure it would be."

With the tips of his fingers, Kasem touched Reham's hand—not to wake but to reassure her. Her skin chilled him. He touched her cold forehead. She did not stir. He pulled back the covers. The sheets were stained in blood.

Leila stared, trembled, looked as though she would faint. Kasem held her, took the baby, placed the child in the cot, slipped a blanket over her.

Leila sobbed. "There was just the two of us. She started bleeding as the baby birthed. I didn't know what to do. She said to fetch you. She said the bleeding would stop. I wouldn't have left if she hadn't told me to. I spent ages looking for you."

Was she blaming him? But maybe he *was* to blame, leaving with Yaqzan for the gorge when she needed him. "There was nothing you could do. What else could you have done?"

"I shouldn't have listened. I should have stayed."

"You did all you could."

"I love her so much. And now it's too late."

The baby cried. Leila went to the cot, wiped the tears from her eyes, picked her up, rocked her, placed the tip of her finger in the child's mouth. The baby sucked herself to sleep. Leila cradled her.

Kasem, once so close to the sisters by their need for him, felt helplessly cut off from Leila by grief, from Reham by death. He heard a rising wind, went to close the windows. When he returned, he found Leila pacing as she rocked the baby. "We agreed if it's a girl we'd call her Neda." She stopped, looked at Kasem. "A child shouldn't stay in a place of death." She wiped her damp cheeks with her hand.

"There's a storm on its way."

"We'll go back to the apiary. The escarpment will give us shelter. Salma always made us go there when storms were bad. In the morning, we'll take care of everything here."

Leila tied a sheet across her chest to carry the baby. They took as much food as they could wrap in a blanket. Kasem collected a skin of fresh goat's milk. They walked in silence against the blowing sands. Thoughts tumbled in and out of Kasem's mind. None of them lasted long enough to register, his mind beset by thoughts of Leila who, barely past being a child, had a child to care for.

The wind intensified. Dry, dust-laden, it scoured their faces and arms, stung their eyes.

At the beekeeper's hut, Yaqzan sat against a wall eating from the plate Kasem had left him. Leila was shocked to recognize the old man. "What happened?"

Kasem did not know where to begin, shrugged, turned away to find somewhere to store what they had brought. They will have time to talk later. Leila placed the baby in a crib of cushions on the floor. She lay beside Neda, closed her eyes, overcome by grief and exhaustion. Kasem lit a candle. Peaceful all through the journey to the hut, Neda now dreamt of milk, woke, cried, woke Leila whose heart pounded like a punching fist.

He fetched the skin with the milk. Leila pinched its mouth to form a teat, fed Neda in drops until she fell asleep. Leila lay back on the cushions by the baby, turned her head to watch Kasem. At the table he untied rope from a bundle, unwound cloth to unveil an old codex. He read the title lettering out loud: *The Book of Knowledge*. He opened it on the table, read quietly by the light of the candle. Yaqzan moved closer to better hear him. Leila closed her eyes to sleep.

Kasem read of the House of Majid, of the Bani Jaber who with the help of the *jinn* discovered the valley, of the ancient and noble Tibu grazers who came from distant oases, lived in peace with local farmers until the war of their expulsion by the Wali. He read of a boy who came from the mountains with his sister—how he served God's shadow, and how time was set loose in the valley. The boy, chosen to be rainmaker, grew to old age and decided to have a child to fulfill his covenant with the Wali.

He stopped reading. The winds from the desert carried sands that crashed like breakers, thundered against the high escarpment walls of the stone plateau. He shuttered the window to keep out the clouds of dust, afraid the sound of the storm would wake Leila and the baby. When he returned, he saw Yaqzan had fallen asleep against a wall. He opened the book several chapters from the end, read silently of Salma saved by the *ghawas* in the lake; of Hashem and his family murdered, and the pale stallion's escape to pound its hooves through Aboud's dreams, to wake him night after night so he could never sleep peacefully; of Nufal's wraith that lingered unseen in coffeehouses and *majlis* rooms to report to Aboud each morning what was said about him; and how at night discomposed by arak and *bango*, the corporal met in visions the *afrit* lords of the desert—the Barbary lord, whose spirit was ape, with flayed servants whose veins and nerves pulsated and quivered on bare, bloodied muscles; Majesty, a dour, wizen lord whose spirit was jackal, who strolled through groves of cacti with men's heads protruding from the sand to flare like wicks when lit; the lord with a viper's spirit who lived in the hulks of oil cans; and the lord whose spirit was crocodile with a mind as dark as the swamps that spawned him; supreme the great lord whose spirit was hippopotamus; a monster of arms, mouth, belly and anus, no eyes or ears, on a mound of his own excrement. But then against the black sky, beyond fields of cacti and severed heads, the pale stallion stomped its hooves to echo across the valley. Its thud-thud shook the stone floor of the great stone plateau and reverberated in Aboud's skull. Still numbed by the arak he drank that night he staggered out of the border post, screamed curses at the creature invisible in the dark. Hearing his shouts of rage the hyenas came to him, collected about him, rubbed against him. He dropped to his knees. They licked and nudged him to the ground. Their spittle dripped on his skin. They tore his clothes, copulated with him, to one day turn him into a hyena.

Kasem folded back the pages to read of how this night he will leave Leila and Neda with Yaqzan to return to the cellblock. The storm will abate and dust clouds settle. Early in the morning he will be put on a truck with the last of the prisoners for relocation to a city penitentiary. Several nights from now, Aboud will promise Zainab Reham's baby if she spends the night with him. The hyenas will go in search of Neda. At the apiary they will kill Leila, take the child.

Kasem stopped reading. He felt an urge to close the book.

He had imagined himself free, thought he always acted out of conscious choice, but if all is written as he reads it, then his life was ordained at the most mundane of levels. But it is probably true, on all consequential matters, he has only ever reacted to whatever came his way. He had lived his life largely as a reflex to the actions of others. And no doubt they too did the same. A chain reaction of stimulus and response, where nobody acted in freedom, though each thought they did. He had lived his days in quotation marks. Everything he had believed and spoken a citation from others. The language he used never fully his, loaned to him at birth. His thoughts shaped by words not his own. His ideas borrowed. His sense of self authored by others.

But he believed what he had read. If he leaves, he will never see Leila again.

He went over to the baby. She seemed so peaceful in sleep. No, he will not leave them. He will not despite, or more correctly because of, what he read. If to be with them meant to risk death, then so be it.

The winds battered the hut, beat against the walls and roof of palm wood. Leila woke from the sound. "We'll be fine here," she said sleepily. "You should report back before they think you are absent without leave."

"I can't go."

"Not if you stay much longer and the storm gets worse."

He wanted to show her what was in the book.

"I never learnt to read."

One day he will teach her.

She thought him joking, smiled.

"I'm staying with you and Neda."

She gazed at him, puzzled by the despair in his voice.

"If I return to the prison tonight they'll make me leave the valley."

"You don't know that."

He told her of what he had read and how the hyenas will soon come for her and Neda.

She stared at him, uncertain whether to believe. Then she said, "I know a safer place."

They packed hurriedly.

Kasem woke Yaqzan. "We have to go."

Leila pulled the *tarha* across her face, held Neda against her breast, covered her with a sheet, stepped out into the flying sand. Kasem led Yaqzan by the end of his staff, carried the bundle they had brought from the house wrapped in a blanket, and the book under his arm.

"Why're you bringing that with you?" Leila shouted over the winds.

He could not leave the book behind. It was his eye into the future and the past.

In the distance a door banged in the wind. Leila thought it the stable gate, worried about the mare and the foal, wanted to return to close it.

"We must hurry." Kasem felt, with a certainty he could not explain, events were moving faster now he had decided to challenge what had been written. He feared the hyenas might already be tracking them.

They struggled along the path up the escarpment, turned off to climb past tall rocky outcrops, continued farther up the side of the stone plateau. Leila heard the beating of the wind on the walls of the beekeeper's hut, thought the mud-brick building could not survive this kind of punishment for long. She worried about the hives, if any were still standing in the shelter of palm-frond mats and flame trees. Salma would never have left them. But then she is not Salma and she has the child to think of. She searched in the dark and the swirling dust for the entrance to the cave of images hidden by outcrops of rock she sheltered in with her sisters. She could not see through the clouds of sand, let herself be guided by memory.

Inside the cave, Leila laid Neda down. The cavern walls provided them shelter from the winds and the flying sand. Inside, the air was still, the sound of the storm muted. Yaqzan settled in the far corner, leant against the rocks to rest. Kasem lit an oil lamp, set it on a ledge. The crimson figures on the wall swayed and floated in the flicker. He gazed at the unfamiliar sight, tried to imagine what the valley would have been like with wild cattle, ibex and gazelle. The light reflected off the rock face, as though the hunters and dancers had their own fire with which to watch him, an intruder to their world. The baby cried itself awake. Leila fed her goat's milk, rocked her until she returned to sleep.

Kasem opened the book, flicked through the pages to the start of chapters to select which to read first. He read accounts of a life he would no longer lead having chosen to be with Leila. The pages crumbled, flowed from the covers in mounds that scattered in drafts that whispered their way through the cave from the winds outside.

The storm thundered against the escarpment. Kasem read as fast as he could through decomposing pages, feared that if he slowed more of them would be lost, skipped back and forth from one chapter to another, sometimes turned a single page, at other times leapt across whole sections. All the while the storm intensified, beyond anything described in the book. Like an hourglass upturned, a torrent of sand poured into the valley.

He kept reading, a gratuitous act, to what purpose? What good could come from reading a story that was almost over? He looked to find the new beginning, certain it must be there in the pages powdering to dust.

Leila sat back against a rock, shielded from the cave mouth, saw the shell Reham once left for Tarek by the well. Its lip a resplendent pink and pearl in the lamplight. She recalled her sister said a secret spoken to the shell was kept for the person who needed to know, and decided as she waited for the storm to settle that she would tell the shell her story, the story of three sisters. Then, maybe, one day, when Neda was old enough to understand, the shell would reveal its secrets to her.

The wind burst through the tree barrier at the mouth of the valley, roared and ripped through mud-brick buildings, wrenched walls from their foundations and buried them with sand and rock, lifted roofs, hurled stone upon stone, wrenched brick from brick, tore fences and shelters, furrowed the village and the truck stop. Winds scoured fields, churned soil with sand, rent earth, drained the waters of the lake, grasped at tamarind and cacti that clung to the ground with roots like talons. The storm beat against the side of the great stone plateau, hammer to anvil, shattered rock as a plough scatters pebbles. Great tidal waves of sand rose over the barriers of trees, dropped into the valley, buried what remained of houses and orchards, as in ages past winds had buried the ancient city of Iram of the many lofty pillars and the people of Thamud with gardens laden with fruit and cities carved into the sides of mountains.

Sabri the baker, spurred on his mule, felled by a blast of wind, lay buried under a wave of sand. Mahmoud the general store owner, struck by flying rocks, lay unconscious as the first wave of the storm blew over. He recovered his senses, saw himself covered in a silvery mass of ants. Pierced by a thousand pinpricks, he screamed and struggled, could not shake them off. He ran, stumbled. With each rise and fall more of the ants swarmed over him, held fast with caliper jaws.

Screeds of sand surged, rose above the valley. Stones and rocks exploded against the sides of the cellblock on the great stone plateau, fractured walls, brought down the roof. An eruption of sand strewed stone and brick, buried rubble. Sand sheets broke against the border post like surf, swelled to engulf the building. Hyenas fled as they inhaled the scent of death. With the dark visor over his eyes, Aboud waited for the amber sky to drop like a flood, to break through the walls of brick and stone, for the page to turn with the fall of the sand, as the book of sky and earth hinged at the horizon closed shut.

PART 4

16

Morning starts clear with a cool breeze from the sea as Tarek leaves Neda asleep in the hut by the ship breakers' yard. In the deep, the expanse of turquoise darkens to blue. At a loading stop with cut-steel sheets a driver waits by his truck, says to Tarek, "Salt Valley? Just follow the track and stone markers. Don't lose sight of the mountains."

The van climbs from the desert floor to the high plateau, follows a single train line until it veers west towards distant peaks patched silver in the early light. Here and there clumps of sparse shrubs and tall desert grass as sharp as shards of glass. By mid-morning hot winds cut across the tabletop devoid of vegetation. The van bounces along stony ground past occasional piles of rocks used by truckers as guiding signs, keeps to the track to avoid sand drifts and pits in the stone plains.

By noon a low mist shimmers pale towards the horizon. Hills wave like reflections in rippling water. The gauge on the dashboard flickers red. With the day at its hottest, Tarek would take to shade if he could find any. Maybe all will be well if he drives slowly until evening and then stops for the engine to cool. Tonight, if the moon is full, he can try to complete the crossing of the stone plateau before sunrise. He cannot recall the phase of the moon the night before to know how much light to expect. What a city boy, not to have noticed and remembered.

In the distance, a dust cloud rises from a solitary truck plying its way from where to who knows where. There must be a village or two scattered about the barren highland, but so far he has not seen any trace of life. He recalls a line of poetry he learnt at school—something about a desert site revived by water like a page awakened by a pen. But this is such barren land. Where would there be water? What to write about on these blank pages of the plateau? This is the void, if anywhere deserves the name.

Late afternoon, the air heavy with the day's heat, the track runs straight to the horizon. No shade or shelter. Nothing stirs. Distant outcrops rise from the west. A smell of burnt rubber from the van's air vents fills the driver's cabin. Tarek stops to check the engine, sees a grey stain around the oil cap, removes the dipstick. Fluid drips and sizzles on the hot engine. He uses a sheet of newspaper from the back of the van to shield his hand as he turns the radiator cap. The radiator billows steam. He knows, without checking further, heat has blown the head gasket. A tide of perspiration breaks out across his back, soaks his shirt. The dry, still air weighs heavy. There can be no chance for rescue here. No choice but to wait. Maybe, with the night, he can drive for a while longer, until he finds help, though he risks flooding the engine with radiator coolant, or blowing the cylinder head and then he is done for. To spend a day under this sun is death.

He squats in the shadow of the van, turns on his phone—no bars, no connection. Not a crackle or buzz of a sound. High overhead in the stillness flights of silver and grey spin and soar. What species of bird? How can they bear to fly so close to the sun? The sky too bright to gaze at, he turns away, checks his watch. The hands motionless, it makes no sound. He shakes his wrist. Of all things, as time runs out the watch stops working—what are the chances? How to estimate such likelihood? What equation could account for this? He feels himself at the limits of reason, removes the watch, shakes it, keeps shaking. Frustration surges, he flings the watch into the back of the van. It clatters on the side, drops to the floor. He throws his head back against the van door, feels the heat sear through his shirt, smells his hair singe, thinks it the scent of death. With the newspaper he wipes his hands coated in sweat and oil from the engine. The page blots in olive stains, turns transparent from the oil. Print smears. In his pocket he finds the braided *dezi* that Leila gave him at Sidi Adi. He had worn it briefly to please her but removed it, thinking it might make Neda jealous of the unborn child. He turns the *dezi* about his wrist, knots it. He will wear it until he returns home, or until death takes him. The admission of mortality causes his chest to constrict and his pulse to run. Not even under torture did he experience fear as visceral, of death as certain. He pants to control his breathing. The ground undulates grey vapours, swells in waves. Distant hills and outcrops sway in scorching light. The world turns liquid as heat dulls his mind. He tries to stay awake, alert to any hope of rescue.

With the sun setting he wakes to a cool breeze, and to whistles and chitter. All around him flocks of tiny birds fill crevices in the rocky ground, beat the sand with wings, hop and spin, peck and scratch before they settle. Barely conscious, he watches them. His body feels as dry as the stone in which they nest for the night.

He drinks a bottle of water, empties a second into the radiator to help make up for lost coolant, leaves himself two bottles to drink later. The margin for survival has just narrowed to a few hours of water. He short-circuits the thermostat so the radiator fan works continuously. Though a drain on the battery, it will keep the van going awhile longer. If it burns out there will be no saving the engine. At this stage anything he does is a gamble. He engages the ignition. The exhaust chugs white smoke. The van crawls forward. He will go as far as he can before the end of night. He drives slowly for about an hour, stops when the gauge on the dashboard shows red, opens the hood to let the breeze cool the engine. If the day's heat does not kill him, the night's chill might. He drives for another hour, then waits in the dark before restarting the engine. The van moves forward, gradually picks up speed, before stalling. He turns the ignition key. The engine screeches. The starter does not engage. Now what? No point in flooding the cylinders. Nothing to be done but wait. Once more feelings of hopelessness return. A little later he can try again. Drive as far as he can in the dark. But, at this rate, not far enough to reach the end of the stone plateau and find shelter. With the morning, he will feel the lash of the sun. The van will stall from the heat. By then he will be out of water. He leans back in his seat, pulls a blanket about his shoulders. Every passing hour lengthens the odds of death. Hope drains from him. He closes his eyes in a torpor induced by resignation—*Maalesh*. That word again, but what else is there to say? But, no, not *maalesh*. He will not sleep his way to death, though that may be easier than struggling to experience life to the last—if death can be experienced, if it has an existence, as such, to be experienced.

Somnolent eyes strain in the grey light of the moon and the low-flying clouds of dust stirred by night winds. To one side of the van, a huddled figure moves, swells, then sinks to the ground. What could it be? What kind of life survives in a place like this? Beyond despair or fear of fresh dangers, he gets out of the van, goes to the bundle. The dust burns and blurs his vision—from its shape, vague in the darkness, it may be a jackal or some breed of dog struck by the day's sun, now dying. It does not resist his touch or try to escape. It must think, at this stage, death a mercy. He lifts it, carries it into the rear of the van, uncaps a bottle of water, pours some into his cupped hand for it to drink, runs a wet palm over its head to soothe its dry, burnt body. The dog's bloodshot eyes brighten with his touch. Tarek does not think it has long to live. He looks to see if anything else moves in the darkness. Surely a dog would not be here on its own? But all is stillness. At least he has company. Death, when it comes, will not find him alone.

Tarek fights off sleep, leans against the side of the van, a blanket pulled about him. He rises from the ground as a figure takes shape in the darkness and comes towards him.

A boy, with a walking staff across his shoulders, squints at Tarek. He whistles and three dogs emerge from the dark. The boy glances at the old dog through open doors in the back of the van.

Tarek stands. "The engine's overheated."

The boy strokes the old dog.

Tarek thinks from her age and that of the other dogs she is likely their mother. The dogs scatter, reappear having gathered a drove of goats out of the night. A dog chases a stray that bolts then turns to join the herd.

"Where's your village?"

The boy shrugs as though to say, what village?

"How far to where you live?"

The boy points with his staff to a mound a distance away.

Tarek offers to drive him in the van.

The boy says he will walk with his dogs and goats.

The engine engages on the first turn of the key. The old she-dog rests in the back on blankets. In the dark, the van moves forward at a walking pace to keep alongside the drove. Tarek drives off the track, careful not to hit a sand pit or damage the underside of the van with rocks. The dogs circle the goats to keep them in a tight clutch, turn the herd one way then another to gather strays. The boy hurries to keep up with the dogs. Tarek wonders what Mona is doing, if awake this late—maybe reading—wishes she were with him, then thinks it just as well she is not. He pictures Neda curled on her side in her bed at home under Teta's quilt. But no, tonight she sleeps with Leila in the hut at the ship breakers' yard. For the first time in hours, he thinks he may see her again, and his heart lightens.

It is almost dawn when they approach the mound—the sky pale with the sun just below the horizon. The van follows the boy and the dogs along the rise of the stone crest. The boy whistles. The dogs drive the herd forward over waves of stone.

"How much further?" Tarek slows the van, knows once the sun rises the gauge on the dashboard will soon show red. "Go round. We'll be on the other side." The boy points the direction with his staff.

Tarek watches the boy follow the last of the goats along a trail over the crest and then out of sight. He drives close to the side of the hill, glances in the rear-view mirror to see the old dog in the back curled nose to tail. "I'll get you home. Maybe my turn next." As they circle the mound of rocks, the cliff edge folds and drops to a valley that flares in the day's first light. A great sheet, like ice, extends to the horizon, refracts light in rainbow colours. A truck waits by the banks of the white plain. This must be Wadi Melleh, Salt Valley. A hut nestles in the curve of the cliff. The boy with a line of goats approaches down the hillside.

Tarek stops the van in the shade of the rock face, opens the hood, disconnects the fan. He carries the old dog in his arms to where the boy stops by the hut. An elderly man comes out, watches Tarek settle the dog on a mat.

"She'll be better once she's eaten," the man says.

From the hut, the boy fetches a bowl, places it by the dog, dips his fingers in the broth, rubs them on the dog's mouth and teeth. He repeats this until the dog lifts its head, starts to eat.

A second man, younger, comes from the hut, introduces himself as the driver of the truck parked by the sheets of salt. He grins as he stares at the van. "You drove here in that?"

"It's blown the gasket on the cylinder head."

The driver runs his finger in the oil and water smeared on the surface of the engine, rubs his fingers together to feel the consistency of the solution, as he would the thickness of a cloth. "You'll need to drain the engine to drive it again." He will be back in a day or so for more of the salt, will bring coolant and oil, also a replacement gasket. Or, if Tarek wants to abandon the van, he can take him to the nearest town to find transport to wherever he came from.

No, Tarek cannot return to Neda without AK. Besides, what can he do without transport? He will stay if that is all right. In truth, he thinks himself too exhausted to go anywhere just yet.

The old man pours water for the she-dog from an urn. "You saved the dog's life. Our dogs are precious to us."

"I'll sleep in the van. I can pay for food and water."

"Meals are what we and the drivers eat when they come to collect salt."

If good for them the food will be good enough for him for a couple of days. He watches the driver with tools from his truck remove the warped gasket. A woman stands at the door to the hut. Tarek thinks the relationship to be father, son, daughter and driver as husband—this corner of the salt sheets a family concern. The driver inspects the cylinder head. "Good, it's the original cast iron. The newer aluminum ones crack in the heat." Tarek offers him money in advance for the purchases. The driver laughs, says he is not worried. He knows Tarek will be here when he returns. As the sun flames along the horizon, the truck departs with a load of salt slabs.

The day births tentatively. The sun, precarious on the edge of the flats, seemingly could roll left or right, even tumble forward onto the salt sheets. The spread of light strips back shadows like an unveiling. On the raised banks of the salt flats Tarek stops to run his fingers through the sand. Tiny crystals scratch his hands, stain them white. This place would make a story for a puppet show. Once there was, though maybe not, a lake the *afrit* lord turned to salt. Better to start with a character—Once there was, though maybe not, a young shepherd boy who lived by a lake of salt. The boy lives with his father. A stranger arrives. Maybe the boy saves the man's life and is offered a wish. What would the boy wish for? What does he know of the world to wish for something better? Maybe he wishes the lake of salt were water, but maybe not. After all, the salt provides him with a living.

In the forlorn hope of making contact, Tarek tries his phone, but still no connection. He steps on the salt sheet, walks on the thick white crust, stops by a pool of water made crimson—he thinks, in all likelihood, from underground deposits of pyrite. Streams run from pool to pool. At white mounds about a metre high, he finds a rusted wheelbarrow. Its bent frame flakes like scabs, the wheel broken from its axle.

A fine mist lifts silver flakes. The sunlight breaks and reflects in shards of light, floating petals rise and drop, take on colours. In the warm breath of the sun, as on a vast canvas with flicks and dabs of reds and blues, butterflies feed on the salt sheet. They take flight as Tarek approaches, flutter, disperse, come together to disperse again—black-and-white tigers, brown-speckled leopards, zebra blues and cabbage whites, small coppers, pea blues. A wave runs over the flats as swarms rise to scatter for the shade of crags and valleys before the sun scorches them with its flame.

The sun swells and rises over the valley. In the far distance he sees men break salt into slabs, tie blocks to the sides of a camel, lead it away towards the horizon. Where did they come from—an oasis in the desert or another valley in the stone plateau? To think people live in such places.

A breeze ripples the crimson pools. The salt flats reflect the sun now fully risen. Tarek walks back to the raised sandbank, ahead of him the stone plateau. He climbs the slope to the tabletop, stops to catch his breath partway up the path, sees the woman by the hut thread weft along the length of a hand loom. She glances at him, then turns back to her weaving. Is she the woman he and Neda bought the salt nugget from? He is uncertain, cannot read her face to know if she recognizes him. Like the boy, her expressions are indecipherable, her mind and mood impenetrable. But what does she see when she looks at him? Is he as unintelligible to her as she to him—each not so much a face as a surface to the other, a mutual opacity? Is his presence to her less of an otherness and more of a nothingness—here, but already forgotten? How often has he driven past boys tending goats, women selling wares, men leading sheep and never given them a glance, as though they were invisible? Maybe, having read herself registered as nothing in the eyes of men like him, the woman sees him as nothing. Yet her brother did rescue him, though maybe only because he showed kindness to a dog. He supposes he owes his life to a discharge of obligation—not that the reason really matters.

Once on the plateau, he turns on his phone. Still no connection. He walks a short distance, stops to check again for reception, paces back and forth, thinks it hopeless. He is nowhere—this expanse an absence. He has come to a period point, a stop. No, maybe only a pause, as he would separate equations by a comma, or place them in parentheses.

In the shade of an outcrop at the edge of the plateau, he sits on a boulder part buried, its face smoothed by wind. He scrolls through the list of contacts on his phone, wonders how many of the names he will see again. He pauses at Yara's number. Is she back at the hospital? And what of his friend's son? Did she ever find him? He will call her once he is back. He would like to get her perspective on what has happened during his days of absence from the city.

Tarek gazes out across the white flats, sees the old man from the hut wield an iron rod to cleave slabs from the salt face. The boy loads the blocks onto a sledge, drags them back to the raised shoreline of sand and rock where the truck had parked overnight. From here, they seem as small as ants foraging a mound for scraps.

When he was last on the great stone plateau he spent his days collecting shreds of newsprint as data for an equation he thought would make sense of the world. He recalls debates in the prison camp with Kasem—because quantum mechanics presupposes radical contingency, freedom is possible. He thinks of the crab-man in the square who disrupted the seemingly inevitable by a choice when no choice seemed conceivable. Did the man understand what he was risking? Did any of them when they climbed into the wheels of the tank or blocked its way to the barricade?

To clarify the thought he would need to formulate it as he would an axiom. But the notion is too vague—so, maybe, work through it as he would compose an equation.

Assume a situation, S, comprises a given circumstance, C, with choice being a subset of possible occurrences, $\{a, b, ...\}$. Then, there is the empty set, $\emptyset$, which can be intuited, imagined, but unknown—a subset of every real set. He needs to write this down, to grasp and develop the conception. From his wallet he removes the paper on which he had previously written the equations of the love poem. On the back of the sheet, he contrives the change in situation as $S \supseteq \{ (\beta . \xi) (a, b, ... \emptyset) / C \}$. The first symbol, β, of the bracketed set represents resistance to change. Suppose ξ, a variable modifier, represents intention, comprising a relationship of dissatisfaction with the status quo, say δ, and the ability to envision something better, call it v.

So, $\xi = \delta / v$. He gazes at the second part of the equation, choices relative to circumstances. If the two terms cancel out, that would mean stagnation, or decay. So, freedom is a function of intensity in Ø, imagination charged with passion. To clarify the basic thought he writes: *Freedom is to conceive and act on a choice that can change the reality from which that choice arises.* He reads the sentence out loud, listens for the sense of the words, likes the implied symmetry of imagination, passion and intention leading to decision, action and responsibility.

He reflects on what he has written, thinks it incomplete. The full set of possible circumstances of any situation is always unknowable, and never solely one's own. Hence, the outcome of an act must always be contingent and replete with unintended consequences. He considers the thought, adds on the next line: *We are each answerable for, and dependent on, the freedom of others.* But who are we answerable to and dependent on if not the people we love? He thinks he has arrived at a knot he is unsure how to untangle—to be free is to love and be loved, and yet to love, one must be free. How to resolve this for sense without infinite regress?

And what of Yaqzan's God? If God is in the universe having created it of His own substance, then God must change as the world changes. But if God is absolute and omniscient, knowing all things for all time, that would mean life is predetermined and God insulated from the world by a state of perfection. Yet, from the equation, the exercise of freedom changes reality and so changes God's knowledge, and thus God changes. So the Creator can be neither fully transcendent nor entirely actual in the world, neither completely interior nor wholly exterior to creation, but in a constant state of becoming. By such deferral God requires our freedom to better know Itself. But also, for God to be in and of the universe and yet free, then creation must also be free and undetermined. Either way freedom is necessary.

He needs time to grasp the implications of his thoughts, misses not having Mona with him to discuss them. Misses both Mona and Neda. In the shade of an outcrop, he watches the man and boy stop work, return to the hut where the woman threads fresh yarn to a shuttle for the hand loom. With legs outstretched, she draws the yarn between the toes of one foot to keep it from tangling. She slides the crossbeam to spread the warp, thrusts the shuttle from side to side, beats down the weft.

The weaving awakens memories of Reham. He recalls making love to her in the cave of images—the different rhythms of their bodies, the rise and fall of their breath. A quickening followed by release and a sensation so completely of the body it slips the mind. The recollection, lambent, dances lightly with him. He wonders if Yaqzan loved Reham. He does not think of the Yaqzan he knows as the husband they betrayed. He would prefer not to think of him as the same person. He realizes in all their travels together he has never mentioned her to him, has spoken of her only to Leila and Kasem. He is surprised by the omission, but more so for having never imagined how Yaqzan ever felt. Such indifference strikes him as a failing, stirs emotions he does not wish to explore. He thinks *I never gave him a thought while I was with her.* He takes a deep breath, shakes off the sensation of a dull ache that runs through his body.

The sun now hot, the air dry, he follows a path down the side of the stone plateau, stumbles on rocks that crumble underfoot. At the van he drinks the last bottle of water, warm and tasting of plastic. He watches a mist rise from red streams like lava through ice. Rainbows ignite on the salt sheets. Tired from the night's drive and the heat, he sleeps.

When Tarek wakes he sees the boy with a shovel digging a pit in the sandy soil at the foot of the escarpment. The boy says the old dog died that morning. At the hut, Tarek lifts the dog in his arms. She is heavier than he remembers, as though death added bulk. The other dogs have caught her scent, follow Tarek. The boy lays the dog in the pit. Tarek collects rocks to mark the grave. The dogs whine, scratch at the soft earth as though to grieve their dead.

The boy takes the path to the salt sheets to where the man stacks slabs. With mallet and chisel, they split the blocks into large tiles, sever them lengthways into tablets, tie a rope crosswise on each, stack them on their ends for when the truck returns. Tarek watches them, feels discomfort at being an observer. They shared what little they have with him. The least he can do is share their labour to acknowledge their world has worth.

On the salt sheets, he helps the boy break the slabs to crosstie them as tablets, loads blocks of salt on a sledge to haul them to where the truck parked that morning. He works in silence, fitting himself to their rhythm, settles into a steady pace of splitting, binding, stacking that obviates the need for words.

With the sun low on the horizon, they stop work. A cool breeze blows across the valley. At a well Tarek washes the salt off his face and arms, pours water, chilled underground, over his matted hair, neck and chest. They return to the hut. The woman hands Tarek flatbread and a bowl of broth. The man and the boy eat, dip bread, drink from the bowls, suck on bones. Tarek does as they do. He feels some comfort at sharing with them, however fleetingly, a sense of community.

The boy takes the broth with more bones to where the dogs shelter in the shade of the escarpment.

Tarek asks the man if he knows where to buy a desert rose for his daughter.

The man nods as he eats. He will look to see if they have any.

Once back in the van, Tarek lies down to rest.

He is woken by the boy, with a bundle wrapped in newspaper. Tarek lays it on a blanket, unfolds the paper that wreathes a desert rose the size of a fist with curved petals. Tarek gazes at the crystal cluster. Its blades fan open from a central whorl, exquisite and delicate. He can appreciate why Neda imagines it magical. He folds the desert rose in a blanket, gathers up the sheets of paper, sees a headline about the protests and the fall of the old dictator. He feels a surge of hope to think he can soon return home. He asks the boy where he got the newspaper.

The boy says he collects litter while grazing the goats. When he was younger, the truck driver identified the letters for him, made their sounds, taught him to read. Alone on the stone plateau, with nothing much to do, he reads the scraps so as not to lose the skill.

At the hut Tarek offers to pay for the desert rose, asks the price.

"Whatever you think is fair." The man pours tea from a small brass kettle into glasses.

"Whatever you ask for."

The man laughs. Never before has he had to bargain down his own price. His unconstrained laugh relaxes Tarek, who thinks it refreshing for being genuine—not the laughter he is accustomed to, the sounding grimace before authority to self-deprecate or degrade another.

With the sunset, the sky turns a deep red, the salt flats darken with streams of black. Like a photographic negative, the colours reverse from day to night. Tarek fills plastic bottles with water from the well, sees the boy walk a team of goats along the side of the escarpment to the stone plateau for grazing. One dog leads as the other two follow the herd. From the hut Tarek hears a storm lamp roar. Its light pulsates through a window.

At night, he sits in the van with only darkness between him and the stars. When with Mona on the balcony of their apartment, the thick city air and street lights obscured all but the brightest constellations. Here, in utter darkness, he watches the universe turn and flow—a shower of meteorites blaze and die. For a moment he feels like a child absorbed by wonder. Then, for no reason he can fathom, tears blur his sight. He wraps himself in a blanket, cries until sleep overcomes him.

Tarek wakes to the sound of an engine's rumble. From the back window of the van he sees the truck roll down towards the salt lake to where the tablets he helped gather and tie are stacked for collection. He rises relieved, splashes water on his face from a bottle, pours it on his head to fully wake.

By the white flats the boy loads salt tablets onto the truck. At the hut the driver drinks tea. He has the head gasket with him. He apologizes for not making it back earlier, but he wanted to be sure he had the right one. Tarek feels such gratitude, wants to hug him, offers to pay what he owes and something extra for the man's troubles.

"When we've got it working," the driver says.

At the van, they drain the engine of water and oil. Dark slurry runs into the sand. They fit the gasket to the cylinder head. In the afternoon, they will refill the engine with oil and coolant, then check for leaks. The driver says he will travel that night to make deliveries by morning, suggests Tarek follow him in the van. They can part ways once they have crossed the stone plateau and the van is safely on the coastal road.

17

In the dry heat of the morning, Omar waits in line for half a tank of gasoline from pumps at one of the few stations still receiving supplies. What extra gas he obtains from the company is not enough for the roadside fares he collects in between assignments. Armed soldiers maintain order. Birds scrape and chitter on the concrete canopy, get on Omar's nerves.

As an attendant feeds the cab's tank, Omar watches the spinning dial on the pump head. He feels on the verge of sinfulness—conflicted by thoughts of the blonde he collected from the hotel days earlier and desire for the boy he smoked *bango* with in his cab. The phone vibrates on the dashboard. Omar glances at it, thinks it might be the boy calling for a ride to the mall, or something more pleasurable. But no number shows on the screen. Disappointed, he answers, immediately recognizes the voice—an officer at State Security—even though he has not heard it in months.

"Nine this evening at my office, and don't keep me waiting."

The call clears Omar's mind of thoughts of the boy and the blonde. A wave of panic breaks out in sweat. He wipes his hands on his shirt.

* * *

That afternoon at a masjid, Omar recites out loud from scripture, applies what he has learnt of accentuation, rhythm, style and clarity. An elderly cleric listens, corrects his intonation.

"One meaning yields to eye, another discerned by ear." The cleric explains the interaction between end-rhyme and the resolution of line tension heightened by the cadence of voice. He speaks of texture and depth that can be gleaned only through skilled recitation.

The balance between sense and musicality eludes Omar. He grows frustrated at his failure.

"The verses should neither be spoken nor sung." The cleric intones the text, links words, lengthens sounds, shortens others. "You must find the voice of the verse."

But there are so many rules to learn before Omar can achieve such skill. A mastery beyond all the laws of language to speak directly to the hearts of men—rules of veiling and unveiling of sounds, of assimilation, doubling and enunciation, of word segmentation and combination, of punctuation and lineation and so much more. And all before he can approach the level of metaphor and meaning. But God has not given him an ear to master the art and science of voice. With the call to prayer he stands, relieved he can stop trying, raises his hands to his forehead in salutation, bows and kneels in supplication to the one Lord of Creation.

In his kitchen Omar recites to Pilgrim his day's lesson. He explains the rules as they pertain to the linking of words in recitation. He speaks of how his cantillation of sacred text is improving. Of course, he has a long way to go before his words can carry the force of conversion, illuminating hearts and guiding men to God. Pilgrim remains still and attentive in the shoebox. Omar feeds him bread crumbs and dry flakes of cheese, tells him of driving a client to the Ben Ezra Synagogue. He is sure the man is a Jew, though is not exactly sure what that means, maybe some kind of an unbeliever, like Tarek.

They have their scripture. God's chosen people.

"Well, maybe once. But not anymore. We the believers are God's chosen. What is the verse? Something, something . . . *created the best of nations.*"

You don't feel yourself comfortable in the man's company.

You're right. I don't.

Then there's the protests and demonstrations.

Those people are insane.

What if you picked one up as a fare?

I wouldn't know them if I did.

But they might recognize you from that night in the square.

They'd want revenge.

You wouldn't be safe.

You're right about that.

You need protection.

But like what? You mean a gun?

For self-defence.

Yes, of course, especially after what he had witnessed of mayhem. To have a gun would be a simple precaution. A gun buys a man respect. Voices multiply in his head, debate how to go about getting a weapon. Yes, God is his witness. He only wants it for self-preservation, nothing else.

At nine o'clock Omar arrives at State Security Central. He signs in at the entrance, as he would at any government building, asks for the colonel who phoned him earlier. He is led to a dimly lit waiting room crowded with young men and women standing or seated on chairs, waiting their turn for interrogation. Their anxiety infects him. He leans against a wall, pulls his scarf up to cover his face. They remind him of Yara, if she was the young woman who berated him in the square.

He argues with himself as a man in uniform calls him from the door. He leaves with a sense of relief, drapes the scarf from his shoulders, follows up a flight of stairs and down a corridor to an office. From across a wide desk the colonel waves him to a seat, offers a cigarette. Omar declines.

"It's been a while." The colonel lights a cigarette, inhales slowly.

"Nothing to report." He struggles to get the last of the argument with the Yara woman out of his head.

The colonel opens a file on his desk, hands Omar a photograph. The image grainy, taken by a traffic surveillance camera, of a man alone in a street, ahead of him a barricade of sheet metal and scaffolding.

"Is that your brother-in-law?"

"You mean Tarek?"

"You have another?"

No, of course he didn't mean it to sound like that. He laughs nervously.

"Is that him?"

If it is a matter of turning Tarek in, Omar really could not care less. After all, the man does not believe in God, and his atheism is probably doing irreparable damage to his daughter, but then the girl is not really Omar's niece, and so not his responsibility, as Mona keeps reminding him. But, of course, his sister is pregnant. Her unborn child ties him to Tarek by blood. Before was then, but now is different—not easy to betray blood. "With the face in profile it could be anybody." Besides, if he does, Mona will most certainly deny him access to her child, stop him guiding it on the path to God, forbid him the opportunity to earn the credits he needs for heavenly salvation. When interrogated in the grave by the angels Naker and Munkar he counts on the child being his alibi for having led a good and godly life. "I just want to be sure." He feels caught between his duty and telling a lie—a sin forbidden by religion. He trusts in God to give a believer a loophole, a way to always do what is right, even when the circumstances are wrong. If only his mind would work faster. "I wouldn't deny there's a resemblance." He struggles to recall a verse that would give guidance and clarity to his thoughts. An authoritative word that would exonerate him before God on the Day of Judgment. The moment stretches. Perspiration collects in his fist clutching the photograph. He wipes his hands on his shirt. Then it comes to him, one of the verses of compassion—*God will not call you to account for thoughtless oaths, but will judge you by the intention of your heart. He is forgiving, forbearing.* "When exactly was this picture taken?"

"Does it matter?"

"He's out of town, left me to look after my sister. As if I don't have enough to do earning a living."

"When did he leave?"

"Some while ago. Not sure when exactly."

The colonel sits back, smokes slowly, watches Omar. "You are certain?"

"Of course I'm certain. I call him and he doesn't even pick up. He knows I'm mad with him. My sister pregnant and abandoned. I never thought him any good. Left me to pay for my sister's bed in the maternity ward. As if I'm drowning in cash." He feels a surge of rage as he recalls his argument with Tarek to accept the money for Mona's stay at the hospital.

"So that's not him?"

Omar shakes his head, still seething, plays over the conversation he had with Tarek.

The colonel presses his cigarette stub into an ashtray. "All right. You can leave."

"I need a favour."

"What kind of favour?"

"Protection."

"Security?"

"Not security, protection."

"I can't issue you a firearm, if that's what you mean."

"Just for peace of mind. So I can sleep at night. I don't feel safe."

The colonel stares at Omar, tears a sheet of paper from a notebook, writes down a phone number, hands it to him. "He'll sell you a handgun. Cash, no questions asked."

Yara makes the bed in Neda's room with sheets Heba washed that morning.

Mona dusts the desk with its collection of matryoshka dolls, sets them neatly in a row.

Yara talks of the days after the president's resignation and the promise of elections when people stopped attending the square, thinking they had won. The army dismantled the barricades. She was held at the field clinic as they checked her identity and membership in the doctors' syndicate. There she saw soldiers force their fingers inside girls' vaginas to rupture their hymen.

Mona gapes at her. "Why do that?"

"Humiliation. To punish them for joining the protests." She spreads a sheet and tucks it under the corners of the mattress, tosses a pillow on the bed, puffs it up.

"You will spend the night here? It's too late to go home."

"Don't be upset, but I'm glad I don't have children. It would be unbearable to bring up a daughter in a place where anything she does is *awra* or *nushuz*." She folds Teta's quilt over the pillows.

"Those words don't mean what they once meant." In her bedroom, Mona sinks into the armchair, stuffs pillows into their cases.

Yara follows her with fresh folded sheets. "Since when do you read scripture?"

"*Awra* meant a man's sin for gazing lustfully at a woman." She shakes out another pillowcase from the pile by the bed. "The meaning's been reversed to make women responsible for men's desires."

"But God permits a man to beat his wife for *nushuz*, for having a mind of her own."

"*Nushuz* means 'deception,' not 'wilfulness.' 'To beat' isn't what the word *darb* means in the verse. The noun means 'path,' the verb, 'to leave.'"

Yara stops tucking the bottom sheet under the corners of the mattress, stares at Mona. "You're saying the verse they poisoned our minds with from when we were children means if a man's wife deceives him he should leave her—and not that he has the God-given right to beat her? You're saying men have been beating women over a misreading?"

"Probably deliberately misread." Mona pushes a pillow into its case, picks up another from the side of the chair.

"So God's not a misogynist after all? Well, who'd have known." Yara laughs, spreads the top sheet.

The cat crawls out from under the bed, stretches, unclenches its claws, curls up at Mona's feet. On the side table is *April March* bookmarked with an old envelope.

"I was reading a novel when I realized we don't have an equivalent for the English word 'couple,' meaning a man and a woman together and equal."

"There are words for twos of this and twos of that."

"Not the same as couple."

"You think a word matters?" Yara folds back the top sheet, helps Mona from the chair to the bed.

Mona settles on the quilt and blankets. "I think its absence symptomatic."

"It's going to take more than words to make a difference."

"The difference won't happen without words." She leans against the pillows, watches through the glass doors of the balcony birds flutter and feed on bread crumbs Heba left by a saucer of water. She thinks them beautiful, free and unconquerable.

Mona wakes to sounds from the window. She lifts herself from the bed, goes to the balcony, opens the shutters. The night breeze is clear and fresh from the river. At the wall that severs the street, young men heave on cables strapped to concrete blocks. A slab shifts by centimetres, then by a few more, then topples, explodes dust from the ground. The earth shudders, releases squalls of birds from trees and nearby buildings. In the street light they spin in panicked flight, swarm, settle back on branches; some rise to new perches on rooftops. Young men tug on cables to shift another block, topple two more, open a gap in the wall wide enough to let through pedestrians and a single line of traffic.

Mona slides a wicker chair onto the balcony. She has not sat out since Tarek and Neda left. She drops into it, leans back against the cushions, gazes at the slabs scattered in the street like alphabet blocks, wonders if elsewhere in the city walls are being brought down. She rests a hand on her belly, comforted by the child's presence, closes her eyes, senses a stirring in the silence about her—so slight, barely an inflection—feels a faint pulse run through her. She shivers, takes a quick breath, waits for a contraction to start, knows it still too soon to wake Yara, asleep on the living room couch. To distract herself she thinks of stories she will read to her child. Stories like the one of when the moon spent her days on earth, drank the milk of ibex and gazelle, returned at night to the sky round and full of light. When the moon saw men hunt, their cruelty frightened her. She hid among the stars, grew thin until she faded in darkness. People felt sorry for the moon, left out bowls of milk for her. Some nights, too thin to be seen, the moon comes down to earth, drinks the milk, then returns to light the sky.

It is early morning as Tarek stops the van past the high gates to the harbour terminal. Ahead, the refugee camp and the great rusted sundial of a ship's hull. He wonders where Neda could be. Maybe still asleep at the ship breakers' camp. Farther along the shoreline the cutting torches flare for the morning shift on the hull of a large steel vessel beached on a sandbank.

He drives along the beach track, parks the van on a hard shoulder of stone, walks to where the rocky ground dips and turns to sand. He sits by a shrub with bare spiky branches. Waves crest and break on the beach in rippling lines of foam. Far in undulating waters bottles bob like shoals of fish. A boy's head jounces, flotsam among the bottles. A plastic crate floats on a tire, dips and lifts with the rolling waves. Tarek sees Kasem on the beach with the dog. It runs to him, wags its tail.

"The kid's amazing, don't you think?" Kasem speaks as though Tarek's absence was barely a pause in their conversation.

Tarek nods. A kid with that kind of determination, he says, could do anything.

"You think?" Kasem stares out to sea.

"Where's Neda?"

"Swimming."

No, Neda—too afraid of the swimming pool let alone open water. Anxious, he looks around. Close to shore, he sees her head among the ripples. She stands, hurries against the ebb of a wave to the beach, throws her arms around him. The dog barks, jumps with fresh excitement.

"I really, really missed you so very, very much."

She wears the amber pendant. Wet and golden, it catches the sun.

He thinks her not the child he left. More assured somehow. Her gaze holds steady as she looks at him. Maybe he has changed, and so sees her differently. "Where's Yaqzan?"

"He's asleep. Auntie Leila and Auntie Salma are with him."

Deep at sea the boy collects bottles in the crate. He swims to the shallows, stands, shakes his head, rains droplets from flailing black hair, stirs in his wake sand clouds in clear water. Beyond the foaming's reach, he drags the crate, leaves a line like a snail's silver trace. "Do you want to buy bottles?"

No, Tarek does not.

The boy drags the crate along the sand to the ridge that leads to his shack.

"I'll go talk to him," Kasem says. "We'll need another *gnawa* now that you're taking Neda from us." He follows the boy up the slope.

Tarek tucks Neda to him. On one side of them the desert, pale in the morning light, on the other the sea with waves that turn like pages.

"You were gone so long I thought you were lost."

"I was lost for a time." He tells her he has the Wishing Rose in the van.

She laughs, hugs him. "I really missed you, and miss Mummy."

Yes, he missed her, misses Mona too.

"Can we go home? Oh, please." Tears run down her cheeks. "It's so wonderful to see Auntie Leila with Auntie Salma, but it makes me feel so sad to be missing Mummy."

He thinks the situation probably safe for Neda, though maybe not so safe for himself even with the fall of the dictator. "I'll get you home."

"No, I want to be with you and Mummy together." She wipes the tears from her face, implores him with a weak smile.

If, once he is back, it seems too much of a risk to stay, he can leave again. He will find a way of explaining why to Neda. "All right, we'll go home."

Neda jumps up and down. "Oh yes, oh yes, we're going home." She hugs her father, stops, steps back. "But now I feel really sad."

He stares at her.

"I will really, really miss Auntie Leila and Auntie Salma too."

"When you're home you can call them."

They drive AK to the ship breakers' camp. In the clearing by the camp's water cistern they see a grey tent with a sign pitched by a Red Crescent truck. Tarek leaves Neda with Leila and Salma in the hut, walks to the tent. A young man in a paramedic's white coat and a blue face mask pulled down under his chin asks if Tarek has come to give blood for the victims of the troubles caught in fighting between army and rebels.

Tarek climbs onto an old metal gurney. It rattles as he rolls up his shirt sleeve, clenches and unclenches his fist to make a vein stand out below where a rubber tube is tied to his biceps. "We just came from the mountains." Tarek watches blood pulse into a plastic sack on a metal stand.

"Want to go back? We're looking for drivers who know the region."

Tarek slowly pumps his fist. It will take him three or four days' driving to get to the mountains, and maybe as many to get back. So this is the choice: He can return home with Neda, or buy time by going to the field clinics in the mountains. If the latter, then either Neda stays here with Leila and Kasem, or they can take her back to Mona. He will talk to them before asking Neda to call her mother to discuss his decision.

The medic removes the needle. A blood drop swells on Tarek's arm at the punctured vein. The medic holds a cotton pad to the wound. "We leave in the morning."

As the sun slips below the horizon, Tarek sits on a dune on the beach, watches the sea a silvery grey in failing light. Above the shoreline, against an orange sky, murmurations of starlings billow, break in waves and scatter like spray. Birds chitter and chorus, gather to settle along the lattice steelworks of piers and cranes beyond the rusted hulk of the beached ship and the wire fences that ring the harbour.

Leila and Kasem, by the crab pools at the water's edge, watch the sunset. They come his way, stop by him. She shows him the shell she had given Neda. "Your daughter forgot it on the beach."

Tarek gazes at it. "Is it the same one?"

"So, you haven't forgotten?"

How could he? There were days he lived to see that shell placed by the side of the well. He takes a deep breath to fill a sudden feeling of emptiness.

Kasem asks if he gave blood.

"They're looking for drivers. They asked me to join them."

Kasem stares at him. "You're not serious."

"If you take Neda back to Mona, you can keep the van until I return."

"If you don't?" Leila asks.

"Then it's yours."

Leila looks askance at him, says she has to put Neda to bed, leaves for the hut.

"I need to buy time until I'm sure the situation's safe for me to return."

"Sounds like a rerun." Kasem takes a cigarette stub from his pocket, flips it between his fingers.

"Meaning what?"

"You're abandoning Neda as you did her mother."

Tarek drops back on the sand, stares at the sky. "Do you have to bring everything round to that one moment?"

"Because I'm right." Kasem searches his pockets for a match.

"I didn't have a choice."

"If you'd asked for time they might have held you over for the next transportation."

"You don't know that."

"The point is you didn't try. You didn't want to risk it. You wanted to be free more than you wanted to be with Reham."

He detects an undercurrent of hurt in Kasem's voice. But, after so many years, what can he say with any honesty that could possibly assuage him? Then there is the issue he has always avoided addressing. "Whatever way you look at it, she was Yaqzan's wife."

"She loved you."

"And he probably loved her."

"He doesn't talk about her."

"Does he talk about Neda?"

"He knows Reham had a child."

Tarek struggles to take a deep breath. "Does he know I loved Reham?"

"That is why he trusts you with her daughter."

Tarek feels a weight press down on him. "Does he think Neda his?"

"He might believe he has reason to."

"But having my child, Reham couldn't have his." He folds an arm across his face, as though to shield his eyes from light too bright to bear. "He must loathe me."

"I think he feels grateful you're taking good care of Neda."

Tarek can barely breathe. Moisture collects behind swollen eyelids. The tension in his chest eases. His breathing gradually returns to normal.

Kasem chews on the filtered end of the unlit stub. "Days ago the army cleared the square. Today they killed a young woman placing a red carnation at a makeshift memorial for those who died defending the barricades."

Tarek's skin chills as he thinks of Yara. "When was that?"

"Early this morning."

He catches his breath with relief. He had sent her a text that afternoon, asking after Mona, and had received a message from her.

"The newspapers say the new marshal is a patriot. But a patriot doesn't kill his own people." Kasem runs his hand through the sand and scatters a fistful to the breeze, gazes out to the darkening sea. "It's a turn in the road to somewhere very dangerous."

Lying still, Tarek watches stars come alight; between them darkness thickens. At the ship breakers' yard the night shift begins. Torches flame in broad red feathers, then sharpen to blue cones to cut through steel decks.

Kasem removes the cigarette from his mouth. "Back then, the way I saw it, you made others pay the price for your freedom."

Tarek thinks Kasem harsh. But no, he says, he did not mean to burden anybody, nor limit their freedom. "I accept we make and are made by our choices. The risks we take—"

"And by our compromises and excuses." Kasem crushes the cigarette stub between his fingers, flakes the tobacco on the sand.

Tarek glimpses through Kasem's eyes an unfamiliar image of himself, feels trapped by it. A surge of frustration at not being understood, an urge to protest, peaks, then subsides. He remains silent, does not want an argument to justify who he was and who he is, or to get drawn into a discussion of obligations and responsibilities. Soon they will part, and he would prefer to do so while still on good terms. "You know the saying: They can crush the flowers, but they can't stop the spring."

"Maybe, but every time and place has its rhythm. Tune yourself to it and the universe goes easier on you." Kasem glances at him, then turns back to the sea, sluggish and black in the night. "With the troubles and a new marshal replacing the old, you're right. It isn't safe for you to return."

Tarek lies still, feels the sand soak moisture from the air heavy with the scent of the sea. At this time of an evening Mona showers, folds her hair in a towel before the bathroom mirror. He feels an overwhelming desire to be with her, thinks that without her he is not himself. "But maybe it is time to go home."

Kasem shakes his head. "I just gave you a reason not to."

"You were right. Not to return would be a rerun of a mistake."

"Going back could be another kind of mistake."

"Sometimes choosing between mistakes is all there is to do."

"I always said you weren't rational."

Tarek laughs. "It's called the Russell paradox, like choosing between identical pairs of socks." He sits up, dusts sand from his hair. He should call Mona.

The next morning Neda cries in Salma's and Leila's arms, hugs Kasem and Yaqzan, says she does not want to leave, then follows her father to AK. On the drive back, with the dog by her side on the passenger seat, she counts down the kilometre signs. "We're home when the numbers reach zero."

He thinks to tell her that zero is not a number but a conjunctive of negative and positive quantities, of real and imaginary values—a statement of unknowability. But decides not to.

With the sun at its zenith they stop for a break and something to eat. Under a crumpled blanket, in the grooves of the floor at the rear of the van, Neda finds his watch. "It's stopped."

"Probably dust in the mechanism. I'll clean it once we're home."

As they sit by the side of the road, eat sandwiches they made that morning, Neda watches a flight of starlings over the turquoise sea swirl across the sky. She asks her father if birds are really the twin spirits of the unborn. He says he thinks not.

She nods as she eats. "It's all a mystery."

Late that afternoon in the van, with the desert rose on her lap, in between periods of sleep she wishes for superpowers like X-ray vision and lightning bolts, and thinks of stories she can tell her friends of her visit to Mount Qaf and Sidi Adi where the Peacock Angel murmurs with the sounds of a subterranean stream, and whispers in a spiral shell she keeps in her pocket.

18

Omar parks by the Rifai Mosque close to the old Citadel. Men on ladders string electric cables between posts across the open courtyard as others hose down tiles of white marble. Banners hung along the sides of raised tents announce the various branches of the Sufi orders preparing to celebrate the saint's *moulid*. Birds chorus from rooftops. Omar walks down the hill through the furniture market, past men and women by stalls selling old mobile phones and electronics to reach the arms dealer. He is taken into a metal workshop, past spinning lathes to a backroom. On a worktable under canvas is a selection of automatic and semiautomatic rifles. "American, French, Italian."

"I need a *fard*. You know, for protection."

The dealer waves his hand at another table with handguns.

The foreign firearms are beyond Omar's means, but the *fard* made locally by backstreet craftsmen are well priced. He selects a revolver that looks like a Colt .45. Its shiny handle decorated with strips of embossed aluminum and nickel alloy. He counts out his money, knows it pointless to bargain. The handgun wrapped in newspaper is slipped into a plastic bag.

* * *

Late morning the dispatcher calls to ask Omar to collect a woman from one of the downtown hotels, tells him the military have announced a lifting of the curfew. With business bad these days Omar is grateful for the news and a chance to earn extra cash from roadside fares. He arrives to see the blonde light a cigarette as she waits in the lobby. She mutters under her breath when she sees him. In the car park says, "I told them I don't want you, crazy man."

Well, that is just too bad. He is the driver the dispatcher sent.

She gets into the car. "Okay, *yalla, yalla.*"

Omar adjusts the rear-view mirror to better see her light another cigarette in the back seat. "I not bad man you speak to like servant."

"*Yalla imshee, imshee.* Go, go." She turns away to look out the side window.

He thought after the other night they could be friends. But, clearly, he was mistaken.

They drive through congested streets, stop at a crowded junction. He tells her of the morning he saw her leaving the hotel with another driver.

"You spy on me, crazy man?"

No, he dropped off a client at the same hotel, just a coincidence, nothing more.

She throws her head back in a gesture of—what? He is not sure, maybe defiance, or insult? He cannot read its significance. Whatever, he thinks it disparaging. To change the subject, he asks if she knows any Jews. Being a foreigner herself, she should know how to tell if somebody is Jewish.

"You want to know *Yehudi,* you ask him."

Yes, of course, he says, that would be one way. But what if he lies, denies it when really he is?

"Why he lie?"

Omar is not sure why. But he might, mightn't he?

"Why?" She glares at him.

"People do lie." Who knows what motives a person may have?

She blows smoke from pursed lips, as though to dismiss his concerns.

Omar gazes at her in the mirror. He wonders why she hates him. Maybe if he paid her she would respect him. What can the clients be to her but money? He stops the cab by her apartment building. "You say ask. I ask, okay."

"What you want ask?"

"How much for you?"

She stares at him.

"I have money, can pay."

"I don't fuck you for any much money." She draws heavily on the cigarette.

"Why?" His face flushes.

"You driver. I no fuck driver." She stares at him as though he has lost his mind, opens the car door, steps out.

He drops his head forward, rests it on the wheel. He remains still, head down, feels the tremor and ache of conflicting emotions. He looks up, stares through the windscreen at the traffic. He needs to collect fares, start to make up money spent on the *fard* and get his mind off the woman.

For the rest of the morning and afternoon Omar collects roadside passengers, keeps away from downtown to avoid wasting fuel with slow-moving traffic caused by still-standing walls and others their blocks tumbled across streets and sidewalks. Everywhere birds rest on storefront awnings, trees and balconies. They flutter and settle. When Omar stops for a sandwich from a sidewalk stall, he calls Mona, hesitates to speak when he hears Yara's voice.

"Who's this?" she asks.

"Omar."

"Mona's at the hospital," she says curtly.

"Which hospital?"

"She's in labour."

Well, yes. He thought as much when Yara mentioned a hospital.

"She's fine, not taking visitors. I'm collecting a few of her belongings."

"Where's Tarek?"

"He's on his way. I've got to go." She hangs up on him.

He stares at the phone, thinks to call back, but with Yara so belligerent he is certain she will not answer. Why didn't they call him? He would have taken Mona. That was the agreement. He rocks in the seat, rests a hand on the holy book on the dashboard so God will take from him the feeling of being disrespected.

Omar drives a fare through the old city, drops him off, waits in congested early-evening traffic as a procession of Rifai dervish wends its way through the narrow streets for the hilltop mosque. Men with snakes about their necks, others with bloodied skewers through the flesh of bare backs sway and spin, follow black flags and banners bearing the names of their orders and home villages. He feels trapped with the long lines of celebrants blocking the roads and causing traffic jams. If he tries to leave it will probably take him an hour or more to get out of these narrow streets, wasting more gas. Once the events get started at the mosque the roads will clear sufficiently for him to make his way back downtown to pick up late-night shoppers. He thinks to call Tarek to find out if he is back and to ask after Mona, but cannot get himself to do so. As he waits in a line of slow-moving cars, his thoughts drift to the boy smoking *bango*. He wonders why he has not called. Did Omar, unintended, cause offence by something he said or did? His thoughts jump to recollections of his humiliation by that whore. He imagines the hurt he could cause her with razors and knives. The suddenness of his rage disturbs him. He should attend the *moulid* by the mosque to seek the calming influence of the saint. It will soon be nightfall and a little time spent there would distract him from the rejection he feels by everyone, from Mona and Yara to the boy and the blonde.

He parks where he can, climbs the hill on foot. In the mosque court-yard in pitched tents men sit or rest on rugs, wait for the evening call to prayer and the start of festivities. Vendors set up stalls along the walls of the mosque. On a raised wooden platform, lashed by ropes, groups of *gnawa* tune their instruments. Several of the men wear *kohl* around their eyes, earrings and bracelets. They smile at him. Their appearance both draws his attention and repels him. He thinks them somehow ungendered. Free in a way that disturbs him.

With the call to prayer over speakers from the minaret loud enough to raise the dead, Omar joins the worshippers overspilling the mosque's main hall. The anonymity of the crowd helps him to discharge the evening's obligation to God without feeling His censure. He prays on a plastic mat on the tiled floor of the courtyard.

As the celebrations start, he sits on the side of a stone basin with thick green shrubs, watches the *gnawa* perform. He rolls himself a joint of *bango* and tobacco, smokes. His mind, at last, stills. His body grows numb. He watches a woman covered in a black *niqab*, only her eyes visible. She gazes at him. He smiles. She approaches him, stands near him. He smokes the joint, then walks unsteadily to where he parked the cab. She follows a couple of paces behind, gets into the back seat.

* * *

Omar, his head thick from *bango*, sits naked on his bed. The woman moves in the darkness of his room, loosens the veil to expose her face. Her eyes lined with kohl, cheeks powdered, lips glisten red. She drops her head towards him, presses her tongue into his mouth, leans against him. He falls back. His shaft stiffens in her hand. She removes the black wrap, keeps on a loose-fitting undergarment, lifts it to squat over him, drips spit on his penis, slides him into her, rises and sinks in gentle motion, rubs her fingers along the stem. He comes, tremors, lies still, struggles to keep his eyes open, exhausted by the day's driving, the brief lovemaking, the *bango*.

"Do you want me to stay?" She rocks gently on him.

He nods. His chest burns.

"You can pay me in the morning."

Too tired, he does not ask her price, knows it will not be much. She kisses and sucks his nipples, strokes him as he drifts in and out of sleep. Once more, he hardens to her touch. She sits on him, takes him until he comes again, then falls asleep with her by his side. Late night, he wakes. She sleeps, kohl smeared on her cheeks. He turns down the sheet, draws up the hem of her gown to look at her naked body. In the street light from the kitchen window through the open door, he sees a sparrow nestled between her legs. He sits back and stares at the soft round shape with a neck folded to one side, reaches down to touch it. It stirs and stretches. She sighs, turns onto her back. Her hands reach for him, draw him down between her legs. The sparrow's neck grows and hardens in his mouth.

When next he wakes she is dressed in the black *niqab*, a veil over her face. She waits in the kitchen to be paid. Omar stumbles out of bed, his head splitting, no longer certain what of the previous night was hallucination and what actual.

* * *

Alone, Omar waits for water to boil for tea, feels himself still in a dream with blurred vision. He stares at the television, turns it off, certain the studio guests on the breakfast show watch him through the screen. He complains to the kettle that it takes too long on the burner. He rocks the almost empty butane cylinder.

He shows the *fard* to Pilgrim to admire the workmanship of nickel alloy along the handle, shows him the magazine with six bullets, cocks the hammer with his thumb. "Single action." Having learnt the words in English from the arms dealer, he enunciates them carefully, releases the hammer, nods seriously. He carries the *fard* around the kitchen to get used to its weight and feel, tosses it from hand to hand, spins it back and forth on his finger like a cowboy. In the toilet, he places it on his lap, worries about the vulnerability of being in such a cramped cubicle should an assailant enter his apartment. He decides to add a hook next to the paper-roll holder to hang the handgun by the trigger guard.

After his first few fares, Omar decides to call Tarek. Rage ignites as soon as he hears his voice. "So now you take my call."

Tarek apologizes, says that while away he ran out of credits, kept his phone turned off so as not to incur long-distance charges. He was visiting a friend. The drive there wasn't easy and the drive back worse because of the troubles.

Omar hears the lie in his voice, demands to know what is going on.

Tarek says he and Neda have only just arrived at the maternity ward.

Omar seethes, certain he is being lied to again. "Has Mona given birth?"

"The doctors estimate delivery sometime tonight."

Omar takes down the address of the hospital, says he will call later, come round if he can. He tells Tarek of the Rifai *moulid*, of how he goes every year to please the saint and gain credit with the Lord.

Tarek, tired from the long drive back, politely feigns interest.

Omar insists Tarek should attend the *moulid* to give thanks and ask for special favours for the newborn. "So the saint may bless the child, protect it against all manner of evil."

In his apartment that afternoon, Omar lies on his bed to relieve a headache he has had all morning from driving congested streets. With the boundaries of sleep and wakefulness transgressed since the previous night, thoughts arise in one state, continue in another. He argues with Pilgrim in the box on the floor. Of course it matters if Tarek lacks religion. "Why do you defend him?" And what of the boy? Why hasn't he called? And what if the blonde reports him to the dispatcher, says he wanted to pay for sex with her? It will be her word against his. He will say it was a misunderstanding because of his poor English. Besides, where is the evidence? He is pious, God-fearing, and she *awra*.

He gets up, rolls himself a *bango* joint, lies back on the bed to smoke. Voices arise to debate, cut across, interrupt and argue with each other in his head—voices around and in him. So many voices he cannot hear himself think—

A man like me above such things as sin   anyone been tempted as much
resist all manner   dare no not at all and but though
like suffocate that's what   better ask   out of you fuck
I would just like that with the bitch   a believer Pilgrim cos if   I can't think

He sobs, takes the shoebox from under the bed into the kitchen, removes the lid, stares at Pilgrim. *What is it you want, Satan?*

Though named for what he is, the cockroach does not flinch, stares back unrepentant with black eyes like hollows. Omar presses his thumb on Pilgrim's back, feels a pulse at the tip of his thumb. Its dark wings twitch under the stiff crust of its back. He intones a line from scripture—*I seek refuge in God from Satan.* Repeats it and repeats it again. But Pilgrim, as stubborn as only the devil can be, will not revoke the chatter in Omar's head. Omar struggles against the onslaught of voices—

> *Don't blame   you're fed   just stop   so what*
> *everybody   just themselves   live a little   they're buried*
> *can't breathe   that's shit   a driver   what*
> *like   didn't   you're   stop.*

Omar pushes down on the exoskeleton, presses against the hard shell. Feels it resist his pressure—*Don't.* He forces his thumb down—*Stop.* Black wings burst apart. White pus pools about the crustacean, coagulates and sticks to his fingers. He stares at the dead cockroach. The voices fall silent. He feels the stickiness between fingers and thumb, inhales the sickly-sweet scent, feels triumphant at killing the devil, terror at having done so.

At sunset, with the curfew lifted, the streets impassable with crowds, Omar parks at the hospital, finds Tarek and Yara with Mona in a room of the maternity ward. Neda slouches in a chair by the side of her mother's bed.

Tarek holds Mona's hand as she sleeps. "Contractions still come and go."

"They gave her an analgesic." Yara sits against the wall, her face pale in the low light of the room. Omar avoids making eye contact with her.

"They think it'll be another couple of hours," Tarek says.

Yara stands. "We should take Neda home. She needs to rest."

Neda protests, says she wants to stay until the baby arrives.

"I'll drive her back," Omar says.

"I'll take you." Yara holds a hand out to Neda. "And I'll bring you here as soon as the baby's born. I promise."

Neda pouts, reluctantly rises from the chair, takes Yara's hand.

Omar ignores Yara, asks if Tarek has eaten.

No, he says, he has not had a proper meal all day.

"Get yourself something. I'll stay with Mona." Omar nods reassuringly.

"I don't know what's open round here at this time of night."

"I'll text you as soon as there's anything."

Tarek nods, gently places Mona's hand by her side so as not to wake her. "I won't be long."

Omar sits in the chair by the bed, watches Mona. He thinks by rights the baby she bears is his. Someday he will take the child to the Rifai *moulid*. He pictures himself with a boy riding on his shoulders. He will teach him to pray, to ask for blessings, to ward off the devil. But then the pregnancy has taken so long. What if there is something wrong? Science has its limits. Only God has power over all eventualities. Only the intercession of the saint can ensure the Lord's intervention. He takes Mona's hand. She is still deep in sleep. He helps her from the bed, puts her coat about her shoulders.

"Where are we going?" Her eyes barely open.

He leads her to the elevator. "Just a short ride."

In the car park he settles her on the back seat of the cab.

She closes her eyes. When she opens them they are in a crowded alley. "Where are we?"

"To get the saint's blessing for the baby."

She pleads he should take her back to the hospital. At any moment she could start back in labour.

"The saint will protect you." He leads her up the hill through the crowds to the mosque. In the courtyard, electric bulbs hang from wires, reflect off stone tiles, cast thick shadows. Children cluster about a man turning a handle on a box of wonders. For a coin they wait their turn to peer into the eyepiece to watch images formed by spinning picture wheels. A vendor at a stall sells sugar-candy dolls wrapped in crimped crêpe paper. In a tent, on a stage, a man adjusts lights behind a screen the size of a single bedsheet, casts images of shadow puppets. In another part of the courtyard *gnawa* beat a hand drum, tune *sentir*, clap *qaraqib*. All about black flags flutter from tents and lampposts. Banners strung between poles proclaim the names of the branches of the Rifai order gathered for the saint's remembrance. Omar thinks it like the Night of Power described in scripture, when angels descend at God's command until the break of day and saints ascend to the seven heavens on steeds of lightning.

In one corner of the courtyard by a tree and shrubs, a man sits on a stool, pierces boys' cheeks with needles. Men in circles sway and chant. A man in black robes spins with arms outstretched. In poor light, it takes Omar a moment to see a skewer pierces both cheeks. Another man turns slowly, presses a long, thin needle against his lower lip, twists it back and forth to breach the skin. Blood wells, then stops at the wound puckered at entry and exit. Others slide blades through flesh pinched at shoulders and chest, raise their arms to spin to the sound of tambourines and *tablas*. Omar wonders if he is capable of such cruelty to himself to reach beyond pain for a state of ecstasy and feels diminished by the thought.

He watches Mona, her mind still in a haze, sees the sickening look on her face, feels satisfaction at her discomfort. She stumbles past whirling dancers. Dervish sway as others chant. Unsteady, she steps into a man draped with snakes about his shoulders. A serpent shoots forward, hisses, bares fangs, its forked tongue lashes at her face. She falls back, steadies herself against a low wall by a jasmine shrub. She rubs her face glistening with perspiration. The *gnawa*, their *qaraqib* and *sentir* amplified by microphones, sing over the clamour. Vendors call their wares. She closes her eyes, rests a hand on her stomach, gasps from the clench of a contraction.

"I need to get back." She repeats herself twice more before Omar can hear her through the surge and ebb of sounds of *gnawa*, recitation of holy texts over loudspeakers, the shouts of vendors and the rumble of the crowd.

"You want to go now?" Surely not with the *moulid* barely begun for the night.

"It's the baby."

Yes, the baby. A child with a mind as soft as clay, ready to be imprinted with thoughts. A child so innocent it could be led to the gates of hell and not know itself damned. He gazes at Mona and thinks he sees her soul dark in the shadows cast by electric lights strung around the mosque. How had he not seen this before? The thought he had resisted for so long. Tarek, his heart hardened against religion, has poisoned her spirit. Enough the damage they have done Neda, depriving the girl of religion, placing her at risk of hell. He cannot let them corrupt the new child. It is his duty to guide and nurture it in the way of belief. An obligation set him by God. A means to gather credits for his salvation with the prophets.

Mona rises, sways, grips Omar by the arm.

They make their way through the crowd down the hill from the mosque to the parked cab.

He drives along the Autostrad.

Mona counts between contractions. "Where are we going?"

He stares intently ahead, does not answer.

"I need to get back." She pushes into the seat as another contraction starts.

He will take her somewhere they can talk. Where she cannot deny the power of the Lord to grant life and death. Where the meaning of eternal damnation will be all too apparent.

They take the exit for the desert road and travel down poorly lit narrow streets to the Jewish cemetery. The cab stalls as it hits a pot-hole. They continue, then stop alongside a broken wall. From under his seat Omar removes the handgun. Mona's face whitens as she sees the *fard*. "For protection," he says. He leads her out into the dark street, tells her to go through a gap in the wall. He waits, glances around to check if anybody watches. Once through the wall he cannot see Mona in the blackness. His eyes gradually adjust to the lack of light. A shadow moves between the gravestones, then more shadows—maybe dogs, shrubs, a low-hanging branch shaken by the breeze. But possibly some-thing more sinister—malevolent wraiths as in stories his mother told him as a child. The *umran* who haunt waste grounds and deserted buildings, whose murmurs can stop the hearts of men—*I appeal for protection from the Lord of Creation from all He created.* Now, he hears voices coming from the graves. Their susurrations call his name, call him to them, while other voices urge him on. His mind reverts to the day's earlier panic. He glances around for Mona. Where has she got to? He struggles over uneven ground, steps into a pool of black water, curses, tries to get away from the voices. Among the gravestones he sees eyes flash, points the *fard*, sees it is a dog, picks up a stone, throws it. The dog yelps and runs. Above the buildings and the expanse of the burial ground the sky shades from grey city haze to black. The voices pierce his skull, grow louder. He screams to drive them out, but still they keep at him, knot his thoughts with words. Voices swell to fill his head, burst from him to fill the space about him. He slips, falls to the ground, crawls in the mud of the seeping pools of sewage, struggles to rise. The voices whisper he will die. His corpse fester with those of unbelievers, fed on by graveyard dogs.

He thinks he sees a figure in the shadow of a stone block. Disoriented, he cannot tell whether it is behind or ahead of him. Has it followed him—hidden in darkness from when he entered the cemetery? He rises, points his handgun. A wraith, or something blown by the breeze. It flits in and out of shadows, peels from grey stone to melt into black, keeps moving. It stops behind an arch. He holds the *fard* ready to fire. When the figure breaks from blackness, he pulls the trigger, feels the pressure against his finger resist once and then again before it gives. The recoil like a door slams on his hand. The sound pounds in his head. The ejected cartridge case hits him in the face, burns. He screams, starts back from the whip and sting of hot metal, doubles forward with pain, drops to the ground. All rage, he crawls to take cover behind a gravestone. Now the voices loud and unrelenting demand he kill. Yes, yes, he must kill the hunted wraith. One bullet spent, five remain, more than enough for *afrit* or man. He looks up over the stone block but does not see any movement—everything still and silent. He creeps forward, darts from gravestone to gravestone, circles behind whatever he thinks stalks him. The next time he fires God will guide his hand. God will decide who lives or dies. He sees a shadow tremor behind a narrow stone wall. He crouches to track it, creeps from headstone to headstone, presses himself flat against the side of an arch, slides down, on all fours crawls forward. He hears a sound, knows he is close to what he hunts. He stumbles, steadies himself, holds the pointed gun as he passes a gravestone, sees to one side a dog dart behind a stone block, ahead of him a dark figure on its knees at a mound of dirt. Omar cocks the *fard*. Voices tell him to fire in case it be a demon, before it looks up and sees him. He resists the urge to kill until he can be certain.

At a rise of freshly turned earth Mona closes her eyes. She grimaces, leans forward. A wave of pain intensifies. She pants as it breaks and rolls through her.

Omar aims the handgun at her, feels an onrush of pleasure, an unfamiliar sense of power—she a broken-winged sparrow, her life at his disposal. The ability to summon death his alone.

She takes a deep breath, braces herself, opens her eyes, fixes him with her gaze, says, "I never forgot."

Her tone, defiant, unnerves him. He stares at her unsure of her meaning.

"Never forgave." She takes another deep breath. With each breath she seems to regain composure.

He shifts uneasily, kneels forward.

"You let them cut me."

He struggles to recall what she could mean. Lashed by the haunting voices, and his struggles with the devil in and among the infidel dead, memory surges and he watches as the blade draws blood from a child held on the bathroom floor, her screams pierce like breaking glass, as though from the gravestones, with shutters closed on the windows, the light like that of the waxen moon risen over cemetery arches by a jasmine shrub, casts shadows where blood runs on the tiles, stains the cement around the floor drain—he sinks into the soft soil, feels its moisture soak to his skin. The straight razor rinsed under running water, wiped on a cloth, slipped back into its sleeve. His mother carried the unconscious child to bed. He blinks, blinks again, returns himself to the present of Mona pregnant in the graveyard.

She stretches forward with her arms on the grave mound, breathes heavily with the start of another contraction. Her face glistens with perspiration.

He leans back against a stone block, gazes at the stars matted by dark matter, an encryption in light of God's will unfolding from a flicker before time to the coming Day of Judgment. His mind clears as the darkness about him stirs. He drops the handgun by his side. A light breeze rustles a bougainvillea, sways clutches of wild grass between unkempt graves. A dog lurks in the shadow of an arch. He recalls a poem he learnt at school. Strange to think, as a boy, he once knew poetry and loved it enough to be persuaded by it—*Tread gently, for the earth is the bed in which rests those you love.* Then, he supposed the earth, moist and tender as an eye, must be full of love for all the dead, itself deserving the love of all that lives. When did he stop thinking that way? When did life become so consumed by rage? When did he seek vengeance in religion? He gazes at the handgun between him and Mona, wonders what purpose he saw in purchasing it when there is God Almighty to protect him. He stares at Mona, as though seeing her for the first time. Tears well in his eyes. He wipes his face with the back of his hand, aware he has failed her as a brother, failed Neda as an uncle. There is nobody he loves and loves him through whose eyes he can recognize himself, and by whose stories he can know himself. He thinks *in place of love I live by prohibitions, equate beauty with sin, ugliness with piety, defer all pleasure to an afterlife*; believes *helpless dirt sinful I am noth- ingness filth wilfulness and rebellion all life and power to Almighty God*. But how can he know God's will and thoughts when he cannot see with the sight of God? Cannot feel what God must feel? He squeezes his eyes shut, rubs them with both hands to scrub away thoughts that carry him to the borderline of faith and doubt, redemption and despair.

* * *

Mona rises, braces herself against a stone block, breathes rapidly, waits for a contraction to tighten, strengthen and release. She steadies herself against a gravestone, takes a step forward, pauses, breathes deeply, then takes another step towards the pale street lights beyond the broken wall of the cemetery.

ACKNOWLEDGEMENTS

Thanks to friends and colleagues at the University of British Columbia's Creative Writing Department, Simon Fraser University's Writer's Studio and the University of Iowa's International Writing Program, as well as to the Canada Council for the Arts for its financial support, and to Harper-Collins for awarding this novel the inaugural HarperCollins/UBC Prize for Best New Fiction.